Praise for *New York Times* bestselling author J.A. JANCE and her riveting J.P. BEAUMONT SERIES

"Jance has a sure hand."

Publishers Weekly

"Once I read the first mystery about this Seattle police detective, I was hooked. . . . Jance's writing is crisp and her characters are authentic."

Louisville Courier-Journal

"Her books keep on sizzling, keep on fascinating, keep on getting better."

Asbury Park Press

"J. P. Beaumont is a star attraction."

Booklist

"J. A. Jance is among the best—if not the best—mystery novelists writing today."

Chattanooga Times

"Jance delivers a devilish page-turner."

People

By J. A. Jance

J. P. Beaumont Mysteries

Until Proven Guilty • Injustice for All
Trial by Fury • Taking the Fifth
Improbable Cause • A More Perfect Union
Dismissed with Prejudice • Minor in Possession
Payment in Kind • Without Due Process
Failure to Appear • Lying in Wait
Name Withheld • Breach of Duty
Birds of Prey • Partner in Crime
Long Time Gone • Justice Denied
Fire and Ice • Betrayal of Trust
Ring in the Dead: A J. P. Beaumont Novella
Second Watch • Dance of the Bones
Stand Down: A J.P. Beaumont Novella

Joanna Brady Mysteries

Desert Heat • Tombstone Courage
Shoot/Don't Shoot • Dead to Rights
Skeleton Canyon • Rattlesnake Crossing
Outlaw Mountain • Devil's Claw
Paradise Lost • Partner in Crime
Exit Wounds • Dead Wrong
Damage Control • Fire and Ice
Judgment Call • Remains of Innocence
No Honor Among Thieves: An Ali Reynolds/Joanna Brady Novella

Walker Family Mysteries

Hour of the Hunter • Kiss of the Bees
Day of the Dead • Queen of the Night

Ali Reynolds Mysteries

Edge of Evil • Web of Evil • Hand of Evil
Cruel Intent • Trial by Fire • Fatal Error
Left for Dead • Deadly Stakes • Moving Target
A Last Goodbye: An Ali Reynolds Novella
Clawback

DANCE OF THE BONES

A J.P. BEAUMONT AND BRANDON WALKER NOVEL

wm
WILLIAM MORROW
An Imprint of *HarperCollins*Publishers

This is a work of fiction. Names, characters, places, and incidents are products of the author's imagination or are used fictitiously and are not to be construed as real. Any resemblance to actual events, locales, organizations, or persons, living or dead is entirely coincidental.

WILLIAM MORROW
An Imprint of HarperCollins*Publishers*
195 Broadway
New York, New York 10007

Walker family tree courtesy of Alison Cook
ISBN 978-0-06-229767-9

First William Morrow premium printing: June 2016
First William Morrow hardcover printing: September 2015

Printed in the United States of America

10 9 8 7 6 5 4 3 2 1

For S-wegi A'an, Red Feathers

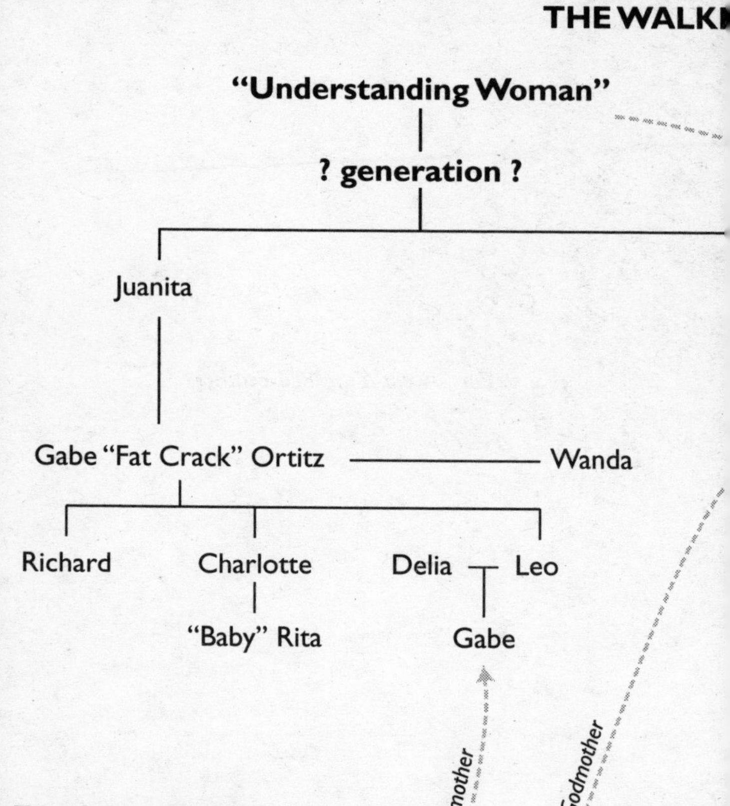

Escalante Family

Clemencia Escalante aka Dolores Lanita Walker
- was bitten by ants and rejected by family.

Delphina (murdered) Escalante

Angie

R FAMILY

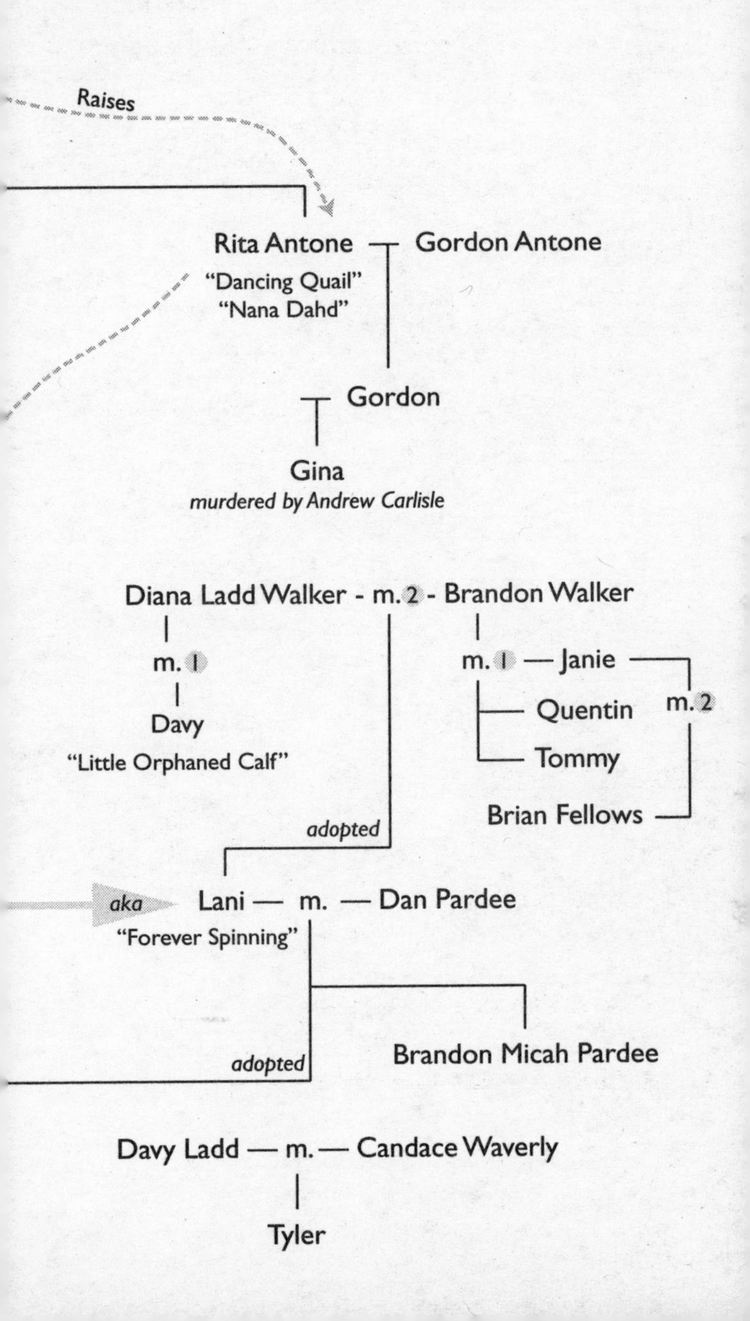

Raises
Rita Antone
"Dancing Quail"
"Nana Dahd"
Gordon Antone
Gordon
Gina
murdered by Andrew Carlisle
Diana Ladd Walker - m. 2 - Brandon Walker
m. 1
Davy
"Little Orphaned Calf"
m. 1 — Janie
Quentin
Tommy
m. 2
Brian Fellows
adopted
aka
Lani — m. — Dan Pardee
"Forever Spinning"
Brandon Micah Pardee
adopted
Davy Ladd — m. — Candace Waverly
Tyler

DANCE OF THE BONES

PROLOGUE

SOZA CANYON, ARIZONA
MARCH 1970

Amos Warren walked with his shoulders stooped and with his eyes and mind focused on the uneven ground beneath his feet. The winter rains had been more than generous and this part of the Sonoran Desert, Soza Canyon on the far eastern edge of the Rincon Mountains, was alive with flowers. Scrawny, suntanned, and weathered, Amos was more than middle-aged but still remarkably fit. Even so, the sixty or seventy pounds he carried in the sturdy pack on his shoulders weighed him down and had him feeling his sixty-plus years.

He had started the day by picking up several top-notch arrowheads. He slipped them into the pockets of his jeans rather than risk damaging them as the load in the pack increased over the course of the day.

The one he considered to be the best of the lot he hid away inside his wallet, congratulating himself on the fact that his day was off to such a great start. Over the course of the morning, he located several geodes. The best of those was a bowling-ball-sized treasure that would fetch a pretty penny once it joined the growing collection of goods that he and his foster son, John Lassiter, would offer for sale at the next available gem and mineral show.

Assuming, of course, that John ever spoke to him again, Amos thought ruefully. The knock-down, drag-out fight the two men had gotten into the night before had been a doozy, and recalling it had cast a pall over Amos's entire day. He had known John Lassiter for decades, and this was the first time he had ever raised a hand to the younger man. The fact that they had duked it out over a girl, of all things, only added to Amos's chagrin.

Ava Martin, Amos thought, *what a conniving little whore!* She was good-looking and knew it. She was a tiny blond bombshell type with just the right curves where they counted. Amos didn't trust the bitch any further than he could throw her.

His next thought was all about John. The poor guy was crazy about Ava—absolutely crazy. As far as John was concerned, Ava was the greatest thing since sliced bread. In fact, he was even talking about buying an engagement ring, for God's sake!

As for Amos? He knew exactly who Ava was and what she was all about. She wasn't anything close to decent marriage material. He had noticed the wicked little two-timer batting her eyes and flirting with John's best friend, Ken—all behind John's back, of course. And two days ago, when John had been out of town, she'd gone so far as to come by his house—forty-five minutes from town—where she had tried putting the moves on Amos.

That was the last straw. Amos was decades older than Ava. He had no illusions about his being physically attractive to her. No, she wasn't looking to get laid; Ava was after the main chance.

She knew John and Amos were partners who split everything fifty-fifty. She probably understood that, for the most part, Amos was the brains of the outfit while John was the brawn. Amos was the one who knew where to go seeking to find the hidden treasures the unyielding desert would reveal to only the most persistent of searchers. He knew what was worth taking home and what wasn't. John was the packhorse who carried the stuff and loaded it into the back of the truck and who carried it into the storage unit.

When it came to selling their finds, Amos had years' worth of contacts at his disposal, all of them listed in his little black book. He had amassed a whole catalog of gem, mineral, and artifact dealers, some aboveboard and others not so much. He also knew which of those might be interested in which items. Amos did the behind-the-scenes wheeling and dealing while John handled direct sales at booths in the various venues. John was a good-looking young hunk, which was always a good bet when it came to face-to-face interactions.

Amos suspected that John had gotten into his cups and talked too much about what they did and how much money they brought in, something Amos regarded as nobody's business but their own. He was convinced that was what Ava Martin was really after—the shortest route to the money. Amos had sent the little witch packing, and he'd had no intention of telling John about it, but Ava had gotten the drop on him. She had told John all about their little set-to. The problem was, in Ava's version of the story, Amos had been the one putting the make on her. With predictable results.

The previous evening, Amos had gone to El Barrio, a run-down bar on Speedway on the east side of I-10. Years earlier, El Barrio had been within walking distance of the house where he had lived. When developers came through and bought up that whole block of houses, Amos had taken his wad of money and paid cash for a five-acre place up in Golder Canyon, on the far back side of Catalina. The house was a tin-roofed adobe affair that had started out long ago as a stage stop. In town, John and Amos had been roommates. The "cabin," as Amos liked to call it, was strictly a one-man show, so John had chosen to stay on in town—closer to the action—and had rented a place in the old neighborhood.

When Amos had gone to El Barrio that night, he had done so deliberately, knowing it was most likely still John's favorite hangout. Amos's mind was made up. He went there for no other reason than to have it out with John. Either Ava went or John did. Amos had been sitting at the bar, tucked in among the other twenty or so happy-hour regulars and sipping his way through that evening's boilermaker, when John had stormed in through the front door.

"You bastard!" the younger man muttered under his breath as he slid uninvited onto an empty stool next to Amos.

John was hot tempered, and Amos knew he was spoiling for a fight—something Amos preferred to avoid. He had come here hoping to talk things out rather than duking them out.

He took a careful sip of his drink. "Good afternoon to you, too," he responded calmly. "Care for a beer?"

"I don't want a beer from you, or anything else, either. You keep telling me that Ava's bad news and claiming she's not good enough for me, but the first time my back is turned, you try getting her into the sack!"

"That what Ava told you?" Amos asked.

"It's not just what she told me," John declared, his voice rising. "It's what happened."

"What if I told you Ava was a liar?"

"In that case, how about we step outside so I can beat the crap out of you?" John demanded, rising to his feet.

Looking in the mirror behind the bar, Amos saw the reflection of John as he was now—a beefy man seven inches taller than Amos, thirty pounds heavier, and three decades younger, with a well-deserved reputation as a brawler and an equally well-deserved moniker, Big Bad John. Amos's problem was that, at the same time he saw that image, he was remembering another one as well—one of a much younger kid, freckle faced and missing his two front teeth. That was how John—Johnny back then—had looked when Amos had first laid eyes on him.

Amos knew that in a fair fight between them, outside the bar, he wouldn't stand a chance; he'd be dog meat. John may not have been tougher, but he was younger, taller, and heavier. By the time a fight was over, most likely the cops would be called. One or the other of them or maybe both would be hauled off to jail and charged with assault. Amos had already done time, and he didn't want anything like that to happen to John. That in a nutshell took the fair-fight option off the table. What Amos needed was a one- or two-punch effort that put a stop to the whole affair before it had a chance to get started.

As the quarrel escalated, tension crept like a thick fog throughout the room, and the rest of the bar went dead quiet.

"I don't want to fight you, kid," Amos said in a conciliatory tone while calmly pushing his stool away from the bar. No one noticed how he carefully slipped his right hand into the hip pocket of his worn jeans, and no one saw the same hand ease back out into the open again with something clenched in his fist. "Come on, son," he added. "Take a load off, sit down, and have a beer."

"I am not your son!" John growled. "I never was, and I'm not having a beer with you, either, you son of a bitch. We're done, Amos. It's over. Get some other poor stooge to be your pack mule."

Big Bad John Lassiter never saw the punch coming. Amos's powerful right hook caught him unawares and unprepared. The blow broke John's cheekbone and sent him reeling backward, dropping like a rock on the sawdust-covered floor. Big John landed, bloodied face up and knocked cold. In the shocked silence that followed, with all eyes focused on John, no one in the room noticed Amos Warren slip the brass knuckles back into his pocket. No, it hadn't been a fair fight, but at least it was over without any danger of it turning into a full-scale brawl.

As John started coming to and tried to sit up, several people hurried to help him. Amos turned back to the bartender. "No need to call the cops," Amos said. "Next round's on me."

As far as the bartender was concerned, that was good

news. He didn't want any trouble, either. "Right," he said, nodding in agreement. "Coming up."

It took several people to get John back on his feet and work-wise. Someone handed him a bar napkin to help stem the flow of blood that was still pouring from the cut on his cheek, but the wad of paper didn't do much good. The damage was done. His shirt was already a bloody mess.

"See you tomorrow then?" Amos called after John, watching him in the mirror as he staggered unsteadily toward the door.

"Go piss up a rope, Amos Warren," John muttered in reply. "I'll see you in hell first."

That was the last thing John had said to him—*I'll see you in hell.* They'd quarreled before over the years, most recently several times about Ava, but this was the first time they'd ever come to blows. In past instances, a few days after the dustup, one or the other of them would get around to apologizing, and that would be the end of it. Amos hoped the same thing would happen this time around, although with Ava standing on the sidelines fanning the flames, it might not be that easy to patch things up.

Lost in thought, Amos had been walking generally westward, following the course of a dry creek bed at the bottom of the canyon, some of it sandy and some littered with boulders. During monsoon season, flash floods carrying boulders, tree trunks, and all kinds of other debris would roar downstream. As the water level subsided and the sand settled, there was no telling what would be left behind. In the course of the day, Amos had seen plenty of evidence—spoor, hoof prints, and paw prints—that indicated the presence of wildlife—deer, javelina, and even what Amos assumed to be a black bear. But there was no indication of any recent human incursions.

At a point where the canyon walls narrowed precipitously, Amos was forced off the bank and into the creek bed itself. And that was when he saw it—a small hunk of reddish-brown pottery sticking up out of the sand. Dropping his heavy pack with a thud, Amos knelt on the sand.

It took several minutes of careful digging with his bare fingers for him to unearth the treasure. Much to his amazement, the tiny pot was still in one piece. How it could have been washed down the stream bed and deposited on a sandy strand of high ground without being smashed to bits was one of the wonders of the universe. Amos suspected that the sand-infused water of a flash flood had buoyed it up before the water had drained out of the sand, leaving the pot on solid ground.

Once it was free of the sand, Amos pulled out his reading glasses, then held the piece close enough to examine it. He realized at once that it was far too small to be a cooking pot. Then he noticed that a faded design of some kind had been etched into the red clay before the pot was fired. A more detailed examination revealed the image of what appeared to be an owl perched on top of a tortoise. The presence of the decorative etching on the pot along with its relative size meant that the piece was most likely ceremonial in nature.

Still holding the tiny but perfect pot in his hands, Amos leaned back on his heels and considered the piece's possible origins. He wasn't someone who had a degree in anthropology, but he had spent a lifetime finding and selling Native American artifacts from all over vast stretches of Arizona's desert landscapes.

Years of experience told him the pot was most likely Papago in origin. Sometimes known as the Tohono O'odham, the Papagos had lived for thousands of years in the vast deserts surrounding what was now Tucson. This particular spot, on the far southeastern flanks of the Rincon Mountains, overlooked the San Pedro Valley. It was on the easternmost edge of the Papagos' traditional territory and deep into the part of the world once controlled and dominated by the Apache. Had a stray band of Tohono O'odham come here to camp or hunt and left this treasure behind? Amos wondered. More likely, the tiny artifact had been a trophy of some kind, spoils of war carried off by a marauding band of Apache.

Since the pot had clearly been washed downstream, there was a possibility that a relatively undisturbed archaeological site was sitting undiscovered farther up the canyon. There were several professors at the U of A who would pay Amos good money as a finder's fee so they could go in and do a properly documented excavation. As to the pot itself? Regardless of where it was from, Amos knew he had found a remarkable piece, one that was inherently valuable. The curators at the Heard Museum would jump at the chance to have a whole undamaged pot for their southwestern collection. Amos knew that most of the pots on display in the museum had been pieced back together, and there was a reason for that.

The Tohono O'odham believed that the pot maker's spirit remained trapped inside her pots. As a consequence, when the pot maker died, tradition demanded that all her pots be smashed to pieces. So why was this one still whole? That made the theory of it being stolen goods all the more likely. Apaches would have no reason to adhere to Tohono O'odham customs. Why free a dead enemy's spirit? What good would that do for you?

Wanting to protect his treasure, Amos put the pot down and then tore a strip of material from the tail of his ragged flannel work shirt. The material was old and thin enough that it gave way without a struggle. He wrapped the pot in the soft cloth. Then, stowing the protected pot as the topmost item in his bag, he shouldered his load and headed back to the truck. It was early afternoon, but he wanted to be back on the far side of Redington Pass early enough that the setting sun wouldn't be directly in his eyes.

Making his way back down the stream bed, Amos kept close watch on his footing, avoiding loose rocks wherever possible. With the heavily laden pack on his back, even a small fall might result in a twisted ankle or a broken bone, and one of those could be serious business when he was out here all by himself with no way of letting anyone know exactly where he was or summoning help. And rocks weren't the only danger.

On this late spring afternoon, rattlesnakes emerging from hibernation were out in force. In fact, halfway back to his truck, a diamondback, almost invisible on the sandy surroundings, slithered past him when he stopped long enough to wipe away sweat that was running into his eyes. That pause had been a stroke of luck for both Amos and the snake. If left undisturbed, snakes didn't bother him. Most of the time, they went their way while Amos went his. But if he'd stepped on the creature unawares, all bets would have been off. One way or the other, the snake would have been dead and, despite his heavy hiking boots, Amos might well have been bitten in the process.

Amos's lifetime search for gemstones, minerals, fossils, and artifacts had put him in mountains like this for decades. Watching the snake slide silently and safely off into the sparse underbrush served as a reminder that snakes, javelina, bobcats, deer, black bears, and jaguars had been the original inhabitants of this still untamed place. Humans, including both the Tohono O'odham and the Apache who had roamed these arid lands for thousands of years, were relatively new and probably somewhat unwelcome intruders. White men, including Amos himself, were definitely Johnny-come-latelies.

Reshouldering his pack, Amos allowed as how he was missing John's presence about then. These days, Amos was finding it harder to go back downhill than it was to climb up. And with the added weight in the pack? Well, he would have appreciated having someone to carry half the load. John may have said they were quits, but as far as Amos was concerned, they were still partners, and they would split everything fifty-fifty.

And there he was doing it again—thinking about John. An hour or so after the altercation that night, when Amos had finally left the bar, he might have looked as though he hadn't a care in the world, but he did. His heart was heavy. Having won the battle, he feared he had lost the war.

Amos and John were no kind of blood relations, but they were peas in a pod. Hot tempered? Check. Too fast with the fists? Check. Didn't care to listen to reason? Check. Forty years earlier, Amos had hooked up with a girl named Hattie Smith who had been the same kind of bad news for him as Ava was for John. A barroom fight over Hattie the evening of Amos's twenty-first birthday had resulted in an involuntary manslaughter charge that had sent Amos to the slammer for five to ten. He recognized that there was a lot of the old pot-and-kettle routine going on here.

Yes, Amos had gotten his head screwed on straight in the course of those six years in the pen. He had read his way through a tattered copy of the *Encyclopaedia Britannica* that he found in the prison library, giving himself an education that would have compared favorably to any number of college degrees. Even so, he didn't want John to go through a similar school of hard knocks. He wanted to protect the younger man from all that because John Lassiter was the closest thing to a son Amos Warren would ever have.

John had grown up next door to Amos's family home. They had lived in a pair of dilapidated but matching houses on a dirt street on what was then Tucson's far west side. Amos lived there because he had inherited the house from his mother. Once out of prison, he had neither the means nor the ambition to go looking for something better. John's family rented the place next door because it was cheap, and cheap was the best they could do.

To Amos's way of thinking, John's parents had been little more than pond scum. His father was a drunk. His mother was a whore who regularly locked the poor kid outside in the afternoons while she entertained her various gentleman callers. On one especially rainy winter's day, Amos had been outraged to see John, a mostly toothless eight-year-old kid, sitting on the front porch, shivering in the cold. He'd been shoved outside in his bare feet wearing nothing but a ragged pair of pajamas.

Amos had ventured out in the yard and stood on the far side of the low rock wall that separated them. "What're you doing?" Amos had asked.

"Waiting," came the disconsolate answer. "My mom's busy."

For months Amos had seen the cars coming and going in the afternoons while old man Lassiter wasn't at home. Amos had understood all too well what was really going on. He also knew what it was like to be locked out of a house. Back when he was a kid the same thing had happened to him time and again. In his case it had been so Amos's father could beat the crap out of Amos's mother in relative peace and quiet. What was going on in the Lassiter household may have been a slightly different take on the matter, but it was close enough.

Without a word, Amos had gone back inside. When he reappeared, he came back to the fence armed with a peanut butter and jelly sandwich.

"Hungry?" he asked.

Without further prompting, the boy had scampered barefoot across the muddy yard. Grabbing the sandwich, he gobbled it down.

"My name's Amos. What's yours?"

"John," the boy mumbled through a mouthful of peanut butter.

"Have you ever played Chinese checkers?"

John shook his head. "What's Chinese checkers?"

"Come on," Amos said. "I'll teach you."

He had hefted the kid up over the low wall built of volcanic rock, shifted him onto his hip, and carried him to his own house. That had been their beginning. Had Amos Warren been some kind of pervert, it could have been the beginning of something very bad, but it wasn't. Throughout John's chaotic childhood, Amos Warren had been the only fixed point in the poor kid's life, his only constant. John Lassiter Sr. died in a drunk-driving incident when his son was in fourth grade. By the time John was in high school, his mother, Sandra, had been through three more husbands, each one a step worse than his immediate predecessor.

Despite his mother's singular lack of parenting skills and due to the fact that the kid ate more meals at Amos's house than he did at home, John grew like crazy. More than six feet tall by the time he was in seventh grade, John would have been a welcome addition to any junior high or high school athletic program, but Sandra had insisted that she didn't believe in "team sports." What she really didn't believe in was going to the trouble of getting her son signed up, paying for physicals or uniforms, or going to and from games or practices. Amos suspected that she didn't want John involved in anything that might have interfered with her barfly social life and late-afternoon assignations, which were now conducted somewhere away from home, leaving John on his own night after night.

Amos knew that the good kids were the ones who were involved in constructive activities after school. The bad kids were mostly left to their own devices. It came as no surprise to Amos that John ended up socializing with the baddies. By the time the boy hit high school, he had too much time on his hands and a bunch of juvie-bound friends.

As a kid, Amos had earned money for Saturday afternoon matinees in downtown Tucson by scouring the roadsides and local teenager party spots for discarded pop bottles, which he had turned over to Mr. Yee, the old man who ran the tiny grocery store on the corner. When Amos happened to come across some pieces of broken Indian pottery, Mr. Yee had been happy to take those off his hands, too, along with Amos's first-ever arrowhead. From then on, the old Chinaman had been willing to buy whatever else Amos was able to scrounge up.

Once Amos got out of prison, he discovered there weren't many employment options available for paroled felons. As a result, he had returned to his onetime hobby of prowling his surroundings in search of treasure. He knew the desert flatlands like he knew the backs of his own hands, and he knew the mountains too, the rugged ranges that marched across the lower-lying desert floor like so many towering chess pieces scattered across a vast flat board—the Rincons and the Catalinas, the Tortolitas, the Huachucas, the Whetstones, the Dragoons, the Peloncillos, and the Chiricahuas.

Now, though, with the benefit of his store of prison-gained knowledge, Amos was far more educated about what he found. He was able to locate plenty of takers for those items without the need for someone like Mr. Yee to act as middleman. He earned a decent if modest living and was content with his solitary life. Then John Lassiter got into trouble and was sent to juvie. Amos, claiming to be the kid's most recent stepfather, had bailed him out and taken him home. From then on, that's where John had lived—in the extra room at Amos's house rather than next door with his mother.

By then Amos could see that the die was cast. John wasn't going to go to college. If he was ever going to amount to anything, Amos would have to show him how. From then on, Amos set out to teach John what he knew. Every weekend and during the long broiling summers, John went along with Amos on his desert scavenger hunts. Most of the time John made himself useful by carrying whatever Amos found. Nevertheless, he was an apt pupil. Over time he became almost as good at finding stuff as Amos was, and between them their unofficial partnership made a reasonably good living.

Not wanting to attract attention to any of his special hunting grounds, Amos usually parked his jeep a mile at least from any intended target. This time, he had left the vehicle hidden in a grove of mesquite well outside the mouth of the canyon. Approaching the spot where he'd left the truck, Amos caught a tiny whiff of cigarette smoke floating in the air.

John was a chain smoker—something else the two men argued about constantly, bickering like an old married couple. This time, however, Amos's spirits lifted slightly as soon as his nostrils caught wind of the smoke. This out-of-the-way spot was a place he and John visited often. Maybe the kid had come to his senses after all and followed him here. Maybe it was time to apologize and let bygones be bygones, and if John wanted Ava Martin in his life, so be it.

Once inside the grove, Amos looked around and saw

no sign of John or of his vehicle, either. That was hardly surprising. Maybe he had chosen some other place to park. There was always a chance John had gone out to do some scavenging of his own.

Amos turned his attention to the pack, unshouldering it carefully and settling it into the bed of the truck. He reached inside the pack, and his searching fingers located the bundle of wadded-up shirttail. Feeling through the thin fabric, he was relieved to find that the pot was still in one piece.

A new puff of smoke wafted past him. That was when he sensed something else, something incongruous underlying the smell of burning cigarette—a hint of perfume. He turned and was dismayed to see Ava standing a mere five feet away, holding a gun pointed at Amos's chest.

"What are you doing here?" he demanded. "Where's John?"

"Don't move," she warned. "I know how to use this thing."

"Where's John?" Amos repeated. "How did you even know to come here?"

"John brought me here several times. You know, for picnics and such. He told me this was where you'd be today."

Outrage boiled in Amos's heart. John had brought Ava to this very special hunting ground, one Amos had shared with no one other than John?

The depth of John's betrayal was breathtaking. Amos took a step forward. "Why, you little bitch . . . ," he began, but he never had a chance to finish his threat.

Ava had told him the truth. She really did know how to use the weapon in her hand. The first bullet caught him clean in the heart. Amos Warren was dead before he hit the ground. The second and third bullets—the unnecessary ones? Those she fired just for good measure, simply because she could. And those were what the prosecutor would later label as overkill and a sign of rage when it came time to try John Lassiter for first-degree murder.

CHAPTER 1

MARCH 2015

They say it happened long ago, that Sun—Tash—came so close to Earth that it was very hot. The corn and wheat dried up, and so did all the other plants. Soon there was no water left. The Tohono O'odham, the Desert People, could make nothing grow. Soon even the food they had set aside dried up and had no taste.

The Indians held a council and decided to send Tokithhud—Spider—to deal with Sun.

Every morning when Sun travels from his home in the East to the West, he makes four jumps. Spider decided to make the same four jumps. At the end of the fourth jump, he spun a web. The web, tokithhud chuaggia, *was so large that, the next day, when Tash made his fourth jump, the web caught him. Spider, hiding nearby, pulled his web so tightly around Sun's legs that he fell over and hurt himself.*

Sun was very angry. No one had ever hurt him before, and he could not believe that the people who had always loved him and sung to him would do such a terrible thing. And so he went away to his house in the East, leaving the Earth all dull and cloudy.

Soon it was very dark. The Desert People worried when Sun did not return. Their food was gone. They could not see to plant. At last the Tohono O'odham sent a message to some of the Little People, the ones who can see in the dark, and asked them what they should do. The Little People said they should divide time into four parts. In two parts they should light big fires so they could see to work in the fields. The other two parts, the ones without fires, would be for sleeping and resting.

But even though they tried this plan and worked very hard, the fires did not give enough light for the seeds to grow.

DR. LANI WALKER-PARDEE, an emergency physician at Sells Indian Hospital, believed in being prepared. The last three things she tucked into her backpack were a well-stocked first aid kit, followed by her somewhat frayed medicine basket and the new one she had made in hopes of giving it to Gabe. After fastening the pack shut she sat down on the edge of the bed, pulled on her hiking boots, and bent to lace them.

"I still don't understand why you and Gabe have to do this," her husband, Dan Pardee, grumbled. The Gabe in question was Lani's godson, Gabe Ortiz. "It's not safe for the two of you to be out there overnight. It's just not."

"I'll have Gabe with me," she said.

Dan hooted with laughter. "Gabe is thirteen. From what his dad tells me, the kid is next to useless these days. If you did get into some kind of confrontation, how much help do you think he'd be?"

Straightening up, Lani sighed and gazed at her husband with a look that was equal parts love and exasperation. "Whether he's a help or not, I still have to do it," Lani said. "I'm Gabe's godmother. Helping out at a time like this is my duty. It's expected. It's what godmothers do. We'll be fine."

Despite her reassurances, Lani could see that Dan remained unconvinced. Theirs was a mixed but generally happy marriage. On occasion, however, things could become complicated, and this was one of those times.

Lani was born of the Tohono O'odham, the Desert People, who had lived for thousands of years hunting and gathering in the desert west of where Tucson is now. Daniel was Apache through and through. The Apache didn't plant and grow. Instead, they traveled in marauding bands, stealing from others. It was no accident that in the language of the Tohono O'odham and in the languages of many other tribes as well, the word for "Apache" and the word for "enemy" were one and the same. On the Tohono O'odham reservation, Dan Pardee, a member of the Border Patrol, was a respected law enforcement officer, but behind his back and by people who didn't know him well, he was often referred to as the *Obb*—the Apache.

Lani attributed the fact that she and Dan—opposites in many ways—had met, fallen in love, and married to the behind-the-scenes workings of Ban—Coyote. Ban had a reputation for being a trickster—someone who loved practical jokes. The irony of Dan and Lani's relationship, an American Indian take on Romeo and Juliet, was apparently one of those.

For years now, Daniel Pardee had worked as a member of the Shadow Wolves, a unit of the Border

Patrol made up entirely of Native Americans who operated exclusively on the Tohono O'odham Nation, patrolling the areas where the international border with Mexico passed through tribal lands. Even though Dan was Apache, he was regarded with a good deal of trust on the reservation not only because of the respectful and honorable manner in which he did his job, but also by virtue of his being married to Lani, who, despite her relative youth, was a well-respected tribal elder.

"Look," Dan argued. "I know how serious you are about your obligations as a godmother, and I understand that the location on Kitt Peak is the same place you went to when you were a girl. I also know that you stayed out there day and night by yourself for a number of days. But the world has changed since then, Lani. Things aren't like they used to be. The desert around the base of Kitt Peak is a dangerous place now—a war zone."

Lani sighed. "But that's the whole problem. Ioligam is where we need to go."

"You can call the mountain Ioligam all you like and claim it as a sacred place, but believe me, the smugglers who are out there—terrorists who are using observation posts, combat gear, encrypted radio transmitters, and AK-47s to protect the cartels' drug shipments—don't see it that way. Too many of the bad guys out prowling the desert night after night are armed to the teeth, and they don't give a crap about the Tohono O'odham belief system. They shoot first and ask questions later. It's not safe, Lani. You can't go. I won't let you."

"Look," Lani said, "with all the Anglos coming and going from Kitt Peak, it's a lot more dangerous on the other side of Baboquivari and in the valley north of Ajo than it will be where we're going. As for smugglers on foot? They're more likely to stick to the lowlands. I doubt they'll bother climbing partway up a mountain when they could just as easily go around it. Besides, it's not a matter of your letting me do anything, Dan," she reminded him gently. "That's not how it works. Gabe's parents asked me for help, and I have to give it to them. This is important. I simply have to go."

Micah, Dan and Lani's four-year-old son, had been sitting on the floor, happily playing with a set of giant Legos, ones his mother deemed safe to play with because they were too large to be swallowed. Now, sensing tension between his parents, he looked up from his solitary game and gave his mother a beseeching look with his striking azure eyes. "Can I go, too?" he asked.

Brandon Micah Walker-Pardee had been named after Lani's Anglo adoptive father, Brandon Walker, and after Dan's grandfather, a full-blooded Apache named Micah Duarte. Part Anglo and part Indian, the boy resembled neither of his parents and was instead a throwback to Dan's Anglo father. Adam Pardee had been a reasonably good-looking Hollywood stuntman who had eventually murdered Dan's mother in a frenzied act of domestic violence.

Smiling, Lani reached down, scooped up her dark-haired, blue-eyed boy, and hugged him close. "Most certainly not," she told him. "You have to stay here and take care of Daddy while Mommy goes with Gabe. We'll be sleeping outside. The ground will be hard and cold. You need to stay here and sleep in your bed where it's warm."

Lani understood that Gabe Ortiz was the real point of contention here. And maybe, just maybe, Dan was slightly jealous of Lani's close relationship with the boy. Now two months short of his fourteenth birthday, Gabe seemed to have come to a critical fork in the road. The kid, one who had always been amenable to direction and biddable by his elders, had suddenly developed a rebellious streak and morphed into a preteen Tohono O'odham version of Dr. Jekyll and Mr. Hyde. Delia and Leo Ortiz, Gabe's frustrated and worried parents, had turned to Lani for help in steering him away from serious trouble. Since Gabe was the grandson of Lani's own beloved mentor, Gabe "Fat Crack" Ortiz, she was determined to do whatever she could to fix the problem.

"I stopped by the garage earlier today and talked to Leo about this," Dan said. "He's afraid Gabe is a lost cause, and so am I. Leo's not even sure Gabe will agree to go."

"He'll go," Lani said determinedly. "I'll see to it that he does. Not going is not an option."

"Then let me go with you," Dan said, "please. If I ask Mrs. Hendricks, I'm sure she'd be happy to look after Micah and Angie. I promise, I'll stay in the background and won't get in the way of whatever you two need to do."

Angie was Dan and Lani's ten-year-old adopted daughter. She was a responsible kid, but she was still far too young to be left in charge of her little brother overnight.

"No," Lani said firmly, "this is a private transaction between Gabe and me. It has to be just the two of us."

Dan was inordinately proud of Lani's role as a physician on the reservation, but he was somewhat less enthusiastic about her status as a traditional medicine woman. Although they had both been raised and educated off the reservation, Lani was the one who seemed to cling to the old ways and honor them, while Dan was more likely to shrug them off.

Still, Dan wouldn't give up. "But why does it have to be now?" he asked. "It's still cold as hell out there at night, freezing in fact. Couldn't all this wait until after it warms up a little?"

"It can't," Lani said simply. "The next time we both have the weekend off, it'll be the middle of May. This has to be done tonight, Dan. Gabe and I will spend the night sharing stories—I'itoi stories. Tomorrow at midnight it'll already be the middle of March. After that, it'll be too late."

Dan knew then that he was licked. When it came to storytelling, Lani was a strict observer of all applicable rules and rituals. Among the Desert People, stories were traditionally called "winter-telling tales." They were to be shared only in the wintertime. That meant they could be told between the middle of November and the middle of March. The rest of the year they were off-limits.

"Got it," Dan said, capitulating at last. "But you will take your Glock, right?"

In the past several months, at least two Tohono O'odham women driving home alone from shopping trips to Tucson had been forced off Highway 86 at gunpoint by bands of illegal immigrants. One woman had been raped by the men who had jacked her car. The other had been beaten and left for dead. After the second incident, Dan had insisted that Lani obtain a concealed carry permit. He had purchased a Glock for her and made sure she knew how to use it.

"Even if you're not worried about smugglers, then have it along in case you run into a snake fresh out of hibernation."

"Yes, sir," Lani said, giving her concerned husband a smile and a mock salute. "Wouldn't leave home without it. Now, how about helping me drag this stuff out front? Leo and Gabe will be by any minute to pick me up."

"You're sure you don't need my help carrying gear up the mountain and making your campsite?"

"Stop worrying," Lani said. "Leo promised to handle all that."

Dan sighed. "All right then," he said. "Have it your way." With that, he picked up Lani's loaded backpack and headed for the front door.

"Do I HAVE to go?" Gabe Ortiz whined. He was lying on the bed, playing with the controls on his Xbox. "Why can't I just stay here? It's going to be cold out there. We'll probably freeze to death up on the mountain."

Delia Cachora Ortiz, hands on her sturdy hips, glared at her son. "You won't freeze, and yes, you have to go. As for why? Because I said so."

As tribal chairman, Delia Ortiz wielded a good deal of influence all over the vast Tohono O'odham Nation. Her husband, Leo, was on the tribal council—a representative from the Sells District. The respect Gabe and Delia were shown outside their home didn't necessarily carry over into what went on inside. Delia knew she bore most of the responsibility for what had happened. Gabe was an only child. She had coddled him, spoiled him. For a time, that hadn't mattered, but once he turned twelve, it seemed as though someone had flipped a switch. Up till then, the boy, named in honor of his grandfather, Gabe "Fat Crack" Ortiz, had always been an excellent student and a good kid. Now his grades had fallen through the floor, and he was palling around with a bad bunch of kids.

Delia and Leo had tried their best to warn Gabe that he was headed for trouble. They had reasoned with him, threatened, and cajoled until they were blue in the face, but nothing they said had the least effect. As a last resort, they had turned to Lani for help, hoping she could somehow work a miracle. The geographical cure she suggested wasn't at all what Delia and Leo had expected. Packing the boy off to what amounted to a boarding-school situation in Tucson sounded like a last resort, but it would be better than his ending up in juvie.

That was what tonight was all about. Lani was determined to take Gabe into the desert and try to convince him to turn his life around. His parents' other option to help him avoid juvie was to send him to live with Delia's mother and attend school on the East Coast. Leo had told his wife straight out that he didn't believe having Lani Walker-Pardee "shake a few feathers" at the boy would do the least bit of good, but Delia was desperate, and a dose of Lani's medicine-woman treatment was their last hope.

"Put down that game, get off your butt, and pack up," Delia ordered. "You'll need a coat, a scarf, and probably some extra pairs of socks."

"You expect me to stay out all night in this weather?" Gabe grumbled. "How's that possible? I don't even have a sleeping bag."

"You won't need a sleeping bag," Delia countered. "Your dad got out a couple of his father's wool blankets for you to use."

The several colorful and tightly woven Navajo blankets that had once belonged to Fat Crack Ortiz were now among Leo Ortiz's most prized possessions. The garage and towing company that had once belonged to Fat Crack had been left to both his sons, Leo and Richard. Over time, Leo had bought out Richard's share of the business. The blankets, though, had been his alone from the beginning, inherited outright. They were kept in a cedar-lined chest, safe from damage by moths and other insects, and were only brought out on special occasions. Gabe should have been honored that he would be allowed to use them tonight, but he was not.

"Great," Gabe sneered. "Those scratchy old things? I'd rather freeze."

"Suit yourself then," his mother told him angrily. "That's totally up to you."

CHAPTER 2

For a long time after I'itoi, the Spirit of Goodness, who is sometimes called Elder Brother, made everything and set Tash on his path across the sky, the days were warm and bright, and every day was just the same. That was good for making corn—huhni—*and wheat*—pilkani—*grow and ripen in the fields, but sometimes the nights in the desert were very cold.*

The People thought about this and decided that it would be nice to have heat whenever they wanted it. They tried to ask I'itoi about it, but Elder Brother was too busy, so the Tohono O'odham decided they must help themselves. They held a council and decided what to do. This is how Fire—Tai—was brought from Tash—Sun.

Early one morning, before Tash started his jumps across the sky, Old Woman—O'oks—was sent with a burden basket—gihwo—*to get some of Sun's heat so the people could have some of its warmth. O'oks went very fast, but even so she was far too slow. By the time she reached the East—Si'al—where*

Tash makes his home, Sun was already far into that day's journey. He was very high in the sky by then and also very hot. When O'oks came home with her burden basket empty, the People asked her to go again, but she refused. The Tohono O'odham shrugged and said that O'oks was too old and slow, and so they sent Boy—Cheoj. When Boy returned, he said that when he was almost there, Tash was so hot that he could not see, and so he, too, had come back empty-handed.

The People thought that this was just another excuse, but they decided that they would wait until the end of Sun's journey, because they wanted the heat for the night. This time they sent Kelimai—Old Man, an elder. Old Man ran all day to get to the place where Tash stays at night. When he came back the next day, he did not have any heat. He said that at the end of the day Tash jumped into a big hole, and that the Desert People would have to send Thah O'odham, the Flying People.

Next the People asked Moth. Hu'ul-nahgi went to the house of Sun, which, as you know, nawoj, *my friend, is in the East on the far side of the Earth. Moth told Sun how sorry the Indians were and how much they needed Tash to return so they could grow their seeds and have food to eat.*

By this time Sun was well, and he was no longer so angry. He agreed to return. But Moth was worried. He asked Sun if he could please walk farther away from the earth so it would not be so hot and make everything dry up.

Sun thought about that and then he agreed. He said that on his first jump in the morning, he would have his niece go with him and kick a ball of red dust to keep the earth from becoming too hot. He said that in the late afternoon, he would have his nephew come along and kick a red ball of dust to make the evenings cooler.

And that is why, nawoj, *my friend, even to this day we have red clouds at sunrise and sunset, because of those red balls of dust.*

Brandon Walker handed over his drink ticket and put a buck in the bartender's tip glass. Then, taking his clear plastic cup of red wine—Turkey Creek merlot—he made his way through the University of Arizona bookstore teeming with the noisy chatter of enthusiastic partygoers. He found himself a quiet corner where he could be out of sight while still keeping an eye on the proceedings around him and also on the group of adoring fans clustered around his wife. Fame seemed to follow Diana Ladd wherever she went, and it was easier for Brandon to keep watch from a distance than it was to be constantly elbowed out of the way.

This cattle-call gathering in the bookstore on Friday evening marked the opening event for that year's Tucson Festival of Books. The reception came first, followed immediately by the Authors' Dinner in one of the student union's upstairs ballrooms across the breezeway. Since Diana was thought to be one of the local literary luminaries, it was only natural that she would be front and center. Her recent biography of Geronimo, *Trail's End,* had turned into a surprise blockbuster. So far it had spent seven weeks on the *New York Times* nonfiction list, clocking in this week at number eight.

The critics had raved about it: "Ladd's lyrical prose transcends the whole idea of scholarly biography and brings a tragic American icon to life on the page."

Brandon tended to focus on positive reviews, and those were the ones he bothered remembering. Diana had taught him to mentally deep-six those that weren't so kind.

He realized that part of what had made Geronimo "come to life" on the pages of Diana's book had to do with the fact that she had spent most of her adult life living among the original settlers of the American Southwest, most particularly among the Tohono O'odham, whose traditional homeland had, since time immemorial, been the vast valley surrounding what was now metropolitan Tucson.

Brandon understood that Diana's deft treatment of Geronimo had grown out of the presence of their son-in-law, Dan Pardee, in their lives. Dan's Apache heritage and the able assistance of Dan's grandfather, Micah Duarte, had given Diana, an Anglo, entrée into the world of Apache oral history and tradition that was accessible to only a select few. Without that, details of Geronimo's life both before and after his surrender might have been treated as little more than footnotes by a less talented writer.

Trail's End, along with Diana's several other books, accounted for why she was being feted tonight at the Authors' Dinner and for the remainder of the weekend. Brandon's role in the festivities was that of escort and backup. Even though he was halfway across the room, he sipped his wine and kept her in view through the crush of people milling around her.

Brandon knew what to watch for—the fans who stayed too long or who monopolized her time and attention, the people who took it upon themselves to lay a hand on her in a more personal way than a simple handshake or greeting. And if someone became too pushy and Brandon happened to miss the warning signs, Diana could always summon him from across the room by using their secret hand signal. A simple touch to her right earlobe would alert him to the fact that one of her fans was being troublesome and needed to be encouraged to go elsewhere.

"Hey, there," someone said from the far side of one

of the movable book shelves behind which Brandon had taken shelter. "How's Mr. Diana Ladd this fine evening?"

Looking around, Brandon was dismayed to see Oliver Glassman making a beeline in his direction. Ollie Glassman was exactly the kind of person Brandon had hoped to avoid. He was a smarmy jerk who had started out as a lowly public defender before becoming the heir apparent in his father's legal defense firm. Managing to manipulate a somewhat thin résumé as a springboard into politics, Glassman had served several terms on the Pima County Board of Supervisors, was currently a member of the state senate, and was rumored to be thinking about running for Congress.

"Matty told me you and Diana would be here tonight. I believe you two are seated at our table. Matty's part of the committee that organizes the dinner, you know," Ollie added.

That last bit of info was entirely unnecessary. Brandon Walker was well aware that Ollie's wife, Matilda Glassman, was one of the movers and shakers behind Tucson's burgeoning book festival. Diana had told him as much, and although Diana tolerated Matilda, she liked the woman almost as much as Brandon liked Ollie. If Diana had known the seating arrangements in advance, she hadn't mentioned them to Brandon. Perhaps she had neglected to do so out of concern that he'd be a no-show. On the other hand, it was possible that she would be as surprised and dismayed as he was.

Ollie took a long pull on his wine, draining half the glass in a single gulp. "What are you doing hanging around in the kiddy-lit section?" he asked. "Thinking about doing some writing yourself?"

In the years Diana Ladd and Brandon Walker had been married, Brandon had done plenty of duty as Diana's escort at book festivals and writers' conferences all over the country. He knew the drill. He also understood some of the pitfalls of being "Mr. Diana Ladd." He had long ago lost count of the people who would look at him agog and ask, "What's it like being married to a famous person?" Another of his least favorite inquiries was a clueless "Oh, are you a writer, too?"

Ollie's inept question was a variation on the latter. Brandon's standard reply was usually: "Diana writes the books; I write the checks." This time, however, an imp took control of his response mechanism.

"Yes," Brandon answered. "I've even got a working title: *So You Want to Be a Sheriff When You Grow Up?* It's a how-to book for kids who are seven or eight, and it's due to be published by a company that specializes in career guidance for grade schoolers."

Ollie frowned and examined the small amount of wine remaining in his glass. "Sounds like a great idea. Do you think they'd want me to do one, too—about wanting to be a defense attorney?

It took some effort for Brandon to keep from cracking a smile. "I'm having an editorial meeting with my publisher next week," he replied. "I'll ask her what she thinks."

The lights blinked overhead, signaling that it was time to head for the ballroom. Catching Matty's eye, Ollie raised his empty glass. With a reproving look, his wife turned her back and returned to the bar.

"I don't know why they have to be so stingy with the wine at these affairs," Ollie muttered. "You pay a fortune to attend, and all they give you is a single drink ticket. What's up with that? But I did want to have a word in private," he continued. "I guess you heard about Big Bad John."

"Big Bad John Lassiter?" Brandon asked. "I haven't heard a word from or about him since the last judge locked him up and threw away the key. That's a long time ago now. What's going on?"

Matilda delivered Ollie's wine. "We're going in soon," she said with a scowl. "Don't be late."

Ollie sighed and shook his head as she stalked away. "The old girl's got her panties in a twist tonight," he observed, downing another gulp of wine. It was evident that sipping the stuff wasn't part of the man's repertoire. "I don't know why she insists on being involved in crap like this when it obviously drives her nuts."

Brandon suspected that wrangling the complexities of the book festival wasn't nearly as much of a problem for Matilda Glassman as wrangling Oliver.

"What about Lassiter?" Brandon reminded him.

"Oh, yes, that's what I need to talk to you about," Ollie answered, "the part about throwing away the key. Have you ever heard of a group of do-gooders called Justice for All?"

Brandon knew a little about the organization. It was composed of people steadfastly devoted to freeing people they felt had been unjustly locked up by the criminal justice system. They utilized modern forensics, including DNA profiling, to win releases for those they believed had been wrongly accused and convicted. Brandon understood there were instances in which innocent folks had been locked up for decades. The problem was, there were also times when the JFA folks' definition of "all" often didn't seem to take the victims of the crimes—either the homicide victims themselves or their grieving loved ones—into account.

After decades of police work, Brandon's feet remained firmly planted on the victims' side of the fence. In retirement, he had signed on with The Last Chance. TLC consisted of a group of retired cops, criminalists, medical examiners, and district attorneys who devoted their time and energy to solving stone-cold homicides—the ones law enforcement had long since abandoned as hopeless. Like JFA, TLC also used modern forensics and technology to bring to account any number of bad guys who thought they'd gotten away with murder.

"Since I work for what some regard as the opposing team, I don't pay much attention to JFA," Brandon said, edging toward the door. "I'm a lot more concerned with closing prison doors than I am with opening them. But speaking of opposing teams, weren't you Lassiter's defense attorney that first time around?"

Ollie nodded. "I was. Public defender the first time around and private for the second one when he appealed that first conviction. The case against him was all circumstantial. I never thought they'd lock him up for 'life without' either time. I'm sure it was all my fault. I was relatively inexperienced the first time and probably didn't do quite as good a job as I should have. Five years later, I was back at the defense table again hoping we'd get him out on a technicality. Unfortunately, that didn't work, either."

"I take it these JFA folks have now parachuted in and done what you couldn't?"

"More or less," Glassman agreed glumly. "They seem to have negotiated a deal with the county attorney. Lassiter could either go for a third trial or he could cop to second degree and get out with time served. I sent my son, Ollie—that's Oliver Junior, who's in the process of taking over my practice—to look in on the situation. Pro bono, of course, just as a courtesy.

"The thing is, Lassiter is saying no-go. He told them he doesn't want a third trial, and he's turned down the plea deal, too. Flat. Said he'd already served more than thirty years for a crime he didn't commit, and he'd be damned if he'd plead guilty to something he didn't do just to have a get-out-of-jail-free card. The JFA folks had made a big deal about working his case, and they're still hoping to save face. At this point, they've avoided making any public announcement that he won't go along with any of it. As for Lassiter? According to Junior, what he really wants right now is a chance to talk to you."

"To me?" Brandon said in surprise. "How come?"

"He evidently remembers you from back then."

"Since I was the cop who put the cuffs on him originally, I suppose he does remember me. But why on earth would he want to talk to me?"

"He said he'd heard you were retired and were busy solving cold cases these days. He wants to talk to you about finding Amos Warren's real killer."

"Sort of like O.J., you mean?"

"More or less. Lassiter told Junior that just because the cops are calling the case closed doesn't mean it's solved!"

Across the room, Diana turned and beckoned to Brandon. "Oops," he said. "Duty calls. We'd best get a move on."

Ollie delayed him for a moment by reaching into the pocket of his suit coat and pulling out a business card. "It's Junior's," he explained. "If you do decide to look into this, I'd appreciate your keeping him in the loop."

Reluctantly, Brandon took the card, slipped it into his own pocket, and then made his way toward the bookstore entrance and up the stairway to the ballroom. Using the table number on his name badge, he found where he was supposed to be. Matilda Glassman was already on hand directing traffic and motioning people into preselected seats. The arrangement left Brandon on the far side of the table from his wife, who was seated next to Ollie, while Brandon was sandwiched between a philosophy professor and the wife of a banker who happened to be a major donor.

The philosophy professor offered Brandon a tepid handshake and turned her attention to the person seated on her left. The banker's wife, clearly out of her element, attacked her salad with a total focus that told Brandon she was beyond shy. He suspected that she, too, would have been far more comfortable seated next to her spouse rather than across the table from him. After a few abortive attempts to engage the woman in conversation, Brandon gave up. Instead, he settled into his own food, all the while keeping track of what was going on across the table.

By then, Ollie, clearly into his cups and despite the daggers being sent his way by his wife, was talking a blue streak. At one point, Diana looked away from him and sent a questioning raised-eyebrow look in her husband's direction. No doubt Glassman had just spilled the beans about Brandon Walker's faux writing career. A moment later, when Diana smiled at him and gave him a slight nod, Brandon knew that she got the joke.

There was something about that shared smile—a moment of silent connection in that crowded, noisy room—that made Brandon's heart sing. The look didn't just cross the table; it bridged the years as well. He remembered the moment in 1975 when he'd first been smitten. He had met Diana years earlier in the course of a homicide case in which her first husband, Garrison Ladd, and Garrison's mentor and former creative writing professor, Andrew Carlisle, had both been suspects. Ladd had supposedly committed suicide, while his co-conspirator had gone to prison.

Years later, Carlisle's early release from prison had put Diana in jeopardy as Carlisle came after her, intent on wreaking vengeance on the woman who had helped send him away. At about the same time, Brandon and Diana had once more been thrown together when Diana's six-year-old son, Davy, was injured in a car accident on the reservation. Brandon had been sent to notify Diana of the incident. Since the boy was an Anglo and couldn't be treated by the Indian Health Service, Brandon had offered to drive Diana to Sells so she'd be able to look after the boy.

In the ER, when it came time for the doctor to put twelve stitches in her son's head, Diana had been forced to bail. Brandon was the one who had stayed at the boy's side. And that night, Brandon had stayed on at Diana's house to help keep the boy awake overnight. That was how he had spent that first night in the house that he and Diana had now shared for years—sleeping on her living room couch.

Yes, Andrew Carlisle had been beyond evil, but without him and his murderous ways, Brandon knew that he and Diana would never have met. In the years since, the two of them had married and raised two amazing kids together—Diana's son, Davy, and an adopted Indian child named Lani. The less said about Brandon's own kids the better, but Davy was now a successful Tucson-based attorney, and Lani was the first ever Tohono O'odham M.D. to practice on the reservation.

As for Diana? In his eyes, although her blond hair had long since turned silver—she preferred the word "platinum"—she was still as beautiful as ever. And even if he had to spend a thousand nights like this, making small talk and enduring the rigors of being "Mr. Diana Ladd," Brandon still counted himself as incredibly lucky to be there with her.

When the after-dinner speeches ended and they headed home toward Gates Pass, Diana nailed Brandon for suckering Ollie Glassman.

"You told the poor man you're writing a book?" Diana asked. "Really?"

"I couldn't help myself," Brandon said, grinning at the very thought of it. "The guy's a jerk."

"That's true," Diana agreed. "I saw him tracking you down during the reception. What did he want?"

That surprised Brandon. He knew he had been keeping an eye on Diana from across the room, but he hadn't realized that she'd also been keeping an eye on him.

"He wanted to talk to me about John Lassiter."

"Big Bad John? Whoa, that's a name out of the dim, dark past."

"Indeed," Brandon agreed.

"So why talk to you about it? I heard they were trying to work out a plea deal of some kind. Evidently two trials weren't enough."

"Wait," Brandon said. "You knew about that—about the plea offer?"

"I read about it in the paper," Diana said with a shrug. "I seem to remember Lassiter's daughter was responsible for bringing in the people from Justice for All."

"John Lassiter has a daughter?" Brandon asked. "What daughter? I didn't know Lassiter had a child."

"He does."

Brandon thought about that. He and Diana read the same papers each day over their morning cups of coffee. Even so, they often came away with totally different sets of information.

"Since you and Michael Farraday were the officers who arrested Lassiter back in the day," Diana continued, "I figured it was just as well to let sleeping dogs lie."

"This particular dog is no longer sleeping," Brandon said. "What did Ollie Glassman want?"

"He says Lassiter asked to see me. He wants TLC to find Amos Warren's real killer."

"Sounds like O. J. Simpson," Diana said.

Brandon laughed aloud at that. "We've been married so long it's no wonder that you and I are on the same wavelength. That's exactly what I told Glassman—just like O.J."

CHAPTER 3

For a long time after Tash returned, things went well. Because of the clouds, it wasn't too hot. Rain, Juk, returned. The Tohono O'odham planted their fields and the crops grew, and every morning and evening, Sun's niece and nephew kicked the dust balls. In a village near the Coyote Mountains lived a woman who braided the grass mats upon which the Desert People sleep. This Braiding Woman, Hihgtpag O'oks, was a fast worker. She could weave as many as four large mats in a single day.

One day while Braiding Woman was working, Nephew-of-the-Sun kicked his red ball so hard that it rolled onto the mat the woman was weaving. The woman quickly picked up the ball and hid it in her dress. When Nephew-of-the-Sun came looking for it, the woman claimed she hadn't seen it. He said that was very strange since he had seen it land on her mat, and some of the dust was still there.

Hihgtpag O'oks—Braiding Woman—still claimed that she hadn't seen it. After a while Nephew-of-the-Sun grew very angry. "If you keep it, something very bad will happen to you, because the red dust ball belongs to Tash." After that the nephew went away.

Braiding Woman was very frightened. She called Nephew-of-the-Sun to come back for the ball, but when he did, she couldn't find it.

On the eighth day after this, around noon when it is very hot and all the animals are sleeping, Braiding Woman became very sleepy. That was strange because she always worked through the day without needing to rest. She asked Cricket—Chukugshuad—to sing to her to keep her awake. Cricket tried, but it was no use. Braiding Woman had to sleep.

AVA RICHLAND, WITH the remains of her blended scotch in hand, sat in solitary splendor in her lushly appointed living room and gazed serenely out through floor-to-ceiling windows at the sunset over the Tucson panorama. From their home, situated on the last buildable lot, high in the Catalinas, she could see almost the whole of the city, stretching for the better part of twenty miles in any direction. Their property line bordered Forest Service land, with the sheer cliffs of the mountain rising skyward less than fifty yards beyond that.

"I built there because of the view," Harold, the man who would be her husband, had bragged back when he and Ava had first met. "Best view in town. No one can ever top it. I made sure of that."

Of course, the view would have been better if it hadn't been for those pesky Dark Sky people. Ava had no patience for what she regarded as a bunch of wild-eyed activists who thought it was so much more important to keep the skies dark for the astronomers at Kitt Peak than it was to have adequate lighting on the city's streets. Especially now, with the arrival of cataracts—particularly the one in her right eye—she was of the opinion that seeing to drive down the street was far more important that seeing what was happening on Mars.

Ava glanced at her diamond-encrusted Datejust Rolex, one that had once belonged to Alvira, Harold's first wife, and saw that it was just now seven. In recent years, she would have been at the University of Arizona campus, rubbing shoulders with all the other Tucson VIPs at the Authors' Dinner for the Tucson Festival of Books. Her good friend Matilda Glassman had always made sure that Ava and Harold were seated at a table with one of the big-name visiting authors.

Ava tended to enjoy those dinners, even if Harold despised them. She had made her way up from some very straitened circumstances, and Ava still got a charge out of being seen in public, where she and Harold were regarded as one of the city's luminary couples. She liked being photographed at charity events, even if her place in the limelight was due to the size of Harold's donations. As far as Ava was concerned, people like Matty Glassman were welcome to hustle around and do the actual work.

This year's Authors' Dinner was going on without either one of them. They'd had tickets, and Harold had suggested that she go without him, but because she knew that Harold's son and daughter-in-law, Jack and Susan, would be there too, Ava had declined. She made it sound to Harold as though she couldn't bear to go without him. The truth was, she didn't want to be in the same room—even a ballroom—with Jack and Susan. Ava disliked the couple, and she knew the feeling was mutual. If she showed up without Harold, Susan was bound to stop by Ava's table long enough to make some catty remark about it being such a shame that poor Harold was once again left to his own devices.

Of course, neither Jack nor Susan ever offered to drop by and stay with "poor Harold." And the man wasn't exactly on his own, either, since his live-in attendant—what was her name again?—was just a few steps away, at the call of a pager.

Ava could see that Harold was growing frailer by the day, and that was a problem. If Harold died—make that *when* Harold died—Ava needed to have her exit strategy completely in place. That was one thing she'd always prided herself on having—an exit strategy. No matter what the circumstances, she was always prepared for the moment when she'd be forced to abandon ship.

Ten years earlier, when she'd nailed Harold, Ava had thought she'd finally found a ship she wouldn't have to abandon. True, Alvira hadn't been entirely cold in her grave before Ava made her move. But Harold was considered a great catch. If she hadn't gone after him when she did, someone else certainly would have.

Harold was at the top of the heap in Tucson at the time, and not just in terms of housing. He was tall, handsome, and rich, and he hadn't yet had either of his two debilitating strokes. Through a series of strategic marriages and at least one tactically brilliant divorce, Ava had been lucky enough to position herself on the fringes of Harold's circle of friends. Younger than most of the other women in the group, she'd had beauty on her side, to say nothing of a sexual appetite Harold was determined to satisfy. He hadn't been quite up to that task, but Ava was discreet about it. What the poor man didn't know about his inadequacies couldn't hurt him.

Ava had taken up with a somewhat older man, thirty

years and counting, fully expecting that after putting in some time reveling in his lavish lifestyle, she'd be left to live out her days as a well-heeled widow. Harold had redone his will shortly after he and Ava married. His kids weren't left out in the cold by any means, but neither was Ava. A short time later, however, his busybody son, Jack—a lawyer himself—had seen to it that the will was rewritten. This time the house and most of Harold's assets were locked up in a complicated marital trust that didn't exactly turn Ava into a pauper, but it meant putting a trustee—who just happened to be one of Jack's best buds—in charge of her purse strings. The trust meant Ava wouldn't be able to make a move on any of those assets—including unloading that huge house in which she had a life tenancy, or even their getaway condo in San Carlos, Mexico—without the trustee's explicit, written permission. As far as Ava was concerned, that was the last straw. She had stopped playing Mother-May-I a long damned time ago!

That was when she began working on this most recent exit strategy. As she had fought her way up from the bottom of the heap, she had been careful not to burn any bridges. She didn't send out Christmas cards to folks from her old life, but she still knew where useful people were and how to get in touch with them. She remained friends with the people she had enlisted to help dispose of the treasure trove she had lifted from Amos Warren's storage locker. Even then, she had been smart enough to realize that she was dealing with top-drawer goods. With access to Amos Warren's little black book, she'd been able to make sure she sold to only the best possible folks.

Ava had started out in the drug trade, back when trafficking had been a wildly profitable freelance operation—back before the cartels got involved and smuggling became a far more dangerous and murderous occupation. She and a girlfriend, or a boyfriend as the case may be, would drive down to Nogales or Naco or Agua Prieta, smile and wave at the customs guy, and be back home with the goods, free and clear, in a jiffy. And she'd always been smart enough at it that she'd never been caught.

Big Bad John Lassiter had been dazzled by her looks. Amos Warren hadn't. Worried that he might turn her in, she'd taken him off the board. The poor sap had probably thought she was bluffing when he saw the gun pointed at him. Too bad. You snooze, you lose.

The fact that Ava had been able to make off with a fortune in artifacts after Amos's death was nothing more than a happy coincidence, one that she had used to good advantage. The resulting money had made possible a complete makeover, one that had given Ava entrée into one of the top-tier escort services in town. From there it had been only a small step to her first upwardly mobile set of marriage vows.

Over the years, however, she hadn't crossed any of the useful people from the bad old days off her list. Guys she knew from her earlier drug-dealing exploits—the ones who were still alive, anyway—were easy to find because many of them were still in prison and could lead her to a whole new generation of useful contacts. Someone she had met in her escort-service days had turned into a very capable forger who could, with a few strokes of a pen, turn a blood diamond into a conflict-free one that was good to go for two to three times what she paid for it initially. And that was Ava's focus these days—smuggling diamonds. Blood diamonds could be bought on the cheap. Certified diamonds went for a bundle, and that was the whole idea—buy cheap and sell high.

Why diamonds? She'd been in the illicit Indian artifact business for a while, but pots were usually too hard to find. Diamonds were easier to come by, and they weighed a lot less. At the moment, nobody, including the cartels, Border Patrol, and the occasional robber, seemed to be looking for diamonds, at least not so far.

A year or so earlier Ava and Harold had been returning to the United States from their condo in San Carlos with a jar full of peanut butter, which Ava had salted with diamonds. South of Nogales, they'd been pulled over by a bunch of gun-toting banditos posing as Federales. The crooks had happily relieved Harold of his wallet and Ava of her purse, making off with close to a thousand bucks in cash, but they had completely missed the diamond-stuffed peanut butter jar sitting in plain sight in the picnic cooler. The crooks hadn't been any the wiser, and for that matter, neither had Harold.

Ava no longer brought the goods across the border herself; that was far too dangerous these days. Now she had a small crew of worker bees to do that part of the job. She figured it would only take a couple more shipments to have enough to make a break for it as soon as Harold corked off, which might well be sooner than later.

The problem was, she had recently learned that a ghost from her past was about to surface. What she didn't need right now was anything at all that would call attention to her earlier life. Unfortunately, according to the newspaper that morning, Big Bad John Lassiter's name was once more in the news. If he ended up back in court, someone might well dig deep enough into the past to learn that a girl named Ava Martin, now Mrs. Harold Richland, had been a prosecution witness in both of John's previous murder trials. That might be enough to bring her entire enterprise crashing down around her ears. There was no way in hell she was going to let that happen.

Ava's drink was gone. She was ready for another. Before she got up to pour it, she kicked off her high heels. Most women her age had given up wearing heels by now, but not Ava. Whenever Harold was up and about, she was careful to dress the part. A dyed-in-the-wool Republican, he had always raved about Nancy Reagan. In Ava's continuing effort to give Harold no cause for complaint, she emulated Nancy in every way—right down to the pearls, the chic size four tailored suits, and the high heels. That evening, though, since Harold had already checked out and gone night-night, she let her stockinged feet revel in the lush living room carpeting.

At the bar, Ava refilled her glass—no ice—and stood staring back and forth between the two trophies she had held back when she had sold off Amos Warren's goods. One was a tiny pot, a miniature olla, that she had kept and treasured from the moment she pulled the cloth-wrapped piece out of Amos Warren's stolen backpack. The other was a serving-tray-sized flat hunk of limestone with the skeleton of what looked like a crocodile fossilized inside it. That hadn't come from the backpack. Ava had stolen it from Amos's house when she'd cleaned that out, too. She wouldn't have had any idea what it was had Amos not gone to the trouble of sticking a helpful label on the back. Printed in fading but still readable ink on a piece of masking tape were the words *Phytosaur, Willcox Playa, 1967,* followed by the initials AW.

For some reason, those two pieces had captured Ava's imagination—the tiny pot and the Gila-monster-sized fossil. After Amos's death, she had revisited the area around the crime scene numerous times. Johnny had taught her enough about searching for artifacts that she had known to go looking farther upstream, and she had lucked out, finding a whole other treasure trove of unbroken pots. Each of those she'd sold to the highest bidder without a second thought.

But Fito, as she called her fossilized treasure, and the tiny pot were hers to keep, and she had never considered selling either one. Instead, she had displayed them together, in one home after another, as she gradually moved up in the world to ever more upscale digs.

In this house, for instance, high in the Catalinas, Ava kept the olla on a clear glass shelf high above the bar, the humble piece of reddish clay keeping company with Harold's first wife's collection of elegant Rosenthal crystal stemware. The rock platter, along with its nightmarish, toothy captive, stood on the counter, propped against the bar's mirror, where it served as a somewhat fierce background to Harold's collection of expensive booze.

Taking the pot down from its place on the shelf, Ava stood there for a time, absently tracing the tips of her fingers over the faint image that remained stubbornly etched there—a tortoise and an owl. She often wondered about them—about why those two images had been placed there together. They seemed so different, and yet here they were in some kind of mysterious juxtaposition.

It was as her fingers slid thoughtfully across those mysterious figures that she reached a final conclusion about what she should do—a decision she'd been wrestling with all day long, since the moment she had seen the article in the newspaper.

After all these years, there was a good chance that Big Bad John Lassiter was about to have yet a third trial for a murder Ava herself had committed. She had dodged that bullet the first two times, but what if new information had come to light, especially something that might implicate her?

"That's not going to happen," Ava vowed aloud to herself as she returned the pot to its place on the shelf. "Not, not, not!"

Taking her new drink in hand, Ava made her way into the bedroom—into *her* bedroom; she and Harold had separate bedrooms these days. Setting her untouched drink down on the counter in the bathroom, she ducked into the attached walk-in closet. In the backmost wall, in the section behind her floor-length gowns, was the wall safe in which Alvira, her predecessor, had once kept her considerable collection of jewelry, which had, of course, been divvied up between Harold's two kids upon Ava's arrival.

Harold could no longer get around well enough to get to the safe on his own. He had no idea that Ava had long since changed the combination, and for good reason, too. That was where she was slowly accumulating her supply of diamonds along with a collection of forged passports, IDs, and preloaded credit cards. It was also where she kept a collection of burner phones. Just because she knew how to get in touch with people didn't necessarily mean that she wanted them to be able to get back in touch with her.

Taking one of those out, she consulted the little black book that also resided in the safe. She found the number she needed and made the call. There was no sense in stalling around about it. She had made her decision.

Big Bad John Lassiter had to go, the sooner the better!

CHAPTER 4

They say it happened long ago that Young Girl—Chehia—from Rattlesnake Skull village, was out walking in the desert where she found a young man who was injured. He was lying under a mesquite tree, crying. Young Girl knew at once that Young Man was Apache, Ohb. Even though she did not speak Young Man's language, Young Girl knew that he needed help.

You must understand, nawoj, *my friend, that the Apache and the Desert People have always been enemies. When I'itoi created everything, he loved the Tohono O'odham, the Desert People. They were friendly and industrious, so I'itoi kept them living close to his sacred mountain, Ioligam, where they stayed busy in their fields, growing corn and wheat, melons and squash.*

But I'itoi found the Apache troublesome. They quarreled a lot and they were very lazy, so I'itoi sent them to live on the far side of the desert. There they found plenty of animals to hunt, but it was hard to grow food. And so, whenever the Apaches grew too hungry, they would ride across the desert to steal the food the Desert People had grown.

When Chebia, Young Girl, found the injured man, she could have just walked away. But he cried so piteously that she did not. Instead, she helped him to a nearby cave and hid him there. Every day, she would slip away from the village and bring him water to drink and food to eat. Soon he grew well enough to return to his own people, but by then Young Man and Young Girl had fallen in love. He asked Chebia to run away with him, but she was afraid to leave her own people.

One day, when she brought Young Man's food, he pointed off across the valley to a place where smoke was rising in the air. "Those signals are signs that my people are coming," he said. "You must run back to the village and warn yours that they are in danger."

LANI'S BODY TENSED with unease as Leo Ortiz turned the Toyota Tundra off the highway and headed down Coleman Road. The three of them—Leo Ortiz, Lani, and Leo's son, Gabe—had driven the whole way from Sells in almost total silence, one broken only by incessant clicks from the video game Gabe was playing on his phone in the backseat.

Off to the left, Lani could see the charco, the water hole, that in her mind still belonged to the long-abandoned village of Rattlesnake Skull. Now, as often happened when she was upset, the almost invisible pin-sized flaws on Lani's face—ones she covered each morning with deftly applied makeup—began to prickle and itch. She knew what was causing the old ant bites to burn—Rattlesnake Skull charco was where all this had started so many years ago. The water hole was where the authorities had found the body of

Gina Antone, a teenage Tohono O'odham girl who had been tortured and murdered by an evil *ohb*-like Anglo named Andrew Carlisle. Garrison Ladd, Lani's mother's first husband, had been a suspect in that case right along with Carlisle.

In the course of the homicide investigation, Diana and the dead girl's grandmother, Rita Antone, had been thrown together. To everyone's amazement and to the dismay of the people on the reservation, the two women—the Indian and the Anglo, the old Tohono O'odham widow and the young Milgahn one—had become fast friends.

On the reservation, Rita Antone, originally from Topawa, had long been known as Hejel Wi i'thag, Left Alone. At the time, Diana, a teacher on the reservation, had been living in a teachers' compound mobile home in the same village. United in their mutual loss and grief, the two women had left the reservation behind and moved to Tucson, where they had worked together to rehab a ramshackle river-rock house in the Tucson Mountains. When Diana's son, Davy, was born, Rita looked after him and became the boy's beloved Nana *Dahd,* his godmother. Years later, when Lani was adopted into the Ladd/Walker household, Rita Antone became Lani's godmother, too.

Lani was eleven years younger than Davy. Even though Rita was elderly by the time Lani showed up, it was Rita who had schooled both children in the sacred traditions and legends of the Tohono O'odham. She was the one who had taught them the endangered ancient art of basketmaking and had pointed out and given names to the various herbs, plants, and fruits that were at home in the Arizona desert. Rita had carefully described how some of the plants were useful in the healing arts while others were used in religious ceremonies. She also made sure they could easily recognize and avoid the ones that were poisonous and even deadly.

And it was through Rita that Lani had come to the attention of Brandon Walker and Diana Ladd.

Lani had begun life on the Tohono O'odham as the neglected child of a jailed father and a runaway mother. Abandoned while still a toddler, Clemencia Escalante, as Lani was known back then, had been left in the care of an impoverished, aged, and exceedingly deaf grandmother in the village of Nolic, which means The Bend. During the summer months, the older children in Nolic had helped look after Clemencia, but once school started, the baby, little more than a year old, had been the only child left in the village.

On a warm September afternoon with her caretaker sound asleep, Clemencia had somehow made her way outside—probably through a door left open to allow a bit of breeze into the rough adobe house. Outside and unsupervised, the child had wandered away from the house. Eventually she had become trapped in a nest of Maricopa harvester ants, whose venom is legendary. There was little doubt that she had screamed as the ants bit into her because she was still screaming an hour or so later when the school bus dropped off the other children. The children were the ones who found her, not the grandmother. Lack of hearing was the reason the grandmother hadn't heard the child screaming, but for the authorities, an even greater concern was that she had failed to notice that the little girl had gone missing.

Close to death from the poison of literally hundreds

of bites, Clemencia had been transported first to the Sells Indian Hospital. When her condition worsened, she was taken to the ER at Tucson Medical Center. At the time, Wanda Ortiz, Fat Crack's wife and Gabe's grandmother, had been the social worker in charge of Clemencia's case.

Clemencia was still hospitalized in Tucson when, on a trip back to Sells from seeing her, Wanda and Fat Crack had stopped by the house to see Rita Antone, Fat Crack's auntie. In the course of the conversation, Wanda had mentioned the situation with the little ant-bit girl. By now the grandmother had been deemed an unsuitable guardian. Even though some of Clemencia's other relatives still lived in Nolic, none of them was willing to take the child in once she was released from the hospital.

"Why not?" Rita had asked.

"They're a superstitious lot," Wanda explained. "They remember the story of Kulani O'oks, the Woman Who Was Kissed by the Bees who, under the name of Mualig Siakam—Forever Spinning—went on to become the Tohono O'odham's greatest medicine woman. They're afraid that the ant bites have made Clemencia a dangerous object, one who will bring Kuadagi Mumkithag, Ant Sickness, to the village."

"What will become of her then?" Rita wanted to know.

"There's an orphanage in Phoenix," Wanda said, "one operated by the Baptist Church. They take in children from any number of tribes."

"Who runs the orphanage," Rita had asked, "Indians or Milgahn?"

"Anglos, I'm sure," Wanda answered with a shrug.

"No," Rita said, speaking with surprising forcefulness. "That cannot be. She needs to be raised here."

Wanda was aghast. It would have been rude, of course, to point out that Rita was far too old to adopt the child and raise Clemencia on her own, but Rita had already come to the same conclusion.

"Mrs. Ladd and Mr. Walker can adopt her," Rita declared. "I'll be here to see that she learns what she needs to know about her people."

"Diana Ladd and Brandon Walker may be great friends of the tribe, but they're Anglos," Wanda had objected. "Tribal courts are discouraging Anglo adoptions these days."

"Why?" Rita had retorted. "Do they think Baptists who run orphanages will do a better job of raising her than these two people will, especially if they have my help?"

In the end and much to Wanda Ortiz's amazement, Rita's wishes had won the day. Brandon Walker and Diana Ladd had become first Clemencia Escalante's foster parents and eventually her adoptive ones. At Rita Antone's insistence, they had given their adopted daughter a new name—Lanita Dolores Walker.

Much later, while Rita and Lani wandered hand in hand along the paths of the Arizona/Sonora Desert Museum, Rita had related the story of how, in a time of terrible drought, a young Tohono O'odham woman named Kulani O'oks had been saved from death by the beating of the wings of the Ali-chu'uchum O'odham, the Little People—the bees and wasps, the butterflies and moths. Rita had gone on to explain how, back when Rita herself had been a child, her grandmother, S'Amichuda O'oks—Understanding Woman—had predicted that someday Rita would find a girl who would grow up to be a trusted medicine woman, someone just like Kulani O'oks, the Woman Who Was Kissed by the Bees.

"You're only a little girl now," Rita had said, "but I hope that you will grow up to be that medicine woman."

"Kulani O'oks," Lani had repeated the words several times, letting the strange and yet familiar collection of syllables roll across her tongue. Suddenly she understood. "Is that why people call me Lani—because of her, Kulani?"

Rita's wrinkled brown face had beamed with satisfaction. "Yes, my child," she had said, "that's it exactly."

A NARROW STRIP of roadway had been carved into the foothills leading up Ioligam's eastern flank. Winter rains had left it rutted, uneven, and washed out in spots. Even in four-wheel drive, Leo's Toyota struggled to make the climb. Closing her eyes, Lani shut out the noise of the laboring engine and prayed that Rita Antone had been right and that somehow the spirit of Kulani O'oks would be with her.

They drove past the small clearing where Fat Crack had pitched the tent while Lani had lived through her sixteen days of exile, her *e lihmhun*—the traditional Tohono O'odham purification ceremony required after the killing of an enemy. Because Lani Walker had indeed taken a human life. Andrew Carlisle, in one last bid for vengeance against Lani's mother, had sent a fellow inmate, Mitch Johnson, to kidnap and kill Lani. In a final confrontation inside Ioligam's network of caverns, Lani had managed to turn the tables on her would-be killer. The crew of experienced rock climbers that had finally removed Mitch Johnson's remains from the depths of the cavern had reported that he had died in a fall.

For years only Lani and Fat Crack Ortiz had known the whole truth about what had happened—that she was the one responsible for the man's death. She had used her bare feet to push a fragile stalagmite loose from its moorings and send it plunging into the depths. Johnson had still been alive and moaning until the rock hit him. Had anyone examined the remains of the rock, they no doubt would have found Lani's footprints on it, but the medical examiner and the detectives—who had zero interest in climbing down into the abyss—had been satisfied with the idea that the fall alone had killed him.

During those long and lonely sixteen days with her face painted black, Lani had fasted during the day. In the evenings, Fat Crack brought her the only meal she was allowed—a dish of salt-free food.

It was during that period of time that she had come to truly understand her relationship to Kulani O'oks, that long-ago medicine woman, whose given name was Mualig Siakam—Forever Spinning.

That was the secret Indian name Rita Antone, Lani's beloved Nana *Dahd,* had given the child long ago just as the old woman had also given Davy, Lani's older brother, his secret name Olhoni—Little Orphaned Calf. As a child Lani had believed that she'd been called Mualig Siakam because of her love of dancing and twirling. It was only on those nights with Fat Crack that she came to understand that Kulani O'oks and Mualig Siakam had been one and the same.

After the confrontation in the cavern, two more secret names had become part of Lani Walker's store of names: Gagdathag O'oks—Betraying Woman, the name of the girl the people of Rattlesnake Skull village had left to die in a cave as punishment for her treachery—and Nanakumal Namkam—Bat Meeter. That was the spirit of Betraying Woman, a ghostly presence that had kept Lani company during the terrible hours she'd been locked in the limestone cavern with a killer. It was the fluttering wings of a tiny bat that had given her the courage to fight back.

Now traveling up that narrow road for the first time in many years, Lani understood she would need help from all those names and spirits if she was to accomplish her goal that night. She would need them, and so would Gabe Ortiz. If Lani's plan worked as she hoped, he would come away from this night with a secret Indian name too—Ali Gihg Tahpani, Baby Fat Crack, in honor of his grandfather, and also after his uncle Richard, who shared the same name but who was simply called Baby.

The Toyota ground to a halt. "This is as far as we go," Leo announced. "Everybody out. From here on we walk."

Lani stepped out onto a shoulder that was so rough she had to struggle to maintain her footing. When Gabe finally clambered out of the backseat, she stood there waiting for him with her hand outstretched.

"What?" he asked.

"Phone," she answered. "Give it to me."

"Why?"

"Because we're leaving it with your dad."

"But what if I decide I want to go home? What if I need to call him?"

"Then you'll have to do it the old-fashioned way," Lani told him. "Try smoke signals."

Reluctantly Gabe handed over the phone. "That's not fair," he said.

"This isn't about fair," Lani replied, dropping the phone on the passenger seat of the truck. "It never has been."

By then Leo was at the back of the vehicle unloading gear from the luggage compartment. Leo gave a snort of suppressed laughter. Lani heard it and hoped Gabe had not.

"*Oi g hihm,*" she said. "Let's go."

"Where to?" Gabe asked.

"There's a clearing up there," she answered, pointing first to a point farther up the mountain and then to a spot nearby where a faint path disappeared into the brush. "It's not all that far, but it's steep. You'll need to watch your step."

"YOU GONNA BE all right now?" Aubrey Bayless asked, pushing John Lassiter's bulky wheelchair into his cell and locking the wheels close enough to the metal cot that the prisoner would be able to manage the last bit of distance on his own.

"I'm fine, Aubrey," Lassiter said, levering his heavy frame out of the chair and onto the narrow bed. "Thank you for bringing me back."

Big Bad John Lassiter was still big, but the bad part had largely disappeared. Multiple sclerosis had turned him into a wheelchair-bound mass of mostly uncooperative muscles. It was hard to tell if he was still bad because, on occasion, he was also virtually helpless. He lived alone in a cell not because he was a danger to himself or others, but because none of the other inmates at the Arizona State Prison in Florence was willing to help him with his ever-increasing physical deficits.

That job usually fell to Aubrey Bayless, a kind, grizzle-haired old black man who primarily functioned as an orderly inside the prison's infirmary. It was there the two men—prisoner and caregiver—had gradually developed a friendship. On those occasions when John wasn't confined to a hospital bed, Aubrey voluntarily helped him in and out of his cell as well as back and forth to the dining room and elsewhere.

"When you gonna agree to see that daughter of yours?" Aubrey wanted to know. "Those guys in the visitors' office tell me she keeps asking and asking."

"How many times do I have to tell you?" John replied wearily. "I don't have a daughter. I signed away my parental rights to that girl the moment she was born."

"You maybe signed 'em away, but I don't think she be listening," Aubrey countered. "They say she even gots the same thing you got. She's what, not even forty years old, and she already stuck on one of them scooters."

That hurt. The idea that MS was hereditary and that he'd most likely passed his own ailment along to an offspring he'd never met seemed grossly unfair. All Big Bad John knew about his daughter was her name—the name her adoptive parents had given her—Amanda Wasser.

Years had passed between the time Amos Warren disappeared and when his remains had been found. By the time John was charged with his murder, his onetime girlfriend, Ava Martin—the one who had caused all the trouble—was years in his rearview mirror. At the time John was taken into custody, he and his then girlfriend, Bernadette Benson, had actually started thinking about getting married. By the time the baby was born, he'd been found guilty and sentenced to life without parole for Amos's murder.

Bernadette had come to the prison visitors' room, hugely pregnant. She had begged him to marry her and give the baby his last name, promising that she'd keep the child and raise it on her own, but John had steadfastly refused. Why give the poor kid the name of a guy who would be spending the rest of his life in prison? Bernadette had no education beyond high school. Without John's support, she was barely scratching out a meager existence working as a waitress.

"Why not give the kid up for adoption?" he had asked her. "Why not let him have half a chance at a decent life?"

Of course, the baby had turned out to be a girl rather than a boy, but Bernadette had come around to John's way of thinking. He'd been surprised when she had put the baby up for adoption, signing away her parental rights at the same time John gave up his. He knew how much Bernadette regretted that decision because she herself had told him so, saying over and over that, more than anything, she wished she had kept the baby after all.

The other thing about Bernadette Benson that had surprised John Lassiter was that, although she had let their child go, she had continued to love him no matter what. For years she had faithfully driven back and forth between Tucson and Florence once a week to spend a few short minutes talking to him through a plexiglass barrier. Bernadette's visits had ceased abruptly in 1983 when she had been fatally injured in a late-afternoon one-car rollover on her way back home from the prison.

John's mind had drifted away. When he came back to the present, Aubrey Bayless was still talking.

"And she be the one who been talking to them JFA

folks about getting your ass sprung out of here. You should be givin' her a chance to at least know you, man. Seems like you owe her that much."

John Lassiter had no idea how Amanda had reinserted herself into his life. He had refused to meet with her mostly because he was too ashamed to do so. He didn't want to have to sit there, as a convicted killer, and look her in the eye. And he had no idea how or why she had managed to persuade the people from Justice for All to go to bat for him, but her efforts on his behalf hadn't and wouldn't make him change his mind about seeing her.

The old Big Bad John would have jumped all over Aubrey and told him to give it a rest and mind his own damned business, but this John Lassiter was painfully aware of how much he depended on the kindness of this good-hearted old man.

"I'm not making any promises," John said as Aubrey backed out of the cell and slammed the barred door shut behind him. "I'll think about it."

CHAPTER 5

Young Girl ran back to the village as fast as she could, but she was too late. Before she could sound an alarm, the Apaches were already there. The men who had been out working in the fields hurried to do battle while the women and children ran to hide.

You must know, nawoj, *my friend, that Ioligam, I'itoi's sacred mountain, is full of caves. Because I'itoi lives in these caves, the Desert People usually stay away from them. The caves are Elder Brother's quiet place, and the People do not want to bother him. But when there is danger, that is where they go.*

That day, as the Ohb descended on Rattlesnake Skull village, that's where the women and children ran to hide—in one of the caves—and the cave they chose was the one where Young Man had been staying. When they found him there, knowing he was Ohb, they attacked him with clubs and beat him very badly even though Young Girl told them she loved him and begged them to leave him alone.

The people of Rattlesnake Skull village were very angry when the Apaches stole all their food. And when the people learned that

Young Man, an Obb, had been living in one of I'itoi's sacred caves and that Young Girl had been feeding him, they held a council to decide what they should do.

BY THE TIME Lani, Leo, and Gabe set out walking, the sun had long since sunk past Ioligam's summit, and that part of the mountain was already shrouded in shadow. Within a few steps, the white buildings atop the mountain that comprised Kitt Peak National Observatory disappeared from view.

As Lani had warned, it was a steep climb. They might have been covered with sweat from exertion, but a chill wind blowing out of the east dried the moisture on their perspiring bodies as soon as it formed.

Even though it had been years since she'd come this way, Lani could have led the way with her eyes closed. She walked past the path she knew would lead to the tiny entrance they had used to enter the cavern on that day so many years ago. She had awakened from a drugged stupor to find herself Mitch Johnson's prisoner. She had traveled to the mountain with him and Quentin Walker, a man whom Lani had never regarded as a brother, although he was Brandon Walker's son. It had taken time that awful day for Lani to realize that, rather than being Mitch's ally, Quentin was as much Mitch's prisoner as she was.

This time, leading Leo and Gabe, she headed straight for what had once been the main entrance to the vast cavern complex and to the part of the mountain that had long ago been brought down in order to entomb a living prisoner.

For years after that day, Lani had refused to go

anywhere near Ioligam. Finally, on the occasion of her twenty-first birthday, she had gathered her courage as well as her brother, Davy, and Davy's good friend and almost brother, Brian Fellows, and the three of them had returned to the mountain. Brian, the son of Brandon Walker's first wife, Jane, and a subsequent husband, was Quentin's and Tommy's half brother. Though there had been no clearing back then, they had gone to the collapsed main entrance armed with tools—pickaxes, shovels, and rakes—for the very purpose of creating one.

Together the three of them had chopped down brush, pulled out the roots, and turned over and smoothed out the disturbed earth, leaving behind a small clearing hidden under a thicket of sheltering manzanita. In one corner of the space they had used a collection of loose rocks to form a small circle in which they had erected a small wooden cross. When the memorial was finished, they had placed a lit candle inside the circle as a remembrance in honor of Betraying Woman.

Lani's old friend and mentor, Fat Crack, was long dead. That day, Davy and Brian became the other two people who knew the truth about what happened to Mitch Johnson. Lani had come here today hoping that perhaps she could share that story with someone else—with Fat Crack's grandson and namesake. Now she wasn't so sure she'd be able to tell Gabe anything at all about her battle with Mitch Johnson.

When Lani reached the clearing and set down her backpack, she was surprised and gratified to see that both the cross and the long empty glass that had once held the candle were still there and undisturbed. Lani smiled to herself when she saw them. Dan might think otherwise, but the fact that those relics remained reassured her that this part of Ioligam was still a sacred place.

Leo was the next to arrive. With a dull thump he dropped the bound bundle of firewood that he had brought from Bashas' store in Sells and set down the plastic gallon jug of water he had hauled up the mountain. Then he wiggled free of his backpack, one loaded with foodstuffs, enamel-covered tin dishes, and utensils that Lani had prepared and packed in advance of the expedition. Gabe, carrying what should have been the lightest load, arrived last, panting and out of breath. As he slumped to the ground, Lani noticed he was munching on something.

"What are you eating?"

He opened a clenched fist to reveal the remains of a half-eaten Snickers bar. Lani knew that diabetes, often called the Tohono O'odham Curse, continued to wreak havoc on the reservation. Her response had been to take a principled stance against the use of processed sugars and flour in her own family.

Gabe had always been short and stocky. Lani, along with Gabe's parents, worried about his diet and the possibility that he, too, might be plagued by the same disease that had cost the boy's grandfather both his legs and eventually his life. It was for that reason the tortillas she had brought along for this trip had been made with flour ground from mesquite beans. Since Lani viewed this as a ceremonial occasion, Snickers bars were definitely not on the menu.

"Where did that come from?" she demanded, snatching the rest of the half-eaten candy bar out of his hand.

A sullen Gabe shrugged. "From the store," he said.

"And how did it get up here?"

"In my backpack," he answered.

"What else is in your backpack?" she demanded. "Let me see."

Within minutes, from among the approved items in his pack—some extra clothing, a canteen, and his grandfather's blankets—Lani unearthed several pieces of contraband: a plastic-bound six-pack of Coca-Cola cans, two bags of potato chips, and three more candy bars. She handed all the confiscated loot, including the remains of the original candy bar, over to Leo.

"Please take these back to the truck," she said to him. "They won't be needed here."

"You're sure you want to do this—that you'll be okay?" Leo asked.

"I'm sure."

"All right then," Leo said. "Delia and I are going to the dance at Vamori tonight, but I'll come back for you in the morning when the dance is over."

Gabe watched sourly as his father disappeared taking the goodies with him. "If I can't drink Coke, what can I drink?" he wanted to know.

"You'd be surprised what a little prickly pear juice and honey can do for a cup of hot water."

"Right," Gabe grumbled under his breath. "I can hardly wait."

Lani ignored his complaints. "Okay," she told him, "it's about time you got off your duff and helped me make camp."

"Why should I?" Gabe objected. "Why do I even have to be here? Why can't I just go back to town with my dad?"

"You're here because I think you should be, and so do your parents," Lani growled back, "and as long as you're here, you're also going to do what I say. Now get busy."

"Doing what?"

In her years as a doctor, Lani Walker-Pardee had encountered her share of surly adolescents, and Gabe was currently running true to form.

"Like gathering some rocks to make a fire pit."

He made a beeline for the first rocks he saw—the easy ones—those surrounding Betraying Woman's cross. "Not those," she told him. "Those stay where they are. Find some others. It'll be dark before long, and we'll need to have the fire going by then."

"Right," he muttered sourly. "Who cares about having a fire?"

"You will," she warned him, "about ten minutes after the sun goes down."

Gabe huffed off to do as he was bidden. Watching him go, Lani felt a hint of despair. Maybe Dan and Leo were right. Maybe Baby Fat Crack Ortiz really was a lost cause.

SITTING ALONE IN my Seattle penthouse, I was a very lonely and glum version of J. P. Beaumont that Friday evening. I sat in the family room in my new leather easy chair and gazed out the window at the setting sun and the busy boat traffic on Elliott Bay far below. From my bird's-eye view, the ferries and lumbering container ships looked like small toys—about the size of the rubber-band-powered plastic toy boats I used to sail on Seattle's Green Lake back when I was a kid.

Though I didn't like to admit it, my beloved recliner's replacement wasn't half bad. It was made of smooth reddish-brown leather and offered the kind of comfort the broken and dying springs in the old recliner could no longer provide. Even so, I wouldn't have gotten rid of the recliner if I hadn't been strong-armed into relinquishing it by Jim Hunt, my once and again interior designer.

I glanced at my watch, sighed, and heaved myself out of the chair. The last thing I wanted to do that night—the very last thing—was go to the Behind the Badge Foundation's Gala and Auction down at the airport Hilton. And I most especially didn't want to go solo. My reluctance had nothing to do with the organization sponsoring the event. After all, Behind the Badge helps maintain Washington's Fallen Officer Memorial. It also supplies much-needed scholarship assistance to the sons and daughters of fallen officers. But the truth is, I would have much preferred whipping out my checkbook and mailing a sizable donation to actually making an appearance.

This was supposed to have been a fun event—a double date of sorts, a foursome made up of my wife, Mel Soames, and me, along with my son, Scott, and his wife, Cherisse. Having aced his stint at the Police Academy, Scotty was now a full-fledged member of the Seattle Police Department. Tickets to the event had been a Christmas present to Mel and me from Scott and Cherisse, and the four of us had planned to go together.

Of course, with everything that had happened just before Christmas, the whole holiday season had turned into something of a bust. Then, at the last minute, Mel had been summoned to Washington, D.C. Homeland Security was putting on an antiterrorism dog-and-pony show for police chiefs from all over the country. Mel, the recently designated chief of police in Bellingham, had initially declined the invitation, saying she didn't have the time or the travel budget to attend.

Then, someone in D.C. had taken a look at their RSVP list and realized that, in terms of diversity, they were on the low side when it came to female attendees. I suspected there were a couple of reasons for that, number one being that female chiefs of departments were still pretty much, as my mother would have said, "scarce as hens' teeth." And the top-drawer ones like Mel took their responsibilities seriously and probably figured they had better things to do with their time than to go trotting off to a meaningless conference in D.C. where they would be treated as little more than window dressing.

The upshot was, early in the week a new batch of invitations had been issued, ones that included Homeland Security coughing up all travel and hotel expenses—for the distaff chiefs. This struck me as an out-and-out case of discrimination toward the male attendees. Nonetheless, Mel had accepted the offer and flown off to D.C. on a red-eye late on Thursday. Her absence left me batching it in Seattle rather than spending a quiet weekend with her in our downtown condo.

With our plans shot to hell, I had called Scott, intending to bail on the party rather than go without Mel. Scott, however, had not only insisted that I come along, he even offered to pick me up so we'd all be able to use the express lanes. With their ETA less than half an hour away, I headed into the bedroom to get ready.

Fifteen minutes later, showered, shaved, and wearing the Montblanc cologne Mel had given me for Christmas, I stepped into my walk-in closet and pulled down the garment bag that held my best suit.

After straightening my pocket square, I slipped one hand into the jacket pocket and noticed an object lurking there. As soon as I felt the contours, I recognized what it was—my Special Homicide badge. Drawing it out of the pocket and seeing the black band still wrapped around it hit me like a ton of bricks. The last time I had worn the suit had been for Ross Connors's funeral.

Unbidden, a whole series of images from that terrible time flashed through my waking mind just as they often do in my dreams at night. First there was the supposedly carefree December evening. There had been flurries of snow as Mel and I headed for Seattle Center intent on a much-anticipated company party that never happened. Mel and I had stood together, frozen to the ground in horrified silence, as a speeding Range Rover, driven by a pair of totally clueless bank robbers, plowed into the side of Ross Connors's town car as his driver attempted to make a left turn off Broad into the Space Needle parking lot.

Now, alone in my bedroom, I recalled the screams of sirens as first responders converged on the awful scene. I remembered heart-stopping moments as, one by one, I realized four people were dead. The two crooks, driving hell-bent for leather without seat belts, had both been thrown clear of their vehicle. They had died instantly.

The town car had been T-boned on the driver's side.

Racing to the vehicle, I checked on both Ross and his driver, Bill Spade, searching for pulses. There were none. The only sign of life inside the town car was in the front passenger seat where Harry Ignatius Ball, my immediate supervisor from the Special Homicide Investigation Team, sat howling in pain. His legs had been nearly severed by the sheet metal from the town car's roof as it collapsed under the weight of a fallen utility pole.

When they hauled Harry away from the scene that night, rolling him first into the KOMO building at Fisher Plaza and then flying him by helicopter to Harborview, I was sure the man was a goner. But the docs at Harborview turned out to be miracle workers. He lost both his legs above the knee, but he lived.

In the aftermath of those events, with Ross barely cold in his grave, the newly appointed attorney general had laid waste to what had been Ross's pet project, the Special Homicide Investigation Team. With little advance notice and less fanfare, S.H.I.T. became a thing of the past, and those of us who had worked there were out of a job.

While the rest of us were being kicked out onto the street, Harry was shut up in a hospital, first fighting for his life and later, in rehab, dealing with the grim realities of his new life as a double amputee. With nothing else to keep me occupied, I had assumed the task of fixing Harry's Eastlake condo and turning it into a place he could use both while he was still mostly confined to a wheelchair and later—how much later I still didn't know—when he would be fitted with a pair of new hi-tech legs.

The rehab job had been a complicated endeavor.

While Harry bitched about his medically necessitated incarceration, I had been in charge of the Harry I. Ball Project, as we called it. Lots of people were ready and willing to make donations, but someone had to be in charge of handling those funds and properly thanking whoever had contributed. My mother would have been proud of all my handwritten thank-you notes.

For the design work, I had enlisted the help of Jim Hunt. There had been permits to obtain, contractors to juggle, materials to be purchased, to say nothing of endless days of design decisions. I didn't care if I ever set foot in a lighting or plumbing fixture store again. Then, once work started, I was in charge of overseeing construction.

The hurry-up remodeling project had come in on time but slightly over budget. Weeks earlier, Harry had finally been released from rehab. He had gone home under the supervision of a capable but nightmare-inducing retired RN named Marge Herndon, whom many regard as a clone of Nurse Ratched from *One Flew Over the Cuckoo's Nest.* She had been my grim-faced, overly bossy drill instructor/taskmaster during my stint of rehab following bilateral knee replacement, but she'd gotten the job done. I had suggested that Harry look into hiring her to help him once he was sent home. I never anticipated what happened once those two tough-minded individuals were thrown together. I had expected they'd initially lock horns and only gradually come to some kind of understanding. Instead, they'd gotten along like gangbusters from the outset, their shared addiction to tobacco having helped seal the deal. And if Harry thought, as I had, that Marge was bossy as all hell, he had so far failed to mention it.

Lost in thought, I had no conscious recollection of sinking down on the side of the bed, but that's where I was when the phone rang.

"Hey," Cherisse announced. "We're here."

There was still a lump in my throat, one I had to swallow before I could reply. "Okay," I said. "I'll be right down."

On the ride down in the elevator, I attempted to compose myself. I realized that Scott and Cherisse were right to insist that I go to the gala. After all, there have been far too many fallen officers in my life for me to take a pass on Behind the Badge, and that's what the evening would be about—remembering those folks and honoring them.

As the elevator descended, I enumerated them one by one, starting, of course, with the most recent—Delilah Ainsworth. Before Delilah came Sue Danielson; before Sue came the big guy, Benjamin Harrison "Gentle Ben" Weston; and before Gentle Ben there was my very first partner in Homicide, Milton "Pickles" Gurkey. Pickles had been on duty when he suffered a fatal heart attack during a shoot-out in the parking lot outside the Doghouse restaurant.

By the time I reached the lobby, I finally had my head screwed on straight. I stepped outside and climbed into the backseat of Scott's Acura. Fortunately for me, Cherisse is a little bit of a thing. Once she moved her seat forward, I had plenty of leg room.

"How's it going?" Scott asked from the driver's seat.

"Fine," I answered. "Just fine."

It was a Mel Soames "fine"—a two-raised-eyebrows "fine." What I meant but didn't say was that I may have been fine *now,* but I sure as hell hadn't been fine a few minutes ago.

"I'm so glad you decided to come along after all," Cherisse said. "It'll be great fun."

"I'm sure it will," I said.

I doubted it would be any kind of fun, but since I was going anyway, I screwed my courage to the sticking place and decided to enjoy it.

CHAPTER 6

The people of Rattlesnake Skull Village were angry with the Apache for stealing their food, but they were even angrier at Young Girl. Even though she had tried to warn them of the attack, they thought she had betrayed them. And so the council changed her name and said that from that time on she would be called Betraying Woman—Gagdathag O'oks.

Young Man had been badly hurt when the women beat him. They carried Young Man back to the cave. Then they brought Betraying Woman there as well along with everything she owned—her pots and baskets, her blankets and awl. Then, leaving Young Man and Betraying Woman inside to die, they asked I'itoi to bring down the mountain and close the entrance to the cave.

Betraying Woman stayed with Young Man until he died, caring for him as best she could. And even to this day, nawoj, *my friend, when you hear the wind whispering through the manzanita—the bush for which Ioligam is named—you will know it is only Betraying Woman singing a song to Young Man.*

Go to sleep, Sweet Ohb. Do not be afraid.
I will not let them hurt you. I will not let them come again
To beat you with their clubs and call you evil names.
No matter what they think, Sweet Ohb, we did not betray them.
They did not listen when I tried to warn them.
They did not listen when I tried to tell them
That you were not the one who stole from them,
That you were not the enemy who spoiled their fields.
No, Sweet Ohb, although we tried to tell them
They did not listen. But do not worry. I will not leave you.
We will stay here together, Sweet Ohb,
You and I together—alone and in the dark.

IT SEEMED TO Brandon that they'd escaped the Authors' Dinner a little earlier than usual. They drove most of the way home in companionable silence. Speedway Boulevard narrowed first from three lanes in each direction, to two, and finally to one as they followed the winding road up into Gates Pass and off onto the dirt track that led to the house.

As the city lights fell away behind them, the stars and a rising moon appeared in a now jet-black sky. When Brandon and Diana married and he had moved in with her and Davy, the house had been a long way out of town, and neighbors had been few and far between. Now the surrounding hillsides were dotted with McMansions, most of them far larger than the river rock relic Diana and her friend Rita Antone had turned from wreckage into a livable home. Their house and pool were far smaller and humbler than those of most of their neighbors, but they were also something most of the others were not—completely paid for.

Leaving the Escalade parked in the detached garage, Diana and Brandon headed for the house. As they did so, Bozo, their aging grand-dog, rose stiffly from his heated bed on the back patio and limped forward, tail a-wag, to greet them. Their son-in-law, Dan Pardee, had been Bozo's original owner, or maybe, as Diana often pointed out, it had been the other way around. Dan had been Bozo's handler in Iraq and credited him with saving his life in combat. When Dan's deployment ended, he had used his own money to bring Bozo home to the United States. They had worked together as a K-9 unit attached to the Border Patrol's Shadow Wolves.

Three years earlier, Dan and Bozo had gone after an illegal border crosser who had been packing two kilos of meth. Fleeing up the side of a mountain, the smuggler had, deliberately or not, sent an avalanche of rocks and boulders roaring down the mountainside behind him. Dan had managed to escape injury by diving out of the way. Bozo wasn't as lucky. A vet had been able to save the dog's life and wire his shattered shoulder back together, but Bozo's resulting limp meant that his K-9 unit days were over. When Dan's next K-9 partner, Hulk, arrived, Bozo had gone into mourning every day when Dan and the new dog left to go on duty. The best solution anyone could come up with, supplied by Lani, had been for Bozo to go live with Grandpa and Grandma.

There was a doggy door in the back of the house, one that Bozo steadfastly refused to use. He much preferred to be outside rather than in, but wherever he was, inside or out, he would wait patiently until a passing human opened the door before entering or exiting. Brandon suspected that the plastic sheeting hitting his shoulder bothered Bozo too much, and Brandon was the one who had insisted on installing a heated dog bed outside on the patio for Bozo to use on these still very chilly desert spring evenings.

"You're making him soft," Dan had objected when he saw the bed. "He never needed anything like that when we were in Iraq."

"He isn't in Iraq," Brandon had countered. "He's a veteran. He's home now. He gets a heated bed. End of story."

And it was.

Brandon unlocked the back door, switched on the kitchen light, and let Diana inside. "You go on to bed," he told her. "Bozo and I are going to sit out here and be quiet together for a little while. Being stuck in crowds of people with all of them talking at once wears me out."

"Suit yourself," Diana said. "But if you're going to be out here very long, turn on your heater, too."

Flicking the switch, Brandon turned on one of the infrared heat lamps that lined the wooden ceiling of the patio and dropped into one of the chairs. Bozo stood beside him long enough to have his ears rubbed. Then, as if realizing they'd be there for a while, the dog limped back to his bed. He circled twice. With a contented sigh, Bozo lay down to sleep while Brandon leaned back to think.

That was what he needed at the end of a far too social evening—a little peace and quiet, with the delicate perfume of orange blossoms drifting on the chilly air.

AFTER LEO LEFT Lani and Gabe alone on the mountain, the first order of business was to build a fire pit. While Gabe reluctantly set about doing that, Lani unpacked the food and dishes. Once the fire was going, she emptied a bowl of precooked beans into the pot to heat. They were tepary beans, the ones the Tohono O'odham had traditionally grown and used long before the arrival of pinto beans.

The beans in question may have been part of Tohono O'odham's ancient customs and traditions, but Lani's manner of transporting them was not. She had loaded them into the backpack inside a sturdy plastic Ziploc container. She realized with some satisfaction, however, that the battered enameled pot she'd brought to heat them was the same one Fat Crack had used to prepare her evening meals during her sixteen-day purification ceremony. The dishes into which she ladled the steaming beans were also the ones she and Fat Crack had used back then.

Tonight she and Fat Crack's grandson ate their food in a cloud of stubborn silence. When it was over, Lani heated some water and made a hot drink of prickly pear juice and water sweetened with honey.

"I'd rather have a Coke," Gabe said.

"I'm sure you would," Lani said mildly, "but sodas aren't the point of this trip."

"What is?"

She glanced at the fire. "Do you remember the story of Betraying Woman?" she asked.

"Not really," Gabe replied.

"You used to know it."

Gabe shrugged. "So?"

"Then maybe I should remind you." She told the story then, from beginning to end.

"So that's what this is about?" Gabe asked sarcastically when she finished telling him the story of Young Man and Betraying Woman. "We're just going to sit around out here in the middle of nowhere and tell ghost stories all night?"

Lani felt discouraged. This should have been a time when she could give Fat Crack's grandson the benefit of some of the old man's wisdom. For years, she had imagined coming here with the boy when he was almost, if not completely, grown, and being able to share the Peace Smoke with him. She had hoped to be able to tell him about her battle with the evil o*hb;* about how Bat and the spirit of Betraying Woman had aided her in the fight; and about how Fat Crack had helped her deal with the aftermath of that awful day.

That's what she had always wanted to do, but somehow Gabe had morphed into a difficult young man who had no patience for or interest in the old ways. It saddened Lani to think that perhaps he had drifted completely beyond her reach.

She took a deep breath. "You used to love the I'itoi stories," Lani pointed out. "When you were little, you used to come to the hospital with me. You liked to visit the patients, especially the old ones. Sometimes you would listen while they told stories, and sometimes you would do the telling."

"I was little then," Gabe countered. "I believed in all that crap back then, along with Santa Claus and other stupid stuff that I don't believe in anymore."

"Why not?"

"Because I grew up."

Lani reached over to her backpack and pulled out her medicine basket. Inside she found the soft leather pouch that held her divining crystals. Lani supposed that those four pieces of lavender-colored rock must have originally come from the wreckage of a geode that had been smashed to pieces long ago. The tiny rocks themselves, as well as the worn pouch that held them, had been passed down from S-ab Neid Pi Has—Looks at Nothing—to Gigh Tahpani—Fat Crack—and from Fat Crack to Lani. She had always supposed that one day they would go to Gabe. At the moment that outcome seemed unlikely.

"Have you ever seen divining crystals?" she asked, emptying the shards of rock into her hand. When she held them up, one at a time, they winked in the firelight.

"So this is what, like reading tea leaves or something?" Gabe asked, his voice dripping with contempt. "You look into them somehow and see the future?"

"It's not exactly like reading tea leaves," Lani said. "Do you remember back when you were in third grade? I went with you on a nighttime school field trip to Kitt Peak, and they let us take turns looking through the telescopes."

"Sure, I remember," Gabe said with a laugh. "For a long time, I thought I'd be an astronomer someday when I grew up. I'm over that, too, by the way."

Ignoring his sarcasm, Lani continued. "When the scientists up there . . ." She paused and motioned with her head toward the collection of invisible buildings on top of the mountain that made up the Kitt Peak National Observatory. "When they look through their telescopes, they use powerful lenses to focus on things that eyes alone could never see. These crystals work the same way. They allow your mind to focus on things that you can't necessarily see. Here, try it."

She passed the crystals over to Gabe. For a long time, he stared down at them. Finally, reluctantly, he held the first one up to his eye, peering through it at Lani.

"What do you see?" she prompted.

"You, of course."

"Be honest now," she said. "Tell the truth. Tell me what you really see. Don't you see someone who's a friend of your parents? Someone who won't mind her own business and keeps telling you what to do?"

Gabe looked crestfallen. "I guess," he admitted.

"Try again. Look at the fire this time," she suggested. "What do you see there?"

He held up the second crystal and peered through it.

"I see a fire," he answered, "a fire and nothing else."

"But what is your mind focusing on as you look at the fire? Are you grateful to be sitting by it, glad of its warmth, or are you thinking something else? Maybe, instead of watching the fire burn, you'd rather be at home, playing with your Xbox or watching TV."

The startled expression on the boy's face told Lani that she had hit the nail on the head. Gabe immediately passed the crystals back to Lani.

"Obviously I'm no good at this," he said.

"All right," Lani agreed. "Let me try." She held one of the crystals up to her eye. "I see a boy who was born in the backseat of a car the night his grandfather was buried. Fat Crack knew before you were born that you would be a boy. He hoped you'd follow in his footsteps."

"And be what, a medicine man?" Gabe asked with a derisive snort. "Right. How much money do medicine men make these days? Where do they go to school?"

"Medicine men go to school in places just like this," Lani said quietly. "They sit around fires and listen to stories—the stories their ancestors used to explain why the world around them—their particular world—was the way it was. Those stories don't have to be scientifically accurate to be true, to contain elements of truth."

Gabe remained unconvinced. "Whatever," he said dismissively, shaking his head.

Lani held up the second crystal. Looking through it, she frowned as she spoke. "I see something strange here—a woman, a white-haired Milgahn woman. I don't understand it, but she's dangerous somehow. You need to stay away from her."

Lani found the idea of an Anglo woman being a Dangerous Object both worrisome and puzzling. Dangerous Objects were an essential part of the Tohono O'odham tradition of Staying Sickness. According to ancient customs, there were two kinds of sicknesses abroad in the world. Traveling Sicknesses, the kinds caused by germs, were the ones Dr. Walker-Pardee routinely treated with antibiotics. Those affected everybody, Indian and Anglo alike. Staying Sicknesses, on the other hand, a kind of Spirit Sickness, were caused by Dangerous Objects and affected Indians only. A Spirit Sickness was usually diagnosed and treated by a Tohono O'odham healer—a medicine man or medicine woman—by means of a combination of traditional chants—*kuadk*—and related devices.

Coyote Sickness, for example, was caused by someone eating a Dangerous Object—perhaps a melon that a coyote had bitten into. Someone suffering from Coyote Sickness could be treated with coyote feces—boiled and turned into a paste, and then rubbed on the patient's body. People with Coyote Sickness could also be treated by a medicine man rubbing the patient's body with a coyote's tail.

Lani knew that as a baby she herself had once been considered a Dangerous Object due to the ant bites that had covered her body. What was disturbing in this instance, however, was that the dangerous object in question was an Anglo. How was that even possible?

Gabe, however, found none of this the least bit mystifying.

"I know who that is," he said, "white hair and all. It's got to be Mrs. Travers, the school principal. She hates my guts."

Without further comment, Lani held up the third crystal. "This one says that you're walking a difficult path right now," she said, "traveling it with some friends. You're about to come to a fork in that path. One fork leads to the PaDaj O'odham—the Bad People—who came out of the South to do battle with I'itoi. If you go the same way your friends do, you'll end up being bad, too."

Gabe turned on her accusingly. "Now you're talking about my friends, the Josés. You probably know about them from talking to my parents and not from looking in that stupid crystal. But you know what else?" he demanded, standing up suddenly and wrapping one of Fat Crack's blankets tightly around his shoulders. "My parents don't get to dictate who my friends are, and neither do you."

With that, he stalked away from the fire and back toward the path.

"Wait a minute," Lani called after him. "Where do you think you're going?"

"Home," he said.

"It's dark, and home is a long way from here," she argued.

"Home may be, but the road isn't. It's Friday night. Someone coming back from town will give me a ride."

"What if you trip and fall?"

"The moon's up now," he told her over his shoulder. "My eyes have adjusted to the dark, and I can see better than I would have thought possible. And just for safety's sake, on my way down maybe I'll ask for some help from that precious I'itoi guy of yours in hopes he'll look out for me."

CHAPTER 7

In the evening when Braiding Woman awakened, she found a tiny baby, a girl, crawling on a mat—the same mat she had been weaving when the dust ball appeared, the dust ball that belonged to Tash.

The baby girl who had once been a dust ball grew very fast. Every four days she was bigger and bigger, until finally she was as large as any of the other children in the village. She had very long, sharp fingernails. When she played with the other children, she scratched them. She would make them bleed by tearing their skin. This happened many times. At last the mothers in the village grew angry. They took their sticks and beat the girl until she lay senseless.

That night, when Braiding Woman went to look for the girl, she could not find her, although she had been told exactly where the child lay.

The next day, this strange girl-child had grown to be a giantess. She went away from the village and into the mountains. There she moved some great rocks and made herself a house. She lived in the house all alone. She killed deer and lions and rabbits and other animals for food. She used their skins to make clothes. The bones and claws of the animals she killed she used for ornaments.

She came to be called Ho'ok O'oks, which means Evil Giantess. She came to be feared by all the Tohono O'odham, and that, nawoj, *my friend, is still true, even to this day.*

A WAVE OF despair washed over Lani as the stubborn boy turned his back and walked away. She knew then that she had failed. Gabe was beyond her reach—too angry and arrogant to listen. Hot tears stung her cheeks. For a moment she was tempted to call and beg him to come back, but she didn't. She simply let him go, reaching instead for the comfort of her medicine basket.

She slipped the crystals back into their pouch and dropped that into the basket. Then, in the flickering firelight, she examined the basket's other contents. First out were two separate shards of pottery—a reddish one with an almost invisible tortoise drawn on it and the other one coal black. The red one had once belonged to Nana *Dahd*'s grandmother, S'Amichuda O'oks—Understanding Woman—while the black one had come from Betraying Woman's cave, deep in this very mountain.

Tradition dictated that a woman's pots must always be broken upon her death in order to release the pot maker's spirit. Lani was sure that Understanding Woman's pots had been broken by her grieving relatives in just that way upon the old woman's death. Betraying Woman, however, had died alone in the cavern, abandoned and unmourned. Her spirit had remained trapped in her long-unbroken pots until Lani herself had smashed them. And these two pieces of pottery, one red and one black, were the only reminders of either of those two long-ago elders.

Next came a tiny bone—as small as a baby's finger. That was the tiny piece of bat wing skeleton that Lani had brought with her out of the cavern. The bone served as a reminder that Nanakumal—Bat—had helped see Lani through one terrible fight, and maybe he would do so again in this battle for Baby Fat Crack's soul.

The next items in the basket were Nana *Dahd*'s basket-makng awl and the leather tobacco pouch Fat Crack the elder had given her. She had gone out in the fall and collected the green wild tobacco leaves—*wiw*. She had dried the leaves and broken them into small pieces just the way the legend of Little Lion and Little Bear said it must be done. She had brought the tobacco along with her today in hope that, before the night was over, she and Gabe would share the Peace Smoke.

Gabe was gone, but perhaps, Lani reasoned, the sacred smoke was still in order. She pulled some of the dried wild tobacco leaves from the pouch and rolled them into a loose cigarette. It took a moment for her fumbling fingers to locate the final item in her basket—Looks at Nothing's ancient lighter. She had taken the old blind medicine man's Zippo to a guy in Tucson, a man with a reputation for rehabbing aging lighters. The brass finish was worn through in spots, but refilled and with a new striking mechanism, the lighter sprang to life at the very first try.

After lighting the cigarette, Lani sat there with the sweet smoke drifting around her as she considered her connection to those two wise old men, one of whom she had never met. It was through them that she knew that the Tohono O'odham never use a pipe—that age-old custom that was part of other tribes' traditions. Originally, the Desert People had used leaves to wrap their ceremonial smokers. Now they bought their cigarette wrappers the same place everybody else did—at either the trading post or else at Bashas' grocery store in Sells.

Lani closed her eyes and allowed herself to be carried along in the smoke-filled air. When she opened her eyes sometime later, it was as though a ghost had arisen out of the ground. That's when she saw a vision of the evil white-haired Milgahn woman once again.

As the hair rose on the back of Lani's neck, she knew two things at once. Evil White-Haired Woman was not the school principal at Sells, and Baby Fat Crack Ortiz was in mortal danger.

GABE STORMED OFF down the mountain, furious with Lani, his parents, and everyone else. It wasn't easy being the son of the tribal chairman. If it hadn't been for the José brothers, who had befriended him early on, his life would have been hell. He and Timmy, the youngest of the brothers, had been fast friends since kindergarten. When one of the older kids, Luis Joaquin, had started picking on Gabe, Tim's brother Paul had intervened on Gabe's behalf.

It would be years before Gabe understood that Luis Joaquin's father had been his mother's opponent for chairman in a recent tribal election. The man was also a bad loser who, long after his failed bid for office, continued to bad-mouth Delia Cachora Ortiz and all her relations to anyone who would listen, including his son.

As a consequence, that first schoolyard skirmish between Gabe and Luis Joaquin and his pals was not the last. Even now, everyone at school—well, maybe not the mostly Anglo teachers—understood that Gabe Ortiz and Luis Joaquin continued to be sworn enemies. As a consequence, Timmy's older brothers still came to Gabe's rescue whenever rescuing was needed.

Gabe's parents worked long, unpredictable hours. Mr. and Mrs. José worked, too, but Mrs. José's mother, Mrs. Francisco, had lived with the family and looked after the kids after school. Early on, Gabe Ortiz had been added to the José after-school mix. On most days, once classes were finished, he would tag along with the others to the Josés' house, where Mrs. Francisco maintained order until the parents came home and also cooked the evening meal.

Mrs. Francisco was a kind old woman who didn't mind having an extra mouth to feed. While her boys chatted away or kicked balls out in the yard, she would pat out and stretch the dough for making the Tohono O'odham staple called popovers—*o'am chu*—which she would slather with red chili and beans to feed her collection of starving boys, Gabe Ortiz included.

For years, Gabe's mother's failed attempts at making popovers had been the topic of running jokes on the reservation. Delia Cachora Ortiz had been raised off the reservation and had the benefit of an East Coast education. When Gabe's grandfather, Fat Crack, had sought Delia out and brought her back to the reservation to serve as tribal attorney, she may have been considered a capable lawyer in Washington, D.C., but back home on the reservation, she spent years being regarded as an outsider.

Fat Crack's approval and unstinting support had contributed to her gradual acceptance and to her eventually being elevated to the office of tribal chairman, but no amount of feather-shaking by a medicine man could improve her pitiful cooking skills. Some people said that Chairman Ortiz suffered from Popover Sickness, and that was why her attempts at making the Tohono O'odham's traditional dish were always such miserable failures. The basis of the dish is supposed to be a plate-sized crisply cooked disk of dough. Delia's versions were anything but crisp, and the soggy hunks usually weren't round, either.

For Gabe, Mrs. Francisco's popovers were a revelation, and it was during those many shared mealtimes, sitting in the José family's large warm kitchen, that Gabe's friendship with Tim's older brothers—Paul, Carlos, and Max—was cemented.

Over a period of several years, the José family had endured a run of bad luck. First their grandmother died. Then, the previous year, their father had been killed and their mother badly injured in a terrible car wreck. It had been one of those horrific multicar pileups that happens during dust storms when visibility rapidly drops to zero. With their mother still in a convalescent facility, the oldest son, Max, had ended up in some kind of trouble with the law and been sent to prison up in Florence. Now the second oldest, Carlos, had taken on the responsibility of holding the family together and keeping Tim from being placed in foster care.

So yes, Gabe thought, the José family might be having some troubles just now, but wasn't that the time when friends were supposed to step up and lend support rather than walk away? That was what Gabe believed, and no matter what Gabe's parents or Lani said, Gabe wasn't going to give up on the José boys, because they were his friends.

Bright stars scattered across the black sky, and a rising moon made it possible for Gabe to see, but he was grateful when he stumbled off the narrow footpath and back onto the rutted road. Away from the warmth of the fire, the air was frigid. His breath came out in visible puffs. Shivering, he pulled the heavy blanket around his shoulders. Doing that helped keep out the biting cold, but it made it far more difficult for him to maintain his balance and negotiate the rugged path.

Across the valley, Gabe could see occasional headlights and taillights coming and going on the highway, but to his way of thinking, the road was still very far away.

Something small and invisible brushed through his hair and then was gone, sending Gabe into a momentary panic. A bat, he realized a moment later, once his heart stopped pounding. It wasn't fair. Why was it that Lani could sit there in the dark by herself and not be afraid, when everything about the nighttime desert made him feel lost and scared.

He was still spooked from the bat encounter when something rustled in the nearby undergrowth. He stopped cold and waited, holding his breath. Suddenly a small herd of javelina burst out of a clump of manzanita, darted across the road in front of him, and clattered noisily down the hill. The fact that the javelina were well known to be terrified of humans didn't help. In this case, Gabe was the one who was frightened. The desert seemed to be full of scary things tonight.

If he asked Lani why the desert night didn't spook her, no doubt she'd tell him that it was because I'itoi was with her. Right. And she'd probably say that's why she knew things that other people didn't. What was the big deal about that? Gabe knew things, too, and I'itoi had nothing to do with it. For instance, he doubted I'itoi had been whispering in his ear last year when he had seen two of his junior high teachers, Mrs. Cadell and Mr. Ramos, together and realized that, although married to other people at the time, they were also in love with each other. When the affair had become common knowledge, the scandal had rocked the whole school district—and especially the teachers' compound where both families lived. None of that had come as a surprise to Gabe. He had kept his private knowledge to himself both before and after it had become public. And it was the same way now with the new principal, Mrs. Travers.

He could tell there was something wrong with her, although he didn't know exactly what. It was a sickness of some kind, and one she didn't want anyone else to know about. That was probably the reason she kept such a close eye on him and made his life miserable—because she suspected that he knew something he shouldn't.

At last Gabe reached the spot where the rutted two-wheeled track intersected with Coleman Road. Walking was easier now because the bladed dirt surface was smoother. The problem, of course, was that it was also far more traveled. He had taken no more than a few steps when he heard the sound of a vehicle approaching from behind.

It wasn't that late, only about ten or so, but still he worried. Some of the people out and about at this time of night could be dangerous. The best case would be for the car to be filled with a bunch of Indians, high school kids maybe, out partying in the desert. That wouldn't be so bad. No doubt they would offer him a ride. But what if the people in the car turned out to be a bunch of smugglers? Gabe knew that the bad guys who brought drugs and people across the nearby border were often armed and dangerous.

Then, of course, there was the last possibility, that the approaching vehicle would belong to the Border Patrol. If one of the Shadow Wolves picked him up, they'd no doubt turn out to be friends of Lani's husband, Dan Pardee. Questions would be asked and Gabe's answers would no doubt lead to more derision about how the tribal chairman's son had been picked up out in the middle of the desert, walking around wearing a ratty old Navajo blanket. That would be good for a laugh, especially from Luis Joaquin.

Not wanting to risk that, Gabe vaulted over the low dirt berm that lined either side of the road and ducked down into a patch of mesquite. Losing his balance, he fell backward against a clump of cholla that had been invisible inside the mesquite. When his full weight landed on the cholla, three-inch-long spines shot through the blanket into his shoulder, backside, and back. Spears of pain took his breath away, and it was all Gabe could do to keep from screaming.

Covering his mouth with his hand, he managed to stifle himself and waited through the agonizing time—the better part of a minute or so—that it took for the vehicle, a green-and-white Border Patrol SUV, to finally reach him and drive past. Once the SUV was gone, Gabe struggled to his feet. The ends of some of the cholla spines still jutted out through his clothing. He pulled out the ones he could reach, then turned his attention to the blanket.

A foot-long branch of cholla along with a dozen smaller balls of thorns were embedded in the tightly woven wool. Without the blanket to keep out the cold, Gabe was already shivering. He needed the blanket's protection, but first he had to remove the spikes. In the dark, with his hand shaking from the cold, that was far easier said than done. He found some rocks and used those to chisel away as much of the cholla as he could. The rocks worked fine on the bigger pieces—the ones he could see—but it would take light and a pliers to remove the spines that remained.

Giving up, Gabe flung the blanket over his shoulders and resumed his painful journey, wincing with every step, as first one spine then another bit into his flesh.

Damn Lani Pardee anyway, he thought. It was all her fault that he was out here in the middle of the night with cactus spikes stuck in his butt. *And damn I'itoi, too!* If he was the Spirit of Goodness, why hadn't he kept Gabe from tumbling into that patch of cholla?

More alone than he'd ever been, to say nothing of hurt and angry, Gabe Ortiz stumbled on through the night, but he knew what he was going to tell his parents as soon as he saw them—that Lani Walker-Pardee wasn't his godmother anymore. After all, he was almost a grown-up now, and grown-ups didn't need godparents.

CHAPTER 8

After Old Man returned without heat, the Indians held another council. This time they asked the Thah O'odham, the Flying People, for help. Oriole—S-oam Shashani—was listening, and he said he would go. The next morning Oriole started off very early. He did not return until very late, and when he did, he was changed. Some of his feathers had turned the color of the sun and others were black. He said that when he came too close to Tash, some of his feathers started to burn. He had to find some water and dive into it. That is why, even to this day, some of Oriole's feathers are black and others are yellow.

After that, several more birds were sent, but none of them could bring heat. The Indians decided that since the small birds could not bring heat, they should try the big birds.

Nuwiopa—Buzzard—was floating around in the sky and listening to the People talking. The Indians called to him and told him that he flew so well that it would be a small thing for Buzzard to go to the home of Tash and bring back some fire. Nuwiopa, too, thought this would be very easy. The next morning he started out. All the people were sure that this time Buzzard would succeed, and so they stopped work and waited.

About noon they saw a tiny black speck, high in the sky. When Buzzard came down, the Indians saw that all his feathers, which had been brown, were now burned black and his head had no feathers at all. It was all covered with blood. The People did what they could to help poor Nuwiopa, but that is how Buzzard is even to this day. He is covered with black feathers and has a head the color of blood.

BATHED IN THE warmth of the overhead heaters and with Bozo snoring contentedly beside him, Brandon Walker savored the quiet and let his mind wander back to the point where Amos Warren and John Lassiter had first come to his attention.

Brandon couldn't remember the exact year—sometime in the late '70s. He and Diana had married by then, but Lani had not yet come into their lives. Whenever it was, he'd been a detective for some time, but it had been a grudging promotion, done over Sheriff Jack DuShane's strenuous objections. Yes, he was a detective, but he was still on DuShane's shit list. That meant Brandon still worked the crap shifts and was given the crap assignments, and that had included his first encounter with what would eventually become the Amos Warren homicide investigation.

The initial call had come in on a hot Sunday afternoon in the middle of August. Brandon had been sprawled on the living room floor teaching the game of checkers to a pair of towheaded nine-year-olds who looked like they could have been brothers but weren't. One was Brandon's stepson, Davy, and the other was

Brian Fellows. His own sons, Quentin and Tommy, had zero interest in checkers.

Brandon had served in Vietnam, far enough from the front lines that he didn't wake up at night quaking from dreams of the war, but close enough to understand the concept of collateral damage. Brandon thought of Brian as the opposite of collateral damage.

Brandon had been devastated when his wife, Janie, had divorced him, taking his two sons, Tommy and Quentin, with her. In the divorce proceedings, she had claimed that her husband neglected her and that she was tired of coming in second to the Pima County Sheriff's Department. The whole "neglect" issue turned out to be nothing but a ruse. Brandon learned later that, long before the divorce came along, Janie had been playing around behind Brandon's back. She was also pregnant with another man's child, a guy who skipped out as soon as he heard a baby was on the way. Brian was born a scant six months after Janie's divorce from Brandon became final.

Brandon had lost the house in the divorce and almost everything else as well. He never missed a single one of his child support payments, but his meager salary at the sheriff's department didn't stretch far enough for him to buy or even rent someplace decent to live. He'd ended up moving back home to live in his old bedroom with his ailing father and his incredibly bossy mother.

Living at home, however, meant that on visitation days, he could splurge and take Tommy and Quentin out to do special stuff. He took them to U of A Wildcat baseball games, which were the ones he could best afford. They also went bowling and saw movies. On those Saturdays when he'd go to pick up his boys, it had broken his heart to see Brian standing sad-eyed and alone as they drove away. One day, on a whim, he'd asked Brian to join them, and the poor neglected little kid had been overjoyed. Much to Tommy's and Quentin's dismay, their annoying half brother became a regular on those visitation excursions with their father.

Three and four years older than their half brother and Brandon's new stepson, Davy Ladd, Tommy and Quentin had as little to do with the younger boys as humanly possible, but Davy and Brian became fast friends. And Brandon, having missed out on much of Tommy's and Quentin's childhoods, enjoyed having a do-over of sorts with Brian and Davy.

On that Sunday afternoon, Brandon had no way of knowing that this second chance at fatherhood would be far more successful than his first attempt with his own sons, and that Brian—a boy who was no blood relation—would one day follow Brandon's footsteps into the world of law enforcement.

"It's for you," Diana said, passing him the phone. "It's the department."

Brandon levered himself into a sitting position. "Detective Walker here," he said.

"Got a dead one for you," Luke, the Dispatch operator said. "A couple of hikers just called in saying they found human remains out near Soza Canyon on the far side of the Rincons. It's probably some Indian who's been dead for a hundred years or so, but it's your problem now."

"Where's Soza Canyon?" Brandon asked. "I've never even heard of it."

"Not surprised," Luke said. "I hadn't heard of it earlier, either. As I said before, it's on the far side of the Rincons. According to my topo map, the spot they're referring to is just barely inside the county line. Soza Canyon evidently drains into the San Pedro River, somewhere east of where the hikers found the body."

"And how do I get there?"

"Drive to the end of Tanque Verde and keep on going. That'll put you on Redington Road, which will take you up over the pass. Just keep following that until you get there."

"How far?"

"The people who called it in said they'd meet you somewhere along the way. They had to drive all the way to Pomerene to find a phone. The first call they made was to the Cochise County sheriff, but someone there pointed out that Soza Canyon is in Pima County, not Cochise. Anyway, they're driving a blue Toyota Land Cruiser. They'll park it alongside the road and lead you in from there."

"Great," Brandon muttered.

"And you'd better bring your hiking boots and some galoshes, too," Luke told him. "They're predicting rain for later on this afternoon, heavier in the mountains than down here."

"What about the M.E.?" Brandon asked.

"I know they've been called, but there's been a fatality MVA up around Marana. They'll send someone out when they can."

Much of southern Arizona is made up of relatively flat or hilly terrain with occasional sections of steep mountain ranges jutting skyward here and there. The Catalina Mountains are generally to the north and east of Tucson, and the Rincons southeast. The two distinct ranges are separated by a low-lying dividing line known as Redington Pass. Heavy summer rains could send devastating flash floods roaring through the gullies and washes that ran in veins down the mountainsides and into the valleys below.

As a detective, Brandon was allowed to take his car home. His ride was a respectable Plymouth Fury sedan with a police pursuit engine that made it fine for chasing down crooks on long stretches of open highway. But on a muddy, rain-flooded road out in the middle of the boonies, the front-wheel-drive vehicle wouldn't be worth squat.

"Any chance of coming in and picking up a four-wheel drive?"

"Nope," Luke answered. "I already asked. They're all checked out for the weekend."

Something jarred Brandon out of his nighttime reverie. He listened, wondering if he'd heard some distant sound, but when Bozo didn't stir, Brandon didn't, either.

HALF AN HOUR or so of walking later, as Gabe was finally approaching Highway 86, he heard the distant hum of an oncoming vehicle. When the turn signal indicated that a pickup—an older-model dual-cab Silverado—was turning onto Coleman Road, Gabe once again ducked out of sight, this time checking behind him for any patches of marauding cactus.

He listened to the sounds of doors opening and closing, of men laughing and joking and relieving themselves. Gabe caught enough of the back-and-forth chit-chat to learn that these were Indians—a group of guys who had gone into town to buy some beer and were now headed back to the village of San Miguel for a weekend of partying. Gabe could tell that the men weren't kids.

They were older—maybe his father's age. They might even be friends of his father's, but just because they knew Leo Ortiz didn't mean they knew Gabe.

Gabe took a deep breath and stepped out into the open. His sudden appearance startled the others, but he had a plausible story at the ready.

"My friends left me here," he said plaintively. "Can you give me a ride?"

"Hebai?" the man closest to the driver's door asked. "Where?"

The fact that the man spoke Tohono O'odham rather than English meant that the men in the group were most likely far older than Gabe's parents. From Gabe's point of view, that was all to the good.

"Komikch'ed e Wah'osithk," Gabe answered.

The men exchanged surprised glances. They probably hadn't expected that he would answer the question in their native tongue and use the traditional name, Turtle Got Wedged, rather than the Milgahn name of Sells.

There was a small pause, then the driver nodded. *"Oi g hihm,"* he said.

Literally translated, *"Oi g hihm"* means "Let us walk." In the everyday vernacular of the reservation it means "Let's get in the pickup and go," and that's exactly what Gabe did—climb in—but before he did so, he took off the spine-riddled blanket and tossed it into the bed of the pickup, where it landed on a tarp-covered load that was most likely several cases of illicit beer.

Squeezed into the backseat between two massive men, Gabe had no choice but to sit there and suffer. There were still sharp bits of cholla spines stuck in his jeans that made squirming in any direction an agony.

To his immense relief, the drive into Sells was done

in almost complete silence. Without a stranger in their midst, the men had been jovial and talkative, but now Gabe's presence seemed to have stifled any desire to talk. As soon as they crossed the low pass just before Sells, Gabe broke the silence.

"*Ihab,*" he said, meaning "Let me out right here."

The truck pulled over at the road that led to the high school. From here it was probably a mile or more to the house, but on the off chance one of these guys did know Gabe's parents, Gabe wanted to be dropped off as far as possible from both his father's garage and the Ortiz family compound.

Gabe was warm when he climbed down from the cab of the truck, but that soon changed. He retrieved his prickly blanket, but even with that slung over his shoulders, he was cold within a hundred yards or so. By the time he reached the house, he was shivering.

With all the windows dark, the house was forbidding rather than welcoming. Gabe wasn't at all surprised that his parents weren't home yet. As part of Delia's duties as tribal chairman, she tried to attend at least one village dance each weekend. The long hours of sitting around fires, dancing, and standing in food lines at feast houses allowed Delia to stay in touch with her constituents, the ordinary people who weren't necessarily sitting on the tribal council. Most of the time, Gabe would have gone to the dance with them.

Gabe stepped onto the poured concrete slab that served as a front porch and walked forward, ready to slip his key into the lock. Before he reached the door, however, he tripped over something and almost fell. Righting himself, he reached down and picked up a small paper bag. When he carried it inside and switched on a light, he saw that the bag held a Costco-sized jar of Skippy peanut butter. Since peanut butter sandwiches were his father's lunch-pail favorite, Gabe's first assumption was that his mother had asked someone who was going into town to pick up a jar for her. At the bottom of the bag, however, Gabe spotted a hand-scribbled note:

Please keep this for Carlos. I'll explain later.
Tim

Gabe stared at the note and then at the jar of peanut butter. It made no sense. Why would Carlos need him to keep that? After a moment, he put down the note, picked up the jar, and opened it. It had been opened before—the foil seal had been peeled away. The problem was, the label on the jar said the peanut butter was creamy style rather than crunchy, but this was definitely lumpy rather than smooth.

Curious, Gabe took the jar over to the kitchen counter, pulled out a tablespoon, and dug a heaping spoonful of peanut butter out of the jar. As he did so, something that was definitely not a piece of peanut caught the light. He put the spoon with the peanut butter inside a wire mesh strainer and used hot water and dishwashing detergent to clear away the peanut butter. What was left in the bottom of the strainer were four brightly glittering glasslike pieces of rock. They reminded him of Lani's pieces of crystal, but he knew at once what they really were—diamonds. Diamonds in a peanut butter jar!

He plucked one of the gems out of the strainer to study it. It seemed as though the diamond worked exactly the same way as Lani's divining crystals. Focusing on the jewel, Gabe realized what was going on. Carlos José and maybe Max, too, had been caught up in some kind of smuggling operation. If that was the case, it meant Lani was right and the Josés were part of the Bad People. It was even possible Tim himself was part of it.

Gabe understood that if his parents found out he was involved in any of this, they would kill him. That was especially true for his mother. The problem was, Tim was Gabe's friend, and he had asked for help. Gabe couldn't just turn his back on his friend. No, tomorrow Gabe would take the jar back to Tim and tell him he'd need to ask someone else for help. In the meantime, though, the jar, the bag, and the note all needed to be kept out of sight. He carried them into his bedroom.

He was standing in front of the dresser, about to put the bag in a drawer, when he realized that he'd stuck the four gems from the strainer into the pocket of his jeans. He had them in hand and was about to return them to the jar when he realized there was no way for Carlos or anyone else to tell how many gems had been concealed in the peanut butter. If Gabe kept them, did that mean he was one of the Bad People, too?

The gems didn't exactly speak to him. What he heard in his head was Lani's long-ago voice telling him one of the I'itoi stories and explaining how four was a sacred number because all of nature goes in fours—four seasons, four directions. Was this the same thing? Was that the reason there had been four diamonds in that single spoonful of peanut butter—not three or five or six, but four? Maybe this was a message from I'itoi, or maybe even the trickster, Ban—Coyote—whispering in Gabe's ear and telling him those four diamonds now belonged to him.

He returned them to his pocket. Then, stripping off his jeans and underwear, he turned to a far more pressing matter—getting the last of those pesky cholla spines out of his bare behind. When he had most of them removed, he got into bed and turned out the light. He was still chilled, and Gabe was grateful to pull the covers up around him. There may have been the sharp end of a cholla spine or two still sticking him, but he had walked too far and was too tired to notice.

He fell asleep and dreamed of bats—hundreds of bats, maybe even thousands. During the dream he noticed something odd. He was out in the desert somewhere all by himself, and although the bats were flapping all around him, for some strange reason, he wasn't the least bit afraid.

CHAPTER 9

After Buzzard returned without Fire, people were still cold at night, and the stories of those who had tried to bring back fire only made them want it more. They held another council and decided that they should send something that flies at night, so they asked Bat—Nanakumal—to go to Tash's house, slip in through a crack, and bring back Fire. Nanakumal said he would try. The next day Bat set off. When he left for Tash's house, he was covered with soft gray feathers.

The People were sure that Bat would succeed, so that night they stayed awake, waiting for him to return.

It was very dark. At last they saw a light coming, and it flashed from side to side and there was a great roar. When the light reached the earth, there was a loud bang. Some of the Indians were frightened and hid, but others said it is Tai—Fire—flashing like the sun. They ran as fast as they could to the spot and found a place where the grass was burning and so was a tree.

One of the men, an elder, ran to the burning tree, took one of the branches, and waved it in the four directions—North,

East, South, and West—so the People would know not to be afraid.

There was still much noise and many flashing lights. The People called the noise Bebethki—Thunder—and the flashing lights, Wepgih—Lightning.

The People were so excited to have Fire that they forgot all about Bat. The next day they went looking for him. They found poor Nanakumal hanging limp in a tree. He had not one feather left. Tash had burned Bat black, all the way to the skin. Bat was so ashamed of how he looked that no one could coax him into showing himself. That is why, nawoj, *my friend, even to this day, Bat comes out only at night.*

As the night sounds of distant traffic hummed in the background, Brandon's thoughts returned to that Sunday afternoon summons that had taken him from Gates Pass in the Tucson Mountains on the far west side of town to the base of the Catalinas on the far east side.

That day, as he drove, he'd kept a wary eye on the weather and the less-than-optimal road conditions. Redington Pass Road was primitive to begin with, and summer rains had made it virtually impassable in spots. Not only that; a wall of white and gray thunderclouds was boiling up on the back side of the mountains, rolling in from the southeast. If a gully washer was in the offing, Brandon knew he'd be lucky to get to the crime scene and even luckier to make it back home. And if the medical examiner's folks were very far behind him, they might be no-shows altogether.

It took the better part of two hours from the time he left home before Brandon finally spotted a light blue Land Cruiser parked alongside the road. A man and a woman stood leaning against each of the front fenders. Brandon pulled up alongside the vehicle and rolled down the window.

"Are you the folks who called the sheriff's department?"

Nodding, the woman stepped forward. She was young and blond, with windblown hair and a peeling sunburned face, complete with a freckled nose. "I'm Suzanne Holder, and this is my partner, Kent Perkins."

Kent didn't seem any too happy. "Took you long enough," he muttered glumly, peering over his shoulder at the tower of clouds marching toward them. "I was expecting lights and sirens. That storm's going to be here any minute."

Brandon put his Plymouth in Park and stepped out of the vehicle, proffering his ID wallet as he did so. "I was told these were skeletal remains," he said, "so it's not exactly a life-and-death situation. As you can see from my ID, I'm Detective Brandon Walker with the Pima County Sheriff's Department. What have you got here?"

Suzanne studied the badge and ID before handing it back. "Don't mind Kent," she said with a laugh. "He's a city slicker from California. He always translates times and distances in terms of freeways."

"So what have you found?" Brandon prodded. "And what brought you out here in the first place?"

Suzanne answered the second question first. "We're grad students in anthropology at the University of Arizona. In the past couple of years there have been lots of unsubstantiated rumors about Papago artifacts being found in this area. The problem is, the San Pedro is a long way from the Papago's traditional haunts. There were far more Apaches here in the past than there were

Papagos. So for the past few weeks, Kent and I have been spending a lot of time out in this area, trying to sort out those rumors once and for all."

"Is there a chance that's what the remains in question are all about?" Brandon asked. "Maybe they're Indian artifacts, too."

"I doubt it," she said.

"How about if I have a look? How far is it?"

"A mile and a half," she answered, "maybe two."

"Can you lead me there?"

"Of course," Suzanne responded. "Kent can wait here and flag down the M.E. Here are the keys," she added, tossing a key ring in his direction.

Suzanne appeared to be several years younger than Kent, but she was clearly in charge, and Brandon wondered if the Land Cruiser wasn't hers as well.

Brandon went back to his car and radioed in to Dispatch. Luke told him that the M.E. van was still a good forty-five minutes out. Brandon figured that was information Kent didn't need to have. Rolling up his window and locking the door on his patrol car, he went around to the trunk. He kept a sports bag back there loaded with spare clothing in case a quick change was needed. Dumping those out, he loaded in gloves, evidence markers, and a supply of evidence bags as well as a camera and extra rolls of film. Then, carrying the bag with him, he crossed the road and followed Suzanne into seemingly trackless desert.

With the coming storm, the temperature had dropped from midday highs of well over a hundred to something maybe ten degrees cooler in a matter of minutes, but from Brandon's point of view, it was still plenty hot, especially with the thickening humidity. He had to bite back the temptation to repeat that old saw about "mad dogs and Englishmen."

It was rough terrain, and Brandon was grateful to have taken Luke's advice about wearing boots. When they had to plow back and forth across a dry creek bed, street shoes would have instantly filled with sand. To begin with, carrying the bag wasn't a problem, but it grew heavier as they went, with Suzanne charging ahead, keeping a stiff pace, and talking as she went.

"Earlier this morning, we had been combing both sides of the canyon," she explained. "By the time we emerged from the canyon itself, it was right around noon and hot as hell. Looking for some shade, we ducked into a grove of mesquite, and that's where we found him."

"What are the chances you stumbled on an ancient burial ground that surfaced during a rainstorm?" Brandon huffed, doing his best to keep up.

"It's not an 'ancient burial ground,'" Suzanne replied. "This guy had a wallet with a driver's license in it. He's also got gold fillings in his teeth."

"You touched the wallet and the skull?" Brandon asked.

"Of course I touched it," she said. "What do you think I am, some kind of sissy? Here we are, come on."

Suzanne led the way into a grove of mesquite. Had the mesquite been left to its own devices, the branches would have grown low enough to touch the ground, but this was ranch land—open range. Grazing cattle had trimmed the lower branches as far up as they could reach. As a result, Brandon was able to remain almost upright as he walked under the trees to where the remains of what would later be identified as Amos Warren lay scattered in dozens of pieces.

The sheltering trees were probably the reason so much of the body remained in one place rather than being spread farther afield. The scavengers who had devoured the decaying flesh had most likely been attracted to the site for that same reason. While there, they were protected from above by a canopy of branches. On the north side, the mountains kept it from view. To the south of the trees, a rugged ridge of what had likely once been molten lava had created a natural basin that, in the aftermath of rain, would create a natural water hole—a charco—that would provide moisture for the trees long after the monsoon season ended.

With thunder grumbling in the background, there wasn't a moment to lose. Brandon made no effort to collect the bones. That wasn't his job. Instead, he put down evidence markers, photographed the bones in situ, then went about the business of gathering evidence—starting with the brittle remains of a leather wallet that contained a faded driver's license years out-of-date and what appeared to be a perfect arrowhead.

If he was packing an arrowhead around as a good luck charm, Brandon mused to himself, *it sure as hell didn't work.*

Brandon's careful search unearthed a few other artifacts. He located a scattered circle of blackened rocks that had most likely once surrounded a campfire. On a long piece of desiccated bone that had once been a forearm, he found an intact watch—a Timex. The hands, still visible behind the dirt-crusted lens, read 2:35.

A few feet away Brandon found a dented canteen,

empty but still covered with ragged bits of canvas. Near that he saw bits of tattered material that might have been a bedroll and what looked like the remains of a leather jacket. Not far from the jacket was another long bone, a rib this time. It had been gnawed along the edges, but through the bone itself was a small, perfectly semicircular hole. You didn't need to be a medical examiner to read the signs. This was the mark from a small-caliber weapon, but Brandon knew that at close range and with the right placement, a shot from a .22 can be every bit as deadly as a .45. Even years after the fact and with no additional evidence, he got the picture. Whoever this poor guy was, he hadn't died of natural causes. Somebody, mad as hell, had nailed him with one shot and maybe more. This was a homicide.

Brandon was combing the ground in a hopeless search for spent bullets when Suzanne called him. "Hey," she said, "over here."

After snapping one last photo of the rib bone, Brandon hurried over to where Suzanne stood. Knowing this was a crime scene, he had donned a pair of gloves and had prevailed upon her to do the same. Looking where she was pointing, Brandon saw a second piece of bone, this one a long leg bone lying near the remains of what had once been a sturdy hiking boot. The boot was marred by grooves from the teeth of gnawing scavengers who had evidently felt protected enough in that grove of trees to dine in place rather than hauling their prizes off to a den.

"Coyotes?" Suzanne asked.

Taken aback that the woman didn't appear to be the least bit squeamish, Brandon nodded before putting down another evidence marker and snapping the next photo. "Probably," he said. "I'm guessing all we'll find are the larger bones. Vultures will have carried off the smaller bits."

"What's going to happen now?" Suzanne asked.

"Once the M.E. does his autopsy and verifies how the victim died, we'll need to find out who did this. Then," Brandon added as the camera shutter clicked one last time, "we're going to put the killer away."

Suzanne said nothing, but Brandon looked up just in time to see her nod. At the same moment, a sharp crack of lightning and a roll of thunder announced the arrival of the long-delayed storm. Struggling against torrential and almost blinding rain, they headed back to the cars. Long before they reached the vehicles, they were soaked through, and the M.E. van was nowhere in sight. A call to Dispatch told them that the M.E. had been forced to turn back on the far side of Redington Pass.

For the time being, there was nothing to do but wait. Then, in a move no one expected, the storm proceeded to stall directly over Redington Pass. Eventually the water in the washes to the south of them receded, while the ones to the north roared bank to bank. That night, the only way back home to Gates Pass was on I-10 via Pomerene and Benson.

It was another two days before Redington Road was again passable. Driving a four-wheel-drive SUV, Brandon led the late-arriving M.E. back to the crime scene. This time, with the aid of a metal detector, Brandon Walker searched the mesquite grove and managed to find and retrieve not one but two spent bullets. They were buried in dirt, otherwise pack rats would have carried them off long ago.

Among the bones the M.E. collected were three rib bones and a sternum that showed the victim had been shot at least three times in the chest. Because of the driver's license they already suspected they knew the victim's name, but it took far longer for dental records to confirm that this truly was Amos Warren, a man who had disappeared in 1970 and been declared missing in 1971. Not long after that, Brandon Walker had found himself hot on the trail of John Lassiter, arresting him and bringing him to justice.

As for Suzanne Holder? It was years before Brandon saw her again. By then he was no longer a homicide detective. He had run against Sheriff Jack DuShane and had won the race fair and square. It was sometime after that, probably during his second term in office, when his receptionist had called over the intercom to say that he had a visitor in the outer office, someone named Suzanne Holder, who wanted to see him.

At first Brandon couldn't place the name, but as soon as she stepped into his private office, he recognized her as the woman from Amos Warren's long-ago crime scene. She was still freckle faced, but her long windblown blond hair was cut in a fashionable bob. The hiking boots and jeans had been replaced by a suit and a pair of low pumps.

"My goodness," he said as they shook hands. "It's been years. How are you doing and what are you doing these days?"

"I'm in town for a meeting," Suzanne said, "but I had to come by and say thank you."

Brandon was bemused. "Thank you?" he asked. "For what?"

"For changing the course of my life," Suzanne answered.

"What you said that day out in the desert about finding the murderer and bringing him to justice really got to me. It was something that seemed far more important than studying ancient artifacts. I could see that tracking that man's killer down gave you a sense of purpose. I wanted to have that same kind of purpose in my life, too. I ended up quitting anthropology and moving over into pre-med. I'm an M.E. now, living and working in Littleton, Colorado."

That meant that at least one good thing had come out of Amos Warren's homicide. Brandon was proud of Suzanne, of course, and gratified that in those few hours on the back side of the Rincons he'd been able to have such a positive influence on her life.

What seemed grossly unfair to him was that guiding a complete stranger onto a better path had been so effortless and easy when having the same impact on his own sons had turned out to be utterly impossible.

Brandon looked down at the sleeping dog. "Life isn't fair, is it, Bozo boy?" he said aloud. "Come on. It's late. Go get busy and then what do you say we hit the hay?"

CHAPTER 10

They say it happened long ago that a boy and girl, a brother and sister, were left all alone when their parents died. They lived in the southern part of the Tohono O'odham's lands. They felt very lonely living there because everything made them think about their father and mother. So they moved to a new place, the village of Uhs Kehk—Stick Standing—which is close to the place the Milgahn call Casa Grande.

The boy had no fields, so he went out hunting and was gone all day. The girl, after grinding her corn on her wihthakud*—her grinding stone—would go out into the desert to find plants for cooking and drying and to find seeds as well. The girl was S'kehg Chehia, which is to say, she was very beautiful.*

But because this brother and sister were alone and had no people and seemed so sad, the people in Stick Standing said they were bad. In this kihhim*—this village—there was a man of great influence, Big Man—Ge Cheoj. Big Man had power over the people because he had large fields. He soon fell in love with* *this new girl who was so very beautiful and so very different from the girls in his own village.*

But Beautiful Girl was always working or out in the desert gathering plants, so Big Man could not see her very often.

THE LIGHTS WERE off and Diana was sleeping when Brandon tiptoed into the bedroom. Bozo was already sacked out and snoring on his bed in the corner. Of the three, Brandon was the only one who still couldn't sleep. With his mind caught up in the case, he tossed and turned, wrestling his covers, battling his pillow, and once again reliving that long-ago crime scene.

Since Brandon had been the first officer summoned to the crime scene, that meant the homicide investigation was assigned to him from the start. At Sheriff DuShane's insistence, Brandon worked the case solo. He understood from the outset that this wasn't a favor. The Amos Warren investigation started out as a ten-year-old case. No doubt DuShane assumed that the homicide would never be solved. By assigning the case to Brandon, the sheriff could be sure that it would count against Brandon's closure rates and no one else's.

DuShane's automatic expectation of failure made Brandon all the more determined to succeed. Knowing that the best he could hope for would be to build a circumstantial case, he went looking into Amos Warren's circumstances.

Over time the victim's history came into focus. He was an ex-con who had gone to prison for killing someone in a bar fight on the night of his twenty-first birthday. After serving his time and being released, he'd been a loner, earning a somewhat sketchy living doing some kind of prospecting rather than having a regular job. Somewhere along the way, he had taken in a young kid from the neighborhood, a neglected boy named John Lassiter.

Since Brandon knew John Lassiter was the one who had filed the missing persons report after Amos Warren disappeared, that's where Brandon started his investigation. Their first meeting went about as well as could be expected.

According to county records, John Lassiter lived in a house on Lee Street in Tucson, a few houses east of Park. It was a modest place, two bedrooms or so, with a screened-in front porch. Because of the neighborhood's proximity to the University of Arizona campus, most of the other houses served as student rentals, but this one seemed to be an exception to that rule. The bearded, burly man who opened the door looked too old and shopworn to be a college student. Brandon estimated the guy was six-foot-six if he was an inch. Already, at nine o'clock in the morning, there was a distinct odor of beer on his breath.

"John Lassiter?" Brandon asked, pulling out his ID.

"That's who I am. Who are you?"

"I'm Detective Brandon Walker with the Pima County Sheriff's Department. May I come in?"

Rather than opening the door, Lassiter stepped outside onto a concrete walkway, pulling the door shut behind him. Folding his arms tightly across his chest, he stood there surly and glowering. "What's this all about?" he demanded.

"It's about a friend of yours—Amos Warren."

"Friend?" he snorted back. "Some friend. What about him?"

"I'm afraid he's dead," Brandon answered. "His recently identified remains were found some time ago on the far side of the Rincons. We've been unable to locate any next of kin. Since you were the one who filed the missing persons report, I thought you might be able to offer us some direction about a next of kin."

Brandon watched Lassiter's face as he delivered the bad news. The two men had once been friends. There was a pause, but no visible reaction crossed Lassiter's face when he heard the news.

"Good riddance then," John said at last. "And he didn't have any next of kin—no wife, no kids, no nothing. So what happened to him?"

"I'm not at liberty to say at this time. What I can tell you is that Mr. Warren's death is being investigated as a possible homicide."

"All right then," Lassiter said with a shrug. "Nothing to do with me. I haven't seen him in years. Where did this happen, down in Mexico?"

"No," Brandon answered. "It happened right here in the States. What made you think he might have died in Mexico?"

"He used to talk about going there someday and being able to live on the cheap. And when he took off the way he did, that's where I thought he went. A couple of years ago, when they finally got around to declaring him dead, I went along with the program, and why not? But I still didn't believe he was dead, not really."

Brandon was caught off guard. "Are you saying Amos Warren has already been declared dead in a court of law?"

Brandon's obvious consternation seemed to amuse Lassiter. "You didn't know about that?" he asked with a grin. "But that's exactly what happened. Three years ago or so and seven years after Amos took off, his attorney, a guy named Ralph Roundtree, initiated proceedings to have him declared dead. The first time I knew anything about it was when Ralph let me know that I was the only beneficiary under Amos's will. That was news to me. You could have knocked me over with a feather."

"What do you mean, it was news to you?"

"After the way he played me? I didn't care if I ever saw the snake in the grass again, and yet he left me everything—like nothing had ever gone wrong between us."

"What exactly did go wrong?" Brandon asked.

Lassiter didn't answer immediately.

"What did he do to you?" Brandon pressed.

Lassiter took a deep breath. "He knocked me flat on my ass, for one thing. In public. In front of our friends. Then there was the supposed partnership thing. That rotten SOB cheated me out of what was rightfully mine. Then, seven years later, I find out he's named me in his will? Big deal. I wasn't exactly impressed. It didn't come close to making up for what he'd done. It may have been ten years after the fact, but friends who cheat friends are lower than low."

Lassiter's voice broke. He turned away and swiped at his eye with the sleeve of his shirt. It was clear that the passage of time had done nothing to diminish the man's hurt at being betrayed by a trusted friend.

"You said you were partners," Brandon interjected after giving Lassiter a moment. "Partners in what?"

"We'd go out into the desert and find stuff—mineral samples, geodes, artifacts, whatever," Lassiter answered. "We'd drag it all into town and sell it. At the time Amos took off, we had a whole storage unit full of stuff set aside and ready to take to market. He made off with all of it. Cleaned out everything and sold it, most likely.

Probably made a killing. Half those proceeds should have been mine."

"You said Amos named you in his will," Brandon said. "What exactly did he leave you?"

"An almost worthless piece of property—five acres out in the middle of nowhere on the far side of Catalina," Lassiter answered. "That's where Amos was living when he pulled up stakes. The land came with a little house that wasn't much more than a one-room shack. He called it a cabin and claimed that it used to be a stage stop, but that could have been so much BS."

"After Amos disappeared, did you ever go up to his place to check it out?"

"Of course I did. I went up there to see if maybe he had tried to sneak into town behind my back, but the place was emptied out, too, slicker'n snot—just like the storage unit. I should have figured. Amos had some valuable stuff of his own that he kept there—stuff he wouldn't sell. That was most likely a lie, too. Anyway, I left the place just like I found it, with the door unlocked and everything. The next time I went back—years later as the supposedly new owner—the house had been burned to the ground. There was nothing left but a couple of walls and a foundation."

"Do you still own the property?"

"Hell, no," Lassiter exclaimed. "Why would I? I never asked for it and didn't want it in the first place. Luckily for me, some crazy-ass developer from back east was chomping at the bit to buy it off me. Claimed he was going to build houses out there in the middle of nowhere for some godforsaken reason. Said it was going to be some hotshot retirement community. I used the money he paid me for that place to buy this one."

"So tell me about the fight the two of you had," Brandon said. "When did it happen?"

"Some night," Lassiter said. "I'm not sure of the exact date. What I am sure is that's the last time I ever laid eyes on Amos Warren."

Brandon knew from the autopsy that Amos Warren had been five foot eleven. John Lassiter was a good seven inches taller than that. If Amos had taken John out, he must have been one tough dude.

"You said Amos Warren clocked you that night," Brandon prompted. "You said he knocked you on your ass?"

For an answer John pointed at a jagged three-inch scar on his left cheek. "Yes," he said, "and left me this to remember him by."

"Where did all this happen?"

"In a place on Speedway called El Barrio. It's still there on the right, just this side of the freeway."

Brandon had seen the place often enough. He drove past it almost every day on his way back and forth to Gates Pass. It looked like a rough kind of joint, and he had never ventured inside.

"So the two of you had a disagreement," Brandon continued. "Was this something about your partnership, or was it something else?"

"It was about a girl, if you must know," Lassiter answered. "Her name was Ava Martin, and she was my girlfriend at the time. We were almost engaged. Amos kept harping away about her not being good enough for me, but the first time he thought I wasn't looking, he made a pass at her and tried to get inside her pants. Hypocritical asshole! She wasn't good enough for me, but it was fine for him to try screwing around with her."

"What can you tell me about the fight?"

"What's there to tell? I told him to knock it off—to stop interfering in my life and to stop messing with Ava. I told him she was off-limits. Next thing I knew, he hauled off and knocked me colder than a wedge."

"Did you ever patch things up?"

"No, we never patched things up. I already told you, I never saw Amos again after that. The last I saw of him, he was sitting at the bar with a smug cat-eating-shit grin on his face and buying a round for every customer in the joint—sort of like a celebration for knocking me on my ass."

"What happened to Ava?"

"What do you think? Maybe Amos was right about her. She dumped me, too, as a matter of fact, just a few weeks later."

"Do you know where Ava is living these days?"

"No idea," Lassiter responded, "and who gives a shit? I heard she moved up in the world. Got herself a husband or two. No matter what Amos said, the girl had some smarts about her. By now she's probably set for life."

"What about you?"

"I'm doing okay," he answered with a shrug. "I've got a fairly new girlfriend now. She's a nice girl, and I don't want her dragged into any of this if that's all right with you."

Brandon nodded. "I don't see any reason why she should have to be, but I do have one more question. You and Amos worked together for a long time. Do you mind telling me how all that came about?"

For the first time, a look of regret passed across John Lassiter's burly face. "Back when I was a kid, my family situation wasn't the best," he said. "My dad was a drunk, my mom whored around, and Amos was our next-door neighbor. When things got too tough at our house, Amos took me in and looked after me. I admit, for a long time he was like a father to me. When I was a teenager and got myself in hot water, Amos was the one who bailed me out and kept me from being shipped off to juvie. But once I got over being a teenager, Amos never noticed. He couldn't see that I had turned into a man and that I didn't need him running my life anymore—telling me what I could or couldn't do, who I could or couldn't date."

Lassiter broke off and took a moment to pull himself back together. "So when do you think this happened?" he asked. "When do you think he died?"

"Probably right after you had that fight," Brandon answered.

"So maybe he didn't take off? Maybe somebody killed him and took all that stuff?"

"Maybe," Brandon answered.

"All this time, ever since Amos disappeared, that's what I've hated him for more than anything—for taking off without a word. But if someone murdered him, maybe he didn't desert me after all. Maybe it's time I rethink that whole thing."

"Maybe so," Brandon agreed. "Desertion is one thing; murder is another. Thanks for your help."

FORTUNATELY FOR ME, Scott Beaumont is currently a very low man on the Seattle PD totem pole. That means he's required to work weekend shifts almost all the time. That reality may have been bad for Scott and Cherisse right then, but it was good for me that Friday night. It meant we left the Behind the Badge gala early on.

My AmEx card had gotten a good workout. Much to

my amazement and even without so much as a sip of the steadily flowing wine, I had gotten into the whole charity auction groove and had come away with several pricey purchases. The first was a trip for four to Walt Disney World—tickets, hotel, and airfare included—that would make a great gift for my daughter, Kelly, and her family. It turns out all four of them, from my son-in-law, Jeremy, right on down, love anything Disney. I'm sure I paid more than I should have for that because the guy I was bidding against was an overbearing jackass. In other words, I couldn't help myself.

The second item was a getaway weekend for two at one of the top-of-the-line B and B's in Port Angeles. I'd overheard Cherisse talking to Scott about how much she'd love to go there for their wedding anniversary. It was part of the silent auction, so she had no way of knowing I had purchased it until that section of the auction closed and I handed the certificate over to her.

"Happy anniversary," I said. "Just make sure he has the weekend off."

As for the third item? That was an immense piece of multiple-layered and thoroughly bubble-wrapped Dale Chihuly glass resting in the trunk. It was bright red, one of Mel's favorite colors. I had no idea where we'd put it—in the condo or somewhere in the new house—but it was ours now. And I bought it for the same reason I bought the Disney tickets—I was bidding against the same guy.

Scott and Cherisse stopped in front of Belltown Terrace. Scott carried the piece of glass art into the building, and the night doorman put a BACK IN A MINUTE sign on his desk long enough to help me get it up to the unit. My phone was ringing as I let him back out the door.

"How's the party?" Mel asked.

"I'm home," I told her.

"Already?"

"It's ten," I said, "so not that early. But if it's ten here, it's one there. What are you doing up so late?"

"The clock may say it's late. My body begs to disagree. I'm not the least bit sleepy. What did you buy?"

To my way of thinking, there should have been a full stop to allow for a new thought and a new paragraph. That's not how Mel Soames works. She goes straight for the jugular.

"Some tickets to Disney," I said.

"And?"

"A getaway weekend for Scott and Cherisse at a B and B over at Port Angeles."

"And?"

I didn't want to tell her about the very expensive red glass bowl. I said, "It's for you, and I'm not telling you. It's a surprise."

"How much did it cost?"

"Same answer. Not telling."

"Spoilsport. Did you call Ralph?"

That counted as another abrupt U-turn in the conversation, with no advance warning. "I didn't," I said. "Not yet."

It was also a sore spot. My friend and attorney, Ralph Ames, had helped start a privately funded and operated cold case organization called The Last Chance, a group that is patterned after the Vidocq Society. The guys who work TLC cases are retired law enforcement and forensics folks—people who were and are, unfortunately, all too much like me.

As soon as Ralph got wind that S.H.I.T. was a thing of

the past, he was all over me, trying to get me to sign on. And every time he asked, I turned him down. My recent experience with a cold case hadn't gone well. Yes, the case got solved—decades too late—but a very talented homicide cop, Delilah Ainsworth, died in the process.

Ralph had been on my case about TLC, and so had Mel. The Harry I. Ball Project was completed, and my next venture into construction—the remodel of our newly purchased fixer-upper in Bellingham—was on hold. There was a major delay in the permitting process, which meant that everything was up in the air. Much as I despise being dragged around looking at appliances and designer plumbing and light fixtures, to say nothing of tile and backsplash materials, doing all those things was better than doing *nothing.* Because that was what I was up to right now, nothing, and it was driving me nuts.

I had come face-to-face with every retired cop's worst nightmare. I had nothing—not one thing—to do. I don't golf. I don't bowl. I don't play chess. I do, in fact, do crossword puzzles, but the older I get, the less time those take. Mel had told me on the way to the airport that she had learned, through Ralph's wife, Mary, that his group was tackling a cold case in Portland.

"I don't want to go to Portland to work a case," I told her. "When you're in Bellingham and I'm here, we're already ninety minutes apart. Being in Portland would add three hours to that."

The part I didn't say aloud, although she probably suspected it all the same, was that I was still shaken by what had happened a couple of weeks earlier when Mel's second-in-command, Austin Manson, had gone off the rails. The man had fully expected to be handed the police chief's job, and when the city council and city manager had settled on Mel, the assistant chief had been beyond pissed. Seething with anger and fueled by too much alcohol, he had caught Mel unawares, knocked her out, trussed her up, and tossed her in the trunk of his vehicle. He had been within minutes of dropping her off a seaside cliff when I, with the help of a cooperative tour bus driver, had managed to come to her rescue.

All that had quieted down now, at least on the surface. The mayor of Bellingham, Adelina Kirkpatrick, had gone to bat for Manson, who happened to be the son of her best friend. As a result, no criminal charges had been brought against the guy. He had been quietly packed off to a rehab facility of some kind. Mel insisted she was over it; I was not. I had felt completely helpless that afternoon. I had known she was gone, and for a while it had seemed as though there wasn't a damned thing I could do about it. It didn't help that I have a recurring nightmare in which I endlessly open the trunk of Manson's car. In the dream, sometimes Mel is there, bound in duct tape just as she had been that day. Other times, I see Delilah Ainsworth's bloody body. And once, just once, the body in the trunk had been that of Anne Corley, my second wife, looking exactly the way she looked the day I shot her to death.

So Mel may have been "over it," but I didn't expect to be for some time. We'd been on the way to the airport when she asked me, "What's wrong?"

I suspect that most married guys see that two-word question for exactly what it is—a minefield. I went for what I thought would be the least damaging answer. "Nothing," I said.

"Don't tell me that," Mel said. "For the past few weeks you've been Mr. Growly Bear himself."

"I'm bored," I had said. But that wasn't a safe-harbor answer, either.

"What are you going to do about it?"

Which put the ball squarely back in my court. "I'll call Ralph," I had said, but I hadn't carried through on that, and now Mel knew it, too.

"You say there's a case in Portland?"

"That's what Mary said."

On the one hand, I was feeling like I'd been ambushed. On the other hand, I knew Mel was right to be worried. I recognized the dangers. The nightmares meant I wasn't sleeping well. And sitting around with nothing to do other than enumerating my many sins of omission—all the things I should have done and didn't—isn't good for people like me. I've been off the sauce for years and haven't had a slip, but that doesn't mean I never will. I'm an alcoholic, after all. I may not be drinking, but I'm not cured.

"Jim Hunt is coming by tomorrow for a full day of furniture shopping. I'll call Ralph when we're done with that," I said. "If not tomorrow, then Sunday for sure."

"Promise?"

"Promise," I answered. For a change, I meant it.

CHAPTER 11

One day Big Man called Ban—Coyote—to help him. You will remember, nawoj, *my friend, that Coyote is often filled with the Spirit of Mischief. Big Man gave Coyote some beads. He told Coyote to go to Beautiful Girl, slip the beads on her wrist, and tell her about Big Man.*

The next morning, Coyote went to the house where the brother and sister lived. Beautiful Girl was cooking. When Coyote tried to slip the beads on her wrist, it made her burn her hand. That made the girl very cross. She scolded Ban. She told him she wanted no beads and no husband, and she wanted no more bother with a coyote.

Coyote carried the beads back to the village and told the great man what Beautiful Girl had said. Big Man was very angry because he was very powerful and used to having his own way. He told Coyote that he must go to the girl the next morning and tell her to take the beads. If she did not, Big Man would kill both her and her brother.

AFTER TOSSING AND turning for what seemed like hours, Brandon made his way into the bathroom to answer yet another call of nature. He glanced at the clock on his way by, but even though it was now after two, when he got back into bed he still couldn't sleep. He was too caught up in remembering the investigation.

The day after his initial meeting with John Lassiter, Brandon had paid his first visit to El Barrio. The bar was one of those low-life dives where time seems to stand still. Cigarette smoke hung thick in the air, with the odor of spilled beer and dried piss adding to the unhealthy mix. The tables were worn and scarred. The vinyl upholstery on the chairs and barstools was torn and duct-taped together in spots.

The customers, mostly regulars propped on sagging stools that might just as well have had their names written on them, were a dodgy-looking bunch of characters, as was the bartender, a man with multiple tattoos and the dubious handle of Unc Flores. Unc recognized Brandon as a cop the moment he walked through the door and long before he ordered black coffee.

Much to Brandon's surprise, there seemed to be a kind of corporate memory lingering in El Barrio's air along with all that cigarette smoke. Once he stated his business, no fewer than four people—Unc included—claimed to have been present the night ten years earlier when Amos Warren had taken out the man they all referred to as Big Bad John Lassiter. That was the first time Brandon heard John Lassiter called that, but it wouldn't be the last. The short-lived fight between Amos Warren and his pal John seemed to have taken on a kind of legendary status. When Brandon mentioned that he was investigating Amos's death, quite a few folks felt compelled to jump into the fray, each willingly sharing his own take on the story.

Since Brandon was still attempting to establish a

timeline for the crime, that was where the conversation started. Members of the peanut gallery in El Barrio all seemed to agree that the fight had occurred in the springtime, but no one could agree on the month or even the exact year. On details of the actual fight they were all surprisingly clear. The timing of events was hazy.

Nevertheless, they all seemed to be in complete agreement when it came to deciding who might be responsible—Big Bad John. Who else could it have been? As for what caused the fight? A woman, of course. Amos and John had gone to war over John's exceedingly attractive girlfriend at the time, one Ava Martin.

"That little bit of a thing was cute as a button," one of the old codgers said, shaking his head. "What a girl Ava was! She had that big old lump of a John Lassiter wrapped around her little pinkie. Led him around by the nose—that's what she did. I thought it was funny as hell."

"More like she led him around by the balls," another one offered.

The next time Unc showed up to refill his cup, Brandon put the question to him. "What do you think?"

Unc feigned innocence. "About what?"

"Everybody else around here seems to be of the opinion that John Lassiter might be responsible for Amos Warren's death. I'd like to hear what you have to say."

"I'm in the 'John Lassiter did it' camp. I've thought that all along, at least ever since we found out about Amos's will. Once that news surfaced, that's when I eighty-sixed Big Bad John Lassiter and told him to get lost."

"Wait," Brandon said. "You knew about the will?"

"Sure I did, almost as soon as it happened. At the

time, my sister Edna was working down at the county courthouse in the recorder's office. She used to come in here now and again, so she knew Amos. When the deed transfer came through, she recognized the name and told me about it. Pissed the hell out of me. Think about it. This old guy goes missing and stays missing. Eventually he's declared legally dead, and—surprise, surprise—his ex-partner ends up being the sole beneficiary under his will. It doesn't take a Philadelphia lawyer to put that one together."

"Did you talk to the cops about your suspicions?" Brandon asked.

"I would have, I suppose," Unc allowed, "if anybody had ever bothered to come around asking the questions, but nobody did—not until you turned up today. In my business, it's never a good idea to go looking for trouble unless it lands smack on your doorstep, especially when you're running a joint like this. But the next time Big Bad John stopped by, I showed him the door and told him he wasn't welcome. He had the unmitigated gall to ask me how come. I told him he already knew how come, and that was that. And you know what? If he walked through that door today, I'd take a baseball bat to the SOB myself."

Brandon left El Barrio that day with a spring in his step and feeling as though he might possibly be making progress. He went back to the office to look for Ava Martin, and she wasn't hard to find. John Lassiter had said that she'd moved up in the world. Based on public records, Brandon could see that was certainly true. At midmorning the next day, Brandon showed up at the spread Ava shared with her new husband. It turned out to be a five-acre horse property just off Houghton Road on the far side of Pantano Wash. County records indicated that Ava was married to a man named Clarence Hanover. Brandon just happened to know for a fact that Hanover was one of Tucson's top-drawer attorneys.

Rather than call ahead, Brandon simply showed up. He parked in the drive of a low-lying stuccoed, fully landscaped ranch house. Stepping up onto the front porch, he rang the bell. There was a long pause before the door cracked open, and a woman peered out.

"We don't want any," she announced immediately, as soon as she caught a glimpse of Brandon's face. She would have slammed the door shut, but Brandon managed to insert the toe of his boot between the door and the jamb.

"I'm not selling anything," he asserted. "My name is Detective Brandon Walker with the Pima County Sheriff's Office. I'm here investigating a homicide."

Ava sighed and opened the door a bit wider. Her blond hair was impeccably styled into a smoothly flowing page-boy. Her makeup was flawless. She wore a tight-fitting cowboy shirt, equally tight jeans, a pair of boots, and enough turquoise and silver jewelry to choke a horse.

"A homicide?" she echoed. "Who's dead?"

"A friend of yours, I believe, or at least an acquaintance—a man by the name of Amos Warren. His skeletal remains were found out in the desert some time ago. After an autopsy, the M.E. concluded that Mr. Warren died of homicidal violence."

Ava sighed again, letting Brandon know that she regarded his arrival on her doorstep as a grave inconvenience. "Okay, then," she said, opening the door. "I guess you'd better come in."

Ava led Brandon into a spacious living room and motioned for him to have a seat on a large cowhide-covered couch, while she sat down on a wooden-armed Eames chair with similarly covered cushions. Between them stood a coffee table constructed of thick glass covering what looked like the splintering remains of an antique wagon wheel. With friends living in real poverty out on the reservation, Brandon found the Hanovers' pricey faux-rustic decor more than a little annoying.

"I'm surprised to hear Amos is dead," Ava said. "What did he die of?"

"This is an ongoing investigation," Brandon answered. "I'm not at liberty to release that information at this time."

"Where did it happen?"

"On the far side of the Rincons. Actually, not that far from here, as the crow flies," he added, pointing, "but it's a long way if you're driving." After a slight pause, he added, "So I take it you did know Mr. Warren?"

Ava nodded. "But not well," she said. "Amos was good friends with the guy I was dating back then, a fellow named John Lassiter. Johnny looked up to Amos, worshipped him practically. Johnny's father died when he was a kid, and Amos acted like a father to him. When Amos left town—at least that's what we thought at the time—it broke John's heart. He went completely off the rails. That's why I broke up with him—he was drinking too much, fighting, and generally getting into trouble."

"You said, 'when Amos left town.' That makes it sound as though you believed the same thing John did—that Amos left of his own free will?"

"Wait," Ava said. "You've talked to Johnny? How is he?"

"Mr. Lassiter is fine, as far as I can tell, but getting back to Amos . . ."

"Oh, yes, that's what Johnny thought and it's what I thought, too—that Amos finally had it up to here with Johnny and just took off. Johnny mentioned there had been some kind of quarrel between them just before Amos went away."

"Do you have any idea what the quarrel was about?"

Ava shook her head. "It was probably about their joint business venture. They collected stuff together, things they found out in the desert and sold to people who deal in those kinds of things—gems and minerals, Indian artifacts, what have you."

"My guess is they even found some turquoise from time to time," Brandon suggested.

Ava looked down self-consciously at the silver and turquoise bracelets dangling on her wrists and at the turquoise-studded belt buckle that would have put more than a few professional rodeo riders' buckles to shame. "That, too," she said. "They always seemed to have plenty of turquoise."

"This so-called stuff," Brandon continued, attempting to put the conversation back on track. "Do you have any idea where they kept it?"

"In a private storage unit inside a warehouse off Aviation Highway. At first Johnny didn't bother checking on the storage unit because he assumed Amos was off in the desert on what they used to call 'scavenging expeditions.' Then, a few days later, Johnny went to the post office to pick up the mail."

"Post office?"

Ava nodded. "Amos kept a post office box to use for business correspondence. He had a key to the box, and so did Johnny. Johnny picked up the mail and there was a letter from a towing company. It turns out Amos had abandoned his truck in the parking lot of a hotel near the airport, and the hotel had it towed. As soon as Johnny knew about the airport connection, he figured Amos had done a runner. That's when Johnny and a friend went to the warehouse. It was empty, totally cleaned out."

"A friend went with him?" Brandon asked. "What friend?"

"His name was Kenneth," Ava answered. "Ken Mangum. He and Johnny hung out together. They played a lot of pool."

"Any idea where Kenneth is now?"

She shrugged. "We lost touch a long time ago. Kenneth and Johnny were sort of roughneck guys. I stopped messing around with them when I decided to straighten up and fly right."

"Let's go back to the storage unit for a moment. Did you ever go there?"

"A couple of times—before it was empty, not after."

"You said it was locked. Do you remember what kind of lock?"

"A padlock."

"One that took a key or was it a combination lock?"

Ava had to think for a moment, frowning before she answered. "I'm pretty sure there was a key."

Brandon made a note of that. He knew for sure that no keys of any kind—car, post office, or padlock—had been found in the vicinity of Amos's bones. But then, they hadn't found a vehicle there, either. Chances were that the padlock key had ended up in the same place as the missing car keys.

Brandon examined his notes for a moment.

"Okay, I know Amos and John duked it out. I've talked

to a number of people—especially folks who were in the bar the night Amos and Johnny had their fight. Several of them seem to be of the opinion that John Lassiter is the guy responsible for Amos's death. What do you think about that?"

Ava shrugged. "I don't know, but after Amos disappeared, Johnny was a wreck and totally out of control. Scary, even."

"What do you mean scary?"

She hesitated a moment before she answered. "He threatened me once," she said quietly. "That's why I broke up with him."

"Threatened you how?"

"With a gun."

"He had a gun?"

"Lots of people have guns," Ava countered. "I have a gun. It's no big deal."

"What kind of gun?"

"I don't know. Not a big one. A .22 maybe? A pistol, not a revolver."

Brandon made an effort to contain his reaction. He had made no mention that Amos Warren had been shot, much less shot by someone wielding a small-caliber weapon. John Lassiter, Amos Warren's disgruntled former partner, had always been Brandon's best possible suspect. Now Brandon knew, via a third party, that Lassiter had been in possession of a handgun at the time of the crime. This had to be a key bit of information. Brandon felt it was also important that when Ava had volunteered the information, it had been in regard to something else entirely, at a time when she'd had no hint from Brandon that Amos Warren had been shot to death.

"You're saying you know the difference between a pistol and a revolver?" Brandon asked.

Ava shot him a withering look. "Of course I know the difference. Just because I'm a blonde doesn't make me stupid."

Touché, Brandon thought. *Well played.*

Ava glanced at her watch. "Look," she said impatiently. "I have a luncheon engagement, and I'm about to be late. If you have more questions, could we please finish this some other time?"

Brandon took the hint. "Of course," he said, rising to his feet. "You've been a big help. If I could just have a phone number . . ."

She gave him the number and showed him to the door. Brandon walked away feeling downright jubilant. He was getting somewhere. Sheriff Jack DuShane be damned, he was going to solve this case. Not then, Brandon told himself, but maybe now.

With that last thought about the years-ago investigation and hours after Brandon Walker landed in his bed, he finally fell asleep.

CHAPTER 12

The next morning Coyote took the beads and went again to the house of Beautiful Girl and her brother. This time Coyote found the girl with her giwho*—her burden basket—ready to go out into the desert and gather plants. She would not even listen to him. She took her basket and left Ban standing there alone.*

When Big Man heard this he was very angry. He went to Wind Man—Hewel O'odham—and asked for his help. And so, while Beautiful Girl was alone in the desert, gathering plants, Wind Man came and found her. With a loud whoop, Wind Man gathered the girl up and took her to the top of a very steep mountain that stands all alone in that part of the country—a mountain the Milgahn call Picacho Peak but the Tohono O'odham call Chewagig Mu'uk, Cloud Peak.

Everyone knows, nawoj, *my friend, that Picacho Peak is very small, but it is also very steep, so steep that no one has ever climbed it.*

In the evening, Beautiful Girl's brother returned to the house and found it empty. He waited and worried. Finally he went out into the village and told the people that his sister was gone, and the people agreed to help him find her.

The next day the people followed Beautiful Girl's tracks out into the desert. They found the place where she had stopped to gather plants, and they found her empty burden basket, but that is where her tracks stopped. The people held a council to decide what to do. Coyote came to the council and said that he'd been passing close to Cloud Peak that day and heard the noise of a woman crying. Ban knew that this was very bad trouble because the woman could not climb down.

At last Beautiful Girl's brother decided to ask I'itoi—the Spirit of Goodness—for help. He called for Messenger, Ah'atha. The brother dressed Messenger in white eagle feathers and sent him to see I'itoi. Spirit of Goodness listened to Messenger and decided to help. He took the seeds from a gourd and planted them at the base of the mountain, then he began to sing. Soon the seeds began to sprout. Before the end of the day the gourd vines had grown so tall that they covered the steep sides of the mountain. Beautiful Girl was able to climb down safely.

WITH THE HELP of several glasses of Pig's Nose scotch, Ava went to bed earlier that evening than she would have otherwise. Several hours later, she was awakened from a deep sleep by the sound of a cell phone clattering noisily across her bedside table. It was another of her burner phones, one that she always kept nearby with the ringer turned on silent and the phone set on vibrate.

"Hello." She didn't need to ask who was calling, because there was only one person who had the number. "What's up?"

"He didn't deliver the shipment."

Ava sat bolt upright in bed. "What do you mean,

he didn't deliver?" she demanded. "Didn't the package make it across the border?"

"It came across the border, all right, but our guy wants more money."

Ava was outraged. "Are you kidding me? He's holding my damned diamonds for ransom?"

"That's how it sounds."

"How much does he want?"

"Twenty thou."

"That's highway robbery—twice what we've paid him before."

"Well," Ava's caller replied with a chuckle. "You know what they say about no honor among thieves. He claims he needs the money. He says his mom is sick, and he's looking after his younger brothers."

"Too bad for him," Ava replied. "Turns out now he's lost his job, too. I want you to take care of this."

"As in . . . ?"

"As in take care of it!" Ava snapped. "As in make a statement. As in do whatever the hell you have to do to get the job done. As in let other people out on the res know that I am not to be trifled with. I want those three José boys wiped off the face of the earth."

"Yes, ma'am, I'll take care of it."

"Before you do," she added, "I want you to make Carlos tell you what the hell happened to my diamonds. I want them back. Do you understand?"

"Yes, ma'am," he said again. "I certainly do."

As he hung up, Ava thought the poor man sounded a bit shocked and more than a little cowed. It must have been hard for him to imagine that she had so casually condemned three members of a single family to death. He shouldn't have been surprised. After all, this wasn't

Ava Richland's first rodeo, and it wasn't the first time she had issued someone's death sentence, either. In fact, now that she thought about it, this probably wouldn't be the last time.

Ava was relieved that she now had other people to do the dirty work for her, so it was no longer necessary for her personally to be the one pulling the trigger. Max José had worked for her for one reason only—because he understood that what she was doing had no connection to the cartels. But if he was behind this and was directing his brothers to hold her up for more money, he had made a fatal error in thinking that she wasn't every bit as dangerous as the cartels.

Ava went into the kitchen and started the coffee. It was just after midnight. Harold wouldn't awaken for several more hours. She knew that three-fourths of the José problem would be handled, but now, while she had a little peace and quiet to herself, Ava needed to make some private phone calls and arrange to deal with Max. What's more, once and for all, she needed to take care of John Lassiter.

The man had already had two separate trials. If Ava Richland had her way, he sure as hell wouldn't have a third one.

AFTER GABE LEFT, Lani sat by the fire for hours, wrapped in her bedroll and gradually feeding the remaining pieces of wood into the flames. Her work as an ER physician meant that she was accustomed to working odd hours, especially nighttime hours. So she didn't try to sleep. Instead, she stayed awake, thinking. For a while she let herself meander through the old stories, the ones she had learned from Nana *Dahd* and from Fat Crack. And since Gabe wasn't present to hear them, she told them to herself—the story of Bat bringing fire as well as the story of Beautiful Girl who would eventually become Evening Star.

Finally, though, her thoughts drifted to Gabe. She wandered through her collection of memories about him, remembering the things about him that had endeared him to her as a child, starting with the night he was born.

Lani and Delia Cachora hadn't exactly been friends back then. When Delia first arrived back on the reservation, the fact that Fat Crack had chosen, doted on, and mentored both of them had caused an odd kind of sibling rivalry to grow between the two young women. They were still wary of each other at the time of Fat Crack's death.

On the day of his funeral, after the nightlong feast in the village of Ban Thak—Coyote Sitting—Delia's water had broken. Lani was still in medical school, but she had realized at once that the baby was coming too fast to make it to the hospital before he was born. That was how Gabe Ortiz became the first baby Lani Walker ever delivered, turning the backseat of Diana Ladd's fully restored Buick Invicta into a makeshift delivery room.

Wanda Ortiz, Fat Crack's widow and the baby's grandmother, had taken the squalling child and dried him on clean towels from the feast house. Then, after wrapping him in one of his father's immense flannel shirts, she had handed him to Lani, who had in turn passed him along to Delia.

Lani still remembered how she had felt in that moment. The baby was a gift through time. He had been passed down from Nana *Dahd*'s grandmother, Understanding Woman, to the next generation, to Rita Antone and Looks at Nothing. They had passed the gift on to Rita's nephew, Fat Crack, who had done the same, passing the baby along to the next generation—Lani and Delia. It had seemed to Lani then, and still did, that the Elders, Kekelimai, had entrusted the care and keeping of this precious child to new hands, with the expectation—the requirement—that he be kept safe.

Gabe had just turned eight when Lani first became aware of how different the little boy was. Lani's mother had been dealing with some health issues, and the mental symptoms had been far more troubling than the physical ones. Although Lani and her father never came right out and discussed the situation, they were both convinced that Diana was losing it—that she was drifting into some kind of dementia situation or perhaps starting down the slippery slope into early-onset Alzheimer's.

The real culprit had been a simple matter of adverse drug interactions, but it was Gabe who had helped Lani understand that Diana was having hallucinations—that she was carrying on long heart-to-heart chats with Andrew Philip Carlisle, the crazed convicted killer who had once tried to murder her and who also happened to be dead. Lani's dad had always credited her medical skills with sorting out Diana's situation, but Lani herself knew that it was Gabe—born long after Carlisle had gone to what she hoped was his just reward—who had brought the matter to her attention.

Instinctively being able to suss out something like that was a medicine man kind of thing. For the next three years, Gabe had followed Lani around like a puppy dog. On Tuesdays and Thursdays after school he would come to the hospital's dialysis unit, where he seemed to function in the dayroom as a pint-sized medicine man, singing the healing chants Lani had taught him and reciting the ancient stories and legends for the patients. Long boring hours in the dialysis unit could be shortened by hearing the stories and legends of I'itoi someone remembered hearing long ago as a child living in one of the villages—in Ge Oithag, Big Fields, or Komlick, Big Flat Place.

Lani had taught Gabe that the I'itoi legends in particular were winter-telling tales and were only to be told between the middle of November and the middle of March. Most of the time Gabe was careful to abide by that rule. Sometimes, when it was July and someone who would not live to see another November wanted to hear the story of Old White-Haired Woman or the story of the Peace Smoke, Gabe would tell the story anyway. It didn't seem to him that I'itoi, the Spirit of Goodness, would mind that in the least.

Only when requested to do so did Gabe visit the rooms of individual patients—the injured, ill, and dying. Even though he had not yet reached *cheojthag*—manhood—and was not yet a fully grown medicine man, the families of patients told Lani that there were times when having Al Siwani—Baby Medicine Man—visit their loved one was better than having no medicine man at all.

Lani had marveled at how, sitting in quiet hospital rooms and without even having access to her sacred divining crystals, Gabe had often known long before anyone other than the doctors about who would live and who would die. He talked to Lani about those things sometimes, but even then he had instinctively known to keep from mentioning them to the people involved. And when Lani had asked how he knew those things, he could never explain it other than shrugging his shoulders and saying, "I just know."

Then, for reasons the divining crystals couldn't or wouldn't tell her, Gabe had started pulling away. He had stopped coming to the hospital. He had started distancing himself from her. And now, much to Lani's despair, her connection to Gabe seemed to be severed. He had walked away down the mountain, leaving her behind along with her last-ditch chance to save him from whatever was pulling at him. It was easy, sitting on the mountain, to ascribe what was happening to the Bad People—PaDaj O'odham—who had come up out of the South to steal the Tohono O'odham's crops and eventually to do battle with I'itoi himself.

So was that what this was all about? Lani wondered. Were the four José brothers with all their family troubles—a dead father and an ailing mother—the cause of all this? Were they somehow a modern-day equivalent of the PaDaj O'odham? And, if so, what did Lani have to do to extricate Gabe from their grasp?

Tossing one more piece of wood onto the fire, Lani slipped into her bedroll. Staring up at the stars, she remembered the story Nana *Dahd* had told her—the one about the terrible time when Andrew Carlisle, the evil *ohb,* had captured both Nana *Dahd* and Lani's brother, Davy, and held them prisoner in the root cellar. While there, Nana *Dahd* had summoned I'itoi to help them by singing a chant—a healing chant—speaking in the language of the Tohono O'odham. Lani had heard the chant often enough that she remembered every word, the same way one remembers a cherished lullaby. And it made her smile to know that while the song had been totally opaque to Andrew Carlisle, Davy had heard the words, understood them, and acted upon them:

Do not look at me, little Olhoni.
Do not look at me when I sing to you
So this man will not know we are speaking,
So this evil man will think he is winning.

Do not look at me when I sing, little Olhoni,
But listen to what I say. This man is evil.
This man is the enemy. This man is ohb.
Do not let this frighten you.

Whatever happens in the battle,
We must not let him win.
I am singing a war song for you,
Little Olhoni. I am singing

A hunter's song—a killer's song.
I am singing a song to I'itoi,
Asking him to help us and guide us in the battle
So the evil ohb does not win.

Do not look at me, little Olhoni,
Do not look at me when I sing to you.
I must sing this song four times
For all of nature goes in fours.

But when the trouble starts,
You must remember all these things

I have sung to you in this magic song.
You must listen very carefully
And do exactly what I say.

If I tell you to run and hide yourself,
You must run as fast as Wind Man.
Run fast and hide yourself
And do not look back.
Whatever happens, little Olhoni,
You must run and not look back.

Then, as seamlessly as if it were a new track on a much-loved CD, the next war chant returned to her as well, with every word and every nuance intact. And as Lani recalled the words, she was once again inside Betraying Woman's hidden cavern beneath Ioligam, trapped there with her own personal evil *ohb.* Mitch Johnson, deputized by Andrew Carlisle to kill her, had been waiting for Quentin Walker—the brother who was not her brother—to return. It was while she and Mitch waited in an ugly, lingering silence that Lani had finally understood what would happen: once Quentin returned, Mitch Johnson would kill them both.

Lani had closed her eyes then, making the darkness of the cavern even darker. And now, sitting outside by the fire, she closed her eyes again. As she did so, all the sensations of that long-ago time came spooling back to her along with the words to the chant. She could smell the sharp, acrid stink of Mitch Johnson's sweat; she could feel the calming touch of the damp soil against her skin; she could hear, somewhere in the far distance, the tiny drip of water; then suddenly and overhead, she felt the gentle touch of a bat's wing, ruffling her hair and telling her what she must do:

Oh, little Nanakumal who lives forever in darkness,
Oh, little Nanakumal who lives forever in I'itoi's sacred cave,
Give me your strength so I will not be frightened,
So I will stay in a safe place where the evil ohb cannot come.

For years Betraying Woman has been here with you,
For years your Bat Strength has kept her safe,
Waiting until I could come and set her free
By smashing her pottery prison against a rocky wall.

Keep me safe now, too, little Nanakumal,
Keep me safe from this new evil ohb.
Teach me to be juhagi—resilient—in the coming battle
So this jiawul—this devil—does not win.

Oh, little Nanakumal who lives forever in darkness,
Whose passing wings changed me into a warrior,
Be with me now as I face this danger.
Protect me in the coming battle and keep me safe.

Even as Lani had sung those words long ago, with Mitch Johnson listening and not comprehending, she had realized that the chant had contained words that were hers and not hers, all at the same time. Her people believed in singing for power, and her words had come unbidden from some ancient magic place, the same place Rita Antone had tapped into as she sang her warrior chant to Davy Ladd even longer ago. It was no surprise that the words gave Lani comfort now—the same kind of comfort and strength they had given her in that earlier time. Somehow she knew that in I'itoi's world, those two other times and this time were all the same.

Realizing she was growing drowsy, Lani looked at the fire and resisted the temptation to add another log. The fire had burned long enough that there would be plenty of coals to last until morning. Then she snuggled into her bedroll. The ground may have been hard beneath her body, but she was too tired to notice.

CHAPTER 13

The brother offered to pay I'itoi for saving his sister, but all the Spirit of Goodness asked for was a bobcat skin to hold arrows. Then Beautiful Girl and her brother went back home. Before many days passed, Coyote came once more to the home of Beautiful Girl with another message from Big Man, saying that the girl must marry Big Man. This time the brother was in the house and heard what Coyote said. The brother told his sister to pay no attention to that no-account Coyote and to get rid of him because he might have mange.

This made Coyote very angry. He said that if Beautiful Girl did not marry Big Man, then the man would come along with the people from his village and kill both Beautiful Girl and her brother. Then Coyote went away.

The brother and sister talked things over. Beautiful Girl said she did not want to marry Big Man. She said she did not want to marry anyone. She said that if trouble came, she would run away to the Eastern Sky—Si'al tahgio Kahchm. She said that she would stay up there in the Eastern Sky and only show herself to those who rose early in the morning to do their work. She said she would smile on the people who rose early and make them smile in return.

The brother, too, said he would rather live in the air, but he said that sometimes he would like to come back to the earth. He said he would like to come back with a bounce and a shake so people would know he was there.

When Coyote went back to the village and told his story, Big Man was very, very angry. He called all his friends together. The next day Big Man and his friends took their bows and arrows and went looking for Beautiful Girl and her brother. The girl saw them coming and tried to warn her brother, but he didn't seem to care very much.

As Big Man and his friends came closer, Beautiful Girl saw there was no hope, so she hurried off to the Eastern Sky just as she had said she would do.

THE RATTLE OF automatic gunfire echoing across the landscape startled Lani awake. The rest of the desert had fallen eerily quiet. Lani held her breath, listening, but she wasn't the only one who sensed danger. So did the Little People—Ali-chu'uchum O'odham—and the insects fell quiet as well. It was oppressively dark. The fire had died down, and the moon had crossed over to the back of Ioligam, leaving that part of the mountain entirely in shadow.

Lani had heeded her husband's advice. She had come on the campout armed and had slept with her Glock under her bedroll. Retrieving it, she stood up and crept over to the edge of the clearing. Concealed by the sheltering manzanita, she peered down at the desert below. For a time—she wasn't sure how long—nothing happened. A long time later another blast of distant gunfire made its way up the mountain.

Lani darted to her backpack and dug through it until she found her cell phone. Although she had confiscated Gabe's phone, she had kept her own, turned off and tucked securely in an outside pocket. It seemed to take forever for the device to finally come online, but when it did, there was no signal, as in zero. She tried sending a text to Dan, but it bounced back as undelivered. The population in this part of the reservation was too scarce to warrant the building of private cell towers, and the tribe couldn't afford to install them, either.

Shaking as much from fear as from the cold, Lani wrapped the bedroll around her shoulders and returned to her lookout point. Even though the phone hadn't worked, the bright light from the screen had momentarily left her night blind. Once she could see again, she spotted a pinprick of light, bouncing here and there in a back-and-forth movement across the desert landscape far below.

In the dark, Lani couldn't be sure, but she suspected the action was in the neighborhood of Rattlesnake Skull charco. Pulling her eyes from the moving light—a flashlight, presumably—she stared off across the valley at a place where the lights from a single vehicle driving westbound on Highway 86 had just rounded the low-lying hill a mile or so from the reservation boundary.

Lani knew that a permanent Border Patrol checkpoint was situated another mile east of the hill, just before the bridge over Brawley Wash. She had heard the gunfire quite clearly, and she knew that sound travels a long way on a still desert night. But she also knew from things Dan had said that the checkpoint guys generally spent the long chilly nights huddled around a space heater inside their guard shack with their music turned to the max. The fact that there were no red lights flashing on the approaching vehicle indicated that this was most likely a private one rather than some kind of patrol car. Or, if it did happen to be an official vehicle—Border Patrol, Law and Order, or Highway Patrol—it was someone doing a routine patrol rather than responding to a specific incident.

As she watched, the flashlight was extinguished. A moment later, a pair of headlights bloomed in the desert on what she was now sure was the near side of Coleman Road, the Rattlesnake Skull village side of the road. She watched, puzzled, as the headlights seemed to move backward along what had to be Coleman Road. When the vehicle reached the intersection with the highway, she thought at first that it was turning right to head into Tucson. That was exactly what Lani wanted to see happen. She glanced at her watch. The illumined dial said 4:16. If the driver turned right and headed into Tucson, the cameras at the checkpoint would maintain an exact record of who had passed that way at that hour of the night.

Unfortunately, the vehicle backed onto the highway, then changed gears and drove in the opposite direction. The whine of rubber on blacktop as the vehicle gathered speed carried across the desert to Lani's mountain perch. She watched and listened until first the headlights and finally the taillights were obscured by the bulk of Ioligam itself. Long after the lights disappeared, she could still hear the whine of tires. So he was driving in a forward gear now, but he had driven for the better part of a mile in reverse. Why would he have done that? Why?

As the sound faded, so did Lani's immediate sense of danger. Whoever had been down there shooting off a weapon was gone now. She staggered back to the fire.

As she sat down to warm herself, she was filled with a smothering sense of foreboding.

Something was terribly wrong. That sense had been with her since she was first jolted awake, but it was only as the fire flared up with newly added wood that she allowed that terrible misgiving to turn into a cohesive thought. Gabe! What about Gabe? When he stormed off the mountain, he must have passed that way, but surely that was hours ago. He couldn't possibly have been involved in whatever had just happened down there. Surely not.

Shortly after the sounds from the one vehicle disappeared, Lani heard another one approaching and slowing. She stood up again and peered down the mountain as this new vehicle turned onto Coleman Road. Searchlights mounted on the roof sprang to life and probed the surrounding landscape. It seemed to her that some of the rays were pointed toward the same spot from which the gunfire had come, but by then the bad guys were gone. There was nothing left to see. In any case, the unsuspecting vehicle continued southward to Coleman Road.

With nothing else to be done, Lani heated a pot of water and made herself a cup of prickly pear tea. Then she sat with her trembling hands cupped around the metal cup, hoping the heat from that would help settle her. At last, seeking reassurance, she reached for her medicine basket.

Her first inclination was to open the pouch that held the *wiw,* the sacred tobacco, but she didn't. Her throat, unaccustomed to smoking, was still raw from the night before. Instead, she located her divining crystals. Had things gone differently that night, she might have given them to Gabe. Since they were still in her possession, she spilled them into the palm of her hand and then, one by one, she held them up, peering at the flickering flame through each hunk of crystal.

She wasn't sure if what she saw was in the crystal itself or if it was only in her mind's eye, but it was the same image she had seen in the sacred smoke—a woman, a Milgahn woman who, despite being Anglo and not susceptible to Staying Sicknesses, was also a Dangerous Object.

Lani understood this even though she couldn't explain it. And without knowing what kind of Dangerous Object the woman was, it was difficult to tell what kind of treatment might be required.

And so, warmed by the fire, and with Morning Star gleaming in the east, Lani closed her fist around the stones and began to sing:

Oh, I'itoi who is also Spirit of Goodness and Elder Brother,
Please hear me as your daughter calls to you
Asking for your help. A dangerous object is loose in the world.
A dangerous object with silver hair and white skin.

I do not know who this woman is, but she is a danger,
A danger to a boy named Gabe Ortiz who is the son of my heart.
Help me to see my way to find this evil woman.
Help me understand why she is a danger.

Help me to protect Gabe, Elder Brother,
In the same way Nana Dahd protected Davy,
In the same way Betraying Woman protected me.
We need your help so the ghostly woman does not win.

As the sun came up over the distant Tucson Mountains in the east, Lani sang the song over and over, always in sets of four, because four is a magic number all by itself; because all of nature goes in fours.

"WHAT THE HELL do you mean, one of them got away?" Ava demanded into the phone. "How is that even possible?"

"Sorry. I was struggling with Paul, and the youngest one got loose. I'm looking for him now."

"Sorry my ass! You should be way more than sorry. What about the diamonds? Did you find them?"

"Not yet, but once I catch up with Tim . . ."

"He's what, twelve years old? Thirteen? You just let him take off and now you can't find him?"

"I know which way he went. I'll find him."

"You'd better," Ava said. "I want my diamonds back, and I want that damned kid taken out. Those asshole Indians stick together like dog shit on a shoe."

"What about Max?"

"What about him?"

"Once he hears about what's happened . . ."

"Don't worry about Max. You take care of the kid and retrieve the diamonds. I already told you, I'll handle Max."

"Yes, ma'am," the man said. "I hear you loud and clear."

Bristling with anger, Ava closed the phone. She heard the nurse out in the kitchen, banging around, starting another pot of coffee, and fixing Harold's breakfast. Ava didn't usually put in an appearance until all that had been handled. Right now, she needed to make sure the Max José problem would be handled sooner rather than later.

The crew she had in Florence had come in handy on more than one occasion. One was a guard; the rest were inmates—lifers, mostly, with nothing more to lose. When they did a job for her, she made sure that all payments went to family members who were far enough removed from the action that nothing could be traced back to the actual doers or traced back to her, either.

Ava's operation was small enough not to attract attention from the cartels, and deadly enough that people usually did exactly as they were told. As for the guy who'd just called her? He was a dead man walking even if he didn't know it yet. Once he recovered her diamonds, he'd be gone, too. The desert was a big place with plenty of hidey-holes where dumped bodies would never be found.

Ava finished her calls, knowing she'd done all she could for the time being, then she went back to bed, hoping to grab a little more sleep. It was going to be a busy day.

SOME TIME LATER, after sunrise, Lani was startled out of her contemplations by yet another gunshot—a single one this time. Once again, she peered off the mountain, scanning the desert for any signs of life. No vehicles were visible. Was this related to what had happened earlier? In the silence that followed the gunshot there was no way to tell.

Leo Ortiz arrived a couple of hours later, at ten past eight. By then Lani had packed up her stuff and Gabe's as well. She'd also doused the fire with the remainder of her water and carefully buried the ashes. She heard Leo's powerful pickup growling its way up the mountain long before the man himself appeared outside the clearing.

Lani had considered hiking down the trail to meet him, but in the end, she simply sat beside the backpacks and waited. When Leo finally showed up, he was panting with exertion. He looked around the clearing and frowned. "Where's Gabe?" he asked.

That was not the question Lani was expecting. Her heart fell. Her stomach clenched. "Isn't he home?"

"He wasn't when we got home this morning. Why isn't he here?"

"He got mad at me and left," Lani admitted. "He said he was going home."

"You let him walk off just like that?" Leo demanded accusingly. "You should have called. It was just a dance. I would have left there in a minute to come get him."

Lani didn't lie and claim she had tried to call. Instead, she held up her useless cell phone. "No signal," she said.

"There's a radio in the truck," Leo said. "I can call home on that."

The trip down to the truck was made in heavy silence. Leo was naturally quiet, but he was also angry, and Lani knew it. As for Lani? If Gabe wasn't home, if he had been the target of some of those gunshots . . . She couldn't bear to consider it.

Leo flipped the two packs he was carrying into the bed of the truck, then went straight to the radio. "He's home," Leo said a moment later. "Delia said he just woke up and scared her to death because she had no idea he was there. He was in his bedroom with the door closed. We didn't bother checking his room when we got home because he wasn't supposed to be there."

Sick with relief, Lani leaned against the passenger door. Gradually her legs seemed to give way beneath her. She slid slowly down onto her haunches until she was sitting propped on the Tundra's narrow running board.

Leo came around to where she was sitting. "Sorry," he said. "He's a teenager and a boy. I shouldn't have blamed you. Come on. Let's get back."

Lani stood up and tossed her own pack into the truck. "There's one more thing we need to do," she said when she again felt capable of speech.

"What's that?"

"I want to stop by the charco."

"What charco?" Leo asked.

"That one," she said, nodding down the mountainside.

"Rattlesnake Skull?" he asked. "How come? People say that place is haunted."

Lani knew that all too well, and one of the haunting spirits was no doubt the soul of Gabe's murdered second cousin, Gina Antone, but Lani didn't feel like going into any of that right then.

"It'll only take a few minutes," she said. "I'm curious about something."

"Don't they always say curiosity killed the cat?" Leo said, letting go of his anger and giving her one of his easy grins.

"Maybe so," Lani said. "But I still want to go. You can stay in the truck if you want. I can hike in and out."

"And let you call me a 'fraidy cat?" Leo replied. "No way."

When they neared the charco, Lani directed him to drive past the turnoff and stop on the shoulder of the road.

As they climbed out of the truck, Leo shot her a questioning look. "What's going on?" he asked. "You look like something's wrong."

"I'm not sure," Lani said. "Let's wait and see. I want to follow the tracks."

Lani had picked up some skill as a tracker from her husband, who had learned that ancient art from his grandfather Micah. Using what Dan had taught her, Lani walked along the road until she saw a place where a single set of tire tracks led off into the brush. A few feet beyond that, she saw evidence of what looked like a struggle and signs of several people walking off into the brush.

"We'll go this way," she said, "but stay to the side of the tire tracks and of the footprints, too."

Just then a shadow passed overhead. Lani looked skyward and saw a single buzzard circling high above them. The morning sun may have been warm, but a chill passed through her body. Having Nuwiopa show up at a time like this was always a bad sign. Buzzards meant death, and the bodies weren't hard to find.

They lay just beyond a parked blue Jeep Cherokee, one Lani suspected might belong to one of the José brothers. The two victims were clearly male. Both bodies had been shredded by bullets. Their hands were bound in front of them with tie wraps, and their heads were covered by paper grocery bags. Both were secured to the base of a nearby cottonwood tree by lengths of cable that looked like those used to lock down bicycles.

Once Lani spotted the bodies, there was no reason to go any closer. It was clear from the cloud of swarming flies that both victims were dead. She stopped in her tracks so abruptly that Leo literally plowed into her from behind. He grabbed her with both arms to keep her from pitching forward and then was startled when she turned in his arms, buried her head in his ample chest, and wept. They stood like that for several moments, with Leo awkwardly patting her shoulder and trying to comfort her.

Leo probably thought Lani was horrified at being confronted by those two bloodied and mangled bodies, but that wasn't it at all. She was weeping in gratitude because neither of the dead victims was Gabe. He was home and safe. Right then, that was all that mattered.

At last she straightened up, wiping her nose and eyes on her shirtsleeve. "I'm okay now," she said.

Letting go of her, Leo started toward the bodies.

"No," she said, grasping his arm. "Leave them."

"But shouldn't we at least check on them?"

Lani shook her head. "This is a crime scene," she said. "I can see from here that they're both dead. There's nothing we can do for them, except call the cops."

CHAPTER 14

Big Man and his friends came to the house. They called out to the brother, and he came out. Everybody aimed their arrows at him, but as the arrows flew, Brother jumped in the air. None of the arrows hit him. The people laughed at him and asked him where his feathers were. They told him he should have wings.

But when Brother came back to earth, the people noticed that the earth trembled under his feet. Three times the people shot their arrows at Brother, and three times, when he came down, the ground shook.

The fourth time the people shot their arrows, Brother jumped into the sky, but this time he did not come down.

And so, nawoj, *my friend, when you are in the land of the Desert People and look toward the Eastern Sky early in the morning, you will see Beautiful Girl, smiling at you from the sky. The Tohono O'odham call her Mahsig Hu'u—Morning Star.*

And sometimes—not often—when you feel the earth tremble, the Milgahn—the Anglos—may call it an earthquake, but you and I will know that it is only Beautiful Girl's brother who has come back to visit.

When Brandon Walker opened his eyes, Diana was standing in the doorway of the bedroom with a cup of coffee in hand. "Up and at 'em, lazybones," she said. "You said you'd be driving Miss Daisy today, and if we want to get to the Second Street garage in time to find a parking place, you'd better get a move on."

Brandon turned over and stared blearily at the clock. It said 8:30.

"What time's your first panel?"

"Ten of the A.M., so we need to head out soon."

Brandon scrambled out of bed, shaved, showered, and dressed. As he slipped his car keys into his jacket pocket—the same jacket he'd worn to the dinner the night before—his fingers encountered the business card Oliver Glassman had given him. Brandon pulled it out and looked at it. He had spent the better part of the night mulling over his own involvement with John Lassiter. Before he got any more deeply involved and before he brought TLC into play, he needed a whole lot more information.

Dropping the card back into his pocket, he went to the kitchen in search of a second cup of coffee.

"By the way," Diana said, "my publicist flew in last night. She'll be meeting us at the first venue, and she's willing to hang with me all day. So if you feel like doing something else instead of showing up at all the panels and signings, that would be fine, as long as you're close enough to come get me when I'm done."

"You're sure you don't mind?"

"Not at all," Diana said with a laugh. "You go to enough of these events that you could probably do a credible job of answering all the questions I'm likely to be asked. So go do whatever you need to do. Consider it your reward for showing up for the cattle call last night."

"Fair enough," Brandon agreed. "Sounds good."

Even though he was only dropping Diana off, getting to the campus was still a challenge. Traffic on Speedway was gridlocked with people trying to turn into the campus while herds of pedestrians, oblivious to the lights, blocked the way. Brandon drove into the bookstore turnaround with bare minutes to spare before Diana's first scheduled appearance.

"I'll pick you up right here whenever you call," he said. With an unexpected free day ahead of him, Brandon headed for the Arizona Inn to treat himself to a leisurely breakfast. Knowing he might need to use the phone, he asked for his food to be served in the bar.

While waiting, he pulled out Ollie Junior's card. Glassman the younger was a defense attorney. Clients who found themselves in the clink would need to be able to reach him. Brandon read through the list of phone numbers on the card and dialed the one listed as a cell. Not surprisingly, he was routed to an answering service, but at least it was a living, breathing person rather than a machine.

Brandon told the woman who he was and why he was calling. Oliver Glassman Junior called him back before Brandon finished the last bite of his whole wheat toast.

"I'm surprised you called," Oliver Glassman Junior said. "When John Lassiter said he wanted to talk to you, I didn't figure he had a chance in hell."

"He may not still," Brandon answered. "Before I go wading into any of this, Mr. Glassman, I want some information."

"Call me Junior. What kind of information do you have in mind?"

"If you can talk to me about this without violating

client confidentiality, please tell me what exactly Justice for All came up with," Brandon requested. "They must have found something serious, or they wouldn't have been able to negotiate a deal."

"Don't worry about the confidentiality issue," Junior answered. "I have John Lassiter's signed permission to bring you on board. As to what they found? Prosecutorial misconduct."

"What kind?"

"It turns out the prosecutor had a prior relationship with one of the prosecution witnesses. He should have recused himself, but he didn't."

"Which witness?" Brandon asked. "And what kind of relationship?"

"A woman named Ava Hanover, at least that was her name at the time of John Lassiter's first trial, but she's Ava Richland now. Back in the day, while she was still Ava Martin and working for an escort service, she and a newbie prosecutor named Eric Tuttle had a little extramarital fling. He was married at the time. She wasn't. Years later, when Ava's name came up on the witness list in the case, Tuttle should have recused himself—both times—but he didn't."

At the time of John Lassiter's trials, Brandon had found it puzzling that the prosecutor had gone for broke both times. Brandon was, after all, the primary investigator on the case—the lead detective for much of it by virtue of being the only detective. The evidence, such as it was, was entirely circumstantial. To his way of thinking, Lassiter should have been charged with second-degree homicide rather than murder in the first degree. Now it all made sense, because by the time John Lassiter went to trial, Eric Tuttle had been the duly elected county attorney.

"All this happened a long time ago. How exactly did Justice for All find out about it?" Brandon asked.

"They do data mining, at least that's how Rosalie Whittier explained it to me."

"Who's Rosalie Whittier?"

"JFA's lead attorney on the John Lassiter case. Somehow JFA tracked down a long out-of-print book called *Lawmen Gone Bad*. Hardly anybody's read it—had a print run of five hundred copies or so—but it's a tell-all book about a previous sheriff, a guy named DuShane. Ever hear of him?"

Brandon Walker remembered Jack DuShane, all right. Sheriff DuShane had been as corrupt as they come. He still remembered the bumper stickers that had blossomed around town at the time. SUPPORT YOUR LOCAL SHERIFF, they said. GET A MASSAGE. That may have been a joke, but unfortunately, it was also all too true. DuShane's involvement with the massage parlor/escort service industry was one of the things that had finally propelled Brandon into running for office against the man and eventually defeating him.

"I know the name well," Brandon said aloud. "DuShane was my boss at one time, but I never heard about the book. You say it's a tell-all?"

"I haven't seen it, but that's what I'm told."

"Why haven't I heard about it, then? A book exposing Jack DuShane's carryings-on should have been big news around here."

"That's what makes all this so interesting," Junior said. "As far as I can tell, the book never saw the light of day. The entire first printing was sold to what was most likely a single buyer who destroyed all the copies."

"What single buyer?"

"No ID on the buyer, but I have a pretty good idea of who it might have been."

So did Brandon Walker. Most likely Sheriff DuShane himself, now retired and living the good life in Palm Springs.

"At any rate, there was never a second printing," Junior continued. "Word is, the author made a good piece of change by just going away and keeping his mouth shut."

"Not blackmail, then," Brandon suggested. "More like hush money."

"Correct."

"How did JFA find a copy?"

"Somebody gave them access to an uncorrected proof. Don't ask me how, but they did, and that's where they came up with the connection between Ava Martin and Eric Tuttle. He wasn't the county attorney at the time, but he and DuShane were evidently good buds."

Who played poker together for years, Brandon thought. If there had ever been a doubt in Brandon's mind about looking into John Lassiter's case, that was the moment it went away.

"Okay," Brandon said aloud, "based on all that, JFA comes in and negotiates a deal that, as I understand it, Lassiter no longer wants."

"He never wanted it to begin with," Junior said. "And he isn't the one who brought JFA into the deal. The person responsible for that would be his daughter, Amanda Wasser."

"Back then I had no idea he had a daughter."

"His girlfriend was expecting at the time he was arrested. The baby was born right after he went to prison for life without. He signed away his parental rights, and the mother gave the baby up for adoption at birth.

Amanda had a health issue in her late twenties and came looking for her biological parents. By the time she did that, her birth mother was dead and you already know about John."

"This daughter, Amanda Wasser, where is she?"

"Right here in Tucson. Turns out she's lived here all her life. She works for the university—at the library, I believe. She's probably off this week since it's spring break, but I doubt she's out of town. I don't believe she travels very much. As I said, she has health issues."

"What kind of health issues?"

"The same thing her father has—MS. I understand it's hereditary."

"Do you have a phone number for her?"

"Sure thing. Let me find it."

"Do you know where she lives?"

"In a condo development off Speedway on the far side of Wilmot, the one with the dying golf course."

It took a few moments before Junior dug up Amanda's address and phone number. "Thanks," Brandon said. "Now, could you do one more thing?"

"What's that?"

"Let John Lassiter know that I'll try to come see him, if not tomorrow then maybe the next day."

"Good-o," Junior Glassman replied. "I'll get a message through to him right away. I'm sure he'll be glad to hear you're on board."

SITTING IN LEO'S truck, Lani dialed 911. After that, it was simply a matter of seeing who would arrive first, Law and Order—the tribal police—or someone from the Pima County Sheriff's Department. While they waited, Lani held her phone for a time, dreading and delaying the call she needed to make. Finally she pressed the button.

"Good morning," Dan Pardee said cheerfully. "We're having breakfast and wondering when we'd hear from you. Since the cat's away, I made blueberry pancakes. Tell Mom how you like them."

"Yummy," she heard Micah crow in the background.

Lani sighed. This was not a conversation she could have on speaker with Angie and Micah hanging on her every word.

"I need to talk to you in private."

"Sure," Dan said. "Just a sec." Lani heard the legs of his chair scrape on the floor. Then a moment later, a door slammed.

"I'm outside now," he said, turning off the speaker. "I can tell from your voice that something's wrong. What is it?"

"Gabe is fine, and so am I," she said hurriedly, "but there was a shooting down by Rattlesnake Skull charco early this morning. It woke me up. When Leo came to get me, I had him stop and check. We found two dead men lying by the charco. Right now we're waiting for the cops to arrive."

"Wait," Dan said. "You said Leo came to pick you up. Where's Gabe?"

"We had an argument," Lani admitted. "He stormed off the mountain, but don't worry. He's okay."

"Don't worry? Are you kidding? This whole camp-out idea was all about helping him, and you're telling me the little shit went off and left you out there on your own?"

Hearing the anger in Dan's voice, Lani glanced toward Leo, who was sitting stolidly in the driver's seat, drumming his fingers on the steering wheel.

"It was fine," Lani said, grateful her phone wasn't on speaker, either. "I'm fine."

An uncomfortable silence passed between Lani and Dan. The next admission would be the worst one, because of Dan's words of warning the day before.

"The bad guys were firing automatic weapons," she said finally. "I had my Glock, but up against whatever they were firing, it wouldn't have been any more effective than a slingshot. You have every right to say I told you so, and plenty of reason to rub my nose in it all you want."

There was another period of silence before Dan asked, "Any idea who the victims are?"

"We found a vehicle that might belong to one of the José boys, but Leo and I backed off without getting close enough to examine the bodies. Both victims had grocery bags over their heads."

"Figures," Dan muttered. "I heard Max was involved in some kind of smuggling operation."

A cloud of dust bloomed farther down the road as a vehicle turned off the highway and sped toward them, red lights flashing.

"Gotta go," Lani said hurriedly. "The cops just showed up. I don't know how long I'll be."

"I'm sure it'll be a while," Dan said. "Don't worry. I'll hold down the fort here. I'm just glad you're safe."

CHAPTER 15

You will remember, Nawoj, *my friend, that after I'itoi divided the water and saved the Tohono O'odham, some of the Bad People—PaDaj O'odham—escaped and went to live in the South. Now these bad people were very lazy—too lazy to plant their own fields. They would come to the lands of the Desert People and steal their crops—their wheat and corn, their pumpkins and melons. Each time they came, the Tohono O'odham fought the Bad People and drove them away, but after a while when the food was gone and the Bad People were hungry, they would come again.*

By now the Tohono O'odham knew that they should put guards in their fields to protect their crops. One day near the village of Gurli Put Vo—Dead Man's Pond—which the Milgahn call San Miguel, the corn was ready to harvest. That morning Hawani—Crow—was sitting in a tree and saw the Bad People coming up out of the ground. Soon they were cutting down all the corn. Crow was so astonished that he called "Caw, Caw, Caw!" The people in the village heard Crow's warning. They came running and drove the Bad People away.

That is why the Tohono O'odham are always kind to Thah O'odham—the Flying People—and never let them go hungry or thirsty, because Crow sounded the alarm.

LANI WAS BOTH relieved and a little disappointed when the first officer to arrive on the scene was one of the Shadow Wolves shift supervisors, Henry Rojas. She was disappointed because she wanted to get through whatever interviewing she needed to do with the investigating officers. But she was also relieved because Henry was someone she knew. He was a Navajo who hailed from New Mexico, while his wife, Lucy, was a Tohono O'odham nurse who worked at the Sells Indian Hospital. Lani knew them both because they lived in the hospital housing complex.

"I understand there's been a homicide," Henry said.

"Two, actually," Lani corrected.

It was hardly surprising that a Border Patrol vehicle was the first to arrive. Law enforcement agencies working on the reservation had the ability to monitor one another's radio traffic. Due to the long distances involved, if an officer got into some kind of trouble, people from other agencies who happened to be in the area could respond and render assistance.

"Any idea who the victims are?"

"There's a vehicle that may belong to one of the José brothers from Sells," Lani answered, "but that's just a guess on my part. We didn't get close to the victims to attempt an identification because we didn't want to disturb the crime scene. Instead, we called it in and came here to wait."

"What made you even think to look there?" Henry asked.

"I heard gunshots during the night," Lani said. "Leo's son, Gabe, and I were camping out up on Kitt Peak. The shots seemed to be coming from somewhere down here, so we stopped to check."

Henry looked questioningly at the backseat.

"Gabe's not here," Lani explained. "He got his nose out of joint and went home during the night."

"Walked?"

Lani nodded.

"Stubborn kid," Henry observed.

"You can say that again," Leo added.

"Whereabouts are the victims?"

Leo gestured with his head. "Over there," he said, "by the charco."

"Mind if I take a look?"

"It's a crime scene," Lani said, "but it's not my call."

The next several vehicles arrived in a caravan. Out in front was a black Suburban that screamed FBI and was FBI. Two agents, one male and one female, emerged from that car and came forward, credentials in hand, to introduce themselves—Agents Angelica Howell and Joseph Armstrong. Behind them was a van belonging to the Pima County Medical Examiner's office. Next came a van with a Pima County Sheriff's Department logo on the door and a four-man CSI team inside. At the very end of the line was a sedan belonging to Law and Order, the Tohono O'odham tribal police.

Henry reappeared, motioned for the others to follow, and then led the group of investigators off toward the charco. Leo and Lani stayed where they were.

"Are they going to want to question Gabe?" Leo asked.

"Probably," Lani answered. "He left long enough

before it happened that I doubt he saw or heard anything, but they'll probably want to check to be sure."

"How long is this going to take?"

Lani sighed. "Probably a long time," she said resignedly. "I don't think either one of us is going to make it home in time for lunch."

Leo nodded. "I'd better call the garage and let them know that I won't be in until later."

WHEN BRANDON CALLED the number Junior had given him, Amanda Wasser was home and answered the phone.

Her response when he introduced himself surprised him. "Brandon Walker," she said. "I believe I recognize the name. Aren't you the original arresting officer, the one who took my father into custody?"

"Yes," Brandon admitted. "That was me."

"So what can I do for you, Mr. Walker?"

"John Lassiter reached out to me through his attorney, Oliver Glassman Junior. I volunteer with an organization called TLC, The Last Chance. We follow up on cold cases. Your father claims he wants TLC to look into Amos Warren's death, and he asked for me in particular."

Brandon more than half expected Amanda would hang up on him. "Thank God," she whispered into the phone. "Finally."

"What do you mean finally?"

"JFA was happy to go after the prosecutorial misconduct angle, but I don't think any of them ever really believed my father was innocent. Of course, with him in prison, no one in law enforcement is interested in revisiting the case, either. Where are you? I mean, are you here in town?"

"Yes."

"Why don't you stop by?"

Without waiting for a second invitation, Brandon drove straight there. The entrance to the development, not exactly a gated community, was half a mile beyond Wilmot on Speedway. Brandon understood enough about golf to know that courses are supposed to be green. That wasn't true here. The greens themselves were green, but that was all. Brandon knew that the cost of water had done in more than one Tucson area golf course, but the crazed golf-cart-driving players on this one didn't seem the least bit perturbed by the conditions on the course.

When he reached the address, he found a single-level unit whose front yard had been turned into a bricked patio surrounded by gaily colored pots on metal stands. Each pot overflowed with a bouquet of colorfully blooming flowers. Amanda Wasser, seated on a bright red scooter, was parked beside one of them. Wearing a sun hat and gardening gloves, she was busily deadheading flowers.

"You must be Brandon Walker," she said with a smile as she stripped off her gloves and held out a hand. "Welcome to my raised garden. Ordinary raised beds don't work for me anymore. I need something higher that gives me access both front and back. When I'm feeling well enough, I like to work the pots myself. When I'm not well enough, I have a yardman. Won't you have a seat? Would you care for coffee?"

"No thanks on the coffee," Brandon said, taking a seat at a patio table with a fully unfurled umbrella. Next to the umbrella was a closed banker's box. "Just had some. What I'd really like is to know about your father."

"John Lassiter is my birth father," Amanda corrected. With that, she tossed her gloves into the scooter's basket, then rode over to join him at the table. "I consider the man who raised me to be my father. By the way, my adoptive parents are both deceased," she added. "They died several years ago and only months apart. My birth mother perished in a car wreck, so as far as relatives are concerned, John Lassiter is the last of the Mohicans."

"What can you tell me about him?"

"Only what's in public records and court records," she said. "I know that he's in prison for murder and that he has MS. That's one thing we have in common—MS. It's hereditary; it's also what started me off on the search for my birth parents in the first place. I'd been having symptoms, and my doctors suggested that I track down my birth family's medical history. I had always known I was adopted, but it came as a big surprise to me to learn that my birth father was in prison just up the road."

"You grew up in Tucson, then?"

Amanda nodded. "I'm guessing that's why my parents kept that information from me—because Florence isn't very far from here. But yes, I've lived in Tucson all my life. I attended Palo Verde High School and the University of Arizona. I'm still there by the way—at the U of A. I'm a reference librarian in the main library."

"I understand from Mr. Glassman that you're the one who brought JFA into the game. Did your father ask you to do that?"

She laughed at that, but it was laughter without humor. "Hardly," she said. "I did that all on my own. Besides, when would he have asked? I've never met the man. He's in prison for life without parole, and he refuses to allow me to visit."

Brandon was taken aback. "You've never met him?"

"Not once."

"Then why did you go to the trouble of enlisting JFA's help?"

"I already answered that. John Lassiter is my last living relative—the only one. If I can get him released from prison, maybe I'll have a chance to get to know him."

"How did all this come about then?"

Amanda shrugged. "I'm a librarian. What can I tell you? When I learned who my birth father was and he then refused to see me, I started doing what librarians do best—research. I went back through newspaper accounts of everything I could find related to Amos Warren's homicide and the resulting criminal trials. I also learned everything I could about John Lassiter and his circle of acquaintances." She reached over, removed the top from the box, extracted a single item—a book—and moved the box in Brandon's direction. "This contains hard copies of everything I found. I've made digital copies as well."

Peering inside, Brandon saw that the box was jammed with files.

"This is the only thing for which I don't have a digitized copy."

She handed him the book. It was a paperback with a plain gold cover. The only words on the cover were *Lawmen Gone Bad, by Randall Hardy.* Uncorrected proof.

"I thought that book was never published?" Brandon asked.

"It was, but only just. It was printed, but all the copies were bought up before they were shipped to the stores. It was pulled prior to publication," Amanda explained.

"Evidently pressure was brought to bear, and the copies that had been printed were shredded. This copy—a galley copy—survived. When I was doing my research, I read the complete papers from beginning to end. Somewhere along the way I stumbled on an item that mentioned Mr. Hardy was working on the book. I made a note of it in case it might be related. When I went looking for it later and could locate nothing about it, I tracked down Mr. Hardy himself.

"He was still living here in town at the time. He'd had several other books published after the first one disappeared. I made an appointment with him on the basis of asking for his papers to be donated to Special Collections at the U of A library. He seemed cordial enough and said I was welcome to what he had. When I made the mistake of asking about *Lawmen* in particular, he went ballistic. He said he'd burned everything that had anything to do with that 'goddamned book,' quote unquote, and that he wished he'd never written it."

"Slight overreaction?" Brandon asked.

Amanda nodded. "That sent me looking. The publisher was a local outfit that went out of business shortly after all this happened. That piqued my curiosity, too. I wondered if the two were related, and that sent me off on a search for the book itself. The book's initial print run was small, so there weren't many review copies printed either—twenty to fifty at most. Fortunately for me, there are people out in the world of dead tree books who specialize in collecting review copies. I paid a lot of money for this one, but that's where I found the connections between the man who prosecuted John Lassiter and sent him to prison and John's onetime girlfriend—Ava Martin."

"I understand Jack DuShane is in here, too?"

Amanda nodded. "He's there as one of the bad guys. By the way," she added, "you're notably absent."

"Sheriff DuShane and I were never on the best of terms."

"When I read the book, I realized that all those folks—the sheriff, the prosecutor, the people running the call girls and the massage parties—were thick as thieves, and I think they all joined forces to pin Amos Warren's homicide on John Lassiter. He was a guy with no connections, which made him an easy target. I went to the sheriff's department and tried to get someone to take a look at all this with a view to reopening the case."

"And you got nowhere?"

"Correct, but maybe you'll have better luck."

"Because I was sheriff once upon a time? I wouldn't count on it. Is your father aware of any of this?"

"I'm not sure. He might have heard about it through Mr. Glassman, but I certainly haven't shown it to him."

"And did you reach any conclusions?"

"Yes, I did. I think Ava Martin bears some looking into. There's a file in there about her, too. I suggest you go through the material on your own and decide for yourself. Just for the record, though, you should be aware that there's at least one other unsolved homicide involved in this case. Kenneth Mangum was one of John's pals—his best friend, actually. Kenneth testified on John's behalf at the first trial and was expected to appear at the second one, but he never showed. He apparently left Arizona and was living in Seattle under the name Kenneth Myers when he, too, was murdered.

"His death is spookily similar to Amos Warren's in that his remains went undiscovered for a number of years. Then, when his body was found, the case was never solved. It's only a few years ago now since those remains were linked up to a missing persons case filed by Kenneth Mangum's mother in Phoenix."

Brandon had been busily taking notes. "I believe it's time for me to go see your father," he said.

Amanda smiled. "I was hoping you'd say that."

"What about this?" he asked, reaching for the box and tapping the lid. "You said I should draw my own conclusions. Does that mean you'll let me go through what you've gathered?"

She nodded. "You're welcome to all of it," she said, "even this." She placed the book in the box before closing the lid. "I'm a librarian, though. That means I want it all back. When all this is over, I may use it to write my own damn book."

Brandon stood up and hefted the box. "Assuming I do see your father—your birth father—is there anything you'd like me to tell him?"

"Yes," Amanda Wasser said. "Tell him that someday I'd like to meet him."

Brandon's phone rang while he was loading the box into the Escalade. Diana's name appeared on the screen. "Hey," he said. "How's the festival going?"

"Busy, and there's a new wrinkle. Someone is holding an impromptu dinner this evening at El Charro downtown. I've been invited. You were invited, too, but I said that after last night you were probably dinnered out."

"You've got that right."

"The thing is, I won't be finished until nine or so. Do you mind coming back into town to pick me up or should I make arrangements for someone to give me a ride?"

"Tell me where and when. I'll be there with bells on."

Brandon glanced at his watch as he got into the SUV. It wasn't noon yet. Rather than having to go back to the festival midafternoon, he now had several hours to do entirely as he pleased. He could go home and spend the afternoon poring through the banker's box, or he could speak to John Lassiter, the person most directly involved in the case. In the end, he literally tossed a coin. Heads, drive to Florence; tails, go home. The coin toss came up heads.

GABE LAY ON his bed, playing with his Xbox. His mom was mad at him. Lani was mad at him. Probably everyone in the whole world was mad at him, including Tim. They often hung out together on Saturdays, usually at Gabe's house rather than at the Josés' place. Without Mrs. José or Mrs. Francisco there to look after things, going to Tim's house wasn't much fun anymore. One of the big attractions in the José household had always been the food. Now, with Carlos in charge, the food at Tim's house wasn't very good.

None of the brothers knew how to make popovers. These days Tim and his brothers lived on sandwiches and take-out stuff from Bashas'—food that didn't need cooking. The kinds of food that would drive Lani nuts, Gabe thought, especially peanut butter sandwiches made with white bread. Thinking about peanut butter made him glance at the dresser drawer where he'd hidden both Tim's mysterious note and the jar of peanut butter. What was that all about? Probably just some brother kind of thing. Tim's older brothers often teased him unmercifully, and maybe the peanut butter was Tim's way of getting back at them for a change.

Gabe sometimes wished he had brothers. Maybe Tim didn't always get along with the ones he had, but at least they were there. Tim wasn't alone, not really—not the way Gabe was alone.

Gabe picked up his phone, the one Lani had taken away from him the day before. His dad had left it on the kitchen counter, and Gabe had found it when he went out to make some toast. He tried calling Tim again. Still no answer. That was odd. If Tim's plans for the day had changed, wouldn't he at least have let Gabe know? Disappointed, Gabe slid the phone back into the pocket of his jeans.

His bedroom door opened, and his mother poked her head inside. He could tell from the frown on her face that she was still angry that he hadn't stayed out on the mountain overnight.

"I have to go to the office for a couple of hours, then I'm going grocery shopping. Your dad's going to be late. There was some trouble out that way when he went to pick up Lani. You're to stay here until he gets home, understand?"

Gabe nodded.

"Oh, and if you talk to Timmy, let him know you're grounded. He can see you at school on Monday, but not for the rest of the weekend. Got it?"

"Okay," he muttered. She left, and he allowed himself a few moments of gratitude. At least she hadn't taken his Xbox away, and she hadn't made him go shopping with her, either. It was bad enough that he'd had to go camping with Lani. If the kids from school saw his mother dragging him around the grocery store on Saturday morning, he'd never hear the end of it.

After his mom left, Gabe kept right on playing. Some time had passed—he wasn't sure how much—when someone knocked on the bedroom door. He was going for a really high score. Thinking the visitor was most likely Tim, Gabe called for him to come in.

A moment later Henry Rojas appeared in the doorway. Gabe knew Henry. He was one of the Shadow Wolves who worked with Dan Pardee. Henry's wife was a nurse at the hospital, and they lived in one of the units at the hospital compound, but as far as Gabe knew, Henry wasn't a good friend of either one of his parents. Among the Tohono O'odham, only relatives and very close friends ever ventured inside someone else's home and, even then, not without an express invitation.

"What's wrong?" he asked.

"I was talking to your friend Tim José," Henry said. "He's in some trouble and asked me to come pick you up and take you to him. Oh, and he wants you to bring along the package he left for you last night."

Gabe tried playing dumb. "What package?"

"You know which package," Henry said. "Now get it and come on. There's not much time."

"I'm grounded," Gabe said. "My mom says I'm not allowed to go anywhere."

"I don't give a rat's ass what your mom wants. Get the damned peanut butter and come on!" Henry's hand went to the grip of the pistol he wore on his hip. "I have a gun and I'm prepared to use it. Get moving."

And so Gabe moved, stumbling toward the dresser and pulling open the drawer like a bumbling sleepwalker. He reached for the peanut butter jar, leaving the bag and the note behind. As his fingers closed around the plastic jar, he knew two things with sickening clarity. One, his best friend was in trouble, maybe even dead. And two, Henry Rojas, the man who stood blocking the doorway? He was clearly one of the Bad People—PaDaj O'odham—the very ones Lani had been trying to warn Gabe about. She had thought the José brothers were bad somehow, but Gabe understood that this man—dressed in his uniform, wearing a badge, and carrying a weapon on his hip—was someone truly evil.

With the jar in one hand and leaving the drawer partly open, Gabe straightened up and turned to face the intruder. Henry Rojas had yet to move. He stood there, still as can be, blocking the doorway.

"What happened to Tim?" Gabe asked.

"Believe me," Rojas said, "you'll know soon enough. Now move."

As Gabe walked past, Henry leaned toward him. "Walk straight," he ordered. "Don't do anything out of line. I've got my Taser right here."

It was only when Gabe looked at the Taser that he realized the man was wearing gloves—surgical gloves. Henry had no intention of leaving any fingerprints behind.

As they stepped outside, there was no one around. It was a quiet Saturday morning. The other houses in the Ortiz compound seemed deserted. No children played kickball in the dirt outside. If women were inside neighboring houses doing chores or washing dishes, there was no sign of them, either. A block or so away, he saw people over by his dad's garage, but none of them was close enough for Gabe to call for help.

Henry marched him over to the passenger side of a truck that was parked just outside—a black Chevrolet with a camper shell on it. It wasn't the Border Patrol vehicle Henry drove when he was on duty. This was private.

Henry opened the door to the cab. "Get in," he ordered.

Gabe tried to twist away, but Henry grabbed his neck in a viselike grip and shoved him headfirst into the cab. Then, before Gabe could right himself, a jolt of electricity from a stun gun shot through his body. When he came to, a second or so later, Henry was removing a hypodermic needle from Gabe's bare arm.

"Hey," he objected, "what are you doing?"

Henry didn't answer. He slammed the door shut, locking it with his key fob, before he walked around the front of the pickup to the driver's door. Gabe tried to unlock the door manually, but his muscles were still disrupted by the stun gun charge. Before he could make them respond properly, they went numb. Suddenly helpless, he fell back against the seat.

As Gabe drifted into unconsciousness, he had a strange thought. Lani had told him that the Bad People always came from the South. Henry Rojas was Navajo. Weren't Navajos from the North?

He'd have to ask Lani to explain that to him the next time he saw her.

CHAPTER 16

They say it happened long ago that in the summers, when it was very hot and the low-lying water holes all dried up, the Desert People would leave their villages behind and go to the foothills at the base of one of I'itoi's sacred mountains—Ioligam, which means Manzanita, or Baboquivari, which means The Mountain That Is Small in the Middle.

The Elders—Kekelimai—say that once the sacred peak of Baboquivari was shaped like the thing the Milgahn—the Anglos—call an hourglass. One day Beautiful Girl's brother returned from the heavens. In the quake that followed his arrival, the top of the hourglass broke off, leaving Baboquivari looking the way it does today, like a spool sitting in the middle of the desert.

BEFORE BRANDON HEADED for Florence, he made a call to clear the way. His younger son, Quentin, an intravenous drug user, had developed hepatitis C, which had morphed into cirrhosis before he had managed to store up enough meds to end it all with an overdose.

During the last year of his life, when Quentin had spent far more time in the infirmary than in his cell, Brandon and Diana had both been constant visitors. One or the other of them had been in the infirmary with him almost daily, providing care and comfort that would otherwise have been delegated to overworked and understaffed nurses and orderlies. Over time, surprisingly enough, they had developed a first grudging but eventually enduring friendship with the warden.

Brandon recognized that Warden Edward Huffman was a conscientious man doing a difficult job, and it seemed likely that Huffman saw Diana and Brandon for what they were, too—a pair of heartbroken parents who, having failed at the task of saving their offspring from himself, were now doing the best they could to see him through to the other side. Maybe Huffman also related to the irony of Brandon's position—that of a former sheriff who had been as helpless at raising his own son as any other father on the planet. For whatever reason, on Brandon and Diana's weekly and finally daily visits, they had been granted a kind of latitude to come and go that most prison visitors were denied.

It had been years now since Quentin died, but Huffman's name and phone numbers remained in Brandon's contacts list. Still parked outside Amanda Wasser's condo, Brandon located the record. Then, since it was Saturday, he dialed the warden's cell phone first.

"Huffman," the man answered.

"Brandon Walker here.

"Long time no see. What's up?"

"I need a favor."

"What kind of favor?"

"I understand John Lassiter has asked to see me, but I

don't want to drive all the way up there if I'm not on the approved visitor list."

"Let me check. I'll get back to you. Is this number all right?"

"It'll work."

While Brandon waited for a return call, he thumbed through his fraying spiral notebook. Yes, he had an iPad. Yes, he used it occasionally, but when he needed to remember something and take notes, he still gravitated toward pen and paper. Glancing at the pages from his interview with Amanda, he underlined the passage about the second homicide—that of Kenneth Mangum/Myers.

Closing his eyes, he was just able to remember the guy, sitting on the witness stand and swearing that John Lassiter had loved Amos Warren like a father and would never have done anything to harm him. Of the witnesses who were called to testify, Mangum was the only one who had failed to be present during the knock-down, drag-out fight in El Barrio, for the very good reason that Ken had been in the county jail at the time doing a six-month stretch on a third DUI conviction.

Mangum had made an impassioned defense for his friend, but the jury had considered the source and had most likely disregarded his testimony completely when it came time to render their verdict.

Brandon's cell phone rang, with Huffman's name showing on the caller ID screen. "I couldn't do this for every inmate, but in all these years, Lassiter's got no bad-conduct problems. I've put your name on the list. When are you coming?"

"Today, if that's possible," Brandon said. "And one more thing. I'd really appreciate it if I could use an interview room rather than the ordinary visitation room. I've got some materials I'd like John to go over, and it'll be easier if we could pass them back and forth across a table."

"Whatever you're bringing in will have to go through security, and you'll need to have someone from the prison sit in on the interview, but I don't have a problem with your using a room. What time should we expect you?"

"I'm leaving right now. Should take me a little less than two hours."

"I'll be sure the room is ready when you get here."

"Thanks," Brandon said.

"You're welcome," Huffman replied, "and say hello to your lovely wife."

When the call ended, Brandon turned back to his contact list, found Ralph Ames's number, and dialed it.

"Hey, Brandon," Ralph said when he answered. "What's up?"

"A guy who's in prison doing life without, a guy I arrested years ago, has contacted me asking for us to look into that case. Even though he's served decades for the crime, he still claims he didn't do it. A group named Justice for All has worked out a time-served deal if he pleads guilty to second degree, but he turned that down. Says he won't take a plea for something he didn't do."

"You're the guy who arrested him in the first place, and now he's asking for your help? That's a little unusual."

"It's the first time it's happened to me," Brandon agreed, "and I have no idea how he knew of my connection to TLC. Still, I'd like to take a look at it. The thing is, I've just been informed that there's another unsolved case—at least I think it's unsolved—that may or may not be related to this one. One of the witnesses from this case, someone who testified on the defendant's behalf, was murdered in Seattle sometime back in the eighties. Isn't there someone you've been telling me about, a friend of yours from up there, that you've been trying to recruit for TLC?"

"Indeed there is," Ralph replied. "His name's J. P. Beaumont. He's a good friend with way too much time on his hands at the moment. He worked for Seattle PD for years and was on a statewide Special Homicide Investigation Team for a number of years after that. Special Homicide was disbanded a couple of months ago. I've been trying to bring him on board, and I've been getting nowhere fast."

"You say he was working for Seattle PD in the eighties?"

"Around then, but I'm not sure of the exact dates."

"The eighties are about the right time frame. Would you mind giving him a call to see if he'd be willing to take a look at the case in question?"

"I have a better idea," Ralph replied. "Beau and I are pals. He can tell me no six ways to Sunday and never blink an eye. I suspect he'll have a lot tougher time saying no to a request for help from a complete stranger. Why don't you call him directly?"

"You don't think he'll mind?"

"If he does, have him take it up with me. I'll text you his contact card."

Brandon's message signal dinged thirty seconds later with Beaumont's contact card. No work phone was listed, only a home number and a cell. Since it was the weekend, Brandon opted for the home number. The phone rang six times before the voice-mail prompt came on.

"Beau here," a male voice said. "You know the drill. At the sound of the tone, leave your name and number. I'll get back to you."

Brandon did as he was told, then he fired up the Escalade and headed for Florence and for what he knew would be an unwelcome trip down memory lane.

AT THE CRIME scene near Rattlesnake Skull village, time slowed to a crawl. There was endless backing and forthing among the various officers about jurisdictional issues and equally endless milling around the crime scene before it was finally time for the FBI interviews.

Naturally Lani and Leo were separated for that process. Leo and Agent Armstrong sat in Leo's pickup while Lani and Angelica Howell stayed in the agents' Suburban. Agent Howell was dismissive and overbearing. Lani had no doubt that Agent Howell saw Lani as a "Native American" woman or maybe even as an "indigenous person" who was bone tired from lack of sleep and worry, who was grimy from sleeping out overnight, and who smelled of woodsmoke. Lani recognized the symptoms. She'd been on the receiving end of that kind of dismissive Anglo arrogance all her life.

"So you were asleep and awakened to the sound of what you believe was automatic gunfire?" Agent Howell asked, with an audible sneer underlining the word "believe."

"It was automatic gunfire," Lani replied. "Anyone who's watched television in the last ten years recognizes automatic gunfire when they hear it."

"And what time was that?"

"When I looked at my watch, it said 4:16," Lani answered, "but that was later, after the second round of gunfire and when the vehicle left the charco and headed back toward the highway."

"Where it turned left toward Sells rather than heading into town?"

"Yes."

"What exactly were you doing out here on the mountain?" Agent Howell wanted to know.

"I was here with my godson, Gabe Ortiz. Leo, the man in the truck, is Gabe's father. He came out this morning to pick me up. I asked him to stop at the charco on the way back to Sells. That's when we found the bodies."

"You knew there would be bodies there?"

"I thought there might be."

"You said you came here with your godson. Seems like it might be a little cold for an overnight campout at this time of year. Where exactly were you?"

Lani pointed back to Ioligam. "Up there," she said. "I can show you if you'd like."

"How old is your godson, and where is he?"

"He's not quite fourteen. As for where he is right now? He's at home. We had an argument, and he left."

"Left how?"

"He walked off the mountain and went home."

"In the middle of the night? In the dark?"

"It wasn't that dark," Lani said. "There was moonlight. There was starlight. You should try it sometime."

Just as Lani had felt the desert go silent after the gunfire, she felt a sudden shift in Agent Howell's focus. "What kind of an argument?"

"Do you have a godmother?" Lani asked.

"A godmother?" Agent Howell asked. "Why would you ask that?"

"Do you?" Lani persisted.

"Of course not. My parents didn't believe in that kind of thing."

"Well, we do here," Lani said. "For the Tohono O'odham, godmothers play an important role. We're part of the child's life; if we suspect that child is straying onto the wrong path, godmothers try to offer guidance away from the bad and back to the good."

"That's what was happening with Gabe?"

Having said that much, Lani had no choice but to continue. "His parents were worried that he was slipping into things he shouldn't, and they asked me for help. That's why we came here—to talk about those things—and that's what the argument was about. His parents were worried about some of the kids Gabe was hanging around with who were pulling him away from the old ways."

"As I understand it, Gabe's mother is Delia Cachora Ortiz, the tribal chairwoman?"

"The tribal chairman," Lani corrected. "We're Indians. We don't have to be politically correct."

If Agent Howell noticed the verbal slap, she didn't acknowledge it. "So you and Gabe argued and he left. What time was that?"

"I have no idea."

"You knew to the minute when the gunshots happened. I should think you'd remember what time a kid walks off into the wilderness on his own."

"Gabe and I came to Ioligam—"

"To what?" Agent Howell interrupted.

"Ioligam. That's what we call Kitt Peak. In our tradition, it's a sacred place. I brought Gabe here to have a serious discussion about the old ways, about right and wrong. That means the time I spent with Gabe last night was done on Indian time. It's time ruled by what's important—by day and night, light and dark, the sun and the stars. It has nothing at all to do with hours, minutes, and seconds. As for the shooting? That didn't happen on Indian time. The shooting was all about your tribe, Agent Howell, and I knew that in the Milgahn world—the Anglo world—knowing the exact hour and minute would be important."

"So Gabe left," Agent Howell said. "What did he take with him?"

"His grandfather's blanket."

"That's all?"

"That's all."

"No food, no water, no cell phone?"

"No, none of that."

"What about weapons? Did Gabe have any weapons with him?"

"Wait, is that where this is going? You think Gabe had something to do with what happened here? He left hours before the shooting happened."

"You said he's home now?"

Lani nodded.

"Did anyone notice what time he arrived there?"

"I doubt it. His parents were at the dance at Vamori last night. They didn't get home until early this morning, just before Leo came to pick us up. They didn't check Gabe's room when they got home because they still thought he was up here with me."

Someone tapped on the driver's window, and Agent Howell buzzed it down. "We've got a tentative ID," Agent Armstrong said. "We need to go. You can finish this later."

Agent Howell turned back to Lani. "Do you have a phone number? How can I reach you?"

"Just call the hospital in Sells," Lani told her. "Ask for Dr. Walker-Pardee. They'll know how to find me."

When Lani returned to Leo's pickup and climbed inside, she saw from the expression on his face that something was wrong. "What is it?" she asked.

"Jimmy Lewis, one of the Law and Order guys, is a buddy of mine. They know who the victims are."

"They're not illegals?" Lani asked.

"No," Leo said, turning the key in the ignition. "They found their driver's licenses. It's two of the José brothers, Carlos and Paul."

"I was afraid of that," Lani said.

Leo nodded. "So was I."

Lani thought of the single gunshot she had heard later in the morning, after the initial volleys of shots. "What about Tim?" she asked.

"There was no sign of him here, but chances are he's dead, too," Leo said. "We have to get back to Sells. I want to tell Gabe before anyone else does."

BRANDON WAS FINE for a while as he headed north on the Catalina Highway. Driving through the bustling business centers of Oro Valley, he couldn't help but remember when Ina had been on the far edge of the city. That was no longer true. As for Catalina? He remembered that as a sleepy hamlet on a two-lane road with little more than a bar, a gas station, and a tow-truck operation. Now it, too, was busy enough to have multiple lanes and multiple traffic lights. Off to the left, between there and I-10, were numerous housing developments and golf resorts. And off to the right, the ridgelines in the distance teemed with newly constructed cheek-by-jowl houses.

He stopped briefly at the red light that marked the entrance to Saddlebrooke, with a thriving "active adult" community that included thousands of retirement homes and more golf courses. No doubt somewhere up there was the property near Golder Dam that John Lassiter had sold to some "crazy" developer who planned to build houses there. It turned out, Brandon realized, that the developer was having the last laugh.

It wasn't until Brandon turned off Catalina Highway and onto Highway 79 that the familiar pall of grief settled over him. His meeting with Amanda Wasser, in which he had learned about her unyielding loyalty to a father she didn't know, had put Brandon's troubled relationship with his own sons in an even worse light.

Tommy had died in his late teens. He and his younger brother, Quentin, had been engaged in the felonious activity of stealing pots from an ancient site in a cavern on the reservation when Tommy had fallen to his death. Wanting to cover up what had really happened, Quentin spent years maintaining that Tommy had simply run away. During that time, before Mitch Johnson's arrival on the scene had revealed the truth about Tommy's death, Quentin had drifted ever deeper into the world of boozing and drugging. His coming down with hep C was pretty much a foregone conclusion, and his frequent run-ins with the law meant that he had finally been given a three-strikes life sentence.

On the surface it was easy to theorize that Quentin's burden of guilt about his brother had been the cause of Quentin's eventually fatal downward spiral, but every time Brandon had driven Highway 79 from Tucson to Florence—every time he had gone to the prison to visit Quentin prior to his death—Brandon had blamed only himself. Today was no exception.

Brandon hadn't been able to prevent his divorce from his sons' mother, Jane, but once that happened, he should have been more actively involved in raising the boys. He should have done more to set them on the right path. He should have done better. He should have fixed it. Brandon's sons were both dead while he was still alive. That wasn't the way life was supposed to work. He grieved for his boys who had died so young and wasted so much of their all-too-short lives.

Drowning in regret, Brandon wasn't the least bit surprised to pull into the visitors' parking lot at the prison and find that the knuckles on his fingers were white from his death grip on the steering wheel. On a sunny Saturday in March, the Arizona State Prison Complex in Florence was the very last place in the universe where Brandon Walker wanted to be.

CHAPTER 17

Each summer the women from the villages would go to the foothills around Baboquivari to gather the fruit from the saguaro— s bahithaj*—from which they make the saguaro wine—*nawait. *For many years, when people from a certain village went to gather the fruit, they were met by the Evil Giantess—Ho'ok O'oks—who lived nearby. You will remember,* nawoj, *my friend, that Ho'ok O'oks had grown out of the dust balls that once belonged to Nephew-of-the-Sun.*

Ho'ok O'oks was a powerful spirit of evil who could make people do just what she wanted. Sometimes she made them give her their best cows. Sometimes she would catch a young child and take it away with her. And although the mothers mourned for their children and pleaded with the Giantess, the children were never returned.

The Evil Giantess had such a lot of hair that when she shook her head, it was like a cloud. The children were all afraid of her. And so it became a custom for one of the women from the village to stay with the children to keep them safe. But this was not easy to do.

There were horses and cattle to be watered and there was wood to be chopped to keep the fires warm to heat the ollas used to cook the cactus fruit before the syrup—sit'ol—*could be turned into wine. All those things meant the women of the village were always busy.*

WARDEN HUFFMAN WAS good to his word. Brandon Walker checked his weapons in one of the lockers provided, then carried Amanda Wasser's box of documents through security. Once clear of that, a waiting guard led him to a nearby interview room, let him inside, and locked the door behind him. Brandon didn't mind. The silence of the locked room was infinitely preferable to the noisy bedlam of the regular visitors' room. His memories of that room—of sitting there trying to converse with Quentin through a yellowed plexiglass barrier—were painful ones Brandon didn't wish to revisit.

The door banged open, jarring him out of his reverie and back into an equally unwelcome present. A uniformed guard ushered a grizzled old black man into the room. "You here to see John Lassiter?" he asked.

Brandon nodded. The man was in uniform. His clothing was more like hospital scrubs than guard attire. The name tag dangling on his lanyard identified him as Aubrey Bayless.

"Mind showing me some ID?"

"How come?"

Bayless shrugged. "Lassiter asked me to check, so I'm checking."

Shaking his head with annoyance, Brandon reached into his back pocket, retrieved his wallet, and held it still long enough for the man to study it.

Finally the old man nodded. "Okay," he said. "Right back."

In the long silence that followed, Brandon remembered taking John Lassiter into custody. The homicide investigation was Pima County's, but the arrest itself had been a joint operation conducted by Brandon and a Tucson PD detective named Michael Farraday. Information from a confidential informant had led them to a seedy bar called the Tally Ho on North Sixth Avenue, one that was low-brow and scuzzy enough to be El Barrio's clone. Once inside, they spotted Lassiter seated at the dimly lit bar, hunched over a pitcher of beer with a shot of tequila on the counter in front of him.

Naturally the place had gone quiet the moment the two detectives walked into the room. Action at the pool tables stopped cold. Lassiter was drunk enough that it took a moment for the sudden silence to penetrate his fog. He was just starting to turn on his barstool when Farraday reached out to tap him on the shoulder.

Big Bad John Lassiter immediately roared to his full height—all six-foot-six of him, without even knowing who they were or what they wanted—and he had come out swinging. He was belligerent enough that for years afterward, whenever they had been together, Brandon had reminisced with Farraday about being lucky and quick enough to dodge Lassiter's powerful right-hand blow. It had taken both detectives to subdue the guy and get the cuffs on him, and all the while, a girl—a young woman really—had been screaming in the background, telling them to stop and begging that they not hurt him. That girl, Brandon realized now, must have been Amanda's birth mother, and she had most likely been only a few weeks pregnant at the time.

The last time Brandon remembered seeing Big Bad

John had been at the Pima County Courthouse at the close of Lassiter's second trial. The verdict was read—guilty—and the judge had remanded him to custody. When it was time to leave, Lassiter had stood up—again to his full height—and had patiently placed his hands behind his back so the guards could cuff him and lead him back to his cell. Even in handcuffs, John Lassiter had been an imposing figure, dwarfing the guards who had swarmed around him like so many midgets. That was who Brandon was expecting to walk through the door, a giant of a man, big enough to match the song. But that wasn't what happened.

When the interview room's door swung open, Aubrey Bayless pushed a wheelchair into the room. John Lassiter's clean-shaven face was familiar, but the rest of him was not. The passing years had turned him into a massive piece of humanity that seemed root-bound in a chair that appeared far too small to hold him. Brandon's first impression was that someone had heated him up and simply melted his body into the chair.

MS, Brandon remembered after a moment. It was the same ailment that had placed Lassiter's daughter on her red scooter. Obviously scooters weren't part of the prison's caregiving protocol.

Aubrey Bayless positioned Lassiter's wheelchair on the far side of the table and disappeared into the background, taking a chair next to the door. For a few moments, Brandon and Lassiter studied each other across the table between them as well as across the years. Lassiter was the first to speak.

"Thank you for coming to see me, Sheriff Walker," he said. "I appreciate it. And please accept my belated condolences about your son. Cirrhosis is a tough way to go. I don't blame him for taking an early out."

Brandon was taken aback. "You knew Quentin?"

Lassiter shrugged. "He and I talked sometimes when we were both in the infirmary. That's how I knew about the work you do for that cold case group, TLC. Quentin told me. That's why I asked for you."

It took a moment for Brandon to swallow the lump that suddenly filled his throat. Words of condolence from Big Bad John weren't at all what Brandon Walker had expected.

"Thank you for that," he murmured. "Thank you very much."

WHEN GABE'S EYES blinked open, at first he thought he'd gone blind. He was in utter darkness. There was no light. He could move his legs, but nothing else. His arms were secured to his sides with something that was probably duct tape. A gag was in his mouth, making it impossible to speak. Gentle swaying from side to side and the sound of tires on pavement told him he was in a moving vehicle, but he had no idea how much time had passed since the stun gun attack, followed by an injection of some kind that had knocked him loopy.

He sniffed the air. It smelled rank—as though someone had peed his pants and probably something worse. Gabe's face went hot with embarrassment. How could he be such a coward? He couldn't even be brave when someone had knocked him out. Then over the sound of the tires he became aware of something else—of someone else. There was another person with him in this dark place, someone who was now sobbing brokenly.

Gabe tried to shift his position, wanting to turn his face in the direction of the sound, but he couldn't. There was an unyielding barrier just above him. In the dark and through his clothing he couldn't tell if the low ceiling was made of wood or metal. Whatever it was, it didn't move, and it was low enough that it didn't allow him to turn over on his side. He could lie flat, staring up into the darkness, and that was it.

Then it occurred to him that perhaps the other person was crying because he or she had no idea anyone else was there in the darkness. It took real effort, but eventually Gabe was able to scoot his body over the few inches of floorboard between them. When he touched the form next to him, the sobbing ceased abruptly. Soon the other person moved as well, coming closer until their two bodies lay side by side.

As they lay there huddled together for comfort, it took some time for Gabe to grasp that they were almost the same size and bound in the same way. With effort, they were just able to touch fingers. When that happened, Gabe's heart filled with inexplicable joy. Some sense he couldn't explain told him who his companion was—Timmy José.

His friend wasn't dead. He was there in the darkness right along with Gabe. They were both trapped, but at least they were together. Tim José wasn't dead and neither was Gabe—at least not yet.

Then, whether it was the darkness, the movement of the vehicle, an aftereffect from whatever had been in the syringe, or a combination of all three, Gabe's eyes closed and he drifted off again.

When Lani and Leo walked into the Ortiz house, there was no sign of Gabe, and Delia was putting away groceries. She was also in a snit. "Your son is in big trouble," she said, turning angrily on her husband.

"Why?" Leo asked. "What did he do now?"

"I grounded him for running off from Lani the way he did," Delia said, "but what do you think happened? I had to work for an hour or so and get some groceries. When I came home, he was gone. I told him he was grounded, and he took off anyway!"

Leo reached for his phone. "Don't bother," Delia said. "I already tried calling him. He didn't take his phone along with him. It's in the bedroom."

Leo stared at her for a moment, then he turned abruptly on his heel and marched down the hall to Gabe's bedroom. When he returned, his face was somber, and he was carrying a paper bag. He put the bag on the table, then he walked over to Delia and took her in his arms.

"I'm afraid it's worse trouble than his just being grounded," Leo said quietly.

"What?" Delia asked anxiously, pushing herself away. "What's going on? What's happened?"

"You know those two dead men out by Rattlesnake Skull charco?"

Delia nodded. "You told me. What about them?"

"They've been identified," Leo answered. "The dead men are Carlos and Paul José."

Delia put her hand to her mouth and sat down heavily

on a nearby kitchen chair. "When you told me about it, I thought they were illegals."

"So did everybody else, but Lani and I both thought we recognized the vehicle as belonging to the Josés," Leo told her. "The problem is, from the way they were gunned down, they must have been into something bad. Gabe may be involved as well."

"Are you serious?" Delia demanded. "How's that even possible?"

"See for yourself," Leo said, pushing a paper bag across the table to his wife. "I found this in one of Gabe's dresser drawers. Look at the note inside."

Delia plucked out the note and read it. When she finished, the slip of paper fluttered away from her fingers and fell to the floor. Leo picked it up and handed it to Lani so she could read it as well.

"The Josés are all involved in some kind of smuggling thing, and now they've pulled Gabe into it, too?"

"That's how it sounds," Leo agreed.

Lani looked at the bag but didn't touch it. "That bag is possibly critical evidence," she said. "Whatever used to be in it probably explains why Carlos and Paul were killed. That means we're going to have to turn the bag over to the FBI."

"But what about Tim José?" Delia asked brokenly. "If his brothers are dead, and he's missing, is he dead, too?"

Lani chose not to speak up about the final gunshot she'd heard, at least not then. She understood the implications better than anyone else, and she wasn't ready to bring those out in the open.

"Tim may not be dead, but he's certainly in danger," Lani said.

"We need to find both Gabe and Tim," Leo declared. "I'd better start looking."

"But don't tell anyone why," Lani cautioned. "At this point there's been no official announcement about the identity of the victims. We know about that now, but we're not supposed to, and we shouldn't let on that we do. As far as anyone else is concerned, Gabe was grounded and took off anyway. That's why you're looking for him—to bring him home."

"But what about the bag?" Leo asked. "Should I put it back where I found it?"

"You can if you want to," Lani said, "but it's really too late. Your fingerprints are on the bag and all our prints are on the note. At some point we'll need to come forward voluntarily and turn it over to the FBI agents working the case."

"But doesn't the bag implicate Gabe in whatever it is the José brothers were up to?" Delia objected.

"It may," Lani said, "but let's cross that bridge when we come to it. First let's find Gabe and see what he has to say."

"On my way," Leo said. "I know most of his hangouts. I'll check those first."

Taking his keys, he hurried out of the house, leaving Lani and Delia together in the kitchen. The two women were close now, so close that it was difficult to remember a time when they had not been friends.

"What happened?" Delia asked. "Why didn't Gabe stay on the mountain with you?"

"Because I brought up his friendship with the Josés," Lani said. "I told him he was going to have to make a choice between doing right and doing wrong."

Delia's eyes flooded with tears. "I guess it's already too late for that, isn't it?"

"Maybe so," Lani agreed, "but I still want to hear what Gabe has to say."

After John Lassiter's unanticipated expression of sympathy about Quentin's death, it took a while for Brandon Walker to regain his interview sea legs.

"I hear you have MS," he said finally.

Lassiter nodded. "There might be better treatments on the outside than they have in here, but as far as I'm concerned, the chair's no worse of a prison than a cell."

"Junior Glassman told me that you wanted to talk to me about Amos Warren—that you want TLC to investigate his death."

"I do," Lassiter said with a nod.

"If so, you'll need to tell me about Amos Warren," Brandon said, leaning back in his chair, "from the beginning. How'd you two meet?"

For the second time in as many minutes, Big Bad John surprised Brandon as the huge man's eyes misted over with tears. When he tried to speak, his voice broke before he managed to force the words to the surface. "Amos Warren was like a father to me. He was the only real father I've ever known. I was mad as hell at him at the time he disappeared, but I didn't kill him. I wouldn't."

It was the same story Brandon had heard years before about Warren taking Lassiter under his wing and looking after him and about the blowup over Ava Martin that had ended the two men's partnership as well as their friendship.

"I met Ava Martin," Brandon said. "I even interviewed her."

"I thought she was terrific," Lassiter continued. "But that's who we were fighting over when Amos knocked me for a row of peanuts. The cheating bastard took me down with a set of brass knuckles that nobody else in the bar ever saw. That's the last time I saw him. I thought he was just out in the desert doing what he always did, scavenging, but when his car got towed from a hotel out by the airport, that's when I went looking. I checked the storage unit and realized he had cleaned it out. Took everything that was there, half of which should have been mine."

"What happened then?"

"I'd been let down by my family time and again, but when Amos pulled the same stunt, it was far worse. I thought he was my friend. I trusted him, and when he turned on me, too, I didn't take it very well."

"What do you mean?"

"For one thing, Ava dropped me, too. After that, I proceeded to get myself drunk and stayed that way. I'd earn some money, cash a paycheck, and go on a bender. When I ran out of money, I'd sober up and work long enough to pay for the next round of drinking. That's pretty much how things stood—right up until just before you and that other detective showed up to arrest me."

"What changed?"

"A couple of months before you came after me, I met another woman—a good one, this time—Bernadette Benson."

"Amanda's mother?"

He nodded. "She was a peach."

"And she stuck by you?"

"Yes, she did—all through the trial and even after I got sent up. She came to see me every week until she died in a car wreck."

"Getting back to Ava. I understand she testified against you at the trial."

"That's true. Amos always said she was bad news. Much as I hate to admit it, I'm pretty sure he was right."

"What about that other friend, someone named Ken?"

"That would be Ken Mangum," Lassiter said at once. "He testified at the first trial. When it came time for the second one, my attorney couldn't find him. He had disappeared into thin air. I heard later that he had died—that he'd been murdered somewhere up north—Portland or Seattle, one of those—but I didn't find out any of that until years after the fact."

"I understand from Warden Huffman that you've had zero bad-conduct problems while you've been here, so it sounds as though you've made some changes."

Lassiter nodded. "That's the thing; once you're inside, you've only got two choices. You either get better or you get worse. I decided to do what Amos did and get better."

"Right," Brandon agreed.

"He did five years of hard time right here in Florence. Read his way through the entire *Encyclopaedia Britannica* while he was at it, initialing the bottom of each page with a pencil when he finished reading it. By the way," Lassiter added, "they still have the same set. Encyclopedias don't wear out because not enough people use them.

"So I did the same thing Amos did—reading it and marking the pages as I went. Doing that made me feel closer to him as I read, like I could understand him better. I read the Bible, too. One is for my mind and the other for my soul. I like the encyclopedia better," Lassiter added with a grin. "The librarian ended up getting so tired of having me underfoot all the time that she lets me take the volume I'm reading back to my cell."

"So you've walked the line as long as you've been here?"

Lassiter nodded. "Pretty much," he agreed. "I did it for Amos—in his memory. That's what he would have wanted me to do, because staying out of trouble in prison is the best way to stay alive. At first, because I was big and tough, competing gangs tried to drag me into one faction or another. I refused to go, and eventually they gave up. Later on, after I got sick, they left me alone completely. That's the one good thing about MS. Most of these guys are too dumb to realize that it's not contagious."

Aubrey Bayless stirred in his corner and pointed at his watch. Glancing at his own, Brandon was surprised to see how much time had passed.

"What's in the box?" Lassiter asked as curiosity got the better of him. "You went to the trouble of bringing it, but we haven't touched it."

"We seem to have run out of time today," Brandon said. "We'll look into the box the next time around. In the meantime, I have one last question. You've been here a long time, more than thirty years. If you didn't kill Amos Warren, who do you think did?"

"Ava," Lassiter answered without a moment's hesitation. "Had to be her. I took her to Soza Canyon a couple of times, just to screw around."

"So she knew that was one of the places you and Amos went?"

Lassiter nodded. "I may have even told her that's where I thought Amos was after the fight in El Barrio."

"Did you mention your suspicions about Ava to either JFA or Junior Glassman?"

"I did, but they weren't interested," Lassiter said. "Those people are all about getting me off, not proving me innocent and finding the guilty party. There's a big difference between the two."

"Yes," Brandon agreed, "a big difference."

If Lassiter was lying, Brandon had to admit this was

a convincing performance. "Look," he said finally, "two separate juries have found you guilty of first-degree homicide. Justice for All has come up with grounds for either a plea deal or another trial. Apparently you're not interested in either one. Why not?"

"Because the plea deal means exactly that," Lassiter said. "It means I plead guilty to second degree and get out with time served. But I won't do that, Sheriff Walker. I won't plead guilty to something I didn't do. Besides, I don't want to get out."

Brandon was taken aback. "You don't? Why not?"

"Look at me," Lassiter said. "I'm the next thing to helpless. Some days I can't even get out of bed by myself. At least in prison they assign people to look after me. Aubrey here, for example," he said, gesturing toward the black man waiting patiently in the corner. "Who would I have to take care of me on the outside?"

"What about your daughter?" Brandon suggested. "I've met her. I know she cares about you and has been working tirelessly on your behalf. She's the one who brought in JFA in the first place. She has MS-related health issues of her own, but I'm sure she'd figure out a way to help you get whatever assistance you need."

"No!" Lassiter roared, bringing his fist down with a surprisingly powerful blow that made the tabletop shudder. A moment later he winced as pain from damaged nerves shot through his body.

"No," he said again, more quietly. "Amanda Wasser is not my daughter; she belongs to somebody else. The people who raised her are her real parents. I relinquished my right to be her father the moment she was born. If they release me, I might end up being a burden on her, and I refuse to do that. I'd rather stay where I am."

"Then what's the point?" Brandon asked. "If you don't care about getting out, why do you want TLC to investigate Amos Warren's homicide?"

"Because I didn't do it," Big Bad John Lassiter said. "And if I ever do meet Amanda Wasser in person, I don't want to look the woman in the eye until the rest of the world knows I didn't do it."

Brandon thought about that for a moment. For reasons he couldn't entirely explain, he realized that he believed the whole thing. He believed that John Lassiter, a twice-convicted killer, wanted to be cleared in his daughter's eyes, no matter what else happened. And since that twice-convicted killer was someone who had once befriended Brandon's troubled son, now proving John Lassiter innocent meant something to Brandon Walker, too.

CHAPTER 18

In this village—this kihhim*—lived a young girl who was always smiling and happy. For this reason she was called Tondam Ge:s—which means Shining Falls. She was a helpful girl who sometimes looked after the fires and sometimes played with the children. Shining Falls said that she was not afraid of the Evil Giantess, and so she was put in charge of the children of the village and told to keep them safe.*

One day, when Shining Falls took the children up to play among the rocks, she slipped and fell. Shining Falls was badly hurt and could not walk. The children were frightened. When they saw the black cloud that was the hair of the Evil Giantess approaching, they began to scream.

Just then, Shining Falls saw a turtle, Large Old Turtle—Ge'echu Komikch'ed. Shining Falls called Turtle and asked him to take the children back to the village, but first Turtle needed to find someone else to send a message because he would have to go ever so slowly with the little children. Turtle called to the children and started with them down an easy way to the village.

AFTER BEING AWAKE much of the night, Ava Richland was still sleeping when her phone rang late that morning. "Did you catch the kid?"

"Yes."

"And the shipment?"

"Got it," Henry said, "but it wasn't easy."

"As much as I pay you, it doesn't have to be easy. Where was it?"

"The kid had passed it along to a friend of his. I've got both of them stashed in a safe place. I won't be able to take care of them until later tonight."

"That is not okay, Henry. Tim José for sure knows who you are, and the other kid can probably identify you as well. They need to be gone."

"I didn't have time. I was working. I had to grab the second kid right in the middle of my shift, and I didn't want to finish off the first one until I was sure he wasn't lying to me about where he had ditched the diamonds. I'll unload the two boys tonight."

"Where are they? What if they get loose? How do you know someone won't find them before you can take care of them?"

"They're bottled up in the bottom of my truck, which is locked up tight in my garage out at the airport. Even if they managed to get loose from their restraints, they won't be able to open the box. It's padlocked shut."

"But what if someone stops by the building? Won't they be able to hear them?"

"Nope, no way."

Ava wasn't pleased with Henry's answer, but there wasn't much she could do about it. "All right," she agreed reluctantly. "What about the shipment?"

"Drop it off at the usual place?"

"That's probably best," she said. "As long as the kids are safe where they are, come by as soon as you finish your shift. You probably want to be paid, and I'm feeling generous today. You've cleaned up what could have been a huge mess for me last night and today. You can expect a substantial bonus."

"Yes, ma'am," Henry said. "I'll be there as soon as I can. But what about Max? I'm worried about him. Once he hears about Carlos and Paul . . ."

"I already told you. Don't worry about Max José. He's handled. He'll be gone tonight, too."

"Okay," Henry said. "The usual place, then. I'll be there."

That's the wonderful power of greed, Ava thought as the call ended. It was the one constant in life. It worked like a charm, and it made people do stupid things.

Ava got out of bed and put on her robe. Then she went in search of Harold. She found him where she expected to, sitting in the sun on the back patio with his walker parked nearby. An untouched copy of the *Wall Street Journal* lay on the table next to him. They still subscribed to it. The paper came every day and Harold made sure that it went with him wherever he was, but he had long since stopped maintaining the fiction of pretending to read it.

It saddened Ava to realize that Harold was a doddering old man now, little more than a husk of the man he had been even as short a time as two years ago. His decline in the past few months had been surprisingly swift. Once she had supposed that she'd have to deal with him before she exited stage left, but that was no longer necessary. Even had he known something, he'd be of little use to any investigators. Besides, having him alive and unwell would give her flexibility in making good her departure with as little hue and cry as possible.

She walked over to the table, kissed Harold on the top of his bald head, and then poured herself a cup of coffee from the carafe on the cup-laden tray the housekeeper had left on the patio table. Then she sat down across from him.

"Good morning, beautiful," Harold said.

That was a good start. At least he seemed to know who she was this morning; that wasn't always the case. Not having to begin by explaining who she was made the coming conversation easier.

"I think I'd like to drive down to San Carlos later today," she said. "It's been months since I've been there. I want to look in on the condo and see to it that everything is in order. I need to make sure the housekeepers are doing their jobs."

Harold frowned and seemed momentarily mystified. "You know," she prompted. "Our place in Mexico—the one on the beach."

Harold's nurse came out then to escort him into the house lest he get sunburned. "I'll be gone for a few days," Ava told her. "I'm going down to San Carlos. If you need anything or if Harold does, Mrs. Sanchez, the housekeeper, can see to it."

"Of course," the nurse said. She didn't wear a name tag, and Ava had no idea what her name was. A succession of home health nurses had come and gone with very little fanfare. There was no reason to try remembering who they were.

With Ava's intentions clear to all concerned, she went about a leisurely job of packing. It wasn't a matter of emptying her walk-in closet. She didn't want to take too much. It was important that everyone believe she didn't plan on being gone more than a couple of days. She did, however, clean out the safe, taking all her traveling money as well as her various forms of forged government ID. Those went into the false bottom of her midsize Louis Vuitton case.

Once she had the last shipment of diamonds in hand, the gems would need to be cleaned and dried. These days she could barely stand the smell of peanut butter, much less the greasy feel of the stuff, but after it was scrubbed away, the last of the diamonds would go into that hidden compartment as well, beneath her casual beachwear clothing, underwear, and day-to-day makeup. The false bottom wasn't good enough to pass muster with a TSA inspection at an airport, but she'd be able to breeze through the highway checkpoints with no problem.

The larger Louis Vuitton bag was loaded and ready to go. It contained her various costume changes—a collection of outfits, along with various wigs, scarves, and makeup. All those, taken together, created any number of disguises that coincided with each of her IDs. The woman who went through one Border Patrol checkpoint would appear to be someone else entirely when she arrived at the next one.

Ava had always known this day would come—a time when she would need to disappear. Now that it was here, she was both excited and wistful. She'd enjoyed living in this place at the top of the heap, but she was tired of having to look after Harold—not that she did the caretaking herself. She was tired of being responsible for him and for his caretakers.

If she'd had clear title to the house, Ava might have hung around long enough for Harold to die so she could inherit the place and live there from then on as Harold's well-set widow. But Harold's son, Jack, had queered that deal. Marital trust my ass! Nope, Ava Richland was leaving, and not on a jet plane, either.

Her intention was to drop her luggage off at the safe house, then drive across the border into Mexico at Nogales in broad daylight. Appearing as Ava Richland herself, she'd be thoroughly inspected and photographed at the border. After that, she'd abandon the car in Nogales, Sonora, with the keys inside. With any kind of luck, it would end up in somebody's chop shop. After walking back across the border with a whole other set of ID, she'd meet a runner who would smuggle her back to Tucson.

As for Ava Richland herself? With the car gone or found stolen, she'd simply go missing. If the media could be believed, hapless American tourists went missing in Mexico all the time, and that's where they would search for her—in Mexico. By the time the search started, she'd be back across the border into the United States, and dropped off at her safe house in Tucson. From there she'd be long gone.

Her unsafe safe house was situated in a dodgy neighborhood on the south side of town—a run-down place she'd picked up as a foreclosure during the real estate collapse. She had bought the place for a song and furnished it on the cheap with secondhand furniture from several of Tucson's many resale stores. The person who had bought the house and the furniture—one of Ava's many stand-in characters—was a frail little old lady named Jane Dobson.

Jane wore colorful muumuus, used a walker, and drove a ten-year-old Acura. She seemed to have serious health issues and never went anywhere without being hooked to a portable oxygen pack in the basket of her walker—one of Harold's rejects. Jane had told both the real estate agent and the neighbors that she had an abusive husband. (Harold would have been so surprised!) That's why she needed a bolt-hole if things ever got too bad at home. As far as the neighborhood knew, the lady in the late-model Mercedes and the Native American man who stopped by periodically and let themselves into her garage? According to Jane, they were her well-to-do younger sister and her nephew, both of whom came by now and then to check on the place for her.

Ava's bags were packed and ready to be carted out to the car when she made one last trip through the family room. Pausing in front of the floor-to-ceiling windows, Ava stared down at the cityscape beneath her. She couldn't help feeling a little sad, actually. She knew she'd never be coming back here. Tucson had been good to her—far better than she could ever have imagined—and she knew she would miss it.

Walking back across the room she passed the bar, and there was Fito. Poor Fito. How she wished she could take that lump of limestone with its toothy captive along with her. Jack and Susan would never be smart enough to sell the piece for what it was worth. Unfortunately, Fito was far too big for Ava to carry.

Then her eye fell on the pot—the tiny pot. Jack and Susan wouldn't know what that was worth either, but what it meant to Ava was far more than any mere monetary value. It was a trophy—a reminder of her first kill, a kill she'd gotten away with then and would still get away with now.

When JFA's attorneys had poked their noses into John Lassiter's case, they must have hoped to have his life sentence reduced to something considerably less than that, but as of today, his life sentence would become a death sentence. Somewhere around five that afternoon, John Lassiter would be a thing of the past, and so would Max José. And once Henry Rojas was out of the way, too, there would be no one left to connect all those dots back to her.

As for Ava? With Jane Dobson's aging Acura decked out in a new set of plates, she would drive to L.A. and to another equally unassuming safe house—a condo in a massive development not far from LAX. On the way she'd stop by a Postal Minders shop off Sepulveda and pick up the collection of packages she'd sent ahead to Jane Carruthers—another of her guises—from one of the shipping centers at the Gem and Mineral Show a few weeks earlier. Lots of people shipped their gem-show purchases home from there, and her packages of blood diamonds had no doubt blended in with the crowd.

Ava plucked the tiny pot from its place of honor on the shelf and slipped it into the pocket of her denim jacket. With all her ducks in a row, she had no reason to leave her good luck charm behind.

She turned down the hall to the guest wing where Harold spent most of his waking hours these days. He was in his easy chair, sitting in front of a TV set watching what appeared to be one of the many Judge Whatever shows. The shows were uniformly mindless and plotless and were enough to keep Harold occupied. The nurse was standing in the doorway as Ava leaned down to give him a quick peck on the cheek. From Ava's point of view, nothing could have been better.

"I'm going now," she said. "I'll see you in a couple of days."

Harold waved at her absently, without really looking away from the screen. "Drive carefully," he said.

She smiled at him and nodded in the nurse's direction. "I will," she said. "I always do."

LANI SHOWERED. THEN, with her hair still wet, she lay on the bed and tried to sleep. Dan had taken the kids and gone off to help Leo look for Gabe. The house was quiet. She was weary beyond words, but sleep wouldn't come. Like Gabe's mother, Lani was appalled that Gabe could be involved in something like this and with people who were beyond dangerous.

Gabe Ortiz and Tim José. She remembered Timmy as a little kid, coming into the hospital because he'd been playing around his grandmother's woodpile and had been bitten by a snake. He'd been cute back then, just as Gabe had been. She heard again the sound of that single early-morning gunshot and understood its heartbreaking significance. The first rounds of gunfire had brought down Carlos and Paul. The final one must have been for Tim—Timmy.

Lani had not yet dozed off when her phone rang. Leo's name appeared on the screen. "Any luck?" she asked.

"Maybe a little," Leo answered. "I've looked everywhere I can think of. I started out by stopping by the José place, thinking Gabe and Tim might have holed up there. Nothing, but I asked around. It turns out nobody's seen Tim since early yesterday evening."

Lani took a deep breath. Leo's last words had just confirmed her worst suspicions about Tim José. "But you said you'd made some progress," she managed.

"Yes," Leo said, "just now when I stopped by the

garage to get some gas, I talked to Martin Cruz and his father. Do you know them?"

"The old blind man with the drunken son?" Lani didn't know the pair personally, but she had seen them often enough, always walking together on the shoulder of the road, the older man limping along with his hand resting on his son's shoulder. Lani had been told that most of the pair's walking trips involved going to or from their preferred bootlegger. "What about them?"

"A lot of the time Joseph and Martin come by the garage in the mornings and sit outside at the picnic table under that big palo verde tree. Martin said they were there today. He claims he saw a pickup—a black pickup—stop by our house. He says Gabe got in and rode off with whoever was driving."

"Did he get into the vehicle under his own steam?" Lani asked. "Or was he forced into it against his will?"

"That's what it sounded like, but I'm not sure how reliable Martin is. The old man is blind, and Martin smells like he's blind drunk. He had no idea about the truck's make and model and couldn't identify the driver. I'm not sure what to do."

"Have you told Delia?"

"I wanted to talk to you first."

"Look, Leo," Lani said. "If Gabe was forced into the vehicle, you and I both know that this is far more serious than Gabe just wandering off on his own. Are those FBI agents still in town?"

"As far as I know. The last I saw their Suburban was parked over by the café."

"We need to report this," Lani said, scrambling out of bed. "Has anyone reported Tim as missing?"

"I doubt it. Who would? Max is in jail. Paul and Carlos are dead. Their mother is in the hospital."

"Then we have to," Lani insisted. "The FBI agents need to know that both Gabe and Tim are missing and that, because of the note, we know Gabe may be tied in with whatever the José brothers have been up to. You go tell Delia. Don't tell her over the phone. Talk to her in person. I'll track down the agents and talk to them."

"Wouldn't you rather talk to Delia?" he asked.

"Sorry, Leo," Lani said. "I'll take the easy duty—Milgahn FBI over a pissed-off Delia Ortiz, any day. After you talk to Delia, you need to let Law and Order know about this, too."

When Lani arrived at the café the Suburban was gone, and only one of the two agents lingered inside. Agent Howell was there; Agent Armstrong wasn't. The first time Lani had met Agent Howell, she had been at a distinct disadvantage. Therefore, it was no accident that she showed up at the café in full M.D. regalia—a pair of scrubs topped by a lab coat and with her name tag fully visible. Clearly annoyed at the interruption, Agent Howell looked up from her computer and then closed the lid abruptly as Lani sat down at the table without waiting for an invitation.

"I came to talk to you about Gabe Ortiz," she said.

"The boy from your campout?"

Lani nodded. "He and the youngest José brother, Timothy, are best friends, and as far as we can tell, they're both missing. With Paul and Carlos dead, I'm worried about Tim. He hasn't been seen since last night, and Gabe was seen possibly being forced into an unidentified pickup earlier this morning."

Leaning back in her chair, Agent Howell frowned. "Just how is it that you happen to know the names of the two victims? That information has yet to be released."

Lani stiffened. Clearly Agent Howell had focused on only one small part of what Lani had said. If that's how the woman was going to play the game, Lani could, too.

"I'm not sure how the names came to my attention," Lani answered with a shrug. "Smoke signals, maybe? The tom-tom telegraph? Does it matter how I know? The point is, I do. The real issue here is that Gabe and Tim are missing."

"I'm assuming Gabe's parents have reported the situation?"

"Gabe's father is probably doing so right about now," Lani answered. "I thought you should know as well, in case the two boys happen to be together."

"That's very kind of you, Dr. Pardee. We appreciate your assistance, and I'm sure the tribal police will be looking into the missing persons situation."

Dismissively, Agent Howell made as if to reopen her computer, but Lani placed her hand on top of the lid. She had fully intended to go into detail about the bag and the note they had found in Gabe's drawer. That was no longer the case.

"I'm not finished," Lani insisted, still holding the computer shut. "Have you spoken to Lorraine José and done the next-of-kin notification?"

"We're not in the habit of discussing investigations with civilians," Agent Howell said icily. "You need to remove your hand from my computer."

"And you need to get over yourself. You need to remember that you're a guest of the Tohono O'odham Nation, and you need to start acting like it. Lorraine

José is one of my patients. I'll be seeing her in a few minutes, and I need to know what to expect."

"Yes, the mother has been notified," Agent Howell said.

"Good," Lani replied. "That's all I wanted to know."

With that, Lani removed her hand, stalked out of the café, and drove straight to the hospital. In the convalescent wing she found Lorraine José, sitting in a chair next to her bed, weeping.

"They used to be such good boys," she said brokenly as Lani sat down on the bed beside her. "What did I do wrong?"

"You did nothing wrong," Lani murmured. "I'm sure you did the best you could."

"Carlos and Paul are dead," Lorraine added, "and now we can't find Tim."

"Does Tim have a phone? Have you tried calling him?"

Lorraine nodded. "We all have phones. Max bought them. When I dialed Tim's number, he didn't answer. I asked the FBI agents if they couldn't trace his phone some way. Because I'm not a signer on the account, they couldn't do it just on my say-so. The one agent, the man, said he'd need to go to town and get a warrant before they could do something like that. I don't know how long that will take."

"What's Tim's number?" Lani asked.

"There are so many, I can't keep them all straight. They're in my cell phone in the bedside table."

"May I?" Lani asked.

"Sure."

Lani retrieved the phone and scrolled through the recent calls list, jotting down numbers as she went—numbers for Carlos, Paul, and Tim. "What about Max's phone?"

Lorraine shrugged. "He probably took it with him when they locked him away up in Florence. He's the one whose name is on the account."

"Has anyone gotten in touch with him about what happened last night?"

"After the FBI agents stopped by, I called Father O'Reilly. He said he'd go to Florence and tell Max. He's probably on his way there now."

Lorraine's sister and brother-in-law turned up just then. Lorraine turned to them hopefully. "Any sign of Timmy?"

"Not yet," the sister said.

Lani pocketed her list of phone numbers and took her leave. Out in the hallway, she used her phone to call the number listed as Timmy's. Not surprisingly, there was no answer. It went straight to voice mail, and Lani knew there was no point in leaving a message.

CHAPTER 19

On the way back to the village, Turtle and the children met Horned Toad—Mo'ochwig. Turtle asked Horned Toad to go tell the women that Shining Falls had been hurt and that he, Turtle, was bringing the children home. Horned Toad ran quickly to carry the message. As soon as the women in the village heard the news, they hurried up the mountain—some to meet Turtle and the children and some to help Shining Falls. But when they reached Shining Falls, the Evil Giantess was already lifting her up.

Ho'ok O'oks told them, "There is no place in your village for someone who is sick. I will take this girl to my home in the mountains, the one that is made of saguaro sticks."

Because they were afraid of the Evil Giantess, the women consented, but they brought a bed and some food to the shelter, and sometimes they sat with Shining Falls.

Ho'ok O'oks told the women it was foolish for them to waste their time looking after a sick girl. "I am a medicine woman," she said. "I will sing the songs and bring the medicine that will make her well."

Ho'ok O'oks went away and returned with a bag of feathers. Some of the feathers were gray, some were white, and some were red. Ho'ok O'oks put the gray feathers around the girl's injured foot, then she waved the red and white feathers over Shining Falls's face. Slowly the girl's eyes closed.

When the women saw this, they decided it was time to return to their work, but the next day, when they returned, Shining Falls was still sleeping.

WHEN I MADE it back to our condo at Belltown Terrace in the early afternoon, I was not a happy camper. I do not like to shop. I have never liked shopping. I hated it back in the old days when Karen and I were married and we didn't have two nickels to rub together. My financial situation has changed remarkably since then, but my attitude toward shopping remains the same. So after spending most of the morning and part of the afternoon being dragged from one furniture emporium to another with Jim Hunt, our interior designer, I was beat and cranky.

And my mood didn't improve when I found a message on my machine from some guy named Brandon Walker, claiming he was a friend of Ralph Ames. He said he was hoping I could give him some help with a case he was working for Ralph's cold case group, TLC.

My initial assumption, of course, was that Mel had somehow ratted me out to Ralph. I suspected that the two of them were conspiring behind my back to bring me into the TLC fold whether I wanted to be involved or not.

Still, I went ahead and returned the call because that's who I am—someone who returns calls rather than ignores them—but I wasn't exactly cordial.

"Brandon Walker?"

"Yes."

"J. P. Beaumont here. You called?"

"I hope you don't mind," he said, sounding genuinely apologetic. "I believe I mentioned this in my message—I got your number from Ralph Ames. Do you know anything about TLC?"

"Some," I admitted with a singular lack of enthusiasm. My terse answers weren't exactly encouraging, and neither was my tone of voice, but Walker plowed on anyway.

"I'm working a case down here in Arizona that may have connections to a cold case from up your way. I'm looking for some help."

"Which case?"

"The dead guy's name is Kenneth Myers," he told me. "At least that's the name he was going by up in Seattle at the time of his death. Down here he was known as Kenneth Mangum. His mother had reported him missing years earlier, but because of the name confusion, it took a long time before someone up there connected your cold case with the missing persons report in Arizona."

"What time frame are we talking about?" I asked.

"Hold on. I have some files here that may include all those details, but I'll need to go out to the car to look through them. Do you want me to call back, or do you want to hang on?"

"Tell you what," I said. "Why don't you call me back in ten?" As soon as the call ended, I immediately dialed Ralph's number. "I'm sure you and Mel have been burning up the phone lines this morning," I grumbled when he came on the line.

"We've done no such thing," Ralph replied. "In fact I haven't spoken to Mel since right after you managed to drag her out of the trunk of that car. What's she up to these days? Keeping out of trouble, I hope."

"I hope so, too," I said. "She's spending the weekend in D.C. at a Homeland Security conference."

"Tell her hello from me when she gets back," Ralph said. "Now, what do you need?"

"What's the deal with Brandon Walker?" I asked.

"He's a good guy who used to be sheriff down south in Pima County," Ralph answered. "He's been a part of TLC not quite from the beginning, but close. He's a neat guy. I like him. His wife, Diana Ladd, is a fairly well-known author. I think she and Mel would hit it off."

Ralph's enthusiasm resembled that of a matchmaker setting up a blind date. I wasn't amused. I didn't figure Brandon Walker and I would ever be best buds, and neither would our wives.

"Tell me the truth, Ralph. Was Walker's call today purely coincidental, or did you and Mel join forces to sic him on me?"

"Mel and I are innocent of all charges," Ralph assured me. "I didn't know a thing about any of this until Brandon called me this morning asking for your number."

"All right," I said grudgingly, "I'll hear him out. In fact, he's calling back right now. Gotta go." I switched over to the other line. "That didn't take long."

"Look," Walker said. "I can tell you're not thrilled to have me intruding on your weekend. This case is an odd one, and if you're not interested in helping . . ."

Odd is something that appeals to me. "What makes it odd?" I asked.

"The initial homicide, the one I'm working on, happened forty-plus years ago. A guy named John Lassiter was convicted—twice over—of murdering a former pal of his, someone named Amos Warren. I was the investigating officer on that original case, and Lassiter has been in prison for thirty years or so. An outfit named Justice for All recently negotiated a plea deal, but he won't take it—because he won't plead guilty to something he didn't do."

"Surprise, surprise," I muttered. "Where have I heard that before? You didn't fall for that old line, did you? Is Lassiter the one asking you to reinvestigate the case?"

"Earlier this morning I talked to Lassiter's daughter, Amanda Wasser. She's the one who got JFA involved, but, yeah, Lassiter asked to see me because of my connection to TLC. The guy who prosecuted Lassiter isn't exactly pure as the driven snow, so I decided to do some asking around. A few minutes ago, I finished interviewing Lassiter himself. I'm going with my gut here, but I think he's the real deal."

Walker may have been a believer, but I wasn't. Busting my butt for a convicted killer wasn't my idea of how to spend a quiet Saturday afternoon. Still, I was a little curious about the unsolved case here in Washington.

"What about the other case you mentioned," I asked, "the one up here? Can you give me any further details on that?"

"I have a box full of paper files," Walker said, "but I don't want to try going over those by phone. Lassiter's daughter has been amassing information on the case for years. That's the box of files I just told you about, but she says she has digital copies of everything she gave me. If you would give me your e-mail address, I can have her send you the digital copies of everything pertaining to the Kenneth Myers homicide."

I gave him my e-mail address. "Tell her she's welcome to send me the stuff, but I'm not making any promises."

The call ended. I made myself some coffee, went into the family room, took a seat in my not-recliner, and picked up my computer. I intended to send Mel a note telling her about what Jim and I had found on our shopping spree along with photos of what we'd ordered, but when I opened my mail program I found a series of e-mails from awasser@roadrunner.net. The first one was entitled *SPD. Archives. KMyers.*

I opened the attached file, intending to glance at it briefly and move on, but I didn't.

The first page was nothing more or less than your basic bureaucratic CYA disclaimer:

> The following information is being sent to Ms. Amanda Wasser in answer to her request under the Freedom of Information Act. It is the policy of the Seattle Police Department to cooperate fully with such requests when releasing information to the public is not considered to be detrimental to ongoing investigations.

The next page included an overview along with photos of the items in the evidence box, and there wasn't much: a frayed leather belt, the remains of a pair of leather shoes, a gold pendant engraved with the names Calliope Horn and Ken Myers, a pair of prescription glasses, and two bullet fragments that were identified as .22 longs. There was no notation that the fragments had been sent out for testing, but that was hardly surprising—that kind of testing costs money. After all, solving cold cases wasn't necessarily a top priority back in the early '90s, and since these were skeletal remains only, the Kenneth Myers case was stone cold from day one.

But this was a new century and a new time in solving cold cases. Before continuing, I made a note to myself to ask my friend Seattle PD assistant chief Ron Peters to have the two .22 bullets sent to National Ballistics Laboratory.

The next scanned page revealed the cover sheet of what I easily recognized as an SPD murder book. In the middle of the page was a struck-through ~~John Doe~~. Written in pen next to it was another name: Kenneth Myers a.k.a. Kenneth Mangum. The next page, the one listing the names of investigating officers, was the one that stopped me cold. Three names leaped out at me: Detective S. Danielson; Detective P. Kramer; and Special Homicide Investigator M. Soames.

Sue Danielson is someone I see often because all these years later she still haunts my dreams. We were working as partners when she died in a shoot-out with her estranged husband. Realistically I know that her death was an act of domestic violence and that it was not my fault. Still, that doesn't keep me from blaming myself and torturing myself with questions about what I could have done that would have meant the difference between Sue's living and dying.

Paul Kramer was and is a jerk—a brownnosing, butt-kissing clown, whose undeserved—as far as I'm concerned—promotion to captain shortly after Sue's death was the catalyst that caused me to pull the plug on my career at Seattle PD.

Then, of course, there's Mel. She's my wife, but one of the jobs she was tasked with on Ross Connors's Special Homicide Investigation Team was searching through multistate missing persons files and trying to match those reports with unidentified homicide victims in Washington State.

Ignoring my coffee, I performed my first duty as one of Ralph Ames's TLC volunteers. I settled in to read.

AGAIN GABE AWAKENED in darkness. This time, the first thing he realized was that the truck wasn't moving. Then, somewhere nearby, he heard a strange buzzing sound. It took a moment for him to recognize what it was—the sound of a cell phone buzzing because the ringer had been turned off. It wasn't his phone. If it were, he would have felt it. That meant the phone belonged to the other prisoner. He still didn't know for sure if his fellow inmate was Tim. What was important was that someone was calling—someone was trying to reach them, but neither of them could answer. Moving closer, he was able to touch his companion's pocket and feel the phone through the cloth. Before he could extricate it, the phone gave one last buzz and fell silent.

Frustrated and helpless, Gabe resumed his former position. "Are you awake?" he attempted to mumble through the tape. What actually came out of his mouth was nothing more than a garbled moan, but an answering moan told him that his companion wasn't sleeping.

That was when Gabe realized that he needed to pee, desperately, and there was nothing for it but to do it, letting the wet warmth run through his underwear and puddle around his butt. When the urine encountered the entrance wounds from the cactus, it hurt like hell. Surprisingly enough, that shocked him out of his strange lethargy.

If he'd been Lani, he might have tried singing a song just then, a song to Elder Brother asking for help, but he doubted I'itoi would be listening. Gabe needed help that was closer at hand.

Then he remembered something important about his friend Timmy. Tim was actually several months older than Gabe. For Tim's birthday, just after Christmas, Carlos and Paul had given their little brother his heart's desire—a switchblade knife. The school campus was, of course, a weapon-free zone. There were signs on every door that said so. That didn't mean, however, that any of the kids paid attention. Timmy, who liked to carve his initials on trees and to whittle little figurines out of pieces of mesquite, took his knife to school with him every day, wearing it tucked inside his sock.

It occurred to Gabe that if Henry Rojas hadn't been smart enough to take his prisoner's cell phone away, maybe he had failed to go looking for a possible weapon as well.

With some effort, Gabe managed to use one of his shoes to peel off the other. Then he ran his sock-covered foot along the pant leg of the person lying beside him. It took only a matter of seconds for him to find it. The knife was here—he felt it under the cloth. If Tim was bound the same way Gabe was, the knife would be out of Tim's reach, but with any kind of luck, maybe Gabe could retrieve the knife and somehow manage to cut them both loose.

Knowing the knife was there and being able to lay hands on it, however, were two different things. It took time to figure out how to approach the problem. Finally, by throwing his legs over Tim's in a way that formed a human X, Gabe was able to slither snakelike far enough down that his fingers touched the handle of the knife. Extricating it from the sock was another whole exercise that left Gabe out of breath, sweating and exhausted.

Back in his original position he had to rest for a bit—rest and think. How much time had passed? Was it day or night? Their cage—that's how he thought of it—was gradually heating up, probably due to the warmth of the two bodies trapped inside it and maybe from sunlight, too—but not direct sunlight. Even in March, if the black truck had been parked in the sun, the boys would have died from heatstroke by now. So where were they then? Gabe suspected the truck was parked inside some kind of shaded structure, far enough off the road that there were no sounds of passing vehicles.

Why do we still have air? Gabe wondered. There had to be some form of ventilation that he couldn't see. Were there ventilation holes that kept them from running out of oxygen? If so, he wondered if that meant that he and Tim weren't the only people who had been transported in the back of Henry Rojas's pickup truck.

Tim moved impatiently beside him as if to say, *What's the holdup?*

Somewhat rested now, Gabe clicked the button. The knife sprang open with such force that it almost shot out of his hand. It was awkward to hold it, but Gabe was gratified to discover that his exertions had somehow weakened the grip of his restraints. He had more range of movement than he'd had earlier. That meant that he should probably be the one wielding the knife blade, even though he'd be working in the dark. And, clumsy as he was, he'd be working with his right hand. If Tim used the knife, he'd be using his left.

Gritting his teeth, dreading that the smallest slip of the blade might mean slicing into Tim's arm, Gabe snuggled over until their two bodies were once again touching. Then, after ascertaining where the tape started and stopped as best he could, he began to pick away with the tip of the razor-sharp blade. He couldn't see in the dark, but biting his lip, he concentrated as though he could and hoped that I'itoi or maybe one of the night-flying bats that had filled his dreams would be there to help him.

As he did so, Gabe felt a surprising sense of joy rise in his heart. He was doing something. He was taking action, and for a change he wasn't afraid.

Maybe I'itoi had heard him after all.

CHAPTER 20

The next day, nawoj, *my friend, when the women came again, Shining Falls was still sleeping. The women tried to awaken her, but she would not open her eyes. The women were frightened. When they tried to question the Evil Giantess, Ho'ok O'oks hid in the black cloud of her hair and would not answer them.*

But there was one thing the Evil Giantess did not know and that the Indian women did not know, either. While Ho'ok O'oks was singing and waving the feathers over Shining Falls's face, she had dropped a single white feather. It was Alichum S-toha A'an—Little White Feather. Shining Falls had put her hand over it, and while she lay sleeping, she held Little White Feather ever so tightly in her hand.

After a time, Little White Feather grew very tired from the weight of Shining Falls's hand and cried out for help. Some White-Winged Doves—O-okokoi—heard Little White Feather's cry for help. It was really a song, and it goes like this:

White Feather, White Feather, child of my mother,
You in the air look down on your brother.
Alone am I here in pain and in trouble.

One of the White-Winged Doves said to the others, "Why, I believe that is one of my feathers calling to us."

You must understand, nawoj, *my friend, that it is the law of the desert that you must always answer a call for help, so the White-Winged Doves circled in the air to try to learn what the trouble was.*

BRANDON WAS SPEEDING south on Highway 79 when his phone rang. He answered it through the Escalade's sound system, and Diana's voice came out through the speakers.

"Have you talked to Lani today?" she asked with no preamble—without asking where Brandon was or what he was doing. That was unusual in and of itself.

"No, why?"

"Gabe's gone missing," she said.

"From Kitt Peak?" Brandon asked. That was the last thing he had known about the weekend's plans—that Gabe and Lani were going to camp out on the mountain on Friday night and that the whole family planned to make a daylong expedition to the book festival in Tucson on Sunday.

"Not exactly," Diana said. "Gabe and Lani evidently got into some kind of hassle, and he walked off the mountain. He made it home, but now no one can find him. Later, after Gabe left, Lani witnessed a shooting—heard it rather than saw it—in which two boys from Sells were killed. It's a mess, and Lani's really upset about it, but I have another panel to go to . . ."

"Not to worry," Brandon said. "I'll call her right now."

He did so. "What's going on?" he asked when Lani answered.

"You're not going to believe it."

"Try me."

Brandon listened patiently to the whole story, but he noticed there were undertones of things not said. "I know Gabe," Brandon said when Lani finally came to a stop. "He's a good kid. And I've met Tim, too. I can't imagine either of them getting mixed up in any kind of smuggling enterprise."

"I believe it all started with one of Tim's older brothers. Max was caught up in it to begin with. Then, after he got sent up for something or other, he must have passed his part of the business on to his younger brothers."

Brandon and Lani had always been close, and he could tell from her voice that she was holding back.

"Okay," he said, after a moment. "You've told me Dan and Leo are out looking for the boys, but I get the feeling that you left out a few pertinent details. How about telling me the rest of it?"

His question seemed to catch her off guard. "How did you know?" she asked.

"You've never been that good of a liar. Now spit it out."

"I don't think Gabe and Tim are just missing, Dad," she said at last. "I think it's worse than that. I'm afraid they're both dead—Tim for sure and maybe Gabe, too."

"Why?"

"Because there was another shot, one I haven't mentioned to anyone but you," she said. "A while after the first two volleys of automatic gunfire, I heard another shot, a single one that time. I couldn't tell exactly where it came from, but it sounded like it was close enough to Rattlesnake Skull charco that it could be related."

"You're saying you think whoever killed Carlos and Paul José may have killed Tim, too?"

"Yes," Lani answered, her voice trembling with emotion. "The poor kid is probably lying out there in the desert in a place where we'll never find the body. I know the FBI agents are aware Tim has a phone, but I'm not sure they'll be in any hurry to put a tracer on it. Finding the phone might not show us where he is now, but it would be a starting point."

"Surely the FBI will get right on that."

"I'm not so sure."

"Why?"

"Remember how you always used to complain about having to work with the FBI?"

"I do, but what does that have to do with this?"

"Believe me, it would have been a lot worse if you'd been Indian instead of Anglo back then," she said. "That female agent barely gave me the time of day. The FBI probably will get around to tracing Tim's phone, but only when they're good and ready and have a properly drawn search warrant in hand. Tim José is an Indian, Dad. When it comes to Indian kids, you could say the FBI has no real sense of urgency. I need to find someone who will go looking for Tim's phone right now. Do you know of anyone who could do that for us, maybe someone from TLC?"

"Not offhand," Brandon answered. "TLC's brief is with cold cases rather than new ones, and I'd hate to think about what will happen if we get caught up in the middle of an active FBI investigation. Still, let me give it some thought. I'm coming up on Oro Valley right now.

I may stop and grab a bite to eat. Give me a call if you hear anything about those boys, will you?"

"Yes," she promised. "I'll be sure to let you know."

"And don't worry," Brandon added. "It'll be okay."

That's what he told his daughter, but it was an outright lie. Brandon had been in law enforcement long enough to understand that if Gabe Ortiz and Tim José had gotten themselves crosswise with drug smugglers, they were most likely already dead, just as Lani feared. Brandon also knew that losing Gabe would break Lani's heart, and she was the one Brandon was worried about.

That's what fathers do where their daughters' hearts are concerned. They worry.

I WON'T PRETEND that reading through the Kenneth Myers murder book was easy. Most of the entries were written in Sue Danielson's back-slanted handwriting. Seeing that again after all those years came as a shock, and it wasn't surprising that it was sometimes difficult to read the words themselves because tears kept blurring my eyes.

The skeletal remains had been discovered in 1990 by a highway department crew clearing brush during the completion of the I-90/I-5 interchange. The case had been assigned to Detectives Kramer and Danielson. There were autopsy notes showing some blunt force trauma, but the presumed cause of death was a shooting; two close-range bullet holes were in the back of the skull, either one of which would have been fatal.

A search of public records for the names on the pendant, Ken Myers and Calliope Horn, had eventually led Kramer and Danielson to a woman named Calliope Horn, who had in turn identified the dead man as someone named Ken Myers, Calliope's former boyfriend, who had gone missing from a transient encampment in 1983.

That piece of information itself went a long way to explain why so little had ever been done. At the time, bum-bashing was more or less a popular spectator sport. Hazing at UDub fraternities often included tracking down bums and beating the crap out of them. If one of them died? It was no big deal because nobody really cared. In fact, I distinctly remembered Kramer waxing eloquent on the topic one day in the break room—talking about how taking down people like that was doing society a favor. I couldn't help but wonder now if he and Sue had been working this very case at the time.

With that in mind, it was no surprise that Sue Danielson had done the lion's share of the work. She was the one who had tracked down Calliope Horn and done the interview. I knew I could go down to Seattle PD and request a look at the interview tape. It wasn't something I was looking forward to, because I dreaded seeing Sue's face again. But it turned out I didn't have to, because Amanda Wasser had worked her Freedom of Information Act magic. The next file I opened included a PDF transcript of the Danielson/Horn interview.

Transcripts are to interviews as raisins are to grapes. They're lifeless and flat. They don't contain the facial expressions and hand gestures that let homicide cops know when someone is lying, but they can still deliver a lot of information, even when done—as this one evidently had been—with some low-cost character recognition program that couldn't make heads or tails of either *Calliope* or *Puyallup.* Fortunately I was able to fill in those information gaps, telling myself all the while that if I needed to see the tape itself, I could always do so. But even with the character-recognition difficulties, I could see that Sue hadn't exactly handled Calliope Horn with kid gloves.

S.D.: For identification purposes, your name is Calliope Maxwell Horn and you were born in Puyallup, Washington?

C.H.: That's right, that's who I am, but why did you bring me here? Am I under arrest? What's going on?

S.D.: You're not under arrest, but tell me. Were you once in a relationship with someone named Ken Myers?

C.H.: Yes, I was. It was a long time ago. Kenny and I were sort of engaged. I mean, I didn't have a ring or anything, but he'd asked me to marry him, and I'd said yes, but then he took off for Arizona. He told me that when he came back he'd have enough money that we'd be set. We'd be able to get our own apartment and start over. That's what he told me, but it's also the last thing he ever said to me. He left, and I never saw him again. But you still haven't explained why I'm here.

S.D.: Are you aware that human remains were discovered last week at the I-90/I-5 interchange?

C.H.: I guess I saw something about that in the paper. But what does that have to do with me?

S.D.: The victim, a male in his late twenties or early thirties, died of homicidal violence, shot in the back of the head with a .22. I'm sorry to tell you that he was wearing a pendant shaped like a heart, with two names engraved on it—Calliope Horn and Ken Myers. If I'm not mistaken, you're wearing a similar item. Is this one engraved the same way?

C.H.: (*nodding*) I still wear it. (*holding up a necklace*) He didn't have enough money for a ring, so he got us matching pendants instead. But are you saying Kenny is dead? That he never went to Arizona? That he died right here in Seattle? That's not possible. He can't be dead. He can't. (*sobbing*)

S.D.: That's how we found you, Ms. Horn, because of the pendant. Calliope Horn is a distinctive name. We were able to locate you through your driver's license records. Unfortunately, we've found no trace of Mr. Myers. No birth records; no driver's license. Are you sure Kenneth Myers is his real name?

C.H.: That's the name he gave me. I didn't exactly ask him to show me his ID. As for his license, he told me he lost it. Because of a DUI, I think.

S.D.: Do you know where he came from? Or do you have any idea who his next of kin might be so we can notify his family?

C.H.: (*shaking her head*) He came from somewhere in Arizona. Phoenix, I think. Or maybe Tucson. I told him Phoenix was a place I'd always wanted to visit. It sounded warm.

I remembered seeing notes in the murder book that Sue had checked with authorities in both Phoenix and Tucson, looking for someone named Kenneth Myers. She'd come up empty, of course, because cops in Arizona knew Myers by the name of Kenneth Mangum.

S.D.: Do you remember when Mr. Myers left town?

C.H.: May 1, 1983.

S.D.: You remember that date exactly after all these years?

C.H.: Yes, I remember it. When you're in love, you remember things like that. At least I do.

S.D.: How did you and Mr. Myers meet?

C.H.: We were both homeless and living in a tent city up on the hillside just east of I-5. A shelter had been cobbled together using old tarps and pieces of canvas. There must have been twenty of us or so living in camp at the time, but I didn't really notice Kenny until we were standing in line for a Thanksgiving dinner offered by the Salvation Army. It was cold and rainy. It was nice to be inside, out of the weather, and to have a hot meal for a change. We got our food, sat at the same table, and then started talking.

S.D.: What happened then?

C.H.: We hit it off and started hanging out together—and drinking together, too. We were both drinkers then. Eventually we started to trust each other, but I don't think either of us ever expected to fall in love. A homeless camp doesn't sound very romantic. (*laughter*) But it was for us. People teased us and said that we walked around in a funny little bubble.

It turned out Kenny and I had a lot in common. We'd both come from broken and abusive homes; we'd both dropped out of high school our sophomore year. We'd both done time. There's nothing like spending time in the slammer to give you something to talk about. (*laughter*) After I got out on good behavior, I couldn't find work. That's how I ended up in the camp—me and plenty of others. Just because you get out of jail doesn't mean you get your life back.

S.D.: What did you get sent up for?

C.H.: I'm sure you've got my record right there in front of you.

S.D.: Tell me anyway.

C.H.: Domestic violence. Manslaughter. I killed my ex. Ray came home drunk and was beating the crap out of me. He tried to choke me. I kicked him in the balls hard enough that I got loose. He liked to play ball with the guys, and his baseball bat was standing in the corner of the living room, behind the front door. I grabbed that and bashed his skull in.

We'd both been drinking that night. I had enough cuts and bruises that it should have been considered self-defense, but I had a worthless defense attorney, and the prosecutor argued that I had hit him more than once after he was down. Which was true. I hit him way more than once.

Taking a deep breath, I had to stop reading for several long minutes. I couldn't continue, not when I knew what had happened to Sue much later. I found myself once again reliving her last moments frame by frame, fighting it out with her enraged and fully armed ex-husband in a battle that had ended with both of them dead.

Throughout the Calliope Horn interview I read enough between the lines to realize that Sue suspected Kenneth Myers, like Calliope's first husband, had died as a result of domestic violence. I couldn't help wondering if she had some inkling at the time—some premonition—that a similar fate awaited her. Probably not. My problem was that I had no such luxury. The curse of hindsight was slamming into every fiber of my being as I read those bare-bones questions and answers.

Finally gathering my roiling emotions, I returned to the text.

C.H.: Now I get it. That's what this is all about and why I'm here, isn't it. You think that just because I bashed Ray's head in that I killed Kenny, too? Am I a suspect? Do I need a lawyer?

S.D.: You're not under arrest, Ms. Horn. You're free to go anytime you wish. We're hoping you can help us locate Mr. Myers's next of kin. So you were both living in the homeless shelter at the time he disappeared?

C.H.: Yes.

S.D.: Did Mr. Myers have a beef of any kind with someone from the camp?

C.H.: No, he didn't, not at all. I wasn't the only one who thought he was a good guy. So did everyone else.

S.D.: Did you have any ex-boyfriends hanging around at the time?

C.H.: No, I didn't. Nothing like that—no boyfriends of any kind.

S.D.: At the time Mr. Myers left, did you report him as missing?

C.H.: No, I didn't. At first I didn't worry because he said he was going to Arizona and that he'd be back in a couple of weeks after he did whatever it was he had to do.

S.D.: How was he planning to travel—by plane? By car?

C.H.: He didn't have a car or a driver's license and he didn't have money for plane fare. I figured he was going to hitchhike.

S.D.: At some point, you must have realized that he was gone for good. Why didn't you report him missing then?

C.H.: Because the cops would have laughed at me. You can't go missing from a homeless shelter. Most of the people in homeless shelters are already missing from somewhere else. Besides, by then, I'd finally tumbled to the fact that he probably had a girlfriend on the side. I figured he'd hooked up with an old flame and that he'd gone back to Arizona to be with her.

S.D.: What girlfriend?

C.H.: I don't know for sure that she was his girlfriend; I just assumed that's what she was. A few days after Kenny left town—after I thought he left town—one of the guys in the camp, Carl Jacobson, mentioned that he'd seen Kenny with another woman the afternoon of the day he left. Carl claimed he saw them sitting together down by the convention center.

S.D.: Did Mr. Jacobson describe her to you?

C.H.: Sort of. He said she was well dressed and classy looking—definitely not homeless. I didn't pay that much attention at the time because, you know, I still thought Kenny would be back when he finished doing whatever it was he had to do. Then later, when he still wasn't back by the end of May, I realized that he was probably gone for good. That's when I finally made the connection with the woman from the convention center.

S.D.: Do you know where we can find Mr. Jacobson?

C.H.: No idea. Homeless people come and go. They don't leave forwarding addresses.

S.D.: So you don't know for sure that Mr. Myers and the unidentified woman were involved in a relationship of some kind?

C.H.: I don't have proof positive, no, but that's what I believe.

S.D.: You said there were two matching pendants—engraved pendants. If you were both homeless, where did he get the money to buy them and have them engraved?

C.H.: Beats me. Probably worked as a day laborer somewhere to get it.

S.D.: You mentioned that Mr. Myers had a drinking problem?

C.H.: We both did, but by early spring we were working on getting sober. Then, all of a sudden, he was gone. When I realized he was gone for good, I fell off the wagon in a big way. I was furious that he'd left me for someone else and was spending the happily ever after he'd promised me with her. That's what I always believed until just now when you told me Kenny was dead. All this time I thought he was alive and well and living with someone else instead of me.

S.D.: Let's talk about her, then—that alleged girlfriend. Did Kenneth ever mention other girlfriends by name?

C.H.: No. We never talked about previous relationships. By mutual agreement those were off-limits. But once he was gone and once I suspected another woman might have been involved, I started putting things together and wondering if maybe she was someone he'd knocked up and she'd come to him looking for child support.

S.D.: Did Kenneth ever indicate to you that he had kids?

C.H.: It never came up and I didn't ask him. Since I didn't have kids, I assumed he didn't, either. By the time I was ready to ask those questions, it was too late. He was gone.

S.D.: How long did it take for you to figure out that he wasn't coming back?

C.H.: For sure by the middle of June. After that, I spent months drinking and got picked up for being drunk and disorderly. The judge ordered me into mandatory treatment. Once I got sober, I realized that since I couldn't count on anyone else to save my sorry ass, I'd have to do the job myself. If my life was going to have any kind of happy ending, finding it was up to me.

Someone from AA helped me get into a shelter run by the YWCA. The people there helped me find a job and start taking classes. First I got my GED and then I enrolled in college. I have my own studio apartment now, and I'm halfway through my junior year.

S.D.: What are you studying?

C.H.: I'm majoring in religious studies. After I graduate, I want to earn a degree in divinity. It's one thing for people in the suburbs to come swanning into some shelter during the holidays to serve turkey dinners and tell themselves that they're doing their Christian duty. I want to minister to the homeless because I've been homeless. I know what it's like.

S.D.: Some people might think you were operating with a guilty conscience.

C.H.: Those people would be wrong.

S.D.: When Mr. Myers said he was leaving, he led you to believe that he was expecting to make a score of some kind? That he'd be coming back with enough money for the two of you to move out of the homeless camp?

C.H.: That's right.

S.D.: Is it possible that he was involved in some kind of illegal activity?

C.H.: You mean like drug smuggling or something? No, Kenny drank, but he didn't do drugs, and I never thought he was a crook.

S.D.: Let me ask you this, Ms. Horn: Did you kill Mr. Myers?

C.H.: No, absolutely not! I swear. Like I said before, I didn't even know he was dead until just a little while ago when you told me. I always believed that he had taken off with another woman.

S.D.: Miss Horn, would you be willing to take a polygraph test?

C.H.: You mean a lie detector test? Of course. I'd do it in a heartbeat.

The interview ended there. And that's when I realized I'd already seen a copy of the results from Calliope Horn's polygraph test. It had been right there in the evidence box. The results indicated that Calliope Horn had known nothing about Kenneth Myers's death. She had been telling the truth.

With those thoughts in mind, I went on to the other

interviews. Calliope Horn's wasn't the only one that had been transcribed into what more or less passed for English. Between the time Myers disappeared and the time his remains were found, the encampment had been disbanded and most of the people who had lived there had moved on to wherever homeless people go when they have to go somewhere else. Only a few of the former residents had ever been identified, to say nothing of located.

Interviews with the few individuals who had been found, especially ones conducted by Kramer working alone, were easier for me to read than the ones with Sue's name on them, but they shed little light on the matter beyond the fact that they all agreed Kenny had disappeared sometime in the spring of 1983. Calliope was the only one who had been able to supply an exact date.

Carl Jacobson, the person who had supposedly witnessed Ken Myers talking to the "ex-girlfriend" and who might have been able to give a description of her, was one of the MIAs. As a consequence, the closest individual to an eyewitness was never interviewed.

Turning off my iPad, I could see why the case had gone cold: No murder weapon. No witnesses. No time of death. No actual crime scene. It wasn't until years later that Mel Soames, using dental records, had linked the Myers homicide up to an Arizona missing persons report on someone named Kenneth Mangum. That report had been filed years earlier by Ken's mother, who was deceased by the time the cops came calling with the bad news that her son had been murdered decades earlier in Seattle.

There was no explanation of why he had left Arizona, moved to Seattle, and changed his name. Yes, Ken

Mangum had done time in jail on a DUI charge—presumably the same one that had cost him his driver's license. That meant that his fingerprints were probably on file somewhere, too, but he'd never been arrested again or linked to any other crimes, and the skeletal remains found at the crime scene hadn't included fingerprints.

Mangum/Myers had died in Seattle. That meant solving the homicide was still Seattle's responsibility. Once the cops there reached out to Arizona law enforcement in an attempt to notify the next of kin, cops in Arizona weren't required to do anything more. In other words, the unsolved case was now cold twice over in two separate jurisdictions. With that in mind and given Seattle PD's lack of enthusiasm for solving bum-bashing cases, I didn't hold out much hope that it would ever be solved. Not by me, not by Seattle PD, and certainly not by Ralph Ames's cold case group, TLC.

CHAPTER 21

The White-Winged Doves—the O-okokoi—circled around until they found Evil Giantess guarding the sick girl who was holding Little White Feather in her hand. The doves knew that there was nothing they could do right then, so they went to a cave on Baboquivari to hold a council and decide what to do.

None of the O-okokoi could come up with a plan, but Turtle overheard them talking. He said that the way to help Little White Feather was very simple. Evil Giantess watched Shining Falls all day, but Ho'ok O'oks herself had to sleep at night. Turtle said that the doves must find one of the white-feathered people who was awake at night. Then Turtle suggested that since Owl—Chukud—was sleeping in the cave, the doves should ask him for help.

Since it was the middle of the day, it was hard for the doves to wake Owl. They had to shout at him and pull his feathers, but eventually he opened his eyes and said, "Whoo, Whoo."

Then the doves told Owl that one of the White Feathers was in trouble and he must help. After Owl heard the story, he agreed that he would go to Evil Giantess and try to steal away the girl who was holding Little White Feather.

You see, nawoj, *my friend, that Owl, too, had many white feathers. If Ho'ok O'oks had used any of the Black Feather tribe or the Blue Feather tribe when she put Shining Falls to sleep, Owl would not be able to awaken her.*

DURING HIS THREE-PLUS decades in the Arizona State Prison, John Lassiter had seen any number of wardens come and go. The weak-kneed ones tended to go sooner than later. Most had been honorable men who did the job to the best of their abilities. Some had been downright corrupt.

The current one, Warden Edward Huffman, was right at the top of Lassiter's warden scorecard sheet. He was tough but fair in the way he handed out rewards and punishments. He had demoted or removed guards who were found to be dealing drugs, goodies, or bribes on the side and had done his best to motivate the ones that remained. He had instituted policies that made it easier for impaired prisoners to exist inside the system. He had found ways to stretch the food budget so things that actually resembled real food and vegetables ended up on the dining room serving trays. At his direction, the evening meal, served at the early hour of four P.M. on Saturday afternoon, was usually pot roast—pot roast with gravy that actually tasted like gravy rather than brown-colored flour.

John didn't have many happy memories from his childhood, but pot roast was one of them. Amos Warren had made killer pot roast. When they were out on a scavenging trip, he'd cook it in a cast-iron Dutch oven, keeping it bubbling for hours over a bed of mesquite coals. When they were in town, he'd use a different Dutch oven, a shiny aluminum one, to cook the roast on top of the stove. Although John watched him do it often enough, he never quite mastered the art of making the stuff, but the cooks at the prison came surprisingly close.

Even on days when he wasn't feeling one hundred percent, John still made the effort to go to the dining room for dinner on Saturdays. By the time a tray came to his cell it was usually dead cold. That evening, even though John was physically drained by his long encounter with Brandon Walker earlier in the day, he asked for an attendant to come wheel him to the dining room. He would have preferred having Aubrey do the job, but Aubrey's shift ended at three. By dinnertime, he was long gone.

Jason, the kid who came to get him, was a new hire. He was competent enough, but he was young and naive. He also talked a blue streak, chattering away like a magpie. John didn't pay much attention because he didn't want to get involved. There was no point. He already knew the guy would be a short-timer.

A strict seating hierarchy was maintained in the dining room. The various gangs stuck together, with their members sitting at predetermined tables. The far corner of the room held the tables for inmates who weren't necessarily affiliated with any of the other groups. It was a form of exile that meant the people who sat there were farther away from the food lines and the trash cans than anyone else. They were also farthest from the door.

John liked to think of his usual table, the most isolated one in the room, as a United Nations of sorts. It certainly wasn't the safest location, due primarily to the presence of two Anglo child molesters, one older—a lifer—and one several decades younger. The two weren't necessarily friends, but they stuck together to watch each other's backs. Everyone else maintained a certain distance, because they knew, without having to say so, who was wearing a target and who wasn't.

There were several arsonists in the group, including two Korean brothers, twins, who had specialized in burning down dry cleaning establishments, and a Vietnamese guy who had torched his own nail salon. His ex-wife, who happened to be inside the salon at the time, perished, which meant her ex-husband was there for a stretch, twenty-five to life. In addition, there were several unaffiliated Indians at the table—a taciturn Hopi, a San Carlos Apache who wasn't friendly with anyone, and a recently arrived young guy who didn't talk much but who was most likely, John thought, Tohono O'odham in origin.

The Vietnamese guy, who went by the name of Sam, was the one with whom John had the most in common. He was the best educated of the bunch and had taken to heart John's suggestion that he read his way through the encyclopedia as a way of passing the time. He was enthusiastic about it and was already halfway through volume C. Their occasional and mostly brief dinner-time chats often centered on esoteric things the two had learned from their individual courses of study.

Jason was still chatting away when he parked John's wheelchair at the end of the table. That was his spot because climbing over the picnic-style bench seating was impossible for him.

"Okay," Jason said. "Gonna go have a smoke. I'll be back for you in fifteen."

The table was generally quiet that evening, but there was nothing out of the ordinary—nothing that hinted something bad was coming. Jason was back from his smoking break and bending over to release the brake on the chair when all hell broke loose. The melee erupted in the middle of the room and soon spread to all corners. Inmates leaped to their feet while metal trays flew through the air and crashed to the floor. As sirens sounded and guards shouted warnings and orders, tables were overturned.

Knowing he was trapped in the corner with no way to escape, John watched as two men emerged from the fracas and started toward his table. With everyone else wildly throwing punches and contributing to the general mayhem, those two moved purposefully but almost in slow motion toward the corner. John's initial assumption was that they were coming for the child molesters. It was only when he saw the shiv slice into Jason's back that John Lassiter realized, too late, he was the real target.

He grabbed his tray and tried to use that as a shield, but the tray only managed to deflect the blow. The shiv plunged first into his side and then into his chest. His chair tipped over, spilling him out of it. He was lying on the floor on his side, looking up and waiting for the next blow, when Sam used his own tray to hammer the side of the attacker's head. The little man's swing was powerful enough to knock the offender unconscious. The shiv fell from the attacker's hand. He toppled over and landed heavily on Jason's too-still body.

Through the din and the milling feet around him, John caught sight of someone else on the floor. It was the young Indian kid—the Tohono O'odham. There was a gaping hole in his neck. He was trying to breathe, but John knew it was no use. He was about to drown in his own blood.

He's dead, John Lassiter thought as his brain finally registered the pain in his own body and the blood pouring onto his hand. *And so am I, but at least I'm out of here.*

Then his world went black.

CUTTING THROUGH THE tape was a long, difficult process. Several times Tim whimpered and jumped reflexively, telling Gabe that the knife had cut into his friend's flesh rather than simply into the tape. But at last, with a satisfying snip, the tape gave way. A moment later, Tim used his newly freed hand to peel the tape from his mouth.

"I'm sorry," he said. "I didn't know he'd come after you. I didn't think he'd come after any of us."

Gabe's muffled reply sent Tim's fingers in search of the tape on Gabe's face as well.

"Who?" Gabe asked when he, too, was able to speak.

Tim was already fumbling for the knife. "Henry Rojas," he answered. "I saw him kill Carlos and Paul. I ran. I thought I'd be able to get away, but he caught me anyway. He said he'd shoot me if I didn't tell him where the jar was. I thought he was kidding. Why would you shoot someone over a jar of peanut butter?"

"It's peanut butter full of diamonds," Gabe answered.

"Diamonds?" Tim asked. "Are you kidding?"

"No," Gabe said, "diamonds for sure."

The blade of the knife slipped. Gabe felt it slice into the side of his arm. A trickle of blood meandered away from the cut. He winced but managed to stifle the cry that rose in his throat. After all, hadn't he just done the same thing to Tim's arm?

"How did he get all three of you?"

"Carlos had already gone to town. He told Paul that he was going to talk to the big boss and ask her for more money. He said that he didn't know where she lived but that someone was going to meet him and take him to her."

"The big boss is a woman?" Gabe asked.

"I think so," Tim answered. "I know Carlos was scared of her. He told us before he left that we should put the jar in a safe place. That's when I brought it over to you even though I knew you were busy last night. I worried about what your parents would say, but then they weren't home, either. So I left the bag on your porch and went home.

"Paul and I played video games for a while, waiting up for Carlos to come back. Finally I got tired and went to bed. I was sleeping when something poked me in the arm."

"A needle?" Gabe asked, biting his lip when the tip of the blade bit into his arm again.

"It was a needle. How did you know?"

"Because he used the same stuff on me," Gabe said. "It's like you're paralyzed or passed out or something."

"Yes, all of a sudden it was like I couldn't move. He picked me up, threw me over his shoulder, carried me outside, and threw me into the back of his Border Patrol SUV. Paul was already there. He wasn't moving, either. And just like that, I was out."

"What happened next?"

"I woke up when we turned off the highway onto Coleman Road. By then he had put tie wraps around my wrists and around Paul's, too. I could see that Paul was already awake. Henry stopped the car in the road by a charco."

"Rattlesnake Skull," Gabe supplied. The knife cut through the last of the tape on Gabe's right wrist. It was a huge relief to finally be able to move his arm. "Close the knife and give it to me," he said. "I'll cut my left hand loose and then work on your right. But first I need your phone."

It took some maneuvering for Gabe to wrestle the phone out Tim's pocket. When he did, it wouldn't turn on. The battery was dead. Hiding his disappointment, he got back to the task at hand.

"Go on," he urged as he went back to working on the tape. "Tell me what happened."

"When Henry got out of the SUV," Tim continued, "he went around to the tailgate and came up with something that looked like an automatic weapon. While he was out of the car Paul whispered that I should run. I was scared. I didn't know how I'd be able to do that. I didn't even know if my legs would work. When Henry opened the door and pulled Paul out, Paul pretended like he was still asleep, but as soon as he was on the ground, he started to struggle and managed to knock the gun out of Henry's hands.

"The door was still open. I got out and ran as fast as I could, but running in the dark with my hands tied was hard. Then I remembered that YouTube video we watched, the one about that girl getting loose from a tie wrap by bringing her arms down from over her head. That's what I did, and it worked."

"But he caught you anyway."

"He had night-vision goggles. He followed me from the highway and nailed me later when I showed up on

Kitt Peak Road. I knew Carlos and Paul were dead by then, and I thought he was going to shoot me, too. He fired one shot just to scare me. He asked about the peanut butter. I told him I left it in a bag on your porch, but by the time we got there, it was gone. You must have already taken it inside. He had to wait awhile before he could get it, and he told me that if it wasn't there, I was dead. But I never thought he'd take you, Gabe. Never."

Even in the dark, working with a freed right hand was incredibly easier than what he had done before. Soon Tim's other hand was loose as well.

"Well, he did," Gabe said. "And just because he has the diamonds doesn't mean he won't kill us anyway."

"What are we going to do?"

"Henry never thought we'd be able to get loose from the tape, but we did. Now we need to find a way to keep him from killing us."

"He has guns," Tim objected. "All we have is a stupid little knife."

"Then we'll need to make that knife work for us." When Gabe heard those determined words come out of his mouth, he wondered where they had come from. The person speaking them sounded brave, and if there was one thing Gabe Ortiz knew about himself, it was that he wasn't brave.

AFTER I FINISHED going through Amanda Wasser's digital files, I sat there for a while longer and thought about them. The first order of business, of course, would be to reinterview Calliope Horn. I still have the last phone book the telephone company sent out. It's so out-of-date now that it's close to being an antique. A check of that showed no listing for Calliope Horn. That was hardly surprising. The Kenneth Myers homicide was twenty-five years earlier. A lot can happen in that amount of time.

Had I still been part of the S.H.I.T., I would have had access to any number of public and private databases and could have used those to track Calliope Horn down on my own. That door was now permanently closed—officially that is. Unofficially, I still had a single ace up my sleeve: my old pal Todd Hatcher.

Todd is a smart guy, a forensic economist. They're the kind of people who look into small things and spot coming trends. One of my first interactions with him had come about when he showed up on the attorney general's doorstep with a dissertation in hand. The paper laid out the long-term adverse financial implications an aging prison population would have on the state budget. I had it on good authority that Todd still had access to all those highly sensitive databases that were now closed to me. Todd is also your basic IT genius. In fact, he's the one who had used off-the-books methods to locate a madman's cell phone, thus allowing me to save Mel Soames's life mere weeks earlier.

This wasn't quite that pressing an issue, but with Mel still out of town, I hoped Todd could help me find Calliope Horn in a timely enough fashion that I could have my interview with her out of the way before Mel came home.

I called Todd and passed along my request. Next I dialed Brandon Walker. When he answered, I could hear the clatter of dishes and the sounds of people talking in the background. "Beaumont here," I told him. "Is this a bad time?"

"No, I missed lunch, so I stopped off for an early dinner, but I'm done now. Did anything jump out at you?"

"At the time of the initial investigation here, detectives spoke to Kenneth Myers's girlfriend, Calliope Horn. She indicated that when she last saw him, he was on his way to Arizona for some reason and that he expected to come home with a sum of money from an undisclosed source—enough money to get them moved out of a homeless camp and back on their feet."

"A score of some kind, maybe?" Brandon asked.

"A score with a woman involved."

"What woman?"

"Not sure," I said. "Calliope didn't have a name, but she suspected it might have been an old girlfriend from Arizona. Kenneth apparently was seen in the company of an unidentified woman here in Seattle shortly before he disappeared. I've got someone looking for Calliope right now. If I can interview her tomorrow, I will.

"Since Lassiter was already in prison, he can't be responsible for Ken's death, but he might have some idea of who was."

"Lassiter pointed me in the direction of someone named Ava," Brandon said, "Ava Martin Hanover Richland. She was John's girlfriend at the time of the homicide, and she also testified against Lassiter at both trials. I know she palled around with Ken, too."

"That's a time-honored way to keep the cops from looking at you," I told him. "You do everything you can to point the finger at somebody else."

"So if you can manage to track down that old girlfriend . . ."

"Calliope," I supplied.

"Ask her if she ever heard Kenneth Mangum Myers mention Ava Martin by name."

"Will do," I said. "I'll have Todd, a friend of mine who's a whiz at data mining, look into Ava's history as well. Could you give me that string of names again?"

While Brandon was repeating them, there was an audible blip in the line. "Just a sec," he said. "I have another call coming in. Can you hang on?"

"Sure." While he was off the line, I made a note of the list of names. One of the things I've learned from Todd Hatcher is that the Internet is no respecter of state lines. Your name is your name. A hit can come from any corner of the country—or of the world, for that matter.

After the better part of a minute, Walker came back on the line. "That was Warden Huffman from the state pen," he said.

His voice was different. I could tell at once that something was wrong.

"What's up?"

"There was a 'disturbance' at the prison a while ago. The guards controlled the situation eventually, and the prison is back under lockdown. Trouble is, two people are dead in the incident, and John Lassiter was severely wounded. He's in critical condition and has been air-lifted to a trauma center in Mesa."

"Somebody tried to take him out the same day you stop by to visit?" I asked. "That doesn't sound like a coincidence."

"Not to me, either," Brandon said. "Anyway, I need to go tell Amanda. I asked the warden if anyone had been sent to notify her. Turns out he didn't even know she existed. She isn't on Lassiter's official next-of-kin list."

"You'll go see her?" I asked.

"I will," he said. "It's the right thing to do."

And that's when I knew Ralph Ames wasn't wrong about Brandon Walker. A lot of people I know—especially guys like Paul Kramer—do their best to avoid having to deal with families of victims. Walker had just volunteered to break some awful news to a family member when it wasn't his job.

"Good luck with that," I said, and meant it. "In the meantime, I'll get cracking on locating Calliope Horn. I'll also have Todd look into this Ava person. It sounds to me as though TLC has just stumbled on a hornets' nest."

CHAPTER 22

The White-Winged Doves took Owl to the place and showed him the sleeping girl, but Evil Giantess was awake and on guard. Once night came, Ho'ok O'oks went to sleep. That was when Owl returned. He flew softly back and forth over Shining Falls, who still lay sleeping with Little White Feather crushed in her hand.

Very gently, Owl fanned Shining Falls with his wings, and slowly—very slowly—Shining Falls's eyes opened. And this is why, nawoj, *even to this day, when someone is asleep and cannot wake up, the Elders—Kekelimai—fan the sleeping one with owl feathers.*

"I'M THIRSTY," TIM moaned in the darkness. "I'm thirsty and hungry and scared. We're going to die."

Gabe was hungry and thirsty, too, but there was no point in talking about it. He had done his best to explore their prison. He had located the ventilation holes that he had known had to be there. They allowed air in but no light. And he had found the seam where the lid closed over them. He had been able to ease the knife blade along it until he encountered what he supposed was a metal hasp. He withdrew the blade as soon as it touched something hard. The knife was their only weapon, and he didn't want to damage it. He slipped it into his pocket. As he did so, his fingers encountered the four diamonds that he had put there hours ago—long before this endless time in the darkness. Gabe couldn't see them, of course, but just having the stones in his hand somehow made him feel better.

"We're not going to die," he declared firmly with a confidence he didn't exactly feel. "We're not going to."

"I could just as well die," Tim went on. "What'll happen to me if I live? My mom is sick. My dad is dead, and so are Carlos and Paul. Max is still alive, but he's in prison. I'll probably end up in foster care somewhere."

Tim's voice sounded funny—like his tongue was thick, like he was mumbling rather than talking.

"What about your aunt and uncle?" Gabe asked. "Couldn't you go live with them?"

"I don't like them," Tim said. "And they have too many little kids. I'd end up being their babysitter."

Moving restlessly in the darkness, Tim's hand came in contact with the back of Gabe's fist. Tim's fingers were hot to the touch, as though he was burning up with a fever. That's when Gabe realized Tim wasn't just thirsty—he was dehydrated, and maybe Tim's assessment was right. If Henry Rojas didn't come back for them soon, Tim might die after all.

Suddenly, without knowing how it happened, Gabe was back in one of those hospital rooms. He had gone to visit an old, old woman, Mrs. Lopez. She was lying in the bed, restless and moaning. The sides of the bed had been put up to keep her from falling. Gabe had reached out to touch her hand and had known in that moment that she was going to die, that this was the last time he would see her.

How had he known that? Gabe wondered. How had he understood Death was coming?

Holding his breath, he reached out now and sought Tim's hand once more. The skin was hot to the touch, but the sense of foreboding and dread Gabe had felt in Mrs. Lopez's hospital room didn't descend on him. If Tim was dying, it wasn't happening right now. It wasn't happening yet.

Then, something else came back to Gabe from that same long-ago hospital room. He had sat down on the floor beside Mrs. Lopez's bed, close enough that her hand could touch the back of his head through the bed rails. Gabe had sung to her that day, a healing song whose words he could no longer remember. What he did remember was that as he sang she had quieted. She had stopped thrashing in the bed, had stopped moaning. He had sung the song four times—for all of nature goes in fours—and when the song was finished and he left the room, she was sleeping peacefully.

Maybe that was what was needed right now—a healing song that would let Tim José fall asleep so he wouldn't notice how slowly time was passing in the stifling darkness, so he would forget how thirsty he was.

Without knowing where the words came from—perhaps from the four stones clutched in his hand—Gabe Ortiz began to sing.

We are here, Elder Brother, two boys in a box.
We are alone in the dark, Spirit of Goodness,

Hungry and thirsty and asking for help.
The man who put us here is not a good man.
He pretends to be good, but he is not.
There is something in him that is evil,
I'itoi, something in him that is bad.
Help us to know what to do, Elder Brother.
Help us to know what to do.

You have given us a weapon, Elder Brother,
A weapon that the bad man didn't see.
The weapon was a gift, a knife, that let us
Cut our bonds, and now we wait,
Wait for that evil man to return. When he does
Help us fight him, Elder Brother,
Help us fight him, that we may live.
We are two boys in a box who need your help,
Elder Brother, two boys who need your help.

Gabe sang the song through four times, and by the time he was done, two things had happened. Tim had fallen asleep, and Gabe himself no longer felt thirsty.

TODD HATCHER WAS good to his word. Within twenty minutes of my handing him the joint Calliope Horn/Ava Martin problem, he was back on the phone. "I found her," he said. "Her name is Calliope Horn-Grover now—Reverend Calliope Horn-Grover. She and her husband, the Reverend Dale Grover, are partners in an outfit called Pastoral Outreach. It specializes in ministering to homeless shelters throughout the Seattle area."

Having just read through the Danielson/Horn

interview, I was impressed that Calliope had somehow made good on her ambitions of becoming a minister to the homeless. Good for her!

"Any idea where they live?"

"Probably only blocks from you," Todd said. "Their address is on Elliott. I have a phone number if you want it."

"Of course I want it." He read off the number, and I jotted it down. "Any luck on Ava?"

"One problem at a time," Todd admonished. "And don't expect miracles."

Duly chastened, I dialed the number he had given me without any idea of what I'd say when someone answered. After all, I wasn't with Special Homicide anymore, and I wasn't with Seattle PD, either. For the first time in decades, I was operating entirely on my own.

"I'm looking for Reverend Calliope Horn-Grover," I said when a woman answered.

"Calliope?" she said. "Yes, that would be me. Who's calling, please?"

"My name is J. P. Beaumont. I've been asked to look into the death of an acquaintance of yours, and I wondered if you could spare me a few minutes."

"Which acquaintance?"

That wasn't such a surprising question. People die in homeless shelters all the time. They live outside in all kinds of weather and often in less than sanitary conditions. I knew from reading the papers that over the previous winter several of Seattle's homeless had fallen victim to cold weather, especially during an unexpectedly frigid cold snap that had roared through western Washington the weekend after Thanksgiving.

"His name was Kenneth Mangum, although I believe you knew him as Kenneth Myers," I added. "My understanding is that the two of you were close at one time."

Her sharp intake of breath told me my assumption wasn't wrong. When she said nothing, I continued, "We could talk on the phone, or I could drop by your home or office. Your address is listed as being on Elliott. My condo is only a few blocks away from there. It's your call."

"Why talk to me?" Calliope asked. "Kenny's homicide has gone unsolved all these years. Why is someone looking into his death now?"

"Because someone who was once a friend of Mr. Myers was viciously attacked during a prison riot earlier today. We're trying to figure out if there's any possible connection between today's attack and the previous homicide."

"What friend?" Calliope asked.

"A guy named Lassiter."

"Big Bad John Lassiter?" she asked.

Even after so much time, Calliope recognized the name right off and without any prompting from me. Sue Danielson had never asked about any connection between the dead man and John Lassiter because, at the time of that interview, there had been no known link between them. Still, when Sue had inquired about Ken's friends, why hadn't John Lassiter's name come up? That's when I realized Sue had asked about Ken's girlfriends but not about his male friends.

"That would be the one," I said.

"And he was attacked?"

"Yes, in prison. He's serving time down in Arizona."

"When did this attack happen?"

"As I said, earlier today."

"Are you a cop?" Calliope asked.

"Used to be," I answered, "but not anymore."

"What's your connection to all this?"

Tenuous at best, I thought, but I didn't want to go into any of the details, not right then. "I'm working in conjunction with a group called The Last Chance—TLC. They specialize in solving cold cases."

"Ken's case is cold, all right," Calliope said with a sigh. "I suppose you're welcome to stop by here if you like, but I don't see how I'll be able to help. And my husband and I have a meeting to go to at seven. We're in the Lofts on Elliott."

"I have the address," I said.

"There's visitor parking in the garage beneath the building."

I knew that, too. The building probably wasn't more than ten blocks away from Belltown Terrace. Getting there on foot would have been easy because the going part was all downhill. Coming back up one of those glacial ridges to return to the Denny Regrade would have been hell, though. Since Mel wasn't there to insist I do otherwise, I drove.

When you live in downtown Seattle, you tend to keep an eye on nearby real estate, if for no other reason than worrying about some building sprouting up and wrecking your view. Mel and I had watched the transformation of a former lowbrow manufacturing plant into an upscale residential property called the Lofts. Thanks to a long succession of bumbling developers, the building had gone through some tough times. Still, buildings in downtown Seattle that come with any kind of parking, and most especially guest parking, don't come cheap. As I parked in the Lofts underground garage and walked toward the security phone by the elevator lobby, I couldn't help but think that Calliope Horn had come a long way from living in a makeshift tarp-covered homeless camp decades earlier.

When I called, a male voice answered and directed me to come to apartment number 502. A glance at the elevator control panel told me that floor number five was the top floor, which meant their unit was also a penthouse. Yes, Calliope Horn had indeed come a very long way.

When I rang the bell, the door was opened by a man in a wheelchair. That shouldn't have surprised me, since the door came equipped with two peepholes—one at the regular height and one a couple of feet lower. One half of the man's face drooped, but he gave me a welcoming smile with the side that still worked, and the grip of his handshake was warm and welcoming.

"Mr. Beaumont?"

I nodded. Having someone call me "mister" still gives me pause. For the greater part of my life, the word "Detective" was an integral part of my name. I still miss it, although I expect I'll get over it one of these days.

"I'm Dale Grover," the man said, "Callie's husband. Come on in." Using a joystick on the arm of his chair, he backed effortlessly out of the way and led me into what turned out to be an impeccably decorated room. There were no rugs on the polished hardwood floor, probably to accommodate the wheelchair. The furnishings were clean-lined and sleek, but comfortable. The place was modern without being either ostentatious or obnoxious. Dale parked his chair next to the far end of a black leather sofa and motioned for me to sit down.

"I'm afraid Callie's just been called to the phone in the office next door. She'll join us in a couple of minutes. Can I get you something to drink?"

"No, thanks," I told him. "I'm fine."

"She mentioned that you were coming," Dale continued. "I believe this has something to do with an old beau of hers, Kenneth."

"Did you know him?" I asked.

"Nope," Dale answered. "Kenny was long before my time. Callie and I met in seminary. We were both starting over. I'd had a stroke in the course of routine surgery—an appendectomy, for Pete's sake. It was supposed to be in and out. Didn't work out that way and I ended up having a stroke. When my wife at the time learned that I'd be stuck in a wheelchair for the rest of my life, she declined to hang around. She told me she wasn't prepared to spend the rest of her life looking after a cripple.

"Before the stroke, I had been a high school football coach. I'd always prided myself on being physically fit and setting a good example for my players. You know what they say, 'Pride goeth before the fall.' Once I was stuck in this, I just couldn't see myself coaching from the sidelines."

"Had to be tough," I offered.

Grover gave me another lopsided grin. "Not really. God works in mysterious ways. Sometimes you have to be hit smack over the head for Him to get your attention. At least, that's how it was for me. Once He did, I could see only one way forward. I decided to ride my wheelchair into the ministry. That's where Callie and I met. She'd had her own personal struggles—including losing Kenny, the guy she had thought was the love of her life. In a way, we met when we were both starting over from square one."

Glancing around the spacious room, I thought that together they'd done a remarkable job of starting over.

"Callie's calling was to minister to the homeless," he resumed. "Since we were teaming up, I decided to make her mission my mission. Fortunately, I had a sizable malpractice settlement from both the hospital and anesthesiologist. That gave us a bit of a nest egg. We still have a fair amount of it. That's important, since most of our parishioners are dead broke. When it comes to tithing, ten percent of nothing is still nothing. We got into this place during an economic downturn and were able to combine two units into one so we'd have some separation from work and home. Cuts way down on the commute."

I had already done a quick calculation on the size of that nest egg. Knowing it had been large enough to allow them to purchase and remodel two units rather than one, I revised my estimate upward.

A pocket door opened at the far end of the combination living room/dining room. A woman stepped through and carefully closed the door behind her. Before my talk with Dale Grover, I had formed a mental image of Calliope Horn-Grover that turned out to be completely wrong. She was a short but formidable-looking woman dressed in a severe black pantsuit topped by a white clerical collar. Her no-nonsense square-toed oxfords looked as though they had been made to kick butt. Her plain face, devoid of makeup, was framed by a wild mane of naturally graying hair. She struck me as a fifty-something woman comfortably at ease with her life, her looks, and her circumstances.

Like her husband, Reverend Horn-Grover greeted me with a genuine smile and a warm handshake.

"I'm Callie," she said. "Sorry to keep you waiting." Then, turning her attention on her husband, she asked, "Did you offer our guest any refreshments?"

"I did," Dale said. "He turned me down."

"Very well then, Mr. Beaumont," she said, taking a seat on the far end of my sofa. "What can I do for you?"

"I just finished reading through the transcripts of the interview you did with Detective Sue Danielson."

"That was a long time ago."

"Yes, it was," I agreed. "But when I mentioned John Lassiter's name on the phone earlier, you recognized it immediately."

"Yes, I did. Kenny considered John Lassiter to be a good friend. He felt Lassiter's imprisonment was a complete miscarriage of justice."

"But you never reached out to Mr. Lassiter?"

Callie sighed and shook her head. "No, I didn't. At first when I thought Kenny had just gone back to Arizona and forgotten about me, I refused to even think about his friends, much less have anything to do with them. Once I learned he was dead—had been dead right here in Seattle for years rather than taking off for Arizona—I was too ashamed. And then . . ."

Shrugging, she broke off.

"And then what?" I prodded.

"Big Bad John was Kenny's friend, not mine. When I learned Kenny had lied to me about everything—including his last name—it seemed likely to me that he might have lied to me about John Lassiter as well. For all I know, Kenny might have been involved in whatever it was that put Lassiter in prison in the first place. Dale and I talked it over and decided the best thing to do was let sleeping dogs lie. And that's what we did. I'm sorry to hear that the man has been seriously injured, though. We'll certainly pray for him."

"You could just as well go ahead and tell him the rest of it," Dale Grover said.

"The rest of what?" I asked.

Calliope took a deep breath. "Dale and I have had twenty-plus years to think about this and talk about it, too," she said. "He came up with a theory that I'd never considered."

"What's that?"

"The way Ken talked about John Lassiter, it was almost as though he blamed himself that his friend was rotting away in prison. A couple of times he said things to me about going back and 'making it right.' But then, almost overnight, he started talking about our having some kind of a big payday coming and about our being able to move into an actual apartment. It was like he expected to come into a sum of money—a lot of money."

She paused and looked at her husband as if pleading for assistance.

"What Callie is trying to say," Dale Grover said, "is we think there's a good chance Kenneth knew who killed Amos Warren. As for that expected payday?"

I could see the pieces falling into place. "Blackmail?" I asked.

Calliope Horn-Grover nodded as a pair of tears slid down her weathered cheeks. "Yes," she said softly. "That's what I think now, too. He knew something about what happened and was maybe even involved in it, and that's where the money would have come from—blackmail."

That's the moment I realized why Calliope was really weeping. It wasn't just because she had lost the "love of her life." It was worse than that. She had always thought of Kenny Myers as the one who got away. Even though he had left her, she had still thought of him as a "good guy" in her interview with Sue Danielson. Now, though, she was faced with the grim possibility that almost none of that was true. And if Kenneth Mangum/Myers had been involved in some kind of blackmail scheme, there was also a chance that he had been involved in something much worse—the murder of Amos Warren.

CHAPTER 23

Speaking softly, Owl told Shining Falls to wake up and follow him. When she tried, Owl could see that she was no longer all asleep, as she had been, but she was not yet fully awake, either.

Evil Giantess had used some red feathers when she put Shining Falls to sleep, and because Owl had no red feathers, he could not bring her completely awake. Owl decided that he would take Shining Falls home with him until he could find some red feathers.

Slowly the girl followed Owl until they came to a water hole surrounded by large rocks. When Shining Falls stepped on one of those rocks, it made a sound. Owl tried to call out a warning, but it was too late. Evil Giantess had heard the noise, and she was awake. Her hair spread out like an evil cloud, and Owl's feet got tangled in her hair. While Owl struggled to get free, Shining Falls fell into the water.

IT HAD BEEN years since Ava Martin Hanover Richland had actually cleaned a house. She had people to do that detestable chore just as she had people to carry out her other orders. That afternoon she did the work herself, however, and she did a thorough job of it, too. Looking up from her vacuuming, she peeled back the top of her latex glove and studied her watch. In an hour or so, John Lassiter would be a thing of the past. An hour or so after that Henry Rojas would be gone as well.

Nodding to herself, Ava went back to work. She had always been careful to keep her life entirely separate from Jane Dobson's, and in that regard, she was nothing if not a chip off the old block. Ava had been twelve years old when her mother discovered, quite by accident, that her husband, Ava's father, was a bigamist with another whole family living in Eloy. A subsequent investigation revealed that there was yet a third family living in Deming, New Mexico.

Ava's father was a long-haul trucker, and he'd been able to keep all the balls in the air for quite some time until a gallbladder attack unexpectedly landed him in the hospital and put him out of commission for a number of weeks—long enough for the other two families to come looking for him. Ava had watched the unfolding drama from the sidelines. She had never been especially fond of her mother, so she'd had scant sympathy for the woman. What had really fascinated her was how her father had managed to pull off the whole escapade. He'd created separate identities complete with checking accounts and social security numbers—one for each family, paying for it by working part-time jobs with three different trucking companies.

That was all a lot easier to do back in the day before computers and cell phones and in-car navigation systems. Ava was careful. She had never brought her cell phone here, and she'd never used her GPS to come to Jane Dobson's house, either. There might be a trace of her travels lingering somewhere in the Mercedes's black box, but she was confident by now her once shiny luxury vehicle had disappeared into some faraway, dusty spot or else it had been reduced to dozens or perhaps hundreds of anonymous pieces.

But that didn't mean there weren't traces of her lingering in the house, and once someone found Henry's body here—however long that took—the cops would be all over the place searching for traces of Jane Dobson. By erasing Jane's presence, Ava deleted her own as well, and that was the reason for her frenetic but very thorough job of house-cleaning. She vacuumed everything. She made sure there were no traces of hair left in any of the sinks, sending a batch of hair-cleaning Liquid-Plumr down the drains.

She wiped down everything, polishing away fingerprints from every conceivable surface—light switches, cabinets, appliances, furniture, silverware, dishes, canned goods in the cabinets, and frozen food in the fridge. From the lack of fingerprints, the cops would be able to tell at once that Jane Dobson had been a crook. What they wouldn't be able to tell was that Jane Dobson and Ava Richland were one and the same.

And once the house was clean, all Ava had to do was wait.

•

WHEN I LEFT the Grovers' condo, I could hardly wait to get back down to my car. I found I had a signal on the top floor of the parking garage, and I called Brandon Walker back immediately.

"Tell me about Amos Warren. Refresh me on the timeline."

"In the spring of 1970, he went out on one of his prospecting/scavenging jaunts in the desert. Weeks later, his vehicle turns up at Tucson International Airport. Ten years after that, his remains are found in the desert twenty miles from the airport."

"That means that the killer must have had an accomplice," I said. "Assuming the victim's vehicle was at the crime scene originally, someone had to help transport it to the spot where it was found."

"We always assumed there was an accomplice," Brandon said, "but we could never get any traction when it came to finding out who it was."

"I think I may know," I told him. "The dead guy up here."

"Ken Mangum?"

"I just talked to Kenneth's old girlfriend, Calliope Horn. Shortly before he disappeared, he told her he was going to take a trip to Arizona and that he expected to come back with an armload of money. Then, the very day he disappeared, Ken was seen in the company of a well-dressed woman—a stranger no one up here had ever seen before. Calliope thought it might be an old girlfriend, and maybe that's true. But what if it's more than that? What if Ken was somehow involved in Amos Warren's death? Or maybe the woman was the one who committed the murder, and Kenneth Mangum/Myers either knew about it or figured it out. What if that windfall he was expecting had something to do with blackmail?"

"That would make sense," Brandon said. "When I talked to Lassiter earlier today, his first suggestion was Ava Martin Hanover Richland. Lassiter's daughter,

Amanda, said the same thing. She tried to point the JFA folks in Ava's direction, but they weren't interested."

"Would blackmail have worked on Ava?" I asked. "Would she have been a likely target?"

"Absolutely. By the time Amos Warren's remains surfaced, Ava Martin had reinvented herself and moved up in the world. She would have had a lot to lose, especially when Lassiter's second trial was about to get under way and even more so now."

Excitement bubbled in Brandon Walker's voice and in mine as well. We were a pair of old hounds who had just caught a scent. It was a very faint scent and one that might not pan out, but it was still there, and we were on it.

"Is there any way to discover if the lady in question was in the Seattle area in the early part of May of 1983?" Walker asked.

"Doesn't seem likely," I answered.

"Maybe I should go pay her a call. Ava and her most recent husband have a house somewhere here in Tucson. The problem is, I don't have an address."

"Let's see what Todd Hatcher can do in that regard. Is it all right if I give him your number?"

"Sure," Brandon said. "Whatever works."

IT WAS LANI'S weekend off, but after her meeting with Lorraine José, she didn't go back home. Instead she retreated into her office at the hospital and closed the door. Before leaving the house to go meet with the FBI agents at the café, she had opened her medicine basket and dropped her divining crystals into the pocket of her lab coat. She put the list containing the José brothers' phone numbers face up on her desk, then she brought out the crystals. She went down the list, one at a time, studying the blurry numbers through the crystals, but that told her nothing. No wavering images appeared in her mind's eye. She had attempted to explain to Gabe how viewing things through the crystals often helped her see things in another light. This time that didn't happen.

Lani's sense of hopelessness and despair deepened. Tim José was most likely lost, she realized. That meant there was a good chance Gabe was lost, too. And there was nothing—not one thing—she could do about it.

Sitting at her desk, Lani stared down at the crystals with her chin propped in her hands. That was when her lack of sleep from the night before finally caught up with her. She dozed off only to be awakened later by a light tap on the door. Jarred awake, Lani looked up to see Dan poke his head inside.

"There you are," he said. "I saw your car on the way past."

"On the way past," Lani echoed. "Where are you going and where are the kids?"

"I called Mrs. Hendricks to come look after them. The FBI got a hit on Tim's cell. The last time it pinged was somewhere out near the airport. Law and Order is calling for volunteers to come search. Hulk and I are on our way there now."

Lani breathed a sigh of relief. The FBI had done its job after all. She scrambled to her feet. "I'll come with you," she said, reaching for her purse.

Dan gave her an appraising look. "Are you sure? You look beat. Shouldn't you have a lie-down?"

"No," she said. "I'll come, too. Has anyone told Lorraine José what's going on?"

"I'm not sure, but I doubt it."

"I'll go tell her, then I'll come help."

"Suit yourself."

Lani hurried into the convalescent wing just in time to see Lorraine José answer a call on her cell phone. Lorraine listened briefly, then, as her face went pale with shock, she dropped the phone, letting it crash onto the tiled floor.

"What is it?" Lani asked, hurrying toward the distraught woman. "What's wrong? Did they find Tim?"

Anguish flooded Lorraine's face. "It's Max," she whispered. "That was Father O'Reilly calling from Florence. There was a riot in the prison a little while ago. Max is dead."

"Dead?" Lani repeated. "How can that be?"

Lorraine shook her head hopelessly. "I don't know. How is it possible that I've lost all my boys, even Tim, on the same day?"

"People are still looking for Tim," Lani said, hoping she sounded more reassuring than she felt. "With any kind of luck, they'll find him."

"Would you ask I'itoi for me?" Lorraine asked. "Please?"

It wasn't a request Lani could ignore. She had slipped her divining crystals back into the pocket of her lab coat as she left her office. Now, sitting on the chair next to Lorraine José's bed, Lani took out the stones, gripped them tightly in her hand, and began to sing. As the song filled the room, Lani was no longer Dr. Pardee. She was Medicine Woman, filled with the spirit of Mualig Siakam, Forever Spinning. Together they were singing for power and singing for all of them—for Tim José and Gabe Ortiz, for Delia and

Leo Ortiz, for Lorraine José, and for the whole community. As Lani sang, she hoped in her heart of hearts that Elder Brother was listening.

AMANDA WASSER LISTENED in subdued silence when Brandon Walker delivered his news about the prison riot.

"This is all my fault," she said when he finished.

"Your fault," Brandon echoed. "How so?"

"You went to see my father at my instigation. A few hours later someone comes after him, killing two people and wounding another? This can't be a coincidence."

"I'm sure you're right about that," Brandon agreed. "There's bound to be a connection. That can only mean that reopening your father's case constitutes a threat to someone."

"Who?"

"Who indeed? There's no statute of limitations on homicide, Amanda. If John Lassiter didn't kill Amos Warren, someone else did, and that killer has gotten away with murder all this time. Whoever did it may be worried that their luck is about to run out."

"You believe my father, then?" Amanda asked. "You believe he didn't do it?"

Brandon nodded. "I do," he said.

"So who's the killer?" Amanda asked.

"You told me earlier that you thought Ava Martin needed looking into. When I asked John Lassiter straight out, 'If you didn't kill Amos, who did?' that was his answer, too—'Ava Martin.'"

"I tried to get JFA to take a look at her," Amanda said. "They were so focused on the prosecutorial misconduct issue that they saw no need to go any further."

"We do," Brandon told her. "In fact, we already are."

"Good," she said. "In the meantime, I need to pack up and get going."

"Going where?"

"To Mesa, where else?" she said. "Since I'm the one who put my father in that hospital, I'm going to go there to see him whether he likes it or not."

"You do know why John Lassiter refuses to see you, don't you?" Brandon asked.

Amanda had turned her scooter and was on her way to the bedroom. She paused and turned back to Brandon. "Why?"

"Because he wants to clear his name first."

Amanda's eyes filled with tears. "Don't you understand? As far as I'm concerned, his name was cleared a long time ago."

BRANDON WAS JUST leaving Amanda Wasser's driveway when J. P. Beaumont's friend Todd called to give him Ava Richland's address. It was somewhere in the far reaches of Tucson's Ventana Canyon, and Brandon was making his way there when his phone rang again.

"Warden Huffman," the caller said when Brandon answered. "This is not an official call, by the way, but I'm hoping you might be able to help us get ahead of this thing."

"In what way?"

"I'm sitting here studying the surveillance tapes," Huffman said. "Over the years I've been around plenty of prison riots. This one simply doesn't add up. I can tell that the action in the center of the room was clearly designed to pull attention away from what was happening in the far corner, which turned out to be a well-organized hit on two individuals."

"John Lassiter and who else?"

"The other victim was a young guy from Sells, Max José. A priest showed up in the middle of all the mess, asking to see Max and saying that he had come, at Max's mother's request, to let him know that his two younger brothers had been murdered near Sells earlier today and that his youngest brother is missing."

"Max is dead now, too?" Brandon demanded. "Are you kidding?"

"Unfortunately not, so here's my question. Can you tell me if there's any connection between the José family out in Sells and John Lassiter?"

"Not right off, Warden Huffman," Brandon answered. "But if I come up with one, I'll let you know."

The GPS led Brandon to a house perched on the mountainside high above the rest of the city. The spectacular window-lined structure seemed to wrap itself around the contours of the mountain. A wrought-iron gate at the end of the driveway was open. He was about to turn in when an aid car, lights ablaze, came tearing down the drive. Brandon pulled aside to let it pass.

When he arrived at the front of the house, a fire truck was just departing. A woman in what appeared to be hospital scrubs stood on the front verandah, wringing her hands. Brandon got out of the Escalade and walked toward her. She turned on him. "Who are you?"

"My name is Brandon Walker," he said. "I'm a friend of the family. I was hoping to speak to Mrs. Richland."

"Mrs. Richland isn't here. That was her husband in the ambulance. He had another stroke. They're taking him to TMC. I've been trying to reach Mrs. Richland to let her know what's going on, but she isn't answering her phone. She's probably out in the middle of the desert somewhere where there's no signal."

"Do you know where she was headed?"

"Their condo in San Carlos, down in Mexico," the nurse answered. "I tried calling there, too. That was strange. When I spoke to the housekeeper, she had no idea Mrs. Richland was coming there today."

"What kind of car does she drive?" Brandon asked.

"A black Mercedes S550."

"Did you notify the authorities in Mexico and ask them to look for her?"

"Not yet. Do you think I should?"

"How bad off is her husband?"

The nurse bit her lip. "Pretty bad," she answered.

"In that case," Brandon said, "if I were you, I'd make that call."

CHAPTER 24

Now Shining Falls, who was neither all asleep nor all awake, lay in a place where the water was very deep. She was not able to move much, but she still held Little White Feather tightly in her hand.

Evil Giantess came to look for the girl, but Owl was free. His feet were no longer tangled in her hair. Owl spread his wings over the water and made it very dark so Evil Giantess could not see Shining Falls lying beneath it.

Finally Evil Giantess gave up and went away.

The next morning the White-Winged Doves went to the village and called and called. At last Shining Falls's mother heard them call and followed them to the big water hole, which is always full of water. It was daytime when they arrived, so Owl was asleep.

The mother of Shining Falls looked everywhere for her child but could not find her. She could not understand why the doves had brought her there.

HENRY ROJAS'S SHIFT that day was pure agony, primarily because he'd had so little sleep the night before. A couple of times during those endless hours, he had tucked himself into out-of-the-way spots in hopes of grabbing a power nap, but sleep wouldn't come. As soon as he tried closing his eyes, images of those two bullet-ridden bodies danced in his head. The only thing that made them disappear was reopening his eyes.

Finally off work, Henry was tired to the bone, far too weary to drive straight into town. He thought about stopping by the garage to check on things but nixed that idea immediately. Instead, he went home to shower—and to think. With Lucy over at the hospital working the night shift, he stood under the shower for a good long time.

He had connected with Jane Dobson years earlier through somebody who knew somebody who knew somebody else. He met with her periodically or stopped by the house to drop off goods and pick up cash. The woman lived in a nondescript house in a marginal neighborhood. Nevertheless, she seemed to have more money than God. She struck him as a sweet little old lady with silver hair who wore colorful dresses, got around with the aid of a walker, and depended on a portable oxygen tank. How was it possible for someone who looked so harmless to be so ruthless? Yes, the José brothers knew too much and they had to go, but still, the idea that Jane had ordered their deaths without so much as blinking an eye came as a shock.

Henry had always let Jane think she was the only game in town. That wasn't entirely true. He had developed a second thriving side business specializing in smuggled prescription drugs. Occasionally, when the meds arrived in his hands before they could be passed along to the buyer, he kept them stored in a safe in his garage out at the airport, along with a growing stash of greenbacks and a number of weapons. He knew that if anyone ever took a close look at the guns, they would lead straight back to what the newspapers were always referring to as "Fast and Furious weapons."

One of the benefits of being on the Border Patrol's front lines, especially as a patrol supervisor, meant that Henry knew what was going on and could make the best of it. He was the one who posted patrol schedules, so it was easy for him to work around them. He also didn't believe for a minute that he was the only member of the Border Patrol who earned way more money on the side than he did on the up and up.

It had been a piece of extreme good fortune that, on the night Jane ordered him to take the José boys out, he'd had his latest shipment of midazolam stashed in his safe awaiting delivery the next time he drove up to Phoenix. A year or so earlier, when he'd delivered his first load of that to a well-heeled customer up north, he'd asked Lucy, his wife, who was also an L.P.N., about it. She'd answered his question without having any idea why he was asking, but that was how he knew the medication's primary use was in paralyzing patients prior to surgery. Henry had a feeling that the guy who bought it from him in boxes containing a dozen vials of the stuff was using it for something a lot more interesting than prepping surgery patients.

The point was, Henry had been in possession of a supply of the medication when he'd needed it most. And because Lucy was a diabetic and on insulin, he'd had easy access to a supply of syringes as well. Once he had collected those, he was good to go.

First he'd set up a meeting with Carlos, assuring him that Jane had agreed to come through with the extra cash. Henry had suggested Rattlesnake Skull charco as the site for their meetup because most people on the reservation avoided the spot whenever possible. The two men had been sitting side by side in the cab of Carlos's Jeep Cherokee having a little chat when Henry had plunged the loaded syringe into the man's bare upper arm. Henry had been both amazed and gratified to see how quickly and thoroughly the drug had worked.

By the time it wore off, Henry had Carlos cuffed and secured to a cottonwood sapling growing on the edge of the charco. After that it was just a matter of collecting the other two brothers and bringing them along for the ride. Henry had come to the meeting with one of his stash of unregistered weapons, knowing and dreading the whole time that he might be forced to use it.

Yes, Jane may have ordered him to do it, but Henry had reasons of his own for being willing to. Henry had needed the José brothers gone on his own account, and Gabe Ortiz as well. They all knew who he was and could identify him. Henry couldn't afford to be sent to prison any more than Jane Dobson could.

Henry's real problem with carrying out Jane's order was that, despite all his years in law enforcement, this was the first time he had ever killed someone. He had assured Carlos and Paul that if they'd just tell him where the shipment was, he'd let them go. That had been a lie, of course, but they'd believed him—or at least Paul had. Once Paul spilled the beans and admitted that Timmy had put the shipment somewhere safe, that was it. Henry had covered their faces with grocery bags before stepping back and pulling the trigger. Then, after barfing his guts out, he'd fired again. Carlos and Paul were dead after that first round of bullets hit them. The second volley was just to be sure. After that Henry had gone looking for the kid, who, in all the hubbub, had managed to get loose and make good his escape.

He'd called Jane while he was looking, thinking she'd appreciate having an update. That had backfired. He could tell she was pissed, but so was he. It was easy for her to sit on her lazy ass in Tucson and issue the orders as long as she had Henry working his own butt off to carry them out.

From Henry's point of view, that was what was wrong with this whole arrangement. He was tired of being bossed around, not just by Jane, but by Lucy, too. He was done. He'd give the woman her damned diamonds, pick up his money, and that would be it. He'd take care of Tim and Gabe, of course. That was a must, but after that, Henry was out of there.

Most of the illegal commerce crossing the border was headed north rather than south, but Henry knew people who could and would help transport him and his wad of cash in the other direction. Why work for a living? Why bust his balls herding a Border Patrol SUV all over hell and gone, when he could shuck the whole thing and live like a king in Mexico?

Yes, Henry thought. It was definitely time for him to ride off into the sunset.

Out of the shower, Henry dressed. He was almost out the door when one last thought occurred to him. Jane had promised him a bonus for cleaning up her mess, but what if she considered him just another part of that same mess? What if Jane was planning on cleaning him up, too? That was definitely a possibility. After all, wasn't

Henry as much, if not more, of a threat to Jane than the José brothers had been?

In that case, Henry had best be on guard. He was determined that Jane Dobson wouldn't take him down without a fight. He already had one weapon on him, but when he went to the garage to pick up the diamonds, he'd grab another one as well. If one gun was good, two were better.

Henry wasn't due at Jane's until after dark. Since he still had time to spare, he sat down and made a single phone call to a number in Nogales. The call that would show on his bill would lead to what was ostensibly an aboveboard shipping and expediting company that specialized in cross-border transportation issues. Inside the company, however, were people who handled far more questionable transportation arrangements.

Henry's call was patched through to one of those. These were people Henry dealt with often. It took only a matter of minutes for him to negotiate a deal that included a time, location, and price for having him and his goods carried across the border and deep into the interior of Mexico. Early the next morning, he'd drive out to the Organ Pipe National Monument, park his truck at the appointed spot, lock it, and walk away.

As Henry hung up the phone, he was in a much better frame of mind. Tim José had been locked in the back of the truck for going on twenty hours, Gabe Ortiz for only half that long. Still, without water, they wouldn't last much longer. A few hours of being parked in a black vehicle in direct sunlight would finish them off. Yes, people would know it was Henry's truck, but Henry would be long gone by then. And so would Gabe and Tim. Other than parking the truck, Henry wouldn't have to lift a finger or pull a trigger. That might not be better for the two boys, but it would sure as hell be better for Henry.

WHEN LORRAINE JOSÉ finally fell into an exhausted slumber, Lani made her escape. Out in the hallway she ran into Lucy Rojas. "What are you doing here?" Lucy wanted to know. "Isn't this supposed to be your weekend off?"

"It is," Lani answered, "but Mrs. José needed me. You've heard about her sons?"

Lucy nodded. "It's terrible."

"Yes, it is," Lani agreed, "so if she wakes up and asks for me, call me immediately."

"I will," Lucy said. "Where are you going?"

"There's a group over at the airport searching for Tim José and Gabe Ortiz. I'm going there to help."

"I hope you find them," Lucy said.

"So do I."

Out in the parking lot, Lani hopped into her Ford Fusion and headed for the airport. That was something of a misnomer, however, since the airport in Sells was an airport in name only, one that saw few planes land or take off in the course of a year. These days it was mostly a hangout for teenagers who went there to neck and drink.

Decades earlier the tribal chairman had been a pilot who had kept his own small Cessna there. At the time the airport had consisted of a single landing strip/runway as well as several outbuildings. When the chairman's plane had crashed, killing all on board, the tribe had stopped doing upkeep on the runway. Most of the outbuildings had been repurposed or rented out. One of those was the sturdy metal Quonset hut that Henry Rojas used as a garage and workshop, leasing it from the tribe for a nominal sum.

Even though few planes came and went these days, the airport's metal cattle guard still kept grazing animals from straying onto the property. As Lani approached, she saw a collection of cars scattered along the fence line. Taking a hint from where the other cars were parked, she stopped along the fence line as well. Leo Ortiz's tow truck was pulled up close to the door of a Quonset hut. Then she saw what looked like the flare of something that might have been a blowtorch. She was shading her eyes and squinting in that direction when someone knocked on the window next to her head.

Startled, Lani looked around. Henry Rojas stood just outside. She rolled down the window. "Have they found something?" she asked.

"I'm not sure," he said, "maybe."

She didn't spot the syringe until it was coming through the open window. She tried to dodge away, but Henry caught her wrist with his other hand and held it motionless while the needle bit through the sleeve of her lab coat and plunged into her arm.

"What the hell?" she demanded. "What do you think you're doing?"

Saying nothing, he maintained an iron grip on her wrist until Lani felt a strange lassitude spread through her body. She tried to yell for help, but the people gathered by the Quonset hut were too far away and totally focused on what was going on there.

The next thing Lani knew, she was being shoved

roughly to one side as Henry moved her from the driver's side to the passenger side by lifting her useless legs over the center console.

As the paralysis closed in, her mind stayed focused long enough for her to realize that he'd given her something powerful. Depending on what it was and the dosage involved, she might awaken in as little as half an hour or it could take far longer. And when she did wake up, would she have her wits about her or would she be stuck in some kind of date-rape-drug confusion and fog?

Henry was behind the wheel now. When they reached the highway, he turned the wheel sharply to the left and sped away.

How soon before someone comes looking for me? Lani wondered. *How long before they realize I'm gone?*

A NOISE AWAKENED Gabe—a metallic noise of some kind that meant someone was coming. If it was Henry, Gabe knew he had to be ready, but where was the knife? It was no longer in his fingers and for several desperate seconds, he was afraid he'd lost it. But then he found it again—right where he'd left it—in his pocket.

Tim José lay beside him, burning with fever and still as death. Gabe could hear his friend's shallow breathing, but that was all. In the coming battle, there would be no help from that quarter. It would all be up to Gabe and nobody else. Henry had left the two boys bound and helpless. He had no way of knowing that they were loose. The fact that Gabe was armed and ready to fight was the only element of surprise the boy had on his side.

Flicking the knife open, Gabe gripped it tightly and

willed his cramped muscles to obey him when the time came. That was when he realized that, for the first time in his life, he didn't need anyone else to do the fighting for him. Gabe Ortiz himself was ready to do battle—ready to kill if necessary—if that's what it took to save Tim's life and his own.

For several long seconds, the only sound in the oppressive darkness was the dull hammering of Gabe's own heart. Then he heard something else, someone shouting his name. The sound seemed to come from somewhere far away. When he tried to answer, Gabe was surprised to find that his tongue was swollen. No words came out of his mouth, only a hoarse croak.

The shout came again. In the background Gabe heard the frantic barking of a dog and the wail of a siren.

"Gabe, where the hell are you?" Gabe heard the desperation in his father's voice and tried his best to answer.

"We're here," he said, "right here." But it didn't seem as though anyone outside the box could hear him.

Then, to his immense relief, there was a sudden shaking and rattling as someone opened the tailgate on the truck. And then a dazzling beam appeared in the darkness as light entered through one of the ventilation holes. A moment later, the box itself moved, as though it was being pulled from the bed of the truck and placed on what felt like solid ground.

"I hear you, Gabe. We'll get you out. Hold on. There's a padlock," his father said. "Somebody get me a fucking crowbar."

Gabe almost giggled at that. He had never heard his father say a bad word before—not ever, not once. That was when Gabe remembered. He and Tim had both soiled themselves. He'd grown accustomed to the stink, but what would happen when other people saw them that way? What would they think? Would they point at them and call them babies?

No, he realized. They would not. He and Tim were supposed to be dead, but they hadn't died. It didn't matter how they looked or smelled. They were alive.

As the hasp gave way, Tim stirred beside him. "What's happening?" he mumbled. "Is he coming back?"

Gabe flicked the knife closed and pressed it into his friend's feverish hand. "No," he said. "It's my dad. They found us."

The lid opened. Fresh air and more blinding light flooded their prison. The first face Gabe saw belonged to his father. "Son," he said, reaching for Gabe. "Come on."

"No," Gabe said. His voice was starting to work now. "Get Tim first. He's worse off than I am."

Several willing hands reached into the box and lifted Tim out. A moment later a single pair of strong arms—his father's—grabbed hold of Gabe and lifted him out, too. The next thing he knew, Leo Ortiz was holding his son against his chest, cradling him as though he were a newborn.

"I thought we'd lost you," his father sobbed. "I thought you were gone forever. We thought both of you were."

Gabe had never seen his father cry. "I'm all right, Dad," he said, wiping away his father's tears. "I'm all right."

Just then he caught a glimpse of Tim on a stretcher with a bottle of some kind of fluid attached to his arm. For just a moment, the knowing spirit that had been with him in those long-ago hospital rooms returned to him. In a flash of joy, he realized long before anyone else that Tim José was not going to die.

Someone in the background—Dan Pardee, Gabe

thought—passed him a bottle of water. He took a tiny sip. It tasted wonderful, better than any water had ever tasted before, but his mouth and throat were so parched that at first one sip was all he could manage.

"I'm okay," he told his father again. "And Tim will be okay, too."

Leo took a ragged breath. "Come on, Dan," he said. "Since you and Hulk are the ones who found them, how about if you give us a ride to the hospital?"

Outside with people milling around and still in his father's arms, Gabe was surprised to discover that it was dark—that the flash of light that had seemed so blinding had come from the fluorescent overhead shop lights in the garage. In the fresh air, Gabe could smell himself. The rank odor was almost overpowering. He was ashamed when his father placed him in the back of Dan's Explorer and crawled in after him.

A woman's face appeared in the window next to Leo. She pounded on the glass and held up a badge. She wasn't someone Gabe recognized, but since her badge said FBI, that wasn't too surprising.

"We need to speak to him," she demanded.

"After," Leo Ortiz said firmly through the still closed window. With that, Dan hit the gas pedal, and they sped away.

They arrived at the hospital entrance less than two minutes later. Gabe more than half expected that Lani would come out to meet them. When she didn't, he decided she was probably busy taking care of Tim.

Leo helped Gabe out of the SUV and was leading him toward the door when Lucy Rojas came running through the door and stopped directly in front of them.

"Is it true what they said," she demanded, "that the boys were in Henry's garage and locked in his truck?"

"It's true," Leo said, trying to brush past her, but she didn't budge.

"Where is he?" Lucy's face was filled with anguish, and Gabe realized that the woman knew nothing about what her husband had been doing.

"I saw your Toyota parked out by the airport," Leo said. "Henry probably saw what was happening and used it to run off somewhere."

Dan Pardee nodded. "That's what I heard, too. They're planning on organizing another search—for him this time."

"But I don't understand," Lucy objected. "What's this all about?"

Gabe was still holding the bottle of water. He swallowed another drink and spoke almost normally for the first time. "It's about diamonds," he said, "diamonds in a peanut butter jar."

CHAPTER 25

The mother of Shining Falls looked and looked for her daughter, but she could not find her. Then suddenly, she heard her daughter's voice. And Shining Falls sounded happy—just the way she used to back when she sang to the children.

The mother followed the sound of the voice. She kept looking and looking. As the light came and went on the surface of the water in the charco, she could see little Shining Falls's face smiling up at her. Sometimes the mother could see her daughter's face very clearly. Other times she could see it only faintly. But always she could see her daughter smiling and hear her singing.

LANI STIRRED AS Henry Rojas accelerated away from the Border Patrol checkpoint. Her shoulders were cramped. Her hands were strapped together with tie wraps while a third one secured her right arm to the armrest on the door. She had no memory of his stopping long enough to cuff her or strip off her coat. Her lab coat had been used to cover the restraints, and no one at this checkpoint had noticed anything amiss. She'd been out cold. She was about to say something when Henry spoke. At first she thought a third person must be in the car with them, but then she realized he was talking to himself.

Dan had told her that during the long hours when he was alone in the car, he often carried on extended conversations with Hulk. Henry didn't have a dog, so he didn't have anyone else to chat with along the way.

Lani twisted in her seat, trying to find a more comfortable position. Then she closed her eyes, feigning sleep. She realized he must have given her something other than scopolamine. She was too wide awake and connected for that. Midazolam, maybe? But where would that have come from? Had Lucy stolen it from the hospital pharmacy? Was she in on this, too?

"Going with some money is better than going with no money," Henry was saying aloud. "Either she gives me enough to get away, or I go to the cops and blow the whistle. It's about time she paid me what I'm worth. She thinks that she can just order me around like she's some high and mighty general while I'm her lowly PFC? Screw that. I'm the one who's been taking all the risks, and I'm the one who's about to lose everything."

What risks? Lani wondered. And she wished she knew who "she" was. Was he referring to Lucy, or was there some other woman involved?

And that reminded her suddenly of the vision she'd had on the mountain—on Ioligam. How many hours ago was that now? Less than a day, but it seemed like years since she had seen that ghostly woman in the smoke, an evil Ho'ok, a witch with silver hair. Was that Henry's mysterious "she"?

And what about Gabe and Tim? Lani had seen the

blowtorch and knew someone had been trying to break into Henry's garage structure out at the airport. Maybe the boys had been there—locked inside. But were they dead or alive? And was Henry Rojas the person who had killed Carlos and Paul José?

Lost in thought, Lani realized that Henry's monologue had changed. "I need to talk to Francisco," he said with some urgency. "And I need him now!"

Lani hadn't realized she'd heard him dialing the phone, so maybe she wasn't quite as with it as she had first thought she was.

A long silence followed. Lani imagined that telephone-hold elevator music was playing from somewhere. She heard Henry sigh in frustration and what sounded like fingers drumming impatiently on the steering wheel. He was still on hold when Lani felt the buzz of her own cell phone in the pocket of her jeans. When she went to the hospital and slipped on her lab coat, she routinely switched her ringer to silent. Sometimes she forgot to turn it back on. And this was one of those times. Between the road noise and the music on his own phone, Henry evidently didn't hear the sound.

Lani whispered a small prayer of gratitude. As long as she had her phone—as long as he didn't realize she had one and took it away—there was a chance someone could figure out where she was.

"Organ Pipe won't work," Henry said a long minute or so later. "Something's come up. We'll have to meet up somewhere else." There was a pause. "How should I know? I'm inside the Tucson sector right now. Just crossed the checkpoint at Three Points. The fewer checkpoints I have to go through, the better." Another pause was followed by "No, not Nogales. Too many people know me there. What about Agua Prieta or even somewhere in New Mexico? There's a lot of empty terrain down by the Peloncillos." Lani heard another voice in the background, speaking loudly enough that his voice carried even without being on speaker.

"Yeah, yeah, I know," Henry said. "Changes in plan mean you raise the price. I'm good with that. Call me back when you have the arrangements in place. The number you have for me works."

Henry ended the call and the car slowed. Lani wondered where they were, but she didn't dare open her eyes. She needed him to continue believing she was still out of it.

AFTER A BUSY and purposeful day, Brandon Walker was surprised to find himself at loose ends. Ava Richland had seemingly gone to ground. With her husband hauled off to TMC, there was no point in hanging around in town. A glance at his watch told him Diana was most likely still caught up in her dinner, so he headed home.

On the way, he tried calling Lani to see if any progress had been made on finding Gabe Ortiz and Tim José, but Lani didn't answer. When he dialed Amanda Wasser's number, she did answer, telling him that she had arrived safely at the hospital in Mesa, but that her father was still in surgery. She promised to call him with news when there was some.

Brandon had just ended that call when a new one came in. "How are you getting on with my friend J.P.?" Ralph Ames asked.

"Surprisingly well," Brandon answered. "He put me in

touch with a pal of his, a guy named Todd Hatcher. In a matter of minutes he was able to track down an address that I needed here in Tucson. That was a huge help."

Ralph laughed. "Todd may be a forensic economist, but he comes with a lot of hidden talents. He's also a great guy. If it weren't for him, Beau's wife, Mel, might very well be a goner now."

"How come?"

"Beau and Mel Soames used to work together on the Special Homicide squad," Ralph explained. "That's where they met."

"Mel Soames," Brandon mused. "Why is that name so familiar? Oh wait, now I remember. She had something to do with putting the Kenneth Myers homicide together with the Mangum missing persons report."

"Sounds like Mel, all right," Ralph said with a chuckle.

"How exactly did Todd Hatcher save Mel's life?"

"When Mel was appointed chief of police in Bellingham, her second-in-command got his nose seriously out of joint. The guy took Mel against her will and was about to toss her off a cliff into the Pacific Ocean when Todd managed to locate her phone so Beau could ride to the rescue."

"So this Todd character is what you might call a forensic economist superhero?"

"You could say that," Ralph agreed, "but don't tell him I said so. He might get a swelled head. In the meantime, I'm glad you and Beau are able to work together. Getting back in the game will be good for him."

"We'll see," Brandon said. "Talk to you later."

He had arrived at the house and pulled into the garage. When he opened the door, Bozo was waiting right outside. Brandon gave the dog a pat on the head.

"Hey, boy," he said aloud. "It's way past your dinnertime. Let's find you something to eat."

With Bozo happily downing his kibble, Brandon took a beer from the fridge and joined the dog on the patio. The sun was down. Evening chill was leaching the warmth out of the dry desert air, so Brandon turned on the outdoor heater before he sat down. Yes, he was tired. It had been a long day, but in the twenty or so hours since he last sat in that same chair, he'd accomplished a lot. Back then he'd been wrestling with the question of John Lassiter's guilt or innocence. Tonight he was squarely on the innocence side of the equation. Last night he'd learned for the first time that Big Bad John had a daughter. Today he'd met the woman and liked her, too.

Brandon glanced at his watch. The fact that Lassiter's surgery had gone on this long was worrisome. Would he make it? And if he did, would he and Amanda manage to eke out some kind of relationship? Brandon understood that outcome was up to him. Would he be able to establish John Lassiter's innocence in a way that would finally make it possible for the man to come face-to-face with his own child?

Brandon's phone rang, and Dan Pardee's name appeared in the window. "Hey, Dan," Brandon said. "How's it going?"

Dan didn't return his father-in-law's greeting. "Have you heard anything from Lani?"

The anxiety in Dan's voice was enough to make Brandon sit bolt upright in his chair and slam his open beer bottle onto the table. Brandon's abrupt mood swing caused Bozo to abandon his kibble and come over to stand close to his master's knee.

"I tried calling her, but it went to voice mail," Brandon said. "Why? What's wrong?"

"She's gone, Brandon." Dan's words came out in something just short of a sob. "We were searching the airport at Sells for Tim and Gabe. She told people at the hospital that she was coming to join us, but she never showed up."

"Sells has an airport?" Brandon asked. "Why were you searching there?"

"The FBI obtained a warrant for Tim José's cell phone. The last ping on that came from somewhere on or near the airport grounds. Hulk and I were late to the game and were sent to the far end of the airport. As soon as we made it back to the main group of searchers, Hulk alerted at the entrance to one of the buildings, a Quonset hut that was locked down tight. Leo Ortiz used a blowtorch to get inside, and that's where we found the boys."

Brandon felt a rush of relief. "Are they all right?"

"They're both at the hospital, being treated for dehydration. Tim is in far worse shape than Gabe is. I think they'll keep both of them overnight at least, but it was when we got to the hospital that I learned Lani wasn't here. Lucy Rojas said she was going to join the search, but she never showed up. She isn't at home, either."

Dan's words had poured out in such a rush that Brandon had to struggle to keep up. "You're saying the boys were locked up in a garage?"

"They were actually imprisoned in a concealed compartment in a pickup that was locked inside a garage. It's a Toyota Tundra with a false bottom on the bed and a camper shell over the top."

"Whose truck?"

"A guy from here on the T.O.—Henry Rojas, who,

I'm sorry to say, happens to be one of the Shadow Wolves. His wife's car was found near the airport. We assumed that Rojas was somewhere near where he'd left her vehicle. Hulk and I helped with that search, too. Hulk picked up a scent all right, but he lost it on the shoulder of the road a dozen car lengths or so from the gate to the airport."

"You think he abducted Lani?" Brandon asked.

"I don't think: I know. I pulled some strings and got the officers at the Three Points checkpoint to review their video feed. Lani's Fusion passed through there half an hour ago with Henry Rojas at the wheel and Lani—or someone who looks like Lani—asleep on the passenger side."

"The guy has to be beyond desperate to pull a stunt like that," Brandon said. "Any idea where he's headed?"

"None. The FBI has posted a BOLO. I gave them permission to go after our phone records, but once again, they're insisting on getting a warrant first. They have to because there may be patient privacy issues with both Lani's phone and her computer. Once they have the warrant, they'll be able to trace her, but for now we're stuck."

"Wait," Brandon interjected. "Are you saying Lani has her phone with her?"

"I can't imagine that she doesn't," Dan replied. "She's a doctor. The ringer is usually turned off, but the woman doesn't go anywhere without her phone. Why?"

"Good-bye, Dan," Brandon said. "I'm hanging up now."

"But—"

"I'll get back to you."

Abandoning Dan midsentence, Brandon searched through his recent calls list. He found the one he wanted—the phone belonging to Todd Hatcher—a few calls earlier on the list. Brandon punched the number. When it rang, a woman answered.

"It's for you," she said, passing the phone along to someone else.

"Brandon Walker," he said when Todd came on the line. "I hope you don't mind my calling you back directly, but we've got a situation here—a serious situation. I need your help."

Only after finishing the call to Todd did Brandon call his wife. Diana was laughing as she answered. "Hey," she said. "This turned out to be fun. You should have come along after all."

"How much have you had to drink?" Brandon asked.

"A couple of glasses of wine," she said. "Why?"

"Do you have a designated driver?"

"Brandon," Diana said indignantly. "What the hell?"

"Do you?" he insisted.

"My publicist is a Mormon girl who doesn't drink at all. So, yes, Mr. Busybody, I do."

"Good. You need to leave the restaurant now and have her drive you straight to Lani's place in Sells."

There was a moment of silence on the phone. "To Sells? Why? What's happened?"

Brandon squeezed his eyes shut. He didn't want to say what was coming next, but he had no choice.

"A man named Henry Rojas is the one who killed Carlos and Paul José," he said. "Now he's taken Lani."

"Are you kidding?"

"Not kidding. Dan says they found Gabe and Tim, and they're okay, but Lani is gone, along with her Fusion. You need to go help with the kids."

"What about you? Can't you drive me? Shouldn't we both go?"

"I'm at the house waiting for someone who may be able to give us a line on Lani's cell phone. I'm going to wait here until I hear back from him."

"Shouldn't the cops be doing that—tracing her phone?"

"Maybe they should," Brandon said, "and maybe they are, but she's my daughter, Diana. Dan was able to learn that Rojas passed through the checkpoint west of Three Points a while ago, coming in this direction. If Lani's somewhere here in town, that's where I'm going to be, too. I'm guessing Dan's on his way to Tucson as well. That's why I want you to be there with the kids, in case . . ."

Brandon stopped talking at that point. He didn't want to think about the worst-case scenario, much less say it.

"I'm on my way," Diana said. "We'll leave right now. But if you find out where she is, Brandon, don't do anything stupid. Promise?"

"I promise," he said.

Brandon had his fingers crossed when he answered. He glanced at Bozo lying nearby on his heated bed. "You won't tell on me, will you, boy?"

The dog thumped his tail. That was all the response Brandon needed.

GABE DID NOT like Agent Howell. She was blond and smelled like some kind of flower, but there was something mean about her. If she was from the FBI, why wasn't she out looking for Lani instead of sitting here asking him stupid questions?

With his parents flanking him, Gabe had told Agent Howell everything he knew: about Tim leaving the diamond-laced peanut butter jar with him for safekeeping; about how Henry had burst into the house looking for it sometime that morning; about waking up in the box with Tim next to him; about how the two of them had managed to get free of their bonds, if not free from the box.

"But how did you know the José family was involved in smuggling diamonds?" Agent Howell insisted.

As far as Gabe knew, the four diamonds he had taken from the peanut butter jar were still hidden in the pocket of his jeans. Gabe had almost died for those diamonds. I'itoi had told him they were his, and he didn't want to give them up.

"I saw one," he said. "I couldn't see what was so important about a jar of peanut butter, so I took out a spoonful and spotted one of the diamonds."

Gabe had actually seen more than one of the stones, but that was a lie he could live with.

"You're sure you had no idea about the diamonds before that?"

"Agent Howell," Delia Ortiz said firmly before Gabe had a chance to reply. "This interview is over."

"But—"

"Gabe has explained that he was helping a friend without the slightest idea of what was really going on. It sounds as if you're coming dangerously close to accusing my son of being actively involved in a smuggling operation, so the next time you speak to him, it will be in the presence of our attorney. In the meantime, I suggest you get the hell out of his room and start doing the rest of your job, like tracking Dr. Walker-Pardee, for instance."

Gabe looked at his mother in surprise. He had never before heard her use her tribal chairman tone of voice outside of council meetings, not even when she was angry. He looked back at Agent Howell. She seemed poised to voice an objection, but then thought better of it.

"Yes, ma'am," she said, slapping her notebook shut. "We're on it."

Gabe waited until Agent Howell left the room before turning to his mother. "This is all my fault, isn't it? If I hadn't walked off the mountain . . ."

"Hush," Delia said, hugging him close. "None of this is your fault."

"Mr. Rojas was going to kill us, wasn't he?"

"Yes," Delia said. "I believe he was."

"And now he's going to kill Lani."

"I hope not," Delia said.

Gabe was silent for a moment. "Where are my clothes?" he asked. "There's something in the pocket that I need to have."

"Those clothes are filthy," Delia objected, but Leo was already on his feet.

"They're out in the tow truck," he said. "I'll go get them."

Leo left the room and returned a few minutes later carrying a black plastic yard waste bag. When Gabe opened it, the stench was enough to make him gag and set his eyes watering, but he found the jeans and gingerly extracted the four diamonds.

"What are those?" his mother asked, eyeing his closed fist.

"They're my divining crystals," Gabe said. "I need them."

HENRY KNEW THAT the cops had to be looking for Dr. Pardee's car by now, so he couldn't just drive around in the bright red Fusion forever, but he couldn't afford to show up at Jane Dobson's house empty-handed, either. He had left the original jar of peanut butter, the one with the diamonds in it, locked in his garage. He needed a replacement in the very worst way. That meant going to a grocery store where there would be people, surveillance cameras, and most likely at least one off-duty cop. Right that minute, though, he was actually more afraid of Jane Dobson's reaction than he was of facing down a shopping center security guard.

He knew the woman kept large amounts of cash in her home because that's how she'd paid him and Max and Carlos José—in cash. He'd hand over the goods, and she'd reach into that huge purse of hers, drag out a stack of bills, and count out whatever was due. That meant she probably also had some kind of weapon. It would be either on her person or else nearby, and she would know how to use it.

So tonight, when Henry handed over the peanut butter jar and she reached for the purse, that was the moment when he'd have to get the drop on her. If he didn't nail her then, he wouldn't get a second chance. And if things went as Henry hoped, he'd have a pile of cash and a new escape vehicle as well. The cops would be looking for a missing Fusion, not Jane Dobson's Acura.

He stopped in the far corner of the parking lot of a down-at-the-heels mall that held a dead gas station, a Fry's, a struggling Target, a barbershop, and a check-cashing store. Pulling in behind a shuttered taco truck, he glanced over at Lani. She was still out cold. That was good. Carlos and Paul had come around a lot sooner than this, but then again, they were almost twice her size, and size probably made all the difference.

His phone rang. "Hey, Francisco," he said. "What's the word?"

"We've got a guy named Manuel who built a new tunnel down in Douglas. That'll get you as far as Agua Prieta. Using that costs an extra five over what I already quoted."

It was a lot of money—money Henry didn't actually have right that minute. "It's okay," he managed.

"You want help going farther south than that, you'll need to deal with Manuel at the time. He's good, but he's not cheap."

"Where do I meet him?"

"Can you make it to Benson by midnight?"

"Sure."

"Exit the freeway at the first Benson exit. There's a dead bowling alley just to the left after you come off the exit. Wait there. Someone will come by, pick you up, and ditch your vehicle. *¿Comprendes?*"

"Got it," Henry said.

He looked at his watch, estimated the distance to the store, and looked at Lani again. He couldn't risk having her wake up too soon and cause some kind of attention-getting fuss here in the parking lot. He only had three syringes left and four glass vials. Would that be enough to take care of both Lani Pardee and Jane Dobson? He certainly hoped so, but if he had to get more physical than that, he would. After all, he had taken out both Carlos and Paul, hadn't he? Maybe the next ones would be easier.

Still, just to be on the safe side, he reached into the gym bag on the floorboard of the passenger side of the vehicle and located one of the remaining vials, then plunged the needle of a loaded syringe into Lani's upper arm. The way she jumped when the needle penetrated the skin made him think that maybe she wasn't as far under as he had thought she was, but he hoped that would hold her for a while. If he left her here sleeping, he might have time to pick up the peanut butter and maybe even some new duds. If someone was sending out an APB on him, it might be a good idea to have a couple of changes of clothes.

CHAPTER 26

When winter came, the Indians returned to their village in the desert. But the next summer, when they brought their horses and cattle back into the foothills, they returned to the deep water hole near Baboquivari. And even before they reached the charco, they could hear the sound of Shining Falls, singing and laughing.

LANI AWAKENED TO the sound of a door slamming shut and the smell of peanut butter in the air. Peanut butter? Why peanut butter? Was Henry hungry and making a sandwich?

She looked around. The car was parked in the driveway of a two-story house with lights on downstairs. There were houses on either side with no lights showing in either one and very little traffic on the street. She guessed that they were in a residential area somewhere in Tucson, but she had no idea where. Then her eye caught the slowly moving lights of a descending airplane. That put them in the southwest side somewhere near Tucson International Airport.

Lani tried pulling her arms loose, but the tie wraps didn't give. Her shoulders were screaming in agony from being trapped in one position for such a long time. How much time had passed since Henry had given her that first shot? Long enough for him to drive from Sells to Tucson. And after the second one? Long enough for night to fall.

Henry Rojas was clearly fleeing for his life. That meant that once he finished whatever he was doing in the house, he would most likely kill Lani. What would happen if she could somehow open the door and fall far enough out of the vehicle so that her body was half in and half out? Maybe a passerby would notice and stop to help. The only problem was that there were no passersby—no cars driving slowly through the neighborhood and no one out walking a dog. And when she did attempt exiting the vehicle, it didn't work. Henry had locked the car. She could reach the door handle, but not the button to unlock the door.

Resigned to her fate, Lani settled back against the car seat as best she could. What would happen to Angie and Micah? Dan was a good man and an excellent father. If she was gone and he was left alone with the kids, he'd do a great job of raising them. She also knew that her parents would do everything in their power to help.

But just thinking about Dan made her want to weep. Only yesterday he had tried to warn her about the dangerous smugglers she and Gabe might encounter out near Ioligam, and he had been right. The dangerous smugglers had been there all right, but it turned out that none of them were strangers, not at all. As for Henry Rojas, someone who should have been above reproach? He was likely the most dangerous of them all. Dan hadn't seen that one coming, and neither had Lani.

She tried to keep an eye on the street. Trusting the drug to keep her sedated, Henry hadn't bothered to gag her. If someone came by, she intended to scream her head off. Otherwise, she knew that her best chance of living was to continue doing just what she'd been doing all along—pretending to be asleep. It seemed unlikely that he'd do whatever it was he planned right here in the car. He'd need transportation of some kind that wasn't filled with either a dead body or blood and gore. She could only hope that at some point he'd have to loosen the tie wraps that bound her. That would be her one opportunity to fight back.

"I'll head-butt that son of a bitch all the way into next week," she swore to herself. "Then I'll run like hell."

AVA LOOKED AT her watch again and wondered what was taking so long. At this point Henry was over an hour late in making the delivery, and she was growing impatient. Or maybe Jane Dobson was the one worrying and watching the minutes tick by. At this point, it was hard for Ava herself to remember exactly who she was at the moment or who she would be at any given time. That was something to bear in mind. As of now, Ava Richland was over. Going forward, Ava would always be someone else.

The problem was, she had a long drive ahead of her tonight. It would take at least five hours to reach the Border Patrol checkpoint northwest of Brawley, California. She wanted to pass through that around midnight, a time when the guards would be tired and traffic would be light. Jane Dobson would drive past the officers in her properly licensed vehicle. Then, somewhere north of there but south of Indio, Jane Dobson would disappear for good, shortly after Ava Richland.

At that point the Acura's Arizona license plate would go in the trunk. Weeks earlier she had commissioned one of her operatives to steal a California plate from a similarly colored Acura. Then, with the stolen plate in place, she would assume the guise of Kate Worthington for the remainder of the trip. And once in L.A., Kate Worthington would also evaporate when Jane Carruthers went into Postal Minders to pick up her preshipped packages of diamonds.

As for Henry Rojas? She hoped it would be days or maybe even weeks before anyone stepped inside Jane Dobson's abandoned house to find his body. Earlier in the day she had asked one of the neighborhood kids for help loading her luggage into her car in the two-car garage. In passing, she happened to mention to the kid that she was on her way to visit her dying mother and wasn't sure when she'd be back.

Waiting for the garage door to open, Ava concentrated on remaining calm. She touched her purse with the toe of her shoe. The extra weight told her that her weapon was where she needed it to be. The Glock semiautomatic was much smaller than the .22 she had used on Amos Warren and Kenneth Mangum. The .22 had originally belonged to her philandering father. Twelve-year-old Ava had found it hidden in the bottom drawer of his dresser the day her mother threw the man out of the house. Ava had taken the gun, hidden it in her own dresser, and used it twice before ditching it in a Dumpster at a gas station somewhere in Portland on her way home from Seattle.

As for this one? It was new. She hadn't spent any time firing it, but at close range, that wouldn't matter. She worried about the sound of gunfire. Occasional gunshots in this dodgy neighborhood weren't all that unusual, but unwelcome attention was something she could ill afford. If she could avoid shooting him, she would.

With that in mind, what Ava was really counting on was Henry's soft spot for tequila. They'd shared a slug or two of that on other occasions when he'd dropped off shipments. This time, she had prepared a special barbiturate-laced bottle of Jose Cuervo. She'd set it out on the coffee table along with a single shot glass, a plate of lime slices, and a shaker of salt. And if that didn't quite do the trick? If something more was required, she was pretty sure she'd be able to make it look like suicide.

Ava had watched the local news at six. She had followed the piece on the reservation shooting with avid interest, but there had been few details. Stories about two unidentified males being gunned down out along the border didn't get much traction these days. Just before the broadcast ended, there had been a brief breaking news alert about a disturbance at the state prison in Florence in which two people had died and one was injured. The smiling young blond anchorwoman breathlessly promised more details on the ten o'clock edition.

Ava fervently hoped that the two dead victims were the right dead victims, but she didn't plan on hanging around long enough to make sure. She'd be well on the road before it was time for the ten o'clock news.

The minutes crept by. She had poured herself a glass of wine that sat untouched on the table next to her chair. There was no point risking having wine before embarking on an all-night drive, but the wine provided camouflage and gave her a reason for not joining Henry in having some of his tequila.

For hours now, the only sound in the house had been the quiet growling of the fridge as the motor switched on and off and the occasional banging of ice machine cubes rattling as they dropped into the plastic bin. The sound she was waiting for was the slow creak of the garage door opening, but that one didn't come. Instead she was jarred by the sound of her doorbell.

Doorbell? Are you kidding? What the hell was the man thinking?

BOZO LAY ON his bed while Brandon paced the patio, waiting and worrying. When Amanda Wasser called to report that John Lassiter was out of surgery and in the recovery room, he was relieved to hear the news, but it was all he could do to keep from snarling at her. He hurried Amanda off the phone because he wanted the line open in case Todd Hatcher called.

He already knew there was no way he'd be able to keep his promise to Diana—no way he'd be able to stay out of it. After all, Lani was his daughter. He didn't want to trust her fate to a bunch of inexperienced patrol officers who might shoot first and ask questions later. And Brandon knew in his gut that Dan Pardee would be on the same page.

Henry Rojas was Navajo and Border Patrol. If Brandon and Dan could get to Henry, they might be able to talk him down or take him down. The problem was, they had to find him first.

When Todd's call finally came, Brandon didn't bother with the niceties.

"Did you find her?"

"Did," Todd said. "Sorry it took so long, I had to jump through several extra hoops, but the phone seems to be stationary in the 5800 block of a street named Calle de Justicia. Do you know where that is?"

"No idea," Brandon said, "but I'll find it."

"The trouble is," Todd continued, "I have the block number but not the actual address."

"Don't worry," Brandon said. "If my daughter's there, I'll find her. You have no idea how much I appreciate this."

Brandon was already heading for the garage when he thought better of it. Turning around, he sprinted back into the house. In the laundry room, he pawed through the collection of bathing suits that stayed there year round. It took a moment to find the tiny thonglike thing that passed for Lani's bathing suit.

Diana was right. Going there by himself was dangerous. Going there without backup was even worse, but it turned out Brandon had just realized he did have backup—backup guaranteed to arrive on the scene at the same time he did.

Bozo was on his bed, eyes closed. "Hey, Bozo," Brandon said. "Do you want to go to work?"

The dog's transformation was instantaneous. One moment he was dozing on his posh heated bed. The next moment the dog was on his feet at full attention, looking quizzically at Brandon as if making sure he had heard right. When Brandon nodded, the dog sprinted for the garage and the Escalade with no sign of the aging animal's game shoulder or crippling limp. Brandon Walker had said the magic go-to-work words, and Bozo was already locked, loaded, and back on the job.

As Brandon fumbled with the GPS, keying in the address, Bozo sat in the backseat, panting over Brandon's shoulder. Once they were under way, Brandon hooked up his Bluetooth and dialed Dan.

"Someone has just located Lani's phone. It's currently pinging in the 5800 block of a street called Calle de Justicia."

"Calle de Justicia?" Dan repeated. "Never heard of it."

"It's not far off I-10 at Craycroft."

"Have you called the cops?"

"Not yet. I'm going there now to check it out visually. It may be the phone's there and Lani isn't. The GPS says it'll take us twenty-eight minutes."

"Who's us?" Dan asked.

"I invited Bozo to come along for the ride—for backup."

"Good call," Dan said. "I've got Hulk with me, too. But don't do anything stupid, Brandon. If you don't call the cops, I will. If anything were to happen to you, Diana would kill me."

His voice came to a strangled halt, and Brandon heard the silent words Dan Pardee couldn't utter. "And so will Lani."

"Really," Dan resumed after a pause. "You can't expect the two of us to go after him on our own."

"I know all about Tombstone courage," Brandon said, acknowledging Dan's warning, "but if Henry is holding Lani hostage, do you want cars with sirens blaring and cops with guns running around all over the place? Besides, by my count, with the dogs in our corner, it's four to one. Where are you?"

"I stopped at Three Points. If Henry's headed to Mexico, Sasabe would be the nearest border crossing.

If he's headed north, he might have cut across to I-10 at Cortaro Road. Okay. I've got the Calle de Justicia address in my GPS. It'll take me forty-five minutes at least. If you want it to be four to one, you'll have to wait until Hulk and I get there."

"Got it," Brandon said. "And for God's sake, do not speed. None of us can afford a speeding ticket right now, most especially Lani."

A FURIOUS AVA marched across the room to the front door, banging her walker on the tile. Henry had parked out on the driveway instead of in the garage? What in the world was the matter with the man? What was he thinking?

At the door she paused for a moment and got herself back under control. A steaming-mad Ava Richland would never pass for an ailing Jane Dobson. Only when she had herself fully in hand did she turn the key in the dead bolt.

Henry stood on her doorstep, holding up a gym bag and looking sheepish.

"Did you get the shipment?" she demanded.

He nodded.

"And Tim's taken care of?"

He nodded again.

"Well, come in then," she said, standing aside. "Why didn't you use the garage?"

"I left the clicker in the other car," he said.

Ava hadn't turned on the porch light. She peered out the door. In the dim light, she caught sight of a strange car parked in the middle of her driveway. She sighed. She'd have to move it into the garage as soon as possible, but for right now, she supposed it was fine to leave it where it was. She didn't want Henry to think she was overly anxious or that anything was amiss.

"That's all to the good, then," she said, trying to sound relieved. "Come have a seat. I know for a fact that you've had a tough couple of days."

"Ain't that the truth," Henry muttered.

Ava smiled her most reassuring smile. "I think this calls for a bit of a celebration, don't you?" she asked. "If you're hungry, I've got a tray of cold cuts out in the kitchen."

"No," he said. "I'm fine."

"Well, at least have a drink with me. I'm drinking wine this evening, but let's have a toast together. What do you say?"

Henry crossed the room ahead of her and took a seat at the end of the sofa that was farthest away from her chair and the side table with her wineglass on it. He set the gym bag down on the floor. Opening it, he dragged the peanut butter jar out of the bag and set it on the coffee table.

"It wasn't easy, but here it is. What about Max?"

"Don't worry about him," Ava said. "Max José is no longer an issue."

She studied Henry. She had met him on any number of occasions over the years. There was something slightly off about him tonight. By her count, he'd done away with four people in the last twenty-four hours, so maybe he had a right to be slightly jittery. After all, Ava herself hadn't been ready to dance the light fandango after she took out Amos and Kenneth. The same thing had been true after she'd helped Clarence step off the bank into that flash flood in Pantano Wash; she hadn't felt altogether perky after that one, either. Right this minute she was relieved that today she was able to walk away from Harold and simply let nature run its course.

She lifted her glass. "A toast," she said, "to you and to a difficult job well done."

With immense satisfaction she watched Henry pour a healthy shot of tequila into the glass and pick up a piece of lime. "A job well done," he agreed.

Ava held the wineglass to her lips, but she didn't swallow so much as a drop.

"Is that a new car out there?" she asked. "I don't believe I've seen that one before."

Her mention of the car was intended as nothing more than an icebreaker. She hoped that if Henry was upset, a little light conversation along with the booze might relieve some of the tension without his necessarily noticing how much liquor was going down the hatch. She was pleasantly surprised to learn that settling on the car as a topic must have been a good idea. Henry quickly poured another slug of tequila into his glass and downed it in a single gulp, following it with a long suck on a wedge of lime. She had worried earlier that even in tequila the barbiturates she'd added might be discernible. Now she could relax. If it tasted strange, Henry Rojas wasn't a sophisticated enough imbiber to notice.

"I know I promised you a bonus," Ava continued, reaching for the purse that was parked beside her chair. "I took the liberty of counting it out in advance. Forty thousand dollars should cover it, don't you think?"

The tension she had noticed in Henry before seemed to evaporate. She didn't know why, exactly. Maybe the tequila was already doing its job. He leaned back on the sofa, looking relaxed, and actually smiled at her. "That should just about do it," he said.

Ava reached into her purse, just as she'd done many times before, but Henry Rojas seemed to be reaching for a weapon of his own. Ava didn't hesitate and Henry never had a chance. The first bullet caught him full in the chest. He tried to rise to his feet. Ava fired twice more, which made for three more shots than she had wanted to discharge. Obviously her carefully laid plans of making his death look like suicide had come to nothing.

Worried that a neighbor might have heard the racket and started peering out windows, Ava abandoned the walker and raced through the kitchen to the garage. She needed to have Henry's car off her driveway and concealed inside her garage before anyone else came snooping around. Outside, she breathed a sigh of relief. No lights had come on in neighboring houses. No one was visible out on the street.

Ava hurried to the vehicle and was dismayed to discover that the door was locked. She had to go back inside and search Henry's bloodied body for a key fob. She pressed the unlock button as she came through the garage a second time. It wasn't until she was seated inside and trying to figure out how to operate the engine that Ava realized with numbing shock that she was not alone. There was someone else in the car with her—a woman.

Ava's fingers went stiff and clumsy as they searched for the ignition button. Once the engine started, she sped into the garage so far that she banged the front bumper on the far wall before braking to a stop.

Ava leaped out of the car and hurried to close the garage door behind her. Then she went to the passenger side of the car and wrenched the door open. As she did so, the interloper was pulled out of the vehicle, landing hard on the concrete floor. Her hands were cuffed together and they had somehow been affixed to the door itself.

"Who are you?" Ava demanded. "What are you doing here?"

Momentarily stunned, the bound woman didn't answer immediately. "Help me," she whimpered finally. "Please help me."

"Of course," Ava said. "Just a minute."

There had been an abandoned workbench complete with tools in the garage when Ava had bought the place. She'd mostly ignored the tools as she came and went, but there was one thing there on the bench that she needed now in the very worst way—duct tape. She picked up the roll, ripped off an eight-inch-long strip, and returned to the passenger side of the car.

Ava kept the tape out of the victim's sight until she knelt down beside the woman who, half in and half out of the car, was struggling desperately against her restraints.

"Hold still," Ava said calmly. "Let me cut you loose."

As soon as the woman quieted, Ava slapped the tape across her face. Then she stood up without noticing that, in the process of her covering the writhing woman's mouth, Ava's prized olla had somehow spilled out of her pocket.

She straightened up and stood for a few moments considering what to do next. She'd have to decide on a permanent solution for the captive woman eventually. She couldn't very well shoot her right here in the garage. There wasn't as much soundproofing here as in the house. But for now, at least, there would be no screaming for help. Ava definitely couldn't tolerate any screaming—not now and not tonight.

CHAPTER 27

Even to this day, nawoj, *if you go to that water hole, you will hear Shining Falls singing. The sound of her voice is so soft and sweet that, if you listen to it long enough, you may fall asleep. Sometimes, even the White-Winged Doves who are always there at the water hole fall asleep, too.*

AVA UNDERSTOOD THAT panic was her enemy. She had put a good deal of time and effort into making sure none of her DNA would be found in the house. She had planned on one final scrubdown of the things she knew she'd touched after the cleaning—her wineglass, Henry's shot glass, the doorknob to the back door. That was why she had sat so still, waiting for him. She hadn't wanted to risk leaving behind any trace evidence, but in her rush to retrieve the car keys and move the car, she'd handled Henry's body without first putting on a pair of latex gloves. She understood that these days it was possible to lift fingerprints and DNA from a victim's clothing. Time and the elements had worked their evidence-destroying magic on the bodies of Amos Warren and Kenny Mangum, but this time she wouldn't have that luxury.

She paused for several long moments in the living room, staring at Henry's still body and worrying, then she did the only thing that made sense. She stripped off all Jane Dobson's clothing, donned a pair of latex gloves, and went to work, removing Henry's bloodied shirt, pants, and underwear and sticking them in a garbage bag. Henry would stay here when she finished; his clothes would be going somewhere else.

BRANDON DIDN'T EXACTLY follow his own advice. He disregarded every speed limit sign he saw. Luckily, he didn't get caught. Twenty-three minutes after leaving Gates Pass he arrived on Calle de Justicia. The houses all had two-car attached garages. A few had an extra car or two parked either in the driveway or out on the street. None of the visible vehicles were Lani's bright red Fusion.

Brandon redialed Todd Hatcher's number. "Is the phone still pinging from the same spot?" he asked.

"Hasn't moved," Todd replied.

"Good," Brandon said. "Thanks."

He went around the block and parked on the next street over, S. Avenida de Aventura. He couldn't very well go into battle with guns blazing. He already knew that Carlos and Paul José had died in a hail of automatic gunfire. That probably meant that he was severely outgunned from the get-go. He was at a physical disadvantage as well. Henry Rojas was a couple of decades younger than Brandon Walker and most likely hadn't had a triple bypass, either. Brandon knew that Bozo could possibly level the playing field some, but he didn't know by how much.

He fumbled in the glove box and found the leash he kept there. He fastened that to Bozo's collar, then the two of them scrambled out of the SUV and onto the pavement.

Over the years, Brandon had enjoyed watching Dan Pardee work with and train his dogs—first Bozo and later Hulk. Brandon had always been fascinated to see how each dog magically became an extension of Dan himself. Over time, Brandon had become acquainted with the simple but useful commands Dan used—find, quiet, get him, wait, off, leave it. He also remembered the dogs' joyous barks after successfully executing one of those commands.

Tonight Brandon worried that a spontaneous bark might warn Henry Rojas that Brandon and Bozo were outside—that they were onto him.

Bozo was already on the ground and shivering with anticipation when Brandon brought out the scrap of material that was Lani's bikini. He held it up to the dog's nose.

"Quiet," he ordered first. Then, a moment later, he added, "Find."

Brandon had no way of knowing if the swimsuit had been laundered. At the very least, it would have been rinsed out. Would there be enough of Lani's scent present for the dog to get a reading? The only way to find out for sure was to try. Brandon and Bozo set out at a brisk pace, with Brandon hoping that they looked like nothing more threatening than a man and his dog out for a late-evening walk.

Looking down at Bozo, Brandon was gratified to see that the dog was on full alert. His ears and tail were up, his head swinging from side to side. Brandon was lost in thought when Bozo made a sudden jerk to the right and lunged up an empty driveway. Taken by surprise, Brandon almost fell on his face as the charging dog dragged him toward a closed garage door. While the dog stood with his nose pressed to the lit crack under the door, Brandon leaned down and whispered in his ear, "Good dog, Bozo. Good find."

Then, hauling back on the leash, Brandon dragged the dog away from the door and far enough down the driveway that he was able to glimpse the house number. Bozo wasn't ready to quit, but eventually he stopped fighting the leash.

"Here's the deal," Brandon found himself whispering to the dog as they walked back around the block to the car. "I'm worried Henry will try to take off before Dan gets here, so we're going to create a deterrent. In a pissing match between a parked Escalade and a Ford Fusion, the F car loses every time, and my Caddy isn't going anywhere. Get in."

Without turning on the lights, Brandon drove the SUV around the corner and parked it at an odd angle in the middle of the driveway in a way he hoped would effectively block both sides of the garage.

Bozo was ready to get out again, but Brandon reasoned they were better off staying inside the vehicle for the time being. They'd be safer, for one thing, and if a resident happened to drive by, they'd be much less visible.

Then, phone in hand, he sent a text to Todd Hatcher:

Parked in front of 5850 S. Calle de Justicia. Dog says Lani is inside the garage. Can you give me any info on residence. Text. Do NOT call.

Finished with that, he sent a text to Dan Pardee as well:

Address is 5850 S. Calle de Justicia. Bozo says Lani is here. Blocking the driveway so he can't get out. Waiting for you to show up before making a move. If he tries to leave before that, all bets are off.

In the time it had taken Brandon to key in the text to Dan, a reply came back from Todd:

Owner of that address is Miss Jane Dobson, age 69. Retired schoolteacher. Drives a 2006 Acura, AZ: License 583-AMV. Sending driver's license photo next.

The photo that appeared a moment later showed a perfectly ordinary-looking woman, maybe a few years younger than Brandon and Diana.

"So what's Henry Rojas's relationship with Ms. Dobson?" Brandon asked, amused by the fact that he was once again conversing with Bozo, who thumped his tail in reply. Dan's replying text arrived at the same time.

On I-10. GPS says I'm five minutes out. Wait for me.

LANI HAD MANAGED to get enough purchase on the car seat with her left foot to push herself up off the floor and into a semisitting position. It wasn't a huge improvement, but it took some of the weight off her aching shoulders. Half an hour later when the door from inside the house opened, Lani expected to see Henry Rojas emerge. He did not.

What came out instead was the silver-haired woman Lani had seen before. This time she was stark naked, except for a pair of latex gloves and a pair of bedroom slippers. In one hand she carried a black plastic garbage bag. The other hand held Henry's gym bag. Lani heard the woman open the trunk of a silver vehicle that was parked next to the Fusion.

Lani figured parading around naked meant one of two things: either the woman was completely nuts or else she had nothing to lose. If it turned out to be the latter, Lani worried that she herself had everything to lose. One thing Lani noticed was the difference between the woman's body and her face. From the face and hair she looked to be close to seventy. Her body was that of someone decades younger. How could that be?

Over the course of the next several minutes, the woman made two more trips back and forth, loading things into the other car each time she came and went. The last time she entered the garage, she was dressed in a muumuu and a pair of chartreuse tennis shoes. She was carrying a walker she apparently didn't need to use. After stowing the walker in the trunk of the vehicle and slamming the trunk lid shut, she walked over to Lani and knelt at her side. Lani noticed that the woman had brought a large purse along with her and that she was still wearing the gloves.

"Okay now," the woman said, "I don't know who you are, but you have a choice here. Henry was considerate enough to bring along some very nice meds. You can either hold still for a shot or two, or else I use my Glock. It's totally up to you."

As she spoke she set three clear glass vials down on the floor next to Lani.

Whatever it was, Lani knew that the medication in the vials was far less potent than Henry had thought. She'd already had two shots of the stuff. But would three more be too many? However, the choice between being given a possibly not-too-powerful drug and being shot in the head at close range wasn't much of a choice at all.

She looked at the needle and nodded.

"Good girl," the woman said. "Hold still now."

Lani watched as the woman plunged the needle into her upper arm with practiced ease. By the time it came to the third vial, Lani noticed that the woman was reusing the second syringe, but the familiar lassitude was already creeping up through her body, and she really didn't care. The last thing she heard was the woman saying, "Okay now. That should do the trick."

Lani felt the drug's rush immediately, noting with some irony that she'd missed her only chance to do any head-butting. Too bad.

Expecting Dan's Explorer to round the corner at any moment, Brandon was dismayed when the garage door started to open. He didn't want to get into some kind of confrontation with either Henry or Jane Dobson on his own. That meant he needed to play for time.

He grabbed for Bozo's leash and was about to exit the Escalade when all hell broke loose. A silver car, driving in reverse, shot out of the garage and slammed dead on into the front bumper of the Caddy. The blow was hard enough to rattle Brandon's teeth, hard enough for the air bag to deploy, but not hard enough to hurt him. And as soon as the air bag deflated, a skittish Bozo came scrambling out of the back cabin into the front.

This was far better than Brandon had hoped. The driver hadn't even glanced in the rearview mirror. He had simply assumed that his driveway was empty and hit the gas. Tough luck for him. Brandon supposed he had seen Henry Rojas on occasion, but would he recognize Brandon in this unfamiliar place in the middle of the night? Maybe not.

But then the driver's door of the other car—Jane Dobson's aging Acura—opened. Jane herself, presumably, stepped out and marched toward him, clearly enraged. There was no sign of Henry.

Brandon still held the leash. "Come on, Bozo. Time for old age and trickery to win out. Let's put on a show."

He opened the car door. With the dog in tow, he staggered out onto the driveway and meandered halfway across the front yard before righting himself and walking tipsily back.

"Who are you?" he demanded of the woman, while swaying drunkenly on his feet. "Where are Adam and Grace?" He slurred the words as best he could. *Grace* came out more like *Grathe.*

"Who are Adam and Grace?"

"I'm staying with them. Isn't this their house?"

"It's my house, you incredible moron. Get that wreck out of my way."

"Oh my," Brandon slurred. "I stopped for a leak and must have hit the wrong driveway. So shorry. Looks like your car took a real hit. Maybe we should try to pull the back bumper forward an inch or so. Otherwise it's gonna wreck your tire."

Bending over, Brandon pretended to examine the Acura's smashed back bumper while he was really trying to see if Henry Rojas was seated in the passenger seat. As far as he could tell the vehicle held no other occupants.

"My car is fine. I don't need your help. Now get that thing out of my way. I was just leaving. If I don't go now, I'll be late."

"Lemme get my insurance info. It's in the car."

"I already told you, I'll handle the damage. Just get the hell out of my way."

The urgency in her voice was unmistakable. Just then a pair of headlights pulled up behind Brandon. Out of the corner of his eye, Brandon recognized Dan's Explorer. "Hey, here's Adam now. He's a mechanic. Maybe he should take a look at your car and see if it's okay."

Bozo had already recognized the car and was barking eagerly as he headed in that direction. Now two cars blocked Jane Dobson's driveway.

When Dan opened the door to step out, Brandon pretended to fall against him. "You're Adam," he whispered urgently. "You live up the street. Bozo says Lani's inside somewhere. No sign of Rojas."

Dan got out of the Explorer with Hulk on his own leash. Brandon passed Bozo's leash to Dan, then stumbled to the passenger side of the Escalade and made a show of rummaging through the glove box.

"Ma'am," he heard Dan saying behind him. "I'm Adam, from just up the street. Sorry about my friend. I'm afraid he's had a bit too much to drink, but you really shouldn't try driving a vehicle with that kind of damage."

"I want you both out of my way. Now!"

There was desperation in Jane Dobson's voice now, along with the very real expectation that whatever order she issued would be instantly obeyed. Brandon turned back toward her carrying a fistful of paperwork, supposedly the insurance documentation that she didn't want or need. He was pretending to be dead drunk. He had parked in the wrong driveway. The accident was clearly his fault, and yet she didn't care about making an insurance claim? There was something wrong about that—something very wrong.

As Brandon stepped toward her, the woman moved back to the Acura's open driver's side door. Leaning inside, she emerged carrying a leather purse. When Brandon saw her shift the purse from her right hand to her left and then reach inside with her right, the hairs rose on the back of his neck. She could have been reaching for a cell phone, but his gut said she wasn't. She had to be reaching for a weapon.

With his Glock in a small-of-the-back holster, Brandon knew there was no way he could manage any kind of gunslinger quick draw. "Gun!" he shouted, hitting the deck and hoping that Dan would do the same.

What Brandon didn't realize—what he hadn't observed in any of Dan Pardee's dog-training sessions—was that, in the world of combat dogs and their handlers, that single word, "Gun!," was an urgent command all its own. Hulk didn't react immediately because his master hadn't issued the command. Brandon had done so, and Bozo was Brandon's dog now. The shepherd's crouch-powered spring covered the distance between him and the woman in a single leap. He knocked her flat and was all over her while the offending gun went spinning harmlessly out of reach.

"Get him off. Get him off!" she screamed. "He's hurting me!"

"Off!" Brandon and Dan ordered together. "Leave it," Dan added for good measure. Obligingly, Bozo stepped away.

Jane sat up and used the frame of the car to pull herself to her feet. The gray wig she was wearing had been knocked askew. Blood flowed from her damaged right wrist.

"That dog is vicious and needs to be put down. I'm calling the cops."

"Please do," Brandon said. "Actually, I can hear sirens, so one of your neighbors must have already phoned it in. Dan, you and Hulk keep an eye on her. Don't let her go anywhere. In the meantime, there's something Bozo and I need to do."

Brandon stepped forward and picked up Bozo's lead. Then he drew a strip of colorful material out of his pocket and held it out to Bozo. "Find," he ordered. A moment later, Bozo was standing at the back of Lani's Fusion barking his head off.

With his heart racing in his chest, Brandon walked over and pressed the trunk release. At first glance, Lani was so still that he thought she was dead. After a heart-stopping moment, he realized she was asleep. Not asleep—unconscious. A moment after that he spotted the tiny but still-bleeding puncture wound on her arm.

He spun around and strode back to the woman, who was leaning against her car. "What have you done to her?" he demanded, brandishing his fist. "If she dies . . ."

Brandon might have gone after her then and there, but Dan barred his way, Dan and Hulk together.

"The cops are here," Dan said. "Let them handle the situation."

"Lani's there. We need to get her out of the vehicle."

"No," Dan told him. "The cops need to see it—all of it."

A patrol car pulled up behind Dan's Explorer, followed by an aid car and a fire truck. The young patrol officer who walked up the driveway toward them was exactly the kind of cop Brandon had worried might walk into this mess—someone who was inexperienced and still wet behind the ears. The name plate pinned to his shirt identified him as Officer Lopez.

"A man named Henry Rojas kidnapped my daughter and locked her in the trunk here," Brandon explained, stepping toward the Fusion. "I believe this woman was his accomplice."

"I didn't!" the woman screamed. "I had nothing to do with it—nothing at all. And that man set his dog on me. Look at my wrist. It's a wonder I'm not dead."

Ignoring the woman's protestations, Officer Lopez followed Brandon and Bozo to the back of the Fusion and peered inside.

"Is that your daughter?" he asked.

Brandon nodded.

"Is she dead?"

"She's still alive, but she needs medical attention. The man holding the other dog is Dan, her husband."

"Any guns here?" Officer Lopez asked.

"I have one," Brandon admitted. "And so does Dan. He's Border Patrol. I'm Brandon Walker, retired sheriff of Pima County. We both have permits. The woman there tried to draw a weapon on us. It's over there on the far side of her vehicle. If it hadn't been for Bozo here, Dan and I would be history."

Lopez nodded. "Sounds like a valuable animal. We had a report of shots fired, but we couldn't get an exact location. When someone called in to report a disturbance at this address, we came here instead."

"You said there were shots fired?" Brandon asked. "I never heard any."

Just then an oversized van with SWAT stenciled on the outside pulled up beside Dan's vehicle, and a team of battle-ready cops spilled out.

Officer Lopez turned to the woman. "Excuse me, ma'am, is there anyone else in the residence? This Mr. Rojas, I believe the name was. Is he still inside?"

"I don't have to talk to you," she said. "I want my lawyer, and I need a doctor."

"What's your name, ma'am?"

"Dobson," she said. "Jane Dobson."

"The wrist doesn't look all that bad," Lopez said. "In fact, it's already stopped bleeding, but do we have permission to search your premises?"

"You most certainly do not!" Jane Dobson said. "You need a warrant."

Unperturbed, Lopez turned to Brandon. "Is it your understanding, Mr. Walker, that Mr. Rojas might still be inside the house and could possibly be in danger?"

When it came to needing a search warrant, the belief that someone might still be in danger was an automatic get-out-of-jail-free card.

Brandon nodded. "We know Rojas drove Lani here, but we haven't seen any sign of him."

Someone Brandon assumed to be the shift supervisor rolled up in an unmarked vehicle, and a uniformed officer named Sergeant Van Dyke stepped out. He and Lopez huddled for a moment. At the end of their discussion, Lopez cuffed Jane Dobson and led her toward his patrol car while Van Dyke ordered everyone else away from the area.

"But what about my daughter?" Brandon demanded. "She needs medical attention."

"I'm sorry," Van Dyke said. "She stays where she is until we clear the residence."

Much as he didn't like it, Brandon knew that was the right call—the only reasonable call. Moments later, the SWAT officers entered the house with weapons drawn. The team leader was back out in less than a minute. "House is clear, but we need the M.E."

"You've got a body?"

"Yup."

Van Dyke turned back to the nearest EMT. "You're good to go," he said.

Brandon followed the medics back into the garage and watched while they carefully removed Lani from the trunk and placed her on a gurney.

"Any idea what they gave her?" one of them asked.

Brandon pointed. "There are some vials over there and a couple of used needles."

"Okay," the medic said. "We'll get them. And don't worry. Her vitals are good. I don't think she's in any real danger."

Brandon had been fine the whole time, but that's when he lost it. He leaned against the interior wall of the garage and let his body slide down until he was sitting on the floor.

Now the medic was concerned about him. "Sir," he barked. "Are you okay?"

"Look after Lani," Brandon muttered. "I'm just a little weak in the knees."

"You're sure?"

"I'm sure."

Bozo evidently shared the medic's concern. Whining, he walked over to Brandon and nosed him on the shoulder. Grabbing the dog's sturdy body with both arms and burying his face in his long fur, Brandon Walker did something he hadn't done in a very long time—he wept.

DELIA AND LEO Ortiz were camped out in the hospital waiting room. Lorraine José was still too ill to come look in on Tim, so Delia was spending time in his room while Leo went in and out of Gabe's.

Right now, with both boys asleep and resting, they sat side by side. "Did you know Lorraine has cancer?" Delia asked.

Leo shook his head. "I thought it was just the car accident."

"She told me tonight that it's liver cancer," Delia said. "Fourth stage. They found the tumor when they were treating her other injuries."

"I didn't know," Leo said.

"She's worried about Tim," Delia continued, "worried about what will happen to him once she's gone."

"Maybe Lorraine's sister will take him."

"What about us taking him?" Delia asked. "Those two boys are close, and they will be even more so after everything that happened today. Besides, Gabe's always wanted a brother."

"Are you serious?"

Delia nodded. "I am," she said. "If Lani was willing to help us with Gabe, we should be willing to help Lorraine with Tim."

"Let's think about it, then," Leo said. "We don't have to rush. We can talk to Lorraine and both boys and see what they think."

"Yes," Delia said, "we'll talk about it after."

Leo's phone rang. He answered it, and Delia studied her husband's stolid face as his expression changed from serious to joyous. "Great," he said. "That's wonderful news, Dan! Thank you for letting us know."

"Know what?"

"They found Lani. It sounds like she's all right. Rojas is dead. His accomplice is under arrest."

"Accomplice?"

"He was working with some woman, I guess." Leo stood up. "I need to go tell Gabe."

"But he's asleep."

"I'll wake him. He won't mind."

Delia nodded. "And I'll go tell Lorraine."

Inside Gabe's room, Leo stood for a moment, looking down in wonder at his sleeping son. Leo and Gabe had talked off and on during the course of the evening. Leo knew about Tim José's knife and about how Gabe had figured out a way to cut them loose. He also knew now that had Henry Rojas opened the box, his son had been prepared to do battle with him. Leo was grateful it hadn't come to that, but he was proud to know that his son was brave and that he was old enough to kill a coyote—old enough to be a man.

Fighting back tears again, Leo reached down and gently shook the boy's shoulder. "Dan just called," he said as Gabe's eyes blinked open. "Henry Rojas is dead, and Lani is safe."

Gabe smiled. "I knew she would be," he said.

"How did you know?"

Gabe reached over and took four tiny transparent stones off his bedside table. "I looked in these," he said. "They told me she'd be fine."

With that, Gabe went back to sleep.

CHAPTER 28

And so, Nawoj, *my friend, even today, if you go out into the land of the Desert People to that deep water hole in the foothills near Baboquivari that is always full of water, you will find that the White-Winged Doves still gather there. And if you stand very still and listen, you will hear Shining Falls laughing and singing. And she still holds Little White Feather in her hand.*

"MOMMY, WAKE UP."

When Lani's eyes opened, she was in a hospital room staring into Micah's unblinking blue eyes. She looked around. Dan and Angie hovered in the background.

"Who found me?" she asked.

"Daddy and Grandpa," Micah said. "Grandma was really mad about that. She said Grandpa should have known better."

Lani laughed. "I'll bet she said a lot more than that."

Dan nodded in agreement. "And in not very grandmotherly terms," he added.

Micah held up his hand. "Where did you get this?"

"Get what?" Lani asked.

He dropped something into her hand. It took a moment for her to realize that it was a tiny olla. She knew from touching the object that this was something ancient and probably very valuable, but maybe dangerous as well. Holding it up to the light to examine it, she spotted the faint images of both a turtle and an owl etched into the clay.

"Where did this come from?"

"You were holding it in your hand when the EMTs carried you out of Ava's garage," Dan answered.

"Who's Ava? That crazy lady?"

Her husband sighed. "It's a long story. Henry Rojas and Max and Carlos José got caught up with a woman named Ava Richland, who was smuggling blood diamonds through Mexico and into the United States. When everything went south, Ava tasked Henry with getting rid of the younger José brothers while at the same time putting out a hit on the older one."

"Which was successful?"

Dan nodded.

"Tim's the only one left?"

Dan nodded again.

"Poor Lorraine."

"What about Henry Rojas?"

"He's dead, too. Ava shot Henry and then loaded you in the trunk of your car. We're pretty sure she was leaving you there to die of an overdose while she drove off into the sunset. The FBI was going after a warrant to track your phone. They probably would have found you before you corked off, but your dad figured out a way to locate you sooner than that—soon enough that Ava didn't have a chance to sneak out of Dodge."

"What's going to happen to Ava?"

"She's in jail on suspicion of five counts of homicide and three counts of attempted homicide, to say nothing of several counts of conspiracy and smuggling. The only case where we know for sure she pulled the trigger is Henry's, but since the others died in the course of the commission of a felony, she's just as responsible as the shooter."

"Did you say five?" Lani asked.

Dan ticked them off on his fingers. "Max, Carlos, Paul, a state prison employee named Jason Swanson, and Henry. The attempteds are you, Gabe, and Tim. She's also a person of interest in two cold cases—the murder of a guy named Amos Warren back in the seventies and a guy named Kenneth Myers who was murdered in the Seattle area in the early eighties. John Lassiter went to prison for Amos Warren's murder. He was attacked in prison at the same time Max José was, only Lassiter didn't die. The detectives are working on the theory that Ava was most likely involved in that hit as well."

"Can I keep the pot?" Micah asked, abruptly changing the subject.

Lani thought about that for a moment. "I'm not sure," she said. "Let me keep it for right now, okay?"

"Okay," Micah said. "But why's there an owl and a turtle on it?"

"Have I ever told you the story of Little White Feather?"

Micah frowned and shook his head. "I don't think so."

"I think the woman who made that pot knew about that story—about how Turtle and Owl helped a girl named Shining Falls. When I get home, maybe I can tell it to you."

"Can't you come home now?"

"I need to talk to my doctor and ask him."

"But you are a doctor. Can't you just tell him?"

Lani laughed and kissed the top of his head. "When you're the patient, it doesn't quite work that way."

As far as Diana Ladd and Brandon Walker were concerned, the Tucson Festival of Books took a big hit on Sunday. After their Saturday from hell, Diana was an understandable no-show at her Sunday panels and signings. And if anyone wondered why, all they had to do was take a look at the front page of the *Arizona Daily Sun.*

Besides, putting on a smiling face with her husband would have been a challenge, since Diana was barely speaking to the man. Yes, she was overjoyed that Brandon and Dan had found Lani and engineered her rescue, but she was not pleased that they had put themselves in danger. The only member of the team who wasn't in the doghouse happened to be the dog. Bozo's timely heroics left him entirely free of blame.

Amanda Wasser called Brandon late in the afternoon. "My father is out of the ICU," she said. "His condition has been upgraded from guarded to serious."

"Have you seen him?"

"Yes."

"And?"

"His first words were 'You look just like your mother.' But that's not why I called. I just got off the phone with Mr. Glassman. Ava Richland confessed."

Brandon was astonished. "She did what?"

"The prosecutor agreed to take the death penalty off the table if she confessed to everything, and she did—to Henry Rojas's death, of course, but also to the murder of Amos Warren. She killed him so she could lay hands on his stuff, and she murdered Kenneth Mangum/Myers because he was trying to blackmail her. And then there's the case of Clarence Hanover . . ."

"Wait, are you telling me that Ava murdered her first husband?"

"Yes, and she got away with that one, too. She pushed him into Pantano Wash during a flash flood. I guess she admitted to his homicide because her attorney convinced her that if anything else surfaced later on, her death penalty plea agreement would go away. In addition to that, she admitted to ordering the deaths of the José brothers and masterminding the prison riot scheme designed to cover the attacks on Max José and my father."

"Does your father know about any of this?" Brandon asked.

"Not yet," she answered. "I called you first."

"Even with Ava taking responsibility, Big Bad John isn't going to want to be released from prison," Brandon warned her. "He's worried about being a burden to you."

"Mr. Glassman says that if all this works out, there should be some wrongful conviction funds to help with my father's continuing care."

"Back to Ava; you say Kenneth tried to blackmail her?"

"He may have pretended to be my father's best pal, but it turns out he was also an accessory after the fact in Amos Warren's homicide. Ava confessed that he helped her retrieve Amos's vehicle from the crime scene. He also helped her remove Amos's goods and transport them from his home as well as from the storage unit. I'm not sure why he bothered testifying on my father's behalf at the first trial, since every word out of his mouth was a lie. Maybe his conscience was bothering him."

Just then something else occurred to Brandon. "When I got to Ava Richland's house yesterday afternoon, an ambulance was just taking her current husband, Harold, to the hospital. Did she try to do him in, too?"

"Probably not. It turns out she was far better off with him alive than dead. Harold's son has created a complicated marital trust that would have left him running Ava's show once Harold passes on. That's most likely why she was leaving town. She'd put together a collection of smuggled diamonds that would have kept her in the manner to which she'd become accustomed. She was planning on going elsewhere and living under an assumed name—several assumed names. It almost worked. If it hadn't been for TLC and you, it might very well have worked."

"It wasn't just me," Brandon objected. "A guy named J. P. Beaumont up in Seattle and his pal Todd Hatcher helped out, too."

"How are the two boys doing?" Amanda asked.

"Gabe was released from the hospital early this morning. Tim is still there, but my daughter tells me he'll be fine."

"And your daughter?"

"She's fine, too."

"I'm so glad," Amanda breathed. "I couldn't have stood being responsible for anyone else coming to grief. I've done quite enough harm as it is."

"You can't blame yourself," Brandon counseled.

"None of this is your fault. Do the doctors say how long John will be hospitalized?"

"Most likely the better part of a week."

"Let him know that I'll be dropping by," Brandon Walker said. "I hate to think of you sitting around in the hospital all by yourself."

"I'm not by myself," Amanda said. "A man from the prison is here with me. His name is Aubrey Bayless. He says he's my father's friend, and he's going to hang around to make sure nothing else happens."

I WAS AT the airport waiting in the cell-phone lot for Mel's plane when Brandon Walker called to give me an overview of what had happened. I knew some of it already because Todd Hatcher had kept me apprised as to how things had played out the night before.

Ava's confession to multiple murders, however, came as a complete surprise. There was a certain righteousness in the fact that Amanda Wasser, the daughter of the man Ava had framed for one of her own murders, was the one who ultimately brought her down. I liked that. It may have been justice delayed by decades, but it was far better than no justice at all.

"And Myers died because he tried to blackmail her?"

As I asked the question, I couldn't help thinking about Calliope Horn-Grover. She may have had her suspicions, but she still clung to the hope that the Kenneth Myers she had known was a good guy. She still wore the pendant he had given her. That left me in a dilemma. Would I tell her about the blackmail scheme or wouldn't I? Would I reveal that, more than just knowing about something, he had been an active accomplice? Right at that moment,

I couldn't say for sure one way or the other. Sometimes we're better off living with our illusions wavering but relatively intact than we are knowing the whole truth.

"That's the story," Brandon continued. "Last night, when they booked Ava into the Pima County Jail, they ran her prints through AFIS. The name Ava Hanover popped up in relation to an arrest on a reckless driving charge near Sacramento, California, on the second of May 1983. The police report there indicates she was trying to drive straight through from Seattle to Arizona and fell asleep at the wheel."

"That gave her both motive and opportunity to kill Kenneth Myers," I said.

"And now we have a confession," Brandon added.

Call waiting sounded. I saw on the screen it was Mel. That meant her plane was on the ground.

"Hey, Brandon," I said. "I've gotta go, but good on you. Sounds like you nailed her."

"We all did, Mr. Beaumont. Thanks for your help."

"Beau," I told him. "Call me Beau."

"Okay," Brandon said. "Next time, I will."

Mel had traveled with one carry-on, so there was no need for her to wait around at the luggage carousel. On the drive back to Belltown Terrace, I repeated everything Brandon Walker had told me.

"Sounds like you and Todd Hatcher have been a pair of busy little bees while I've been gone," she observed.

"Busy, yes," I agreed, "and I'll be the first to admit it's been fun."

"So on your first at-bat with TLC, you obviously hit it out of the park," Mel observed. "You saved a young woman's life and took down someone who's clearly a criminal mastermind."

"Todd Hatcher is the one who hit it out of the park. All I did was put him in touch with Brandon Walker."

"I just gave you a compliment," Mel said. "You're supposed to say thank you."

So I did.

There was a long silence in the car. Traffic was heavy. It was raining like crazy.

"So what do you think?" Mel asked at last.

"About what?"

"About TLC? Are you going to work with them again?"

I thought about it for a moment. "I just might," I said. "I didn't do much, but what I did felt damned good."

CHAPTER 29

They say it happened long ago that I'itoi, Elder Brother, came down from Baboquivari. He went to the villages of the Desert People, sat with them around campfires, and told them stories. He told them about how he created the water and the earth. He told them where Wind Man and Rain Man came from. He told them about the Man in the Maze and how the Desert People had emerged from the center of the earth.

The people loved Elder Brother's stories so much that after I'itoi returned to his mountain, that was all the people wanted to do—sit around and listen to the stories over and over. No one wanted to feed and water the cattle. No one wanted to plant the corn and melons. The men stopped going hunting and the women stopped cooking and minding the fires. Soon there was no food. Everyone was hungry, and the Desert People started fighting among themselves.

Up on Baboquivari, I'itoi heard all the quarreling and wondered what all the fuss was about. When he learned what had happened, he was very sad, for you see, nawoj, *my friend, although telling stories is good, you must do other things as well.*

And that is why, even to this day, among the Tohono O'odham, the time for telling stories is only from the middle of November—Kehg S-hehpijig Mashath, the Fair Cold Month—to the middle of March—Chehthagi Mashath, the Green Month. Those are the cold months, the time when the snakes and lizards go to live underground. That's why the stories of the Desert People are winter-telling tales. If a snake or lizard overhears a story, they can swallow the storyteller's luck and bring him harm.

IT WAS FRIDAY again, a whole week later. Once again Leo Ortiz drove Lani and Gabe past Rattlesnake Skull charco at the base of Ioligam. Lani had been both surprised and gratified when a chastened Gabe had shown up in her office earlier in the week, asking if it would be possible for a do-over of their campout. Hopeful that the events of the previous weekend might have somehow penetrated some of the boy's defenses, Lani had agreed on the spot. With both Dan and her slated to work that weekend, it had taken some serious scheduling readjustments to make it work.

So now Lani, Gabe, and a very grumpy Leo were once again lugging their goods up the side of the mountain. "After everything that happened, I don't understand why you have to come here again," he grumbled as he dropped his bundle of firewood. "Couldn't you camp somewhere else?"

"Stories have to end where they begin," Lani said quietly.

Leo simply sighed and shook his head.

The changes in Gabe were remarkable. This time there was no surliness on his part. He hadn't played video games on his phone during the drive from Sells, and he handed it over without a murmur of complaint to his father as Leo left. He set about building the fire pit without being told and waited quietly while Lani heated their simple supper.

It was after sunset when they settled down beside the fire. Gabe had been quiet during most of the evening and Lani didn't want to push him. She knew he had things he wanted to say, and she didn't want him to rush.

"I guess it's too late to tell I'itoi stories," he said. "I saw the snake."

A rattler, still lethargic from hibernation, had crossed the path ahead of them on their hike up the mountain. Lani nodded. "I saw him, too."

"Why did you let him go?"

"Why do you think?"

"Because the Tohono O'odham only kill to defend themselves or to eat."

Lani smiled. "That's right. The snake wasn't bothering us, and I had no intention of eating him."

"I was going to kill Henry Rojas," Gabe admitted at last. "I had Tim's knife. If Henry Rojas had opened the box, I would have."

"I know," Lani said, "and if you had, you would have been stuck out here for sixteen days. Your parents would have been fit to be tied. So would Mrs. Travers. She wouldn't like you to miss that much school."

"Is Mrs. Travers sick?" Gabe asked.

Lani gave him an appraising look before she answered. "She's my patient, Gabe. I can't talk about that."

"If she goes to the Indian hospital, does that mean she's an Indian?"

"I can't talk about it."

Until that moment, Gabe had always believed Mrs. Travers was an Anglo. Gabe nodded. "Okay," he said.

After that, he was quiet for a time while the wind whispered softly through the manzanita.

"Mrs. José came to see me in the hospital," Gabe said. "She's your patient, too. I knew it already, but she told me herself that she's dying."

Lani didn't respond one way or the other.

"My parents said that if that happens, Tim might come live with us. What would you think of that?"

"It might be good for both of you," Lani said. "Just because Tim's brothers did bad things doesn't mean he's bad. Maybe you could help him."

"Maybe," Gabe said. "I hope so."

He tossed another log on the fire, but the boy still seemed troubled, and Lani suspected there was more to come.

"Henry Rojas was a bad man," Gabe said at last. "Do you think Mrs. Rojas will stay in Sells? I heard that she's thinking about moving back to the Navajo."

Lani nodded. "That's what I heard, too. After everything that happened, I don't blame her. I don't believe Lucy had any idea about what Henry was doing behind her back. And the evil Anglo woman he was working with—the woman who had the José brothers smuggling diamonds for her—reminds me of the Evil Giantess in the story of Little White Feather. Do you remember that one?"

"I remember some of it," Gabe said. "I think you told it to me a long time ago."

Lani smiled. "I'll tell it to you again someday—next winter maybe."

"I had a dream last night," Gabe continued after another pause. "It was a weird one. I think it was about the people that evil woman killed—not just Carlos and Paul and Henry, but the other people, too."

"Tell me about it."

"I was walking through a cemetery—a Milgahn cemetery somewhere in town, not here on the reservation. The graves opened up and skeletons started coming out of them. They made a circle around me, and even though they were only bones, I could tell them apart and knew all their names. They were holding hands and dancing. I should have been afraid, but somehow I wasn't. That's what was so weird. I wasn't frightened."

"That's one of the things a medicine man or a medicine woman can do," Lani said. "They can look at a dream and see what it means. The bones were dancing because after all this time the person who murdered them is finally facing justice. They were happy. You weren't frightened of them because they weren't scary."

"Do you think I'll ever be a real medicine man like my grandfather was?" Gabe asked.

"I think you can become one," Lani replied. "You'll have to study hard and learn a lot. Your father told me you said that I gave you some divining crystals."

Gabe lowered his head. "That was a lie," he said. Reaching into the pocket of his jeans, Gabe pulled out four tiny stones and held them out to her in the palm of his hand, where they sparkled in the firelight.

"You didn't give them to me. I found them in the jar of peanut butter Tim left for me. I took out a spoonful of the peanut butter, and when I washed everything else away, these were what was left. I'll give them back if you tell me I should, but they worked," he added. "That night when I was in the hospital, I used them. When I held them in my hand and sang to them, they told me you would be all right. That you would be safe."

Another long silence followed. "I don't think you need to give them back," Lani said at last, taking Gabe's outstretched hand and closing his fingers around the glittering diamonds. "I think you should keep them. Put them back in your pocket and keep them safe. You know how the Ohb would take scalps when they defeated their enemies?"

Gabe nodded.

"They took them as trophies. And that's what these diamonds are—they represent a piece of the evil Milgahn woman. You have a trophy, and so do I."

"You do?" Gabe asked, putting the diamonds back in his pocket.

"Yes," Lani said. She reached into her backpack and pulled out her medicine basket, the one she had woven during her sixteen days of exile. Removing the tightly fitting cover, she extracted the tiny pot and passed it to Gabe. "Can you see the design?"

Gabe held it close to the fire and peered at it closely. "An owl and a turtle?" he asked finally.

"Yes, those are from the story of Little White Feather as well. Owl and Turtle were the first to help Shining Falls when she came under the spell of the Evil Giantess. I believe this is an ancient pot, Gabe, maybe even as old as the ones that belonged to Betraying Woman, the ones I found in the cave. It was made by someone who knew and loved the story of Little White Feather. The evil Milgahn woman had this pot with her on the night she shot Henry Rojas. It must have fallen out of her pocket, maybe when she was putting the duct tape on my face. And now I'm giving it to you."

"For me?" Gabe asked in surprise. "To keep?"

"No," Lani said, "I'm giving it to you to break." She brought out one of Dan's white hankies and laid it across a rock. "I want you to break it on this. Don't smash it. I want you to crack it open very gently like you would if you were breaking an egg. Once you do, I want you to wrap the pieces up in the hankie, take them home, and glue them back together. By breaking the pot, you'll be setting free the spirit of the woman who made it. And once you glue it back together, you'll have a place to keep your divining crystals."

Frowning in concentration, Gabe did as he was told. When he tapped the clay pot gently on the hankie-covered rock, it split apart into four distinct pieces.

"See there?" Lani grinned. "All of nature goes in four. And once you've tied the hankie shut, you can put it in this."

Once again she reached into her backpack. This time she pulled out the second medicine basket, one she had woven with love in hopes of one day giving it to Gabe.

His jaw dropped in disbelief. "A medicine basket?" he asked. "A medicine basket of my very own?"

"Heu'u," Lani said softly. "Yes, your grandfather, Fat Crack, and an old blind medicine man named Looks at Nothing would be very proud."

Life has shifted for JP Beaumont. After a tragic accident that devastated and ultimately disbanded his Special Homicide Investigation Team, he has a lot of unanticipated free time on his hands. He's keeping busy with the renovations on the new house that he and his wife, Mel Soames, the newly appointed Chief of Police in Bellingham, Washington, have bought. But when Beau shows up one afternoon to find Mel's car there but no sign of her, his investigative instincts kick in. Suddenly he's back in the game except this time, his heart is on the line as well as his professional dignity.

Keep reading to join Beaumont as he faces one of his most harrowing trials yet in the novella "Stand Down"

As the machine spat out the last drops of coffee that Monday morning, a tiny whiff of hairspray wafted down the hallway from Mel's bathroom and mingled with the aroma of freshly ground beans and the distinctive fragrance of Hoppe's #9 gun-cleaning solvent. While she was down the hall getting ready to go to work, I was in the kitchen cleaning our weapons—her standard-issue Smith & Wesson and her backup Glock, along with my own Glock as well.

It's what I did these Monday mornings—clean our weapons—while she got ready to go to work in Bellingham and while I got ready to do whatever it is I do these days. I don't suppose the architect who designed our penthouse condo imagined that our granite countertop would often double as a gun-cleaning workshop, but then again, where else would I do this necessary, lifesaving task—the living room? It only takes once to learn how completely a tiny piece of pistol innards can disappear into the hidden reaches of a plush living-room carpet. And cleaning her weapons every Monday morning was my small contribution toward keeping her safe.

The hairspray told me that within a minute or so, my wife, Mel, would emerge from her bathroom dressed, made up, properly coiffed, and ready to go out into the world as the city of Bellingham's newly hired police chief.

While I was married to my first wife, Karen, we'd shared a single bathroom, with a single washbasin and a combination tub and shower. By the time Anne Corley, my second wife, came into my life, however briefly, I still had a single bathroom, but it contained two washbasins, and a tub/shower combo. Shortly after Mel Soames and I tied the knot, it became clear that even a deluxe bathroom, one with two basins, a tub, and a stand-alone shower, simply wouldn't cut it.

Mel had solved the problem by collecting her lotions and potions and decamping to the far end of the hallway and turning the guest bedroom, bathroom, and closet into her private domain. At the time, since we were both working the same shifts for the same outfit, having separate bathrooms worked for us. Now things had changed. She had a relatively new job. As for me? I was struggling with the uncomfortable realities of being newly and quite unwillingly retired.

Mel came down the hall, looking very official in her spiffy police chief's uniform and a pair of sensible, low-heeled pumps.

"Good morning, gorgeous," I told her. I knew she had a meeting with the Bellingham mayor, the city manager, and city council that morning, and I also knew she was dreading it. "Girls in uniform always turn me on."

She stopped and glared at me. "Don't lie," she said. "You know I look like hell."

The truth is, and much to my surprise, she did look like hell. There were dark shadows under her eyes that even deftly applied makeup didn't quite cover. I had spent the night lying next to her in bed as she had tossed and turned her way through the hours. During my years in law enforcement, including twenty or so at Seattle P.D., I had never once entertained the idea of climbing the treacherous career ladder from being an ordinary cop to becoming one of the brass. Mel was different. She had been on the cop-to-brass path in a previous jurisdiction when those plans had been derailed by a complicated divorce. That detour had brought her to Washington State, where we had met.

Second chances don't come along all that often. This time one had. Earlier the previous fall, Mel had been offered her dream job as chief of police in Bellingham, Washington, a small city some ninety miles north of Seattle. The moment the job was offered, I knew she wanted to take it, so I supported her in that decision. I had, however, tried to warn her that making the transition from being part of a team of investigators to being top dog in a new department wouldn't be an easy one. It turns out I was right.

Previously, Mel and I had both worked for the Washington State Attorney General, Ross Connors, on his Special Homicide Investigation Team or, as we had been perversely proud to call it, the S.H.I.T. squad. Ross had been the best boss either of us ever had, bar none. He had expected his people to deliver excellent results while, at the same time, giving his teams of investigators an amazing amount of autonomy. Ross was a political animal, but politics stopped at the door to his office.

I knew even before Mel sat down at her desk that she would find herself in a political quagmire and probably with a dearth of support from the rank and file. Unfortunately, that was proving to be the case. Mel's second-in-command, Assistant Chief Austin Manson, evidently thought the chief's job should have been his for the asking, and he hadn't been happy when she was chosen over him. From what she'd said, I had gleaned that Manson was a much-divorced kind of guy with a rancorous and still-ongoing child-custody battle in his background, along with a few anger-management issues besides. Mel had spent the whole weekend distant and preoccupied. I suspected Manson was the root of the problem, but she hadn't been willing to discuss it. I hadn't brought it up, and neither had she.

Now, even without being Mirandized, I understood that in this dicey situation, anything I said could and would be held against me. Besides, handing out a dose of "I told you so," bright and early in the morning, is never a good way to start a new day or week. I couldn't come right out and tell Mel that she should just bust Austin Manson back to the gang and get it over with. And I sure as hell didn't see myself in the role of Sir Galahad, riding in on my white charger to intervene on her behalf, so that morning, I took the line of least resistance.

"Coffee's ready," I said noncommittally, shoving

her newly cleaned weapons across the counter. Once she had stowed them in their appropriate holsters, I handed over Mel's favorite mug, loaded with fresh coffee. "This should do the trick."

Mel gave me the benefit of a small, rueful smile. "Thanks," she said, taking a tentative sip. "Coffee is just what the doctor ordered."

That hint of a smile was enough to make me hope that, as far as dealing with women is concerned, maybe I was getting older and wiser.

"What's on your agenda today?" she asked. She had left piles of unfinished paperwork on the dining-room table before we'd gone to bed the night before. She gathered it into a single stack and shoved it into an open briefcase. The stack was bulky enough that closing the case was a bit of a struggle.

"Late this morning, I'm scheduled to drive up to Arlington to meet with the contractor and take a look at the final estimate."

Two and a half months into her new job, Mel was still spending four nights a week at a dreary Execu-Stay Hotel in Bellingham. Once she accepted the job, we had decided that, although we didn't want to give up our penthouse in downtown Seattle, we'd find someplace nearer to her workplace as a second home. As spouse-in-chief, I had been tasked with finding us suitable digs in the Bellingham area that would allow us to stay there when she was working and come and go from Seattle as often as we wished.

Initially, Mel had voted for another condo. I was looking for something else. After decades of high-rise living, I was ready for a pied-à-terre with . . . well . . . a little actual terre. I wanted a covered patio where, rain or shine, I could walk outside and barbecue steaks for dinner without messing up the kitchen. I also wanted a place where, if the grandkids came to visit, we could put up a volleyball net or fly model airplanes.

My first few meetings with Helen Tate, the Realtor, hadn't gone well. She had evidently checked up on the value of our home in Seattle on the Web, and I could see the dollar signs swimming in her eyes the first time she showed up to take me looking at properties. She had been somewhat dismayed when I fell in love with a vintage-but-dilapidated three-bedroom midcentury modern. Located in the Bayside area of Fairhaven, with a spectacular, cliffside view, it was listed as a "fixer-upper." With plenty of sixty-year-old plumbing issues, lots of dry rot, and a sagging roof, not to mention a collection of more recent but steamy dual-paned windows that had long since lost their seals, the place should have been listed as a tear-down. There was only one problem with that—I wanted it.

The original owner, a widower, had recently been carted off to an Alzheimer's' facility. His son, who lived out of state, simply wanted to dispose of the place with the least possible amount of effort and fuss.

The thing is, I could tell that underneath all the filth and trash, the house had good bones. The spectacular view of the bay, the interior courtyard, and the expansive windows all beckoned to me. There was so much glass that, once the fogged windows were replaced, we'd be able to see right through the house from back to front. You can get those kinds of views in high-rise condos occasionally, but finding them in a house was unusual.

Even so, I hoped it would be possible for Mel to see

past the neglect to the house's buried charm. Something about the old place felt familiar and inviting and made me want to bring the derelict back from the dead. That stormy day in February, when Mel agreed to meet Helen and me at the house during her lunch break, both the Realtor and I held our collective breaths as Mel, dressed in her uniform and heels, wandered thoughtfully from room to room.

"I see what you mean," Mel said at last, picking her way through yet another minefield of debris as she returned to the living room. "The place does have good bones, but it's going to take a lot of work. Are you sure you're up to it?"

I nodded.

"What happens to all this stuff?" Mel asked, gesturing at the piles of junk surrounding her.

"The owner's son lives out of town. He doesn't want any of it, and he doesn't want to have to deal with it, either," Helen explained. "He's ready to be done with it."

"We'd be buying the place as is, contents and all, no contingencies," I added. "That means whatever is left here, we'd have to haul away, and whatever's broken, we'd have to fix. I've already called Jim Hunt to see if he'd be willing to come take a look and give us some suggestions."

Mel eyed me speculatively. "Jim Hunt, as in the guy who designed both your bachelor pads?"

I nodded, guilty as charged. After Karen divorced me, I had moved into a unit at the Royal Crest in downtown Seattle with little more than the clothes on my back and the one piece of furniture that Karen had allowed me to take—my recliner. One of the secretaries at the department had referred me to Jim, and he had done a complete job of creating a livable condo from a barren shell, up to and including linens and pots and pans. Our only disagreement was over the recliner. He wanted it gone, but I was adamant. The recliner was mine, and I was keeping it. In the years since it had been recovered more than once.

Mel wandered over to the spot where a baby grand piano peeked out from under a mountain of magazines and newspapers. "You say everything stays, even this?" she asked, pausing long enough to open the dust-laden lid and play a scale. Even I could hear that the piano was hopelessly out of tune.

Helen nodded. "That, too," the Realtor said helpfully.

"All right, then," Mel said. "I'm headed back to work. As long as the piano is included, you've got my go-ahead to make an offer. When you talk to Jim, see if he knows of a good piano guy who could haul this poor old thing out of here, refinish it, and tune it up. Obviously, it can't stay here if the place is about to turn into a construction zone."

Talk about an assumed close! I learned all about those back in my youth, when I was selling Fuller Brush to earn my way through school. We were trained not to say, "Do you want this brush?" but, rather, "How do you want to pay for this, cash or check?" That was long enough ago that credit cards still weren't an option. It was also typical behavior for Mel Soames. When I asked her to marry me, she hadn't come right out, and said, "Yes." Instead, her response had been more on the order of, "Well, okay. When?"

I don't think that was the reaction the Realtor expected. She was still standing in an openmouthed daze, as Mel walked out of the house, closing the door behind her.

"You're buying it, then?" Helen asked. "Just like that?"

"It's looking good."

I waited for Jim to arrive before making a formal offer. He's a tall, good-looking, narrow guy—maybe even skinny. He's about my age but fared better in the knee lottery than I did since his are still original equipment. He has an enviable head of silvery hair combined with the good looks of an aging movie star. He's also gay and attempting to cut down on his smoking, but in the thirty years we've known one another, neither of those issues—smoking or sexual orientation—have impacted our friendship. He goes his way; I go mine. And he thinks Mel is terrific.

Jim showed up a while later in his shiny white Mercedes C230 and spent the better part of two hours prowling the place before rendering his verdict. "I think we could make do with this," he told me, "but, if you want my help, there's one condition."

"What's that?" I asked.

"The only way I'm tackling this job is if you agree to get rid of that damned recliner. Finally."

When I called Mel to report Jim's single demand, she had jumped at it.

"If he can get you to let go of that ugly old thing, then make an offer on the house and tell me where to sign. I'm there."

And so we did. Once the deal was finalized, the former owner's son and a grandson had dropped by long enough to gather up several boxes of clothing and a few mementoes, then they drove away without so much as a backward glance, leaving behind seven decades' worth of accumulated trash and a houseful of dead and dying furniture and mountains of out-of-date foodstuffs. Some of the canned goods had exploded, leaving behind the distinctive aroma of decay, which would only disappear once we'd stripped the wallboard down to the studs.

That's what we were working on now—the reno. The trash had been hauled away. The piano had been collected by a piano restorer and carted off to be refinished, tuned, and stored until it was safe to come back home.

Originally, the house had been insulated with layers of cedar shavings that, over time, had been reduced to little more than dust. After evicting a family of raccoons that had taken up residence in the attic, we vacuumed out the smelly remains. With that gone, along with the reeking wallboard, the place smelled almost civilized. Jim had come up with an elegant redesign. By sacrificing the third bedroom, he was able to give Mel and me a master bedroom suite that included two separate bathrooms and two walk-in closets.

The master-bedroom plans alone were enough to send Mel over the top with delight, but after that, the project seemed to have stalled out. The challenge now was nailing down a busy contractor and getting him to commit to doing the job in a timely fashion. That was what I was hoping to accomplish today. Only then would we be able to apply for permits and start actual construction.

"I know about the meeting with Jim and that contractor later today," Mel said with a frown, "but aren't you also scheduled to see Harry? He's due to be released from rehab anytime now, isn't he?"

Making Harry I. Ball's house wheelchair accessible was currently my other pressing home-remodeling issue. While waiting for the project in Bellingham to get under way, I—along with Jim's help—had been running point on the renovations to bring Harry I. Ball's house into compliance with his current wheelchair-bound status. His project, too, had been plagued with delays. Now, even though we were down to finishing touches, they all had to be completed, inspected, and signed off on before Harry could be released from rehab to go home.

I nodded. "The foreman told me yesterday that they expect to be done by the end of this week. That's the goal, anyway."

"And you've got Marge lined up to look after him once he's back home?"

Marge Herndon was the crusty retired RN Mel and I had first encountered when I'd hired her to come look after me after my bilateral knee-replacement surgery. The woman was about as warm and fuzzy as a Marine Corps drill sergeant, but she knew how to get the job done, and she had kept me on the straight and narrow as far as rehab was concerned. Harry Ignatius Ball, aka Harry I. Ball, was a tough customer under the best of circumstances. Now, stuck in a wheelchair, with both legs amputated above the knee, I knew he would be a demanding and difficult patient.

"She's willing," I answered. "She's supposed to show up this morning to meet him for the first time, then we'll see what happens. If those two lock horns, it could turn into World War III."

Standing with one foot out the door, Mel turned back long enough to give me a genuine grin. "I'd love to be a mouse in the corner when that happens. Between Harry I. Ball and Marge Herndon, my money's on Marge—all the way. She managed you just fine, and I'm betting she'll be able to handle him, too. Harry won't know what hit him."

"Drive carefully," I warned her, giving her a goodbye peck on the cheek. "It rained hard overnight. They're saying to watch out for standing water on the roadways."

While Mel took the long elevator ride from our aerie down to the parking garage far below and drove up four sets of ramps to street level, I went out on the balcony and stood waiting for her to emerge. If Mel had known that I did that every morning, rain or shine, when she left for work, she would have thought I was being a sentimental fool, but I couldn't help myself. Now I knew how it felt to be the spouse of a cop heading out the door for a day of confronting the bad guys. For the first time in my life, I understood what it meant to be the one waiting at home, knowing that my beloved would be at work some ninety-one miles and at least two hours away in good traffic. More if anything went wrong along the way. Yes, karma is definitely a bitch!

So is change.

I walked back inside and made myself another cup of coffee. Then I sat down on the living-room window seat and looked out at the Space Needle. That iconic piece of Seattle's skyline has taken on a whole new and much darker meaning these days. It was where all of our lives had taken a sudden turn in a new and unexpected direction.

THINGS HAD STARTED going haywire almost three months earlier, on the Friday, two weeks before Christmas. Mel was back in her bathroom getting ready for our evening out while I sat in this same window-seat perch looking at the red and green lights, including the glowing Christmas tree that topped the Needle's flying-saucer-shaped roof. Ross Connors had scored the Needle's lower level for a Special Homicide Investigation Team Christmas party. If Ross had been using state funds for the event, he probably would have had to call it a "Holiday Party," but since he was paying for the whole thing out of his own pocket, he would, as he told me, call it whatever the hell he wanted.

The people from all three S.H.I.T. squads—the ones in Spokane and Olympia as well as our Seattle-based one—along with their spouses/partners were invited. Ross was also springing for hotel rooms where necessary. We all knew what the real deal was. It was really a thinly disguised post-election celebration. When the polls had closed the previous November, and when all the votes were counted, Ross Connors had won again despite all the predictions to the contrary. He was still the Attorney General because countless people had crossed party lines to vote for him. The problem was, Ross was the exception. All the other statewide office holders, including the governor himself, now belonged on the "opposite side of the aisle." I hadn't a doubt in my mind that Ross's Christmas party was a poke in the nose at all those folks—a way of letting them know that he was the last man standing.

As for his people, those of us privileged to call Ross Connors "boss"? We really were "his people." Ross had used that same considerable political savvy that had won cross-party-line voters in creating S.H.I.T. He had collected a diverse set of people—always the ones he thought most skilled in getting the job done—and had molded us into a cohesive whole, a team in every sense of the word. If this was a Christmas party, we were all going, and that included the two guys in the organization who describe themselves as "non-observant" Jews.

The event was due to start promptly at six. It was five fifty-five when Mel emerged from her private domain at the far end of the hall. Dressed in a long, ruby-red dress with her long blond hair swept up onto her head, she would have been at home on any Hollywood red carpet. So would the shoes—amazing bright red stiletto heels made by a guy named Jimmy something. They matched her dress perfectly. In four-inch heels, she was only slightly shorter than me. In honor of the evening, she was carrying a small, glittery clutch rather than one of her more customary suitcase-sized purses.

I had sat there, waiting for her and holding her coat. Standing up, I slipped it over her shoulders and inhaled a hint of perfume.

"It's spitting snow," I said. "How about if we take the car and use the valet?"

"Come on," she said. "It's only three blocks."

The thing is, I was well acquainted with almost every inch of those three blocks. Doing rehab in the aftermath of my knee-replacement surgery, I had done more walking than ever before, trudging alone through Seattle's Denny Regrade neighborhood. I knew full well that the Space Needle was a mere three blocks away from Belltown Terrace's front door, but I also understood that those three blocks are lined with mature trees whose roots have, over time, played havoc with nearby sidewalk surfaces. Not only is the concrete lumpy and bumpy in spots, it's also riddled with cracks and iron drain covers that are the natural enemy of misplaced feet, especially ones in very high heels.

"Besides," Mel said, "it'll be fun, and I promise to hold on to your arm for dear life."

"Right," I said, "as in the blind leading the blind."

Someone once told me, "Happy wife; happy life," so we walked, laughing and talking through spattering snow that we both knew would never stick. We crossed Broad at Second then walked up the north side of the street as far as Denny, which we crossed at the light.

Walking along the grassy berm between Denny and the Pacific Science Center, we were almost at the valet parking entrance at the bottom of the Space Needle and the Chihuly Glass Garden when I heard the first hint of sirens—lots of sirens.

When you live downtown, you grow accustomed to sirens. You learn to differentiate between those of the fire engines and aid cars at the Seattle F.D. station over on Fourth. There are the short bursts from patrol cars that usually indicate traffic stops. Those are especially annoying in the wee hours of the morning, just after the bars let out, when the traffic guys are busy taking drunks off the street. But this was different. This was something more. It sounded like a car chase to me, coming southbound toward us along Elliott. Suddenly, sirens blossomed all around us as police vehicles from all over the city converged on the area. There were cars coming northbound on the avenues from downtown and cars coming down from Queen Anne Hill.

Car chases are inherently dangerous. The potential for tragedy—for death and serious injury—is always there, whether it's on a deserted highway in the middle of the night or on a city street in broad daylight. A car chase during rush hour on a dark and rain-slick city street was insanity itself. Someone else must have come to that same conclusion. The sirens went silent, and I surmised that orders to break off the chase must have been given. The cops got the message. They backed off, all of them. Unfortunately, the crooks didn't.

Let's just say that guys who set out to make a living by robbing banks usually aren't the sharpest pencils in the box. The only place smart bank robbers show up is on scripted television shows. And bank robbers who would pull off a heist in Ballard then head into the city center in rush-hour traffic, hoping to make good their escape, exhibit a particularly astounding brand of stupidity. But that's what these two dimwits had done. They had somehow convinced themselves that if they just made it into the downtown core, they'd be able to blend into traffic and disappear.

In the old days, bank tellers would slip dye packs into the crooks' tote bags that would stain the robber and render the money unusable. These days, tellers have access to packets of bills that come pre-equipped with GPS locator chips. All the teller has to do is activate the chip before slipping it into the bag, and voila. That money is invisibly findable with no car chases necessary. I'm sure that's one of the reasons the chase was called off. The chip was working. The good guys had all the time in the world to track the bad guys down.

So far the two boneheads hadn't figured that out. I heard the squeal of tires behind us as they came screaming up past Western and onto Denny. Then, to my amazement, a set of headlights weaving in and out of oncoming traffic, turned off Denny and onto Broad with other drivers slamming up onto sidewalks in desperate attempts to escape harm. Obviously, the maniac behind the wheel hadn't gotten the memo that Broad is no longer a through street.

Instinctively, Mel and I both headed for higher ground although Mel didn't start up the grassy berm until after she'd pulled off those damned shoes. We were standing side by side when the robbers flew past us, herding their stolen Range Rover between rows of stopped cars and tearing off mirrors and door panels as they went. The Range Rover slewed sideways directly in front of us then accelerated up Broad.

I knew what was going to happen long before it did. A vehicle turned off Fourth. Then, with oncoming traffic apparently stalled, the unsuspecting driver made the left-hand turn into the Space Needle's valet parking area. The speeding Range Rover, driving in the wrong lane, smashed into them midturn, T-boning them, hard.

You can go to movie theaters and watch all the computer-generated mayhem you want, but none of that compares to the real thing—to the terrible crash followed by the sickening, grinding sound of twisting metal coming to rest. And then, out of the sudden silence that followed the carnage came the haunting sound of not one but two wailing car horns. They sounded like sentinels announcing the end of the world, or at least the end of the world as we knew it.

By then, Mel and I were both moving, toward the action rather than away from it. There would be other cops in the neighborhood soon, but we were closer than anyone else, and in what would soon turn into a massive traffic jam, we'd get there before anyone else could, too. If the crooks, whose car was closer, managed to exit their vehicle and tried to take off on foot, we'd be able to restrain them.

Not surprisingly, neither of them—dumb and dumber—had been smart enough to wear a seat belt. They had both been ejected from the vehicle. We found them lying on opposite sides of Broad. I located the first one on the north side of the street, lying with his head cracked open like a broken watermelon on the sharp edge of the curb. I didn't need to check for a pulse to know he was a goner.

The other guy, the passenger, had slammed full-tilt into a metal utility vault on the far side of the street. Mel reached him at the same time several passersby did. She knelt briefly and dropped out of sight. When she straightened up, she caught my eye and gave me the thumbs-down. So that one was dead, too—no great loss there. Subsequent computer-generated reconstructions of the collision estimated that the two dunces were doing seventy and still accelerating when they slammed into the turning vehicle. There was no sign that the driver ever touched the brakes.

Knowing those guys were dead, Mel and I turned our attention toward the other damaged vehicle. It was only then that we realized, with growing horror, that what we were seeing, stalled in the middle of Broad, were the still-smoking remains of Ross Connors's Lincoln Town Car.

Even months later, recalling that horrific scene that changed all our lives was enough to shock me back to real time. I set down my coffee mug and headed for the shower. An hour or so later, when I left Belltown Terrace, I turned right on Second and drove all the way down to Olive and used that to make my way up to Harry's rehab facility on the far side of Capitol Hill. That's the official name for that particular neighborhood, but due to all the hospitals based there, locals generally refer to it as Pill Hill.

In the old days I would have turned right on Broad and over to Fifth to make that trip. Not anymore. For one thing, the city's traffic engineers have fixed it so Broad no longer goes anywhere useful. Besides, I avoid Denny and Broad as much as possible. That's where the accident happened. It's where Ross Connors and his driver, Bill Spade, lost their lives, and it's also where Harry Ignatius Ball lost both his legs.

Just glancing up either of those streets is enough to bring back vivid memories of that nightmarish scene. Ross's aging Lincoln Town Car had been hit so hard that both people on the driver's side of the car—Bill at the wheel and Ross seated directly behind him—had died on impact, crushed to death when the stolen Range Rover plowed into the passenger compartment, ending up with the Rover's front bumper crushed up against the Town-Car's drive shaft.

Momentum from the collision carried the two conjoined vehicles into a nearby light pole with enough force that the pole toppled over. It landed on the roofs of both cars, crumpling metal like so much tissue paper and sending a jagged edge of roof into Harry's lower thighs, nearly severing his legs. The weight of the pole on top of the roof was the only thing that kept him from bleeding to death on the spot.

I had reached in through the wreckage and checked both Bill and Ross. Neither of them had a pulse. They were gone. By then, Mel was on the far side of the car, reaching in through the shattered passenger window and trying to comfort Harry, who was howling in pain. Looking at his legs, I was sure he was a goner, too.

The nearest fire station, at Fourth and Battery, was only five blocks away, but in the sudden snarl of stalled traffic, it could just as well have been in Timbuktu. It seemed to take forever for them to get there with the jaws of life. In fact, an EMT, a young woman, jogging from the station and carrying a first-aid kit, arrived long before anyone else or any other equipment. She was small enough to maneuver inside the tiny space left in the vehicle and somehow managed to fasten two tourniquets around Harry's upper thighs, thus saving his life but dooming his legs. In the meantime, I was left with nothing to do but wish I could slam my fist through someone's face, preferably that of the stupid driver, who was already dead.

Mel and I had set out for the Space Needle just minutes before the party was scheduled to start. It turned out that Ross, too, had been making an uncharacteristically late entrance. I found out later that Harry's car had developed a fuel-pump issue on his way into the city from Bellevue. When he'd called Ross to let him know he'd be late, Ross had insisted that he and Bill drive over Lake Washington on the I-

90 bridge, pick Harry up, and bring him to the party. I've always been struck by that old saying about no good deed going unpunished, but having Ross and Bill dead because they'd done nothing more than give Harry a ride was too much.

The jaws of life were not yet on the scene when I realized that if most of the other partygoers were already upstairs, I was the one who would have to deliver the bad news. And so I did, pushing my way into the Space Needle lobby and through the line of holiday revelers waiting for the elevator. People protested vigorously as I fought my way to the head of the line and flashed my badge in front of the boyish-faced operator.

"Skyline Banquet level," I snarled at him. "Now!"

Without a word, he allowed me into the elevator, barred the other waiting passengers by means of a velvet-covered rope, closed the door on them, and pushed the buttons. We rode up in utter silence. "Wait here," I ordered. "I'll be coming right back down."

Just inside the door stood a waiter holding a tray of glasses filled with bubbling champagne. I was tempted to grab one of them. In fact, I was tempted to grab them all and swill them down one after another. Instead, I stopped short and scanned the room.

It took a moment for me to locate Katie Dunn, Ross's secretary. She was talking to Barbara Galvin, Harry's secretary and the cornerstone for Unit B of Special Homicide. Finding both women together was a stroke of luck. Katie must have caught sight of the look on my face. She turned away from Barbara and hurried toward me, with Barbara, also sensing something amiss, close on her heels.

"Beau," Katie asked, frowning, "whatever's the matter?"

With no time to lessen the blow, I blurted it out at once. "There's been a car accident down on the street. Ross is dead, and so's his driver. Harry may not make it, either."

Katie's face drained of all color. "Oh, no!" she whispered. "Ross is dead?"

I nodded. Without a word, Barbara sprinted for the elevator.

"Go with Barbara," Katie said to me. "I'll hold the fort here. Keep me posted."

When I entered the elevator, Barbara was already there, white-faced and furious, screeching into the operator's face. "Go, damn it! What on earth are you waiting for? Go now!"

But I had made a believer of the poor guy. He waited until I stepped on board before pushing the DOWN button. By the time we hit the ground level, Barbara was out of her sequined heels. Holding them in one hand and a tiny beaded clutch in the other, she sprinted out of the elevator and left me in the dust as she pushed through the crush of people waiting for the long-delayed elevator.

I caught up with Barbara only because she was stopped short by a uniformed cop trying to maintain a perimeter around the crash site. "She's with me," I told him, holding up my badge. "Let her through."

We reached the wreckage while firefighters were still maneuvering the jaws of life into position. Despite protests from more than one first responder, Barbara shoved Mel out of the way. "Don't you die on me, you bastard!" she yelled at Harry, snatching his hand from Mel's. Bad as things were, Harry focused his eyes on Barbara's face and favored her with a tiny grin.

"Do my best," he whispered. "I'll do my best."

Believe me, the relationship between Harry I. Ball and the reformed punk rocker, Barbara Galvin, had nothing to do with an office romance. It was more like a love/hate, father/daughter kind of thing.

At that point, one of the firefighters simply picked Barbara up and carried her away from the wreckage, bringing her over to where Mel and I had taken refuge on a piece of sidewalk slick with shattered glass. "Keep her here and get her shoes back on," the man growled at us. "We need this woman out of our way!"

Another firefighter appeared behind him. "Okay," he said. "We've got permission to land the chopper on top of KOMO."

The snarl of traffic, growing worse by the minute, made transporting Harry to a hospital by ambulance a nonstarter. The building for the local ABC affiliate, complete with a helipad on its roof, was almost directly across the street. In moments, they had Harry out of the crushed vehicle and onto a gurney, rolling him across the street and toward the building to the helipad. Once at Harborview Hospital, a team of the ER docs tried valiantly to save his legs. It didn't work. His legs were gone, and soon, so was everything else, S.H.I.T included.

Within weeks of Ross Connors's funeral and while Harry was still in the hospital, the governor—the one from the "other side of the aisle"—had appointed a new attorney general, whose first order of business was to disband Special Homicide altogether.

Suddenly we were all out of a job. Well, not all of us. Mel was one of the younger ones, and she'd already decided to make the move to Bellingham before the axe fell. But the rest of us—the old duffers—were out of luck. For right now, I was keeping busy wrangling construction projects. What I'd do later on when all the plaster dust settled was something I mostly avoided contemplating.

I found a parking place on Cherry and trudged half a block in the wrong direction to find the applicable pay station, grumbling to myself the whole way about the loss of old-fashioned parking meters. They might have eaten every bit of change out of your pocket in the blink of an eye, but at least they were right there by your car. You didn't have to go searching for them.

I was back on Boren and about to walk through the automatic doors into the lobby, when Harry hailed me by name. Turning, I saw his wheelchair parked some fifty feet away from the door under a bus-stop-like shelter designed to keep smokers away from the building and out of the rain, at least, if not out of the cold. I had wheeled him up there more than once, so he could have a smoke.

Coming closer, I saw that Harry wasn't alone. Standing nearby was Marge Herndon herself, the hoyden who had looked after me during my bout with postsurgical rehab. She was smoking like a chimney, and so was Harry. He looked happier than I'd seen him in months.

"Hey," he said, waving his burning cigarette in her direction. "Thanks for putting me in touch with Margie here. She came by just now to introduce herself. She got here a few minutes early. The woman is a gem."

Are you kidding? They'd barely been introduced, and Harry was already calling her Margie? I had known the woman for months without ever getting beyond the basic Nurse Ratched stage. And he thought she was a "gem"? I regarded the woman as an absolute terror, one who had run roughshod over me for what had seemed like months rather than weeks.

I nodded in Marge's direction. "Good to see you," I said.

"Same here," she muttered tersely in a way that told me that even though Harry had scored big with her, I had not.

I knew in that moment that, once again, Mel had been right, and I was wrong. In the course of a single cigarette, or maybe two, Marge Herndon had Harry I. Ball eating out of her hand.

It was enough to piss off the Good Fairy.

Clearly, since Marge and Harry were getting along like gangbusters, my planned introduction as well as my continued presence weren't required. I chatted for a few minutes, then, excusing myself, I found my car, complete with paid-for-but-unused parking time, and made my way down the hill to I-5, where I headed north.

JIM HUNT HAD located three possible contractors for us. This one, Don Hastings, the last one on the list, lived in Smoky Point, a tiny ex-burb north of Everett.

Don had done jobs for Jim Hunt several times in the past, and he and his people had done quality work. He had also handled projects in towns stretching from Everett all the way to the Canadian border. That meant he had contacts and working relationships with people in planning departments from here to there. Those connections were bound to streamline the permitting process. More to the point, he had a crew based in Arlington that was finishing up one job and would be ready to tackle another within a matter of weeks.

We'd taken proposals from the two other construction outfits—so we had three estimates altogether. Jim had warned us that the one from Hastings would most likely come in as the priciest one of the three in terms of up-front cost, but I've learned over time that you get what you pay for. And I'd already made up my mind to sign on the dotted line long before I found my way to Don's office, located in a converted garage next to his residence on the outskirts of town. I stayed long enough to meet the man in person and write a deposit check that would put the wheels in motion, then I headed north again, leaving Don and Jim Hunt huddled together over a stack of plans spread out across a drafting table.

Once on I-5, I tried calling Mel to let her know the deed was done, but when her phone went straight to voice mail, I didn't bother leaving a message. She was probably busy, and I'd be there soon enough to give her the news in person.

Although I was glad to have the project out of my hands and in the care and keeping of a competent professional, I was a little blue about it, too. I had been so preoccupied with dealing with the housing issues that I'd had little time to think about what I was going to do with the rest of my life.

Between my years at Seattle P.D. and the ones with S.H.I.T., I'd spent almost all my adult life in law enforcement. It's not just a career. It's a mind-set and a way of life. There are far too many stories out there of ex-cops who, having pulled the plug on working, end up taking their own lives. Of course, that wouldn't be me. For starters, I had Mel. I was determined to spend every possible moment with her. She had her own career path now—a complicated career path—but what the hell was I supposed to do with my spare time? Take up golf, for Pete's sake? That seemed to be working for my friend, Ralph Ames who, along with his wife, Mary, was now living—and golfing—at a development called Pebble Creek which is somewhere in the Phoenix metropolitan area. Ralph had tried unsuccessfully to interest me in golfing. It just didn't take.

Twenty miles out of Bellingham, I dialed Mel's number again. This time I did leave a message. "Hey," I said. "I signed the contract with Don Hastings. Things moved faster than I expected. Since I'm sort of in the neighborhood, I thought I'd see if we could grab a quick late lunch. Call me when you have time. I'm about twenty minutes out."

It was frustrating to know that Mel was in a complicated situation at work and that, other than offering her moral support, there was little I could do about it. As far as I could tell, Mel's tenure as chief had been completely devoid of a honeymoon period. It had become clear all too soon that Mel's selection by the city council and city manager had been made over the mayor's strenuous objections. Mayor Adelina Kirkpatrick was a typical small-time politician. The mayor was a lifelong Bellingham resident who knew where all the bodies were buried while

Mel was new to town. Mel had learned that the mayor had fully expected Assistant Chief Austin Manson to be handed the job of chief, a move that had been thwarted by both the city manager and the city council. That meant Mel's relationship with the mayor had started out on the wrong foot and had stayed that way.

Midway through Mel's second week in office, there had been an officer-involved shooting in Bellingham at a lowlife bar on the waterfront, a rough place called the Fish Bowl. For most of my working life, that term—the Fish Bowl— had referred to the window-lined office on the fifth floor of Seattle's Public Safety Building where Homicide Captain Larry Powell long held sway. So the irony of the bar's name touched my funny bone. On the surface, the shoot-out shouldn't have been all that serious. For one thing, nobody died.

Mel had been locked up in a meeting with the mayor and the city manager at the time of the incident. At the mayor's insistence, pagers and other electronic devices were not allowed inside her office. That struck me as odd all by itself. I warned Mel that anyone that concerned about electronic eavesdropping was either a conspiracy freak or else s/he had something to hide. As far as Mayor Kirkpatrick was concerned, it might have been a little of both.

Some people stream music on their phones and tablets. Once Mel ended up in Bellingham, I spent a lot of time tuned into a radio station there. I also programmed my iPad so breaking news alerts from there would be sent to me as they occurred. The day of the shooting, with Mel locked in the mayor's office, I knew about the incident before she did. As soon as the news alert showed up on my screen, my heart went to my throat. As police chief, Mel shouldn't have been out on any kind of patrol, still I didn't breathe easier until I had called her office, checked with her secretary, and learned that Mel was still upstairs in a meeting. Whew!

Over the course of time—that day and subsequent ones—the details emerged. A young cop, Officer Dale Embry, had been patrolling the waterfront area when a guy came running out of the Fish Bowl and flagged him down, alerting him to a developing domestic-violence situation inside the bar. Embry radioed for backup then hurried inside. The bartender's estranged and enraged husband, armed with a butcher knife, was threatening to murder his soon-to-be-former wife and anyone stupid enough to get in his way.

Embry entered the premises with his weapon already drawn. When Embry told the guy to drop his knife, the guy swung around and started for him. I know firsthand that when you're facing an assailant armed with a knife, you're caught in a chaotic situation, and you're not exactly thinking straight. Adrenaline is pumping; your heart is hammering off the charts, and you're hoping to God it's not your last day on planet earth.

Embry pulled the trigger. The shot should have taken the guy down. It didn't, but only because someone else took him down first. One of the customers, armed with a barstool, clobbered the irate husband and put him on the floor. The only other casualty turned out to be the mirror behind the bar, which shattered into a million pieces.

The assailant was knocked out cold. An ambulance

was summoned and hauled him off to the ER with a possible concussion. When departmental supervisors arrived on the scene, a group that ultimately included Assistant Chief Manson, Officer Embry was sent home on administrative leave.

In officer-involved shootings where a weapon is discharged, administrative leave is standard procedure. When Mel came out of her meeting, however, and learned it was a done deal, she was not pleased. Yes, she hadn't had her pager along in the meeting, but she was offended that Manson hadn't bothered to come upstairs himself or even send someone up to let her know about the incident while it was still unfolding. She took the position that, by issuing the leave order himself, Manson had undercut her authority.

In the heat of the moment, she had called Assistant Chief Manson out about it and given him a dressing-down. Later on that day, she paid a call at Officer Embry's home, encouraging him to use his leave time constructively in a way that would turn him into a better cop. After that visit, she had attempted to apologize to Manson, but he wasn't having any of it. The damage was done. Manson was pissed, and apparently he planned to stay that way.

The problem was, I could see both sides of the issue. This was a routine situation and a routine call on Manson's part. If Mel had been a more seasoned chief, she wouldn't have felt compelled to assert her authority in such a heavy-handed fashion. Perhaps she shouldn't have reacted the way she did initially, but now it was too late. Rather than having Manson as an ally, she had turned the man into a sworn enemy.

When Mel had accepted the job, I think she had

imagined herself as being the kind of skilled leader Ross Connors had always been. The problem was, when it came to building S.H.I.T., Ross Connors had been able to go out and handpick the people he wanted on his team. It had been an older, wiser, and dedicated group, with little, if any, deadweight. In her new department, Mel didn't have the luxury of handpicking her people. She had to work with what was already there.

Two months later, Embry was back from his leave. Due to the Fish Bowl incident, Mel was stuck with both an extremely loyal but peach-fuzzed young cop and a grizzled veteran who wouldn't give her the time of day and didn't miss a trick when it came to badmouthing Mel behind her back. In terms of departmental morale, guess which one carries more weight?

One evening, over dinner, I had made the tactical error of venturing an opinion on the subject. As a result, Assistant Chief Manson was no longer a topic of conversation between Mel and me. He was the elephant in the room—the taboo place where neither of us dared to tread.

I was coming up on the Fairhaven exit when I tried Mel's phone one last time. By then, I was slightly annoyed. Obviously, my idea of treating her to a surprise lunch wasn't going to happen. Consequently, I turned on the directional signal. Exiting the freeway, I left another message.

"You're probably too busy for lunch," I said. "There's no sense in my coming down to the department and being under hand and foot. I'm turning off at Fairhaven. I'll wait at the house until you get cut loose. Maybe I can take you out to dinner instead of lunch. If you're really lucky, you might even talk me into spending the night."

I drove over to Bayside and down the steep driveway that leads to our house. Mel's Porsche Cayman was tucked in behind a massive construction Dumpster that had taken over a big portion of the concrete slab that had once been a detached garage. The rest of the garage structure, afflicted by a terminal case of dry rot, had been red-flagged as a hazard, knocked down, and the splintered remains hauled away during the first week of our renovation efforts. Mel had worried that perhaps it was an omen about the inadvisability of the entire project. Jim Hunt had attempted to reassure her by explaining that in sixty-year-old wood-frame buildings, dry rot was simply the natural order of things, especially in the rainy Pacific Northwest.

I wasn't surprised to find her car parked there. Mel had told me that when things got too stressful at work, she'd grab a sandwich from Subway and drive out to our place, where she would eat lunch in her car, take a few deep breaths, and relieve the pressure by watching the birds out on the bay. I suspected that once the workers showed up, and construction kicked into high gear, parking there for lunch wouldn't be nearly as peaceful.

Given all that, I half expected to see her sitting in the car, but she wasn't, so I walked on down to the front of the house and stepped up onto the sagging front porch. The door was locked, so I used the key and stepped inside.

"Mel?" I called into the echoing skeletal shell. "Are you here?"

She wasn't. The house was empty. Leaving the front door ajar, I went back outside and walked across the sloping front yard until I came to a halt at the fence that marked the end of our property.

"Mel?" I called down the bluff, "where are you?" Again, there was no answer.

Mel is physically fit, but clambering around on a steep hillside even in a uniform and low heels didn't seem in character unless, of course, someone else had been in trouble. Then all bets were off. For the first time, I felt the smallest frisson of concern.

"Mel," I called again, shouting this time. I peered off down the bank. At the condo in Seattle, we keep two pairs of binoculars parked on the sill next to the window seat. We used them for occasional bits of bird-watching, for viewing the Fourth of July Fireworks, and occasionally, during snowstorms, for being entertained while watching hapless drivers attempt to make their fender-bender way up and down Broad. Unfortunately, I didn't have a pair of binoculars here with me now at a time and place where I really needed them.

If a boat had overturned, I knew Mel would have wanted to lend a hand, but it seemed unlikely that she would have gone down the bank on foot. It seemed far more reasonable that she would have used her phone to summon help. Besides, there was no sign of wreckage out on the water or on the steep bank at the water's edge. And no sign of life either—no sign of movement.

There was a rough, steep trail that ran in breath-taking switchbacks down to the water. It might have been usable by mountain goats, but I didn't think it was something that should be tackled by an old codger with a pair of fake knees. When I walked over to the path and studied it closely, I saw no sign of any recent footprints. If Mel had gone down the bluff, she hadn't used the path.

I stood up and looked down at the bay again. There was a stiff wind blowing in off the water. The sky above may have been a robin's egg blue, but the sea itself was gray-green and dotted with rolling white-caps. It looked dangerous—and threatening.

Genuinely worried now and still staring down the hillside for any sign of movement, I plucked my phone out of my pocket and dialed Mel's cell phone again—with predictable results. The call went straight to voice mail. Then I dialed Mel's office, not her direct line, but the one that was usually answered by Kelly, the receptionist stationed just outside Mel's door.

"Is Chief Soames in?" I asked when Kelly answered. "This is her husband calling."

"No, she isn't here," Kelly answered, "and I'm a little surprised. She was supposed to do a live radio interview at one. I've tried calling her cell, but she doesn't answer. It's not like her to miss an appointment like this."

No it's not, I thought grimly. "If you do hear from her," I said aloud, "ask her to give me a call."

Before ringing off, I gave Kelly my cell-phone number, then I hurried back up the hill. Ignoring the wide-open front door, I headed straight for the back of the house and to the spot where the cars were parked, with mine directly behind hers. Some ancient cop instinct must have kicked in. As I approached her vehicle, rather than grabbing the door handle and pulling it open, I bent down and shaded my face enough so I could peer inside.

That's when my heart almost came to a stop. Mel's purse lay half-open on the passenger seat. Next to it lay an unopened Subway sandwich—her favorite, no doubt, tuna with jack cheese and jalapeños. Next to the sandwich, I caught sight of what looked like the grip of a weapon. Her Smith & Wesson maybe? There was her cell phone, too, but what really took my breath away was what I saw on the passenger floorboard—a shoe—a single, abandoned shoe, one of the low-heeled black pumps Mel routinely wore to work. If she had been in the driver's seat, and the shoe was in the passenger footwell, that indicated there must have been a struggle of some kind.

I stepped away from the vehicle without touching it—holding my hands in the air as though I'd been ordered to do so by a traffic cop. If something had happened to Mel—if someone had forced her out of her vehicle—I had to stop being a worried husband and transform myself into a detective. I looked around. The cars were parked below the crest of the hill out of view from the level above and shielded from the neighbors on either side by a thick screen of trees. It seemed unlikely that there would have been anyone close enough to witness whatever had happened.

Fighting panic, I fumbled to pry my cell phone from my pocket. My fingers seemed like frozen stubs as I forced them to dial.

"Nine-one-one," a calm-voiced woman answered. "What is your emergency?"

"It's my wife," I said. "I think someone's taken her."

"What do you mean by 'taken?'" she asked.

I tried to keep my voice steady. "My wife is Mel

Soames," I said. "She's the police chief here in Bellingham, and she's missing."

"Calm down, sir. What do you mean 'missing'?"

I wanted to reach through the phone and throttle the woman. How could she be so stupid?

"I mean her car is here. Her purse is here. Her weapon is here. She isn't. I think she's been kidnapped."

"Where are you?" the operator asked.

Taking a deep breath to control my temper, I gave her the address. "All right," the woman said. "I'm sending units your way. Do you have any idea how long she's been gone?"

I walked around to the front of the Porsche and leaned over close enough to the hood to hear if there was any clicking from the engine. There was nothing—not a sound—and there wasn't any heat rising from the hood, either. That meant that the car had been parked long enough for the engine to cool completely.

"No idea," I said into the phone, "but probably an hour at least."

While waiting for a patrol car to arrive and to avoid disturbing any possible evidence, I forced myself to stay away from the vehicle. I walked past the house, through the front yard, and all the way back down to the fence, where I stood stock-still, staring out to sea. Anyone seeing me right then might have assumed I was simply admiring the water view. I wasn't. I was peering into an abyss at the appalling possibility of losing what I held most dear and knowing that if Mel was lost, I was, too.

That's when it hit me. If a woman goes missing, who's the first suspect? The husband or else the person who calls it in. In this instance, that would be yours truly twice over. I thought about how I had forced myself to sound calm during the 9-1-1 call, and then I thought about all the other 9-1-1 recordings I had heard over the years—the ones where some chump calls to report that he found his dead wife, the wife he just murdered, lying on the floor in the living room. Usually, the killer will mention that he's tried reviving her even though the autopsy will reveal that she died hours before the 9-1-1 call. Instead of trying to bring her around, he's spent the interim attempting to clean up the crime scene.

I was that guy now, the calm one on the phone. When officers did show up, I'd be the first one they interviewed and the first one under suspicion. I knew what that meant, too. While investigators were busy investigating me, whoever had done it would have plenty of time to get away.

That thought brought me up short. Who had done it? Was the unknown assailant someone who just happened to come by? Was this a crime of opportunity, or was it something else, something planned and deliberate? And if it was the latter, who had it in for Mel Soames?

I could think of only one answer to that question—the guy who had been passed over for the job of chief, Austin Manson. Mel's phone was there in the car. Otherwise, I could have used our Find My Device app to locate her. But what about Manson, where was he, and, if he was the culprit, was Mel still with him?

The house was at the far southern end of Bellingham in a low-crime area. That explained why it was taking time for a patrol car to arrive on the scene. I took out my phone again and redialed Mel's office. "I'm looking for Austin Manson," I told Kelly, identifying myself again and hoping against hope that word of my 9-1-1 call hadn't yet filtered upstairs from the emergency operator.

"Sorry, Assistant Chief Manson is out sick today," Kelly informed me. "Can anyone else help you?"

I'm not generally a very good liar, but right then that's exactly what I needed to be—a capable and believable liar. "I wanted to surprise Mel by inviting Assistant Chief Manson to dinner with us tomorrow night," I said. "Do you happen to have either a home number for him or else a cell?"

Kelly gave me both, texting them to me because I had no other way to write them down. Did I turn around and try calling either one? No, I did not. Instead, my next call was placed to a guy named Todd Hatcher.

Todd is a self-styled forensic economist whose playbook includes access to untold databases. He also has an uncanny way with computers. In S.H.I.T., Todd had functioned as Ross Connors's unseen right-hand man, and now Todd was the one I turned to for help.

"Hey," Todd said when he answered the phone. I could hear the noisy sound of a child wailing somewhere near the background—most likely Todd and Julie's two-year-old daughter, Danielle. "Long time no see."

A momentary silence followed. I was remembering the last several times I'd seen Todd—first in the flashing-light chaos beneath the Space Needle minutes after Ross Connors's car wreck; at the funeral for Bill Spade, Ross's driver; and finally outside the packed gymnasium at O'Dea High School, which had been the only place deemed large enough to hold

Ross Connors's funeral. From the odd catch in Todd's voice when he spoke again, I suspect he was recalling those same scenes.

"What's up?"

Standing in the chilly midday sunlight, I heard the distant sound of an approaching siren. There wasn't much time. I told him what I needed as quickly as I could.

"You think this sour-grapes guy Manson may be behind what's happened?"

"I do. He called in sick today. If I try to tell one of his officers that I think the assistant chief is the one responsible for all this, the cop will most likely fall on the floor laughing. Maybe I'm wrong. Maybe Manson isn't behind it at all, but I still want to know where he is as of right now."

"Beau," Todd began, "do you think . . . ?" I could hear the coming barrage of caution before Todd ever managed to spit it out, and I cut him off in midsentence.

"I'm texting you his numbers right now," I told him urgently. "Please, Todd, see if you can locate Manson's cell."

"As long as we don't have a warrant, anything you find won't hold up in court."

"Mel's life is in danger. That means we can get around the need for a warrant. Besides, I'm not a cop any longer," I snarled at him. "I don't give a rat's ass about admissible evidence."

I disconnected then, forwarded the numbers to him, and started back up the slope, just as a patrol car came down the driveway and screeched to a stop with one final bleat from the siren.

When the cop emerged from the car, I took a look

at his baby face and figured he would be something less than useless. Then I saw his name tag—Officer Dale Embry—the young guy from that officer-involved shooting months earlier. I don't know how many sworn officers there are in Mel's department, but when I realized who he was, I felt as though I had just won the lottery.

"What seems to be the problem?" Embry asked.

"It's my wife," I said, pointing at Mel's car. "I think she's been kidnapped."

There probably aren't that many Caymans running loose in Bellingham. As soon as Embry glanced at the vehicle, a look of shocked recognition spread across his features. He immediately spoke into the radio attached to the shoulder of his uniform.

"Officer needs assistance," he said. "Chief Soames is missing."

I'm not sure if the emergency operator had deliberately withheld that piece of information from her radio transmission or if it had simply been an oversight on her part, but I knew Embry's call would bring a stampede of officers, most likely none of whom would turn out to be Assistant Chief Manson. I also knew that if I let my car be trapped in the driveway, it might take hours for me to get it loose again. I couldn't risk that.

"Let me move my vehicle out of the way so the detectives and CSIs can access her car."

Embry was very young, bless his heart—young and naive. I learned later that he was also an Eagle Scout and a Boy Scout troop leader. He hadn't yet learned that most people can look you straight in the eye and lie through their teeth. The prospect that his chief had been kidnapped left him totally out of his depth, so he was happy to let me. Once back up on street level, I heard the sounds of multiple sirens approaching, and so I simply vanished, driving out of the Bayside neighborhood and slipping quietly into the parking lot of a nearby apartment building. I was gone before any other officers arrived on the scene. With any kind of luck, it would be quite some time before Embry figured out that I hadn't come back down the driveway along with everybody else.

I'm not a man given to praying, but that's what I did—I prayed my heart out. I was still in the apartment parking lot and in the middle of my long heart-to-heart chat with the Man Upstairs when my phone rang, with Todd Hatcher on the line.

"That was quick," I said.

"Completely illegal but quick," he responded. "I got a ping off Manson's phone. He's currently in the parking lot of the scenic overlook at a place called Larrabee State Park. It's on Highway 11, about six miles south of Fairhaven at milepost fourteen. Depending on how fast you drive, it should take ten to fifteen minutes to get there."

"I'm on my way. What kind of vehicle does Manson drive?"

"I thought you'd want to know that," Todd said, "and I have it for you. It's an '06 Chevrolet Malibu."

During that drive, Formula 1 drivers had nothing on me. I made it to the overlook parking lot in just under seven minutes. Driving there, I realized it was probably close to the same spot where Mel, while working for S.H.I.T, had located the remains of a missing guy who'd fallen to his death on a Sunday afternoon while taking a leak on his way home from an afternoon of heavy drinking.

Somewhere along the way, I realized that I'd gone off and left the front door to the house unlocked and wide open. With cops all over the place, I didn't suppose that was much of a problem, for the remainder of the afternoon anyway. Besides, since the place had already been stripped bare in preparation for the remodel, how much damage could anyone do?

Todd had said that the overlook was right around milepost fourteen. I slowed down about a half a mile out so I could approach the place under the flag of your ordinary day-tripper out seeing the sights. When I pulled into the parking lot, there were only two other vehicles visible. One was a white Chevy Malibu, parked at the far end of the lot. In the middle of the space was an immense luxury tour bus loaded with a group of Japanese tourists, who were in the process of cleaning up after a chilly, windblown picnic lunch. Pretending to throw away some trash, I blended in with the group and discovered that most of them spoke English surprisingly well. I engaged a couple of them in conversation long enough to learn that they had spent the weekend sightseeing at the Skagit Valley Tulip Festival. Now they were taking the scenic route north to Vancouver, B.C., before catching their flight back to Tokyo.

I usually grumble about tourists. The hordes of camera-wielding dolts who stream off cruise ships and into downtown Seattle and the Regrade these days can be downright provoking. They may drop millions of dollars into the cash registers of local merchants, but my big gripe is that they tend to walk four and five abreast, effectively blocking traffic on any given side-walk at any given time.

This particular batch of tourists, however, I regarded as an absolute godsend. Manson had probably come here thinking he'd have plenty of time and privacy to send Mel plunging from the parking lot to certain death on the wave-pounded rocks far below. My hope—my slenderest smidgen of hope—was that the picnickers had delayed him long enough that Mel was still alive.

A man I suspected of being the tour-bus driver stood off by himself, smoking a cigarette. The passengers might have been Japanese, but I could tell by his flannel shirt and baseball cap that the driver was dyed-in-the-wool American.

Taking a steadying breath, I walked toward him, not knowing as I went what I would say or even exactly what I wanted to accomplish. On the one hand, having the tourists present provided cover for me and kept Manson from making his next move. On the other hand, I was armed, and, most likely, Manson was, too. If the confrontation ended up turning into some kind of shoot-out, I didn't want to be responsible for putting a busload of innocent Japanese visitors in jeopardy.

The driver stubbed out his cigarette as I approached. "How's it going?" he said.

Those three words were ordinary enough—casually welcoming of a stranger, but, at the same time, a bit on the wary side, as though to say he thought I might turn out to be an okay guy while still warning me not to try getting too chummy. I needed a quick way to start a conversation, and so, even though I quit smoking literally decades ago, I came up with the only possible topic that had any hope of working.

"Got a smoke?" I asked.

There's an instant bonding among smokers these days. Smokers are so accustomed to being treated like pariahs—glared at, ridiculed, and reviled—that when they find other like-minded individuals, they tend to let down their defenses. I had seen that phenomenon at work earlier that very morning in the interaction between Harry I. Ball and Marge Herndon. They met, they lit their respective cigarettes, and were instantly pals for life.

After a moment's hesitation, the driver reached into his pocket and pulled out a pack of cigarettes—a brand I didn't recognize. From an arm's length away, I could see that the writing on the package was in Japanese. What I couldn't see from that distance was if the indecipherable characters included any of our country's nanny-state grim health warnings.

"A gift from one of my passengers," he explained, noticing that I was studying the packaging. "They brought their own along on the trip, and that's a good thing. It means they don't mind if I stop for cigarette breaks. They want them, too."

He tapped a cigarette out and held the package in my direction. Then he took one for himself and lit both with a lighter he extracted from the pocket of his jeans.

I took a puff. After so many years of not smoking, that first fiery lungful of nicotine hit me like a ton of bricks. It took real effort on my part to suppress a sudden fit of coughing.

"I've got a problem," I said.

"Oh, yeah?" Cigarette bonding goes only so far. Wariness crept back into his voice. "Like what?"

"You see that car over there in the corner?"

"You mean the Malibu with the guy sitting in it? He showed up a while ago. He's been sitting there the whole time without getting out of the car. Made me wonder what he was up to."

"And well you should," I told him. "The guy behind the wheel works with my wife and hates her guts. She's gone missing. I think he might have kidnapped her from our new house in Fairhaven. I believe she's locked in the trunk and that he brought her here to kill her. As soon as he has a chance, I suspect he's going to shove her off the cliff."

That declaration provoked a fit of coughing—from the driver, this time, rather than from me. "You're kidding," he gasped when the spasm subsided. "It's March. What is this, some kind of weird April Fool's joke?"

"It's no joke. My name is J. P. Beaumont. I'm a retired homicide cop. My wife's name is Melissa Soames, but she goes by Mel. She was recently appointed chief of police in Bellingham. Austin Manson is her second-in-command. He's pissed beyond measure that she got the top job, and he didn't. He's known to have a temper."

"Pissed enough to kill her?" the driver said, shaking his head in disbelief. "No way!"

"Way," I said.

"If he kidnapped her, how come you know about it? What makes you think he brought her here?"

"We got a ping off his cell phone."

The driver ground out the remains of his half-smoked cigarette. "I'd better get my people out of here pronto," he said. "Before the cops show up, and this picnic turns into the shoot-out at the OK Corral."

"Wait," I said. "Please. I need your help."

He gave me what Jeremy, my son-in-law, calls the stink-eye. "What kind of help?"

"The fact that you and your people have been here is probably the only thing keeping him from making a move. I need you to stay. Round up your people. Get them loaded onto the bus, but please don't leave. If things go to hell in a handbasket, and there is a shoot-out, chances are we're talking handguns. I doubt he'll be armed with a high-powered rifle. Your bus should be far enough away that the passengers shouldn't be in any danger."

"But they might be," the driver pointed out.

"Yes," I agreed. "They could be."

"You and he might be armed with handguns only," the driver continued, "but the cops who show up will come with rifles and shotguns at the ready and with bulletproof vests, besides. My poor people have nothing," he added, nodding in the general direction of the bus. "Zilch. They'll be sitting ducks."

This was the part where things were getting dicey—the place where I would either lose him completely or win him over. It could go either way.

"The cops aren't coming," I said. "As I said, I'm Mel's husband. Right now, I'm most likely suspect *numero uno* as far as the cops are concerned. They're probably searching for me high and low."

"They don't know you're here?"

I shook my head. "The problem is, while everybody else is wasting their time looking for me, I'm afraid Manson is going to kill her. You and I may be her only chance."

I said my piece then fell silent and waited. For a long time, the only sound in the graveled parking lot was the soft roar of waves breaking on rocks far below. I was afraid he would simply turn and walk away. He didn't. Straightening his shoulders, he looked me square in the eye.

"What do you need me to do?"

It was all I could do to keep from hugging the guy. I said, "Get your passengers loaded into the bus. Tell them to take cover as best they can—to sink down below window level as much as possible."

The driver grinned then. "That shouldn't be a problem. Most of 'em aren't any bigger than a minute."

"By the way, could you lend me another cigarette?"

"Lend?" he replied. "Are you saying you'll buy me a pack when all this is over?"

The cigarette-smoker's bonding was back, big-time. The driver and I were on the same page. We were a team. He pulled out his pack and passed me a single cigarette.

"Pack? Hell," I declared, "I'll buy you a whole damned carton."

"What are you going to do?"

"I'm going to walk over there, tap on the window, and ask for a light."

"If he works with your wife, won't he recognize you?"

"I doubt it. Manson knows Mel; he doesn't know me. We've never met. When he rolls down the window, I'm going to take him down. While I'm doing that, you get on the horn to 9-1-1. Tell them there's some kind of altercation going down here at the state park. You're welcome to say I'm involved or not, your call. Say you believe people's lives are in danger and to get here fast."

There was a pause. Finally, he said, "What if things don't go your way?"

"Then take your bus and your people and get the hell out of here because if I don't succeed in nailing the bastard, my wife's done for, and so am I."

After an even longer pause, the driver nodded and held out his hand. We shook. "Good luck," he said. "I'm rooting for you."

With that, he headed for his bus, and I turned toward the Malibu. It was parked at the far south end of the lot, with the passenger side snug up against a guardrail made of a long length of log rather than metal. Given the distance down the cliff on the far side of that slender barrier, I would have much preferred metal.

Forcing myself not to rush, I sauntered up to the Malibu's driver-side door and rapped sharply on the glass with one hand while holding up a cigarette in the other. Then I bent down and mouthed three understated words through the closed window, "Got a light?"

Before Manson could reply, I slipped my right hand into my jacket pocket and closed my fingers around the plastic grip on my Glock. Manson must have been dozing when I tapped on the window. He started awake at the sudden noise and reached for something I couldn't see—a gun most likely. After a moment and to my immense relief, he seemed to relax. The window rolled down.

Manson looked at me through bloodshot eyes.

"Whaddyu want?" he demanded as a blast of boozy breath spilled out of the car, leaving its stink in the cool, crisp air around us.

I reasoned that if Manson was going to shoot first and ask questions later, he would have done so already. Luckily for me, the bus was still there and still acting as a deterrent because it meant there were all kinds of possible witnesses on the scene. Even drunk as a skunk, Manson knew better than to gun someone down in cold blood in front of a spellbound audience.

"Got a light?" I repeated. "I must have blown a fuse or two in my Mercedes. Neither of my lighters work, and I'm dying for a smoke."

Manson gave an exaggerated sigh, then he reached over and punched the lighter button on his dashboard. With his right hand. Amen! That probably meant he was right-handed. It also meant that a hand holding a lit lighter wouldn't be holding a gun. Couldn't be holding a gun. I studied him while we waited for the lighter to heat up. Manson was in his midfifties, wore his hair in a graying crew cut, and was reasonably fit. He could have been me a few years ago, up to and including the booze-fueled breath.

I waited until he held out the lighter, then I pounced. I dropped the cigarette, grabbed his wrist with both hands, and twisted for all I was worth. Then I bodily dragged his resisting body out through the open window.

"What the hell?" he yelled, fighting to free himself. "Let go. I'll kill you, you asshole."

Manson's big problem right then was that he was still drunk, and I wasn't. I dropped him onto the ground from window height and heard the air swoosh out of his lungs. Once he was on the ground gasping for breath, I was there, too, twisting his arm into an impossible pretzel behind his back in a way that was only a half inch short of pulling his shoulder out of its socket.

"You bastard," he howled when he could speak again "Whoever you are, you are a dead man."

"No, I'm not, Manson," I told him cheerfully, "but you're done. Stand down!"

Out of the corner of my eye, I saw the bus driver sprinting toward us from across the parking lot. "Thought you could use these," he said, arriving out of breath and gasping but holding up a handful of industrial sized tie-wraps. "You'd be surprised how often they come in handy on the bus. And I called the cops just like you said. They're on their way."

Moments later, with both of Manson's hands properly cuffed behind his back, I stood up, more grateful than ever for Dr. Auld, the orthopedic surgeon over at Swedish Hospital who had replaced my original out-of-warranty knees with properly working new ones. Manson was still on the ground, grumbling and railing. Meanwhile, I slipped the Glock out of my jacket pocket and back into its holster. No shots had been fired. There was no reason to have a weapon on display when the cavalry showed up.

That's about the time I first heard a fierce thumping noise coming from inside the trunk. Mel was alive! Tears of relief sprang from my eyes as I searched the interior of the Malibu for the trunk release. A second later, the bus driver and I stood in front of the open trunk, staring down at my wife.

She was alive but helpless, duct-taped from head to foot. A long strip of tape covered her mouth. It hurt me to pull the sticky gag as well as a layer of skin off her face, but it didn't bother her. In fact, I don't think she even noticed.

"Where's Manson?" she demanded furiously, once she was free of the gag. "Just wait until I get my hands on that bastard!"

"Manson is handled," I assured her. "He's not in custody just yet, but he's handled. What about you? Are you all right? Are you hurt?"

Still focused on Manson, she didn't answer, but as I helped her sit up, I saw a streak of dried blood that ran from her right temple all the way to her chin. Most likely, Manson had used something heavy to clock her over the head and knock her out.

While I loosened the restraints on Mel's legs, peeling off strips of shredded panty hose along with every piece of duct tape, the bus driver worked at freeing her hands. Once Mel was free from the tape, we attempted to stand her upright, but she immediately toppled over. Luckily, we caught her before she landed on her face. Her lower limbs were so numb, it was impossible for her to stand on her own.

"Who's this?" she asked, nodding toward the driver, who was gripping her other elbow.

"Name's Sam," he told her with a grin. "That's my bus over there. I'm the bus driver."

"Today I think Sam is short for Good Samaritan," Mel declared.

We all laughed uproariously at that, as though she had just cracked the best joke ever, and maybe she had. Then, as suddenly as our outburst of laughter had erupted, it ended. Limp with relief, Mel fell weeping against my shoulder. "Manson was going to kill me," she sobbed brokenly. "He said if he couldn't have the job, I sure as hell wouldn't have it, either."

"I know," I murmured comfortingly into her ear. "I know."

I tried to pretend I was holding her tightly against me in order to keep her from falling, but that wasn't the only reason—not by a long shot. I didn't want to let go of her ever again.

After a time, she pried herself loose from my grasp. "Where are we?" she asked, frowning.

"Larrabee Park on Chuckanut Drive, a few miles south of Fairhaven."

"How did you find me?" she wanted to know. "How did you know to come here?"

I didn't answer the question, but she figured it out anyway. "Todd?" she asked a moment later.

I nodded.

"And he located Manson's cell phone without having a warrant?"

I nodded again.

"Well," she said, "we can't just throw him under the bus, can we?"

When Sam objected to her use of that particular terminology, Mel quickly corrected herself. "I mean, we can't tell the cops about any of this. If they find out what Todd can do, they'll be all over him. He might even end up in jail."

"You're right," I agreed. "It's probably for the best if we don't make any mention of him or his participation."

"What then?" Mel asked. She fell silent, but soon

she brightened. "Wait a minute," she said. "I know how to handle this."

Reaching into the jacket pocket of her very rumpled uniform, she pulled out a spare set of keys. Mel Soames is notorious for losing track of keys—car keys, house keys, you name it. As a consequence, she never goes anywhere without two complete sets—one in her purse and one in her pocket. She held the key ring up, in the air jingling it triumphantly in front of my face. "We'll tell them you used this."

Months earlier, for Christmas, I had given her a collection of small squares of plastic tiles, containing locator chips. With the devices attached to her key rings, no matter where she misplaced one of them, we could use our iPhones to find it.

"Those are designed to work inside houses or apartments," I objected. "It would never cover this much distance."

"Technology is mysterious," Mel declared. "Nobody else knows that for sure, and what they don't know won't hurt them."

Sam saw that as a signal to take his leave. "I'd better go check on my passengers and let them know everything's all right," he said, backing away from us.

It was a good thing we'd already made arrangements about handling the locator beacon because, at that point, a string of cop cars with lights flashing and sirens blaring came streaming into the parking lot. Someone grabbed up Austin Manson and hustled him away, first into the back of a patrol car and later into a newly arrived ambulance.

I expected that investigators would immediately separate Mel and me while someone else went to talk to Sam. That's what cops usually do—they separate witnesses and suspects in an effort to keep them from comparing notes and collaborating as far as their various stories are concerned. I was grateful that Mel and I had managed to get our stories straight before the new arrivals got there.

But before we could be separated and interviewed, something unexpected happened. A white Buick sedan nosed its way into the crush of cop cars, and a woman I later learned was Mayor Kirkpatrick bounded out of the car and started throwing around her considerable weight. I have no idea how she learned about what was going on as fast as she did. Maybe she was monitoring police scanners. Maybe someone called her directly to let her know.

She hustled up to Detective Walsh, the officer in charge. "Is it true?" she demanded. "Is Austin Manson behind all this?"

Walsh was a cop with a duty to protect the integrity of both the crime scene and the investigation. Even so, he couldn't help but acknowledge the woman's authority. Rather than doing his job and ordering her away, he simply nodded. There was so much deference in the gesture that I more than half wondered if the old bat had been his Sunday school teacher once upon a time.

"Austin's mother, Mona, is a good friend of mine," Mayor Kirkpatrick continued. "He's been staying with her ever since his last divorce and becoming more despondent every day. She called me earlier this morning, worried that he had stormed out of the house in such a state that he might do something to harm himself or others."

"Nice of you to let us know," Mel muttered under her breath.

Another vehicle pulled into the lot—a media van. As people sprang out, expecting to set up their equipment, Mayor Kirkpatrick immediately shooed them away. "No cameras and no microphones," she announced firmly before any of the media folk could unpack. "We're dealing with a mental-health issue, and we're required by law to respect the patient's privacy. Isn't that right, Detective Walsh?"

To my amazement, the reporter scurried back to the van without a single word of objection. When it came to wielding influence, Adelina Kirkpatrick was a marvel. Within moments, the entire press corps beat a hasty retreat.

I looked back at the detective. He was clearly torn—torn between doing the right thing as a professional cop and knowing which side his bread was buttered on; between the old guard, the mayor, and the new guard, Mel; between Manson, a guy he'd come up with through the ranks, and Mel, his new chief. The old guard won hands down.

"Yes, ma'am," Walsh said.

Mel was offended. "A mental-health issue?" she stormed. "Are you kidding me? Is that how you expect to handle all of this? Austin Manson attacked me, kidnapped me, and threatened to kill me, and you expect me to forget about all that and let you sweep it under the rug by saying he suffered some kind of psychotic breakdown? You're engaging in an illegal cover-up and expecting me to go along with it?"

"As I said, Austin's mother and I are best friends," Mayor Kirkpatrick explained. "Mona will see to it that her son gets the best possible treatment. Sending him to jail certainly won't fix it. And in this day and age, when police departments operate under so much suspicion, letting word get out that one of our sworn officers has gone on a potentially murderous rampage isn't going to do your department any favors, and it won't do my administration any good either."

"But . . ." Mel began, but Mayor Kirkpatrick talked right over her, speaking loud enough now for all the officers within earshot to hear what she was saying.

"Chief Soames has just informed me that Assistant Chief Manson was threatening suicide earlier today. She, with the aid of her husband . . ." She stopped and looked at me, pleading for assistance.

"Beaumont," I said helpfully. "J. P. Beaumont. Mel wanted to keep her own name, you see."

Mel jabbed me in the rib with her elbow while Mayor Kirkpatrick continued on her merry way.

"She and Mr. Beaumont here have just now managed to subdue him. Assistant Chief Manson is about to be transported to a facility where he'll be given the kind of treatment he requires. In the meantime, let's give Chief Soames and Mr. Beaumont a round of applause!"

Enthusiastic clapping echoed through the parking lot around us. For once in her life, Mel was caught flat-footed and dumbstruck besides. She had been completely outmaneuvered by a politician who had somehow succeeded in turning Mel Soames into a reluctant ally. With Manson gone, maybe the undercurrent of objection to Mel's tenure as chief would be gone as well.

By the time the applause ended, Detective Walsh

was nowhere to be seen. The incident had been publicly declared over and done with. Mel was furious, but I, for one, was grateful. Yes, letting it go that way amounted to crappy police work, but I was glad the mayor had stopped the process before the interviews started and before Mel and I had been forced to perjure ourselves. Besides, the whole shebang had turned into a nonevent. No one had died in the incident. No weapons had been discharged. No one was going to jail. It was a done deal.

The tour bus left shortly after the ambulance departed. Before the bus drove away, I jotted down Sam's name and address so I could send him his promised carton of cigarettes. I didn't mention to Mel I had been forced to smoke a cigarette in my effort to save her life. Since she herself was a relatively recent ex-smoker, she most likely would have thought I volunteered.

Half an hour later, Mel and I left the now-empty parking lot where, as far as the rest of the world was concerned, nothing at all had happened. We went back to the house on Bayside. We stopped by Mel's car long enough to collect her missing purse, phone, and shoe. The other black pump had turned up in the trunk of Manson's Malibu, as well as Mel's backup weapon.

With Mel properly shod again, we went around to the front of the house, stripped off the crime-scene tape, and went inside. Mel took advantage of the relative privacy of our expansive wallboard-free living room to peel off her tattered panty hose. When we left the house again, after closing and locking the front door, Mel tossed the remains of her panty hose on top of a pile of construction debris in the Dumpster parked next to her Porsche.

Then, driving two cars, we headed into Fairhaven, found parking places on the main drag, and were shown to a quiet corner table in Dirty Dan Harris's, a small bistro that has the reputation of being the best restaurant in town.

We placed our order for an early dinner and sat there holding hands across the white-linen tablecloth. We both knew how close we'd come to losing it all that day, and we were very grateful.

"This isn't over," Mel said determinedly. "I should have Walsh's ears for this."

"It'll be better for you if you don't," I advised. "With the mayor all over him, the man was caught between a rock and a hard place. He knows he was in the wrong. In terms of having the trust of your rank and file, as well as having his long-term loyalty, resolving it without turning it into a public outcry is a better bet. Without that trust, you're going to end up being a short-timer."

Mel thought about that. "Maybe you're right," she said.

Our food came then, and we tore into it. We had both missed lunch, and we were starving. It wasn't until we were sharing a dessert of bread pudding that things turned serious again.

"Where do we go from here?" Mel asked.

"Well," I said, "I assume that tomorrow morning, you'll go back to being Chief of Police although, for my money, I'd just as soon you refrained from being locked in another car anytime soon."

"What about you?" Mel asked.

"What do you mean what about me? I'm not exactly

sitting around letting the grass grow under my steel-belted radials. I'm finishing up Harry's project and will be starting on ours as soon as his is out of the way. I can only handle one housing crisis at a time. I'm sure Jim Hunt will be dragging me hither and yon looking at plumbing fixtures, slab samples, and lighting options."

"That may be what we need you to be doing right now," Mel allowed, "but I don't see much of a future in it. You don't plan on spending the rest of your life supervising construction projects, do you?"

"No," I admitted. "It's something I can do in a pinch if I have to, but you're right. It's not really me."

"There you go," Mel said, nodding, leaning back in her chair and giving me one of those questioning, raised-eyebrow, Mr.-Spock looks that I find so endearing. "So what are you going to do with the rest of your life?"

It was a serious question—one I had been dodging for months—so I did my best to laugh it off. "Bowling, maybe?" I asked. "Or what about golf? Golf seems to be working just fine for Ralph Ames."

Ralph came into my life about the time my second wife, Anne Corley, shot through my world like a speeding comet and transformed my existence. Ralph was Anne's attorney to begin with and became mine in the aftermath of her death. We've had a client/friend relationship for decades, one that continues even now that he's semiretired. Mel leaned forward in her seat and gave me one of her most beguiling smiles. I knew at once that I'd stepped into a trap although it hadn't yet sprung shut.

"I'm so glad to hear you mention Ralph," Mel said. "What about TLC?"

TLC, aka The Last Chance, is Ralph's baby, the same way S.H.I.T. once belonged to Ross Connors. It started years ago when one of Ralph's already well-heeled clients, a woman named Hedda Brinker, hit a huge Powerball jackpot. Hedda's daughter, Ursula had been murdered years earlier, and at the time the crime was as yet unsolved. Hedda wanted to use her jackpot winnings to start a privately operated cold-case organization. Hedda's original vision was that Ralph, operating in the capacity of her attorney, would set things in motion and then step away. Instead, he had remained at the helm.

After the shuttering of Special Homicide, Ralph had suggested that I should maybe think about joining up with TLC. Every time he mentioned it, I had turned him down. Unfortunately, my last cold-case experience had been an ill-fated effort that had resulted in the death of Seattle Homicide Detective Delilah Ainsworth. I knew too well how otherwise good intentions could have fatal consequences. Only three people knew how much Delilah's death had rocked my world— Mel; my AA sponsor and former stepgrandfather, Lars Jensen; and Ralph Ames.

As far as I was concerned, I was out of the homicide business, especially when it came to cold cases.

"Being a homicide cop is in your blood," Mel insisted. "Just look at what you did today. You were back in your element out there and saved my life in the process. You're a savvy guy, mister. You know what you're about, you've still got the moves, and I know TLC would be lucky to have you."

"What are you saying then?" I asked. "No bowling and no golf?"

We both laughed at the very idea. Laughter came easily that evening, and it's no wonder.

"Yes," she agreed, "no to both, so are you going to call Ralph about this, or should I?"

It was the old Fuller Brush assumed-close routine all over again—How do you want to pay for this, cash or check?

"Let me think about it," I said. "Give it a little time. Let me get this housing stuff under control, then I'll give Ralph a call."

"Promise?" Mel asked.

"I promise," I said.

And just like that, I knew I was toast. I also knew that TLC was definitely in my future because Mel was right. Over-the-hill or not, being a cop isn't only what I do. Like it or lump it, it's who I am.

NOVELS OF SUSPENSE BY
NEW YORK TIMES BESTSELLING AUTHOR

J.A. JANCE

Featuring Sheriff Joanna Brady

JUDGMENT CALL

978-0-06-173280-5

When Joanna Brady's daughter, Jenny, stumbles upon the body of her high-school principal in the desert, the search for justice leads straight to her own door. Now Joanna is forced to face the possibility that her beloved daughter may be less than perfect when a photo from the crime scene ends up on Facebook. A photo only one person close to the crime scene could have taken.

REMAINS OF INNOCENCE

978-0-06-213471-4

Sheriff Joanna Brady has her hands full investigating the suspicious death of a developmentally disabled man when another case rocks the department—a shocking murder involving Liza Machett and a mysterious fortune in hundred-dollar bills she found in her dead mother's house. Now Joanna must solve two disturbing cases fast, before more innocent blood is shed.

Available wherever books are sold or please call 1-800-331-3761 to order.

JB2 0515